"A KISS AND YOU MAY GO"

His mouth met hers. A tiny jolt went through her but she kept her lips tightly pinched together, her body instinctively resisting.

Gabriel's head lifted. The grip on Cassie's wrists tightened by a hair. "Come, Yank, you must do better than that."

His mouth closed over hers once more. The fleeting thought chased through her mind that this kiss was like none other, and then her mind seemed not her own. His lips were warm and compelling, starkly primitive yet oddly persuasive, draining her of strength and will.

"Will you not change your mind, Yank?" A fingertip traced the graceful arch of her throat. "I promise you a night you'll not soon forget."

If You've Enjoyed This Book,
Be Sure to Read These Other
AVON ROMANTIC TREASURES

Gabriel's Bride

Samantha James

An Avon Romantic Treasure

AVON BOOKS ◆ NEW YORK

GABRIEL'S BRIDE is an original publication of Avon Books. This work has never before appeared in book form. This work is a novel. Any similarity to actual persons or events is purely coincidental.

AVON BOOKS
A division of
The Hearst Corporation
1350 Avenue of the Americas
New York, New York 10019

Copyright © 1994 by Sandra Kleinschmit
Inside cover author photograph by Almquist Studios
Published by arrangement with the author
Library of Congress Catalog Card Number: 93-90816
ISBN: 0-380-77547-6

First Avon Books Printing: May 1994

AVON TRADEMARK REG. U.S. PAT. OFF. AND IN OTHER COUNTRIES, MARCA REGISTRADA, HECHO EN U.S.A.

Printed in the U.S.A.

RA   10 9 8 7 6 5 4 3 2 1

I would like to dedicate GABRIEL'S BRIDE to those wonderful people who made it possible . . .

To Lyssa Keusch, for her support and enthusiasm, and for being so fantastic to work with.

To my family—Ed, Kelly, Sara, and Jami—for their patience and understanding through so many deadlines . . . I love you all.

And last but not least, to Peggy, Iona, and Joyce . . . you're the best, ladies!

Gabriel's Bride

Prologue

Tall, ivy-clad gates announced the entrance to Farleigh Hall. A long, winding drive wound its way amidst formal, terraced gardens and yew-hedged walks. But it was Farleigh Hall itself, with its stately brick facade and sprawling grandeur, that inevitably commanded the eye of the beholder. Beyond the wide, curving stone steps, high, mullioned windows draped with shimmering gold silk stretched endlessly on either side . . . it was at once a sight both formidable and awe-inspiring.

At the east end of the manse, two young children sat beneath the watchful guidance of their tutor, Mr. Findley. More and more often their attention strayed to the window of the schoolroom, which was slightly ajar in deference to the warm June afternoon. Stout and sturdy boys of ten and six they were, the elder as fair as the younger was dark, both with eyes the same piercing gray as their father.

And it was their father for whom the pair waited so anxiously, fidgeting at their cherrywood table, until at last Mr. Findley rolled his eyes heavenward and threw up his hands.

"Off with you now!" he said crossly. "I could be filling your heads with porridge for all the two of you would know! Your father won't be back from London before nightfall, but who am I to tell you differently? Education is indeed life's most coveted prize, but do either of you realize it? I think not!"

He cast a last disparaging glance at the boys, muttering under his breath about the vagaries of fate with an equal mix of envy and frustration. For although their minds might someday be empty as a poor man's kettle, such would not be the case with their pocketbooks . . .

Not for the sons of the seventh duke of Farleigh, a man who was among the wealthiest in all of England.

At that precise moment, the clatter of coach wheels sounded on the drive outside. Mr. Findley ignored it, his mettle pricked still further.

Outside, the carriage rounded the last graceful curve of the drive. The elder lad bounded down the wide stone steps. Although his brother struggled to keep pace, his thin legs pumping furiously, he lagged far behind. He had scarcely breached the wide double doors when the carriage door burst open. A handsome man, impeccably dressed in an elegant striped silk frock coat and pale pantaloons, leaped lightly to the ground.

"Papa!" Bright, eager eyes gleamed up at him. "We missed you! As much as I enjoy my riding lesson with Ferris, I'd much rather you taught me instead."

The duke's gaze settled upon his golden-haired son, roving the aristocratic features that so reminded him of another . . . Lord, but the boy resembled his mother!

He laughed. "And I, too, Stuart. Indeed, our lessons were oft on my mind while I was gone—why, so much so that I couldn't resist bringing this back for you."

The duke gestured to his footman, and again the sound of hoofbeats was heard. Another rider appeared, but it was the small white pony that trailed behind that widened Stuart's eyes.

"Papa!" he breathed. "You have brought me my very own pony! Why, I shall name him White Dancer!"

An indulgent smile curved the duke's lips as he led the pony forward. "Of course I brought you a present. Nothing is too good for the future duke of Farleigh, you know."

Neither of them had noticed young Gabriel, who now darted forth. "A pony!" he cried, beaming. "Papa, you have brought us a pony!" In his eagerness he thrust a hand up in front of the pony's nose.

But the suddenness of the move frightened the animal; he reared up and back, instinctively striking out with his forelegs. Stuart leaped back, only narrowly escaping the flashing hooves.

The duke whirled on the child. "The pony is for your brother, boy, not you! And for pity's sake, watch yourself! You know better than to startle a horse. Your brother might have been killed!"

Stuart glanced at his father. "He meant no harm, Papa." His tone was earnest. "He only wanted to see the pony. Didn't you, Gabriel?"

The child called Gabriel said nothing. He suffered his father's silent disapproval, his dark head bowed low. His bottom lip trembled; all the life had flickered from his eyes.

"Yes, I suppose you're right." The duke did not bother to hide his irritation. "But he would do well to be more like you, Stuart. Your brother is a bit of a nuisance at times."

The younger lad's shoulders slumped further. Thinking to cheer him, Stuart glanced at his father. "Papa, what present have you brought for Gabriel?" he asked curiously.

The duke sighed. "Dear me. Wills and I were so caught up in trying to find your pony, I fear it quite escaped me. No matter—I shall try to remember the next time." He crooked a finger at his elder son. "Come along now, Stuart. We've much to discuss, for I've decided you shall accompany me on my next trip to London."

His chest swelling with pride, Stuart stepped up smartly beside his father. The duke turned as if to walk away. Then, as if it were an afterthought, he stopped and patted Gabriel on the head—like a favored pet—then turned and walked away, Stuart at his side.

But the boy was neither favored, nor a pet. He was only a child who did not understand why his father slighted him so.

But his mother knew.

Inside the house, a fold of the silk draperies slid silently back into place. Unbeknownst to the three of them, Lady Caroline Sinclair, duchess of Farleigh, watched from afar. There was a melancholy sadness about her as she turned away, for she was aware, in that way only a mother is, that the lad had been wounded. She alone understood the wistful yearning in her son's eyes, the ache in his soul. She could have wept, for the boy was always so eager to please, so anxious for his father's attention. But Edmund was blind to his son's devotion. Indeed, he scarcely knew the boy existed.

For the duke's favorite was his firstborn.

And Caroline greatly feared that a second son was no better than a second *wife* . . .

Bitterly she recalled that long-ago day Edmund had come to her. "Stuart needs a mother," he had said. "And it seems I need a wife." Oh, how bold he had been! So dashing, so arrogant and strong-willed! But Caroline had spared not a care, for she had loved Edmund Sinclair from the moment she had set eyes on him—and to think he had chosen her above all others! Her foolish heart had brimmed with joyful hope. Surely he would come to love her. Surely someday . . .

And so she strived mightily to be a loving, dutiful wife in all things, that he might come to love her in return. But she had come to realize that although her love would forever dwell with the man who claimed her heart, his forever dwelled with one who now lived with the angels . . .

Edmund was not incapable of loving—how much easier to bear were it so!

She pressed trembling fingers against her forehead. She must be strong, if not for her own sake, then for Gabriel. She could stand the hurt, the pain—anything for this child of her heart, for indeed, he was all she had—all that she might ever have. Her heart heavy with her burden, but determined such weakness would not show, she hurried down the gallery and out into the sunshine.

The boy remained where he was, still and silent. Small and alone. Forgiven . . . then forgotten.

But the child did not forget, nor forgive; with gentle insistence he eased himself from his mother's loving embrace. To her surprise, he would accept neither pity nor comfort. There were no tears, only a hint of stoic pride despite his tender years. For Gabriel was very much his father's son . . .

Far more than any of them realized.

Chapter 1

Charleston, South Carolina
1815

A torrential summer rain poured from the sky, drenching to the skin those dauntless souls who ventured outside, and turning the already rutted, stinking streets into a sea of mud. But inside the taproom of Black Jack's Inn, the air fairly seethed with the pulse of life and raucous, masculine laughter.

Although it was only a few blocks from the waterfront, Black Jack's was one of the better establishments of the city. It boasted excellent food, clean sheets, and respectable service, all at a fair price.

On this particular wet, dreary night, the table in the far corner was occupied by two well-dressed men, one with hair as dark as the midnight hour, the other slender and chestnut-haired. After weeks at sea, they'd decided to forego the ship's cramped quarters for the pleasures of a warm, comfortable mattress.

"To a safe trip back to England—and to the earl of Wakefield and his future bride!"

The laughter-filled voice belonged to one Sir

Christopher Marley. Lord Gabriel Sinclair, however, was not so eager to join the toast. And little wonder, for his impending nuptials were hardly to his liking . . .

They were most certainly not of his doing.

He stared into his glass as if it held the secrets of the world. These last weeks had blurred into a dream—sweet heaven, a nightmare.

Stuart was dead, a casualty of the battle of New Orleans.

Stuart. An unseen hand seemed to close about his heart and squeeze. In truth, his brother's death was something Gabriel had never once considered. He and Stuart had never been truly close, and the years had found them drifting further and further apart. Gabriel had left Farleigh the day of his mother's funeral, and he'd not been back. In truth, he had turned his back on his father and set about building a successful shipping business of his own. And in so doing, Gabriel had turned his back on all that he was.

Bitter remembrance seared his heart. Needless, his father had not sought him out, even when he'd left to march with the English forces against Napoleon. No, not once in nearly five years had his father deigned to call upon him. Indeed, it was as if he never existed . . .

But all that had changed with Stuart's death.

It was inevitable, perhaps . . . Gabriel's mind slid back in time, back to his last meeting in his father's London study when he'd learned his brother was dead.

His father had not changed. He was as arrogant, as imperious . . . as cold as ever.

"You are now the earl of Wakefield, the next duke of Farleigh," his father said in that frigid, formal tone Gabriel remembered so well—and hated so intensely. "'Tis your duty to marry, to give me a grandson so that our family name does not die out."

Duty. God, but the word was suddenly vile. In truth, Gabriel had known precious little of duty, for that was the role for which Stuart had been groomed.

He forced himself to relax, then smiled lazily. "Oh, I've many uses for women, Father, both in the bedroom and without." He paused, taking a perverse delight at his father's expression, visible proof of his displeasure. He gave a short laugh and continued. "Fortunately, none of them have ever included marriage."

Brows the color of iron drew together over Edmund Sinclair's eyes. His hair, still well in abundance, was streaked with the same iron-gray. Gabriel did not flinch from such piercing regard, the way he had done so often as a child. "Ah, yes, so it would seem." The duke's tone was icily distant. "I've been kept apprised of your . . . activities. It seems you've had many a mistress yet never a wife."

Gabriel's smile vanished. The man had dared to spy upon him! He glared at his father, only barely able to conceal his temper.

"With a title comes responsibility, Gabriel, as well as respectability. In light of your . . . behavior, I believe the first step should be to remedy the situation. You must take a wife. Now. From your own lips, you've indicated no preference. I, therefore, propose a solution. Since Stuart can no longer wed Lady Evelyn, it seems only logical that you take his place."

Gabriel had known, of course, of Stuart's betrothal to Lady Evelyn, only child of the duke of Warrenton, whose estate bordered Farleigh in Kent.

"Indeed," his father had gone on, "I see no reason why the wedding should not take place as planned."

For an instant, Gabriel had been too stunned to reply. It was only later that he realized he should have expected such haughty presumption—after all, this was his father with whom he was dealing.

The urge to walk away was almost overpowering. Lord, he'd been tempted to do exactly that, to shirk his so-called *duty* and to hell with his father. Yet something stopped him . . .

Gabriel was many things, but never a fool. Farleigh was a grand estate, and a future dukedom was a powerful lure indeed . . .

Perhaps, he decided grimly, this was Fate's way of seeking to erase those miserable years of his youth.

"Well?" Oh, but his father's note of impatience was far too familiar. "Have you nothing to say, Gabriel? If so, then I must assume you have no objection to wedding Lady Evelyn."

Gabriel clenched his fists at his sides. "Father," he said evenly, "the years have not changed you. You possess no will but your own. You *acknowledge* no will but your own. Would it truly matter to you if I harbored some objection?" Even as he spoke, his mind was otherwise encumbered. He needed time to consider, time to decide one way or the other . . .

One thing stood out high in his mind. If he chose to wed Lady Evelyn, it would be done not to please his father, but himself.

As Gabriel expected, the duke chose to ignore his jibe. "Very well, then. Warrenton and his daughter have already agreed to the match. Therefore, we shall share this news immediately—"

"No. I have business in America. My ship leaves at dawn tomorrow. I fear I must insist we wait until my return."

The duke's dislike of Yankees was known far and wide, and little wonder, considering the fate that had befallen his first wife, and now Stuart . . . The duke's lips tightened. "I see no reason to delay," he began.

"Ah, but I do. Surely a wait of several months would be more appropriate in light of Stuart's demise. Besides, I hardly think it proper that the *ton* be apprised of such an event without my presence in the flesh." Gabriel shrugged, his tone one of reason and utter calm. "Surely a few months will make little difference."

The duke's jaw clamped tight. His eyes were a cool, pale reflection of his son's. "You are right, of course," he said at length. "We will make the formal announcement as soon as you have concluded your business and returned to London."

His father was furious, Gabriel acknowledged smugly. The victory was a small one, but a victory nonetheless. As such, he would do well to enjoy it.

A heaving guffaw from behind Gabriel brought him back to the present. What was it Christopher had said? *To the earl of Wakefield and his future bride.* Recalling the toast, Gabriel raised a darkly slanted brow in lieu of his tankard. The way he felt right now, he'd just as soon take as his wife an ugly hag than do as his father wanted.

"We've only just arrived," he said lightly. "Are you so anxious then to depart without sampling all Charleston has to offer?" One corner of his hard mouth came up. "As I recall, our last visit to Charleston left nearly every maid in the town yearning for the thrust of an English blade!"

Though Gabriel was sometimes distant, often remote, Christopher had known his friend far too long to overlook his brittle smile. "Something," Christopher said slowly, "is troubling you."

Troubling him? Why, what should he care that Fate had cast him back into his father's path? A mocking smile twisted Gabriel's lips.

"I will soon be wed to a woman whose lineage is among the oldest in all of England. You are right, Christopher. Let us toast the alliance between the house of Warrenton and the house of Farleigh." He raised his glass high. "To the mighty and the damned!"

This time it was Christopher who looked on as Gabriel proceeded to drain his tankard of every drop of ale. He pictured in his mind the pale ethereal blond who would wed his friend. He sighed. What he wouldn't give to be in Gabriel's shoes! But to a lowly baronet, the lovely Evelyn was as far out of reach as the stars.

"Lady Evelyn is hardly a troll, Gabriel. Faith, she is as comely as any! Were I you," he chided, "I'd find marriage to her no hardship at all."

Gabriel said nothing. He had already inherited Stuart's title, he thought blackly. Why not his wife as well?

In truth, it was not the marriage itself that Gabriel found so distasteful. Christopher was right, he realized. He supposed Evelyn was pretty enough. And perhaps it was well and good that she was quiet and mousy and half-terrified of him. She would do as she was told, and would not dare to question him. And did it truly matter that he would soon have a wife? Marriage and fidelity were hardly synonymous. Society accepted that a man slept where he chose, and with whom he chose. No, his life need not be any different than before.

Nonetheless, a seething resentment seized hold of him. What grated was that his father had commanded he marry. And it was just like his father to expect that his every wish be obeyed, blast his arrogant, autocratic hide!

For a moment his brooding silence lingered. "I did not expect to have to marry out of duty," he said at last. "Indeed," he did not bother to hide his annoyance, "I did not expect to have to marry at all."

When the innkeeper hurried over to serve them a sumptuous round of beef swimming in gravy, baked yams, and honeyed ham, Christopher silently studied his friend. From the time they'd met at Cambridge, Gabriel had been wild and reckless, ever the rebel. Even then the state of affairs between Gabriel and his father had been bleak. But there was now a hardness within him, a brooding hardness that had been there until his mother had died.

Indeed, Christopher could have sworn that Gabriel blamed his father for his mother's death . . . Yet Caroline had died of an accident—a tragic one, to be sure—but an accident nonetheless.

But Christopher did not ask why Gabriel might hold his father accountable. For there were some boundaries even he dared not cross.

Christopher shook his head. "Few of us eagerly enter the marriage market, my friend. I fear 'tis usually a case of needs must."

Gabriel gave a harsh laugh and reached for his fork. "On that, you are right. Women complain that 'tis men who possess all the freedom. But marriages are made to acquire that which one does not hold. 'Tis ironic, is it not, that if a woman possesses much in the way of beauty, she usually manages to marry a fortune. And if she already has a fortune, she needn't marry at all. But a man . . . well, if a man wishes to produce an heir, he must find himself a wife!"

Christopher's blue eyes filled with mirth. "Perhaps the lady—and marriage—will tame you." His friend chuckled. "Indeed, I find the possibility rather intriguing!"

Gabriel smiled, his first genuine display of humor. "Intriguing, yes," he drawled. "But likely?" He shook his head. "I think not." Gabriel was well aware his reputation as a rakehell was hardly undeserved. Of vice he knew much, of virtue, precious little.

"In fact," he continued lightly, "I suggest we occupy ourselves with the pursuit of far more pleasant matters. Why, who knows what new fields have bloomed in our absence?"

His gaze swept the taproom, his meaning unmistakable. Christopher was only too glad for the diversion. A barmaid had just moved to clear the tankards from a table recently vacated. Generous-hipped and raw-boned, she had round brown eyes and plump red cheeks. On seeing she had captured their attention, she flashed a beaming smile and leaned forward across the table. Her bodice gaped wide, offering an unimpeded view of bare, ample breasts.

"Ah," Christopher murmured. "A display of female charms that is hardly platonic, wouldn't you say?"

"Indeed." Gabriel was mildly amused by the barmaid's ploy. Clearly the wench was willing. She was young, and appeared to have good teeth. But she was a bit ungainly . . . "I fear," he murmured, "she's rather clumsily made for my tastes."

Christopher laughed. "No doubt she'll make some man a good farmer's wife."

It was then that Gabriel saw her—the other barmaid. She was hurrying from the kitchen, tying an apron about her waist.

And this one was far from ungainly. Her hair seemed the same rich color as the firelight, a striking combination of amber and gold. But it was caught up in a knot on her nape, pulled so severely tight that the skin on her forehead was stretched taut. He found himself possessed of the notion that she sought to hide her beauty.

Christopher's gaze trailed his. On seeing where Gabriel's had settled, he raised a thick chestnut brow. "Ah," he murmured, rubbing his chin. "Now there's a maid I vow is as pleasant to kiss as to look upon. Nature has not failed her, my friend. Why, I daresay such beauty could carry her far . . . no farmer's wife, this one, eh? No doubt she could aim far higher."

Gabriel was not disposed to answer. Nor did he need to, Christopher decided. Gabriel's intense scrutiny of the girl told him all he needed to know. He heaved a silent sigh of regret, for the thought of pursuing a dalliance with the wench was captivating indeed, but Gabriel had spied her first so he would quell any frivolous pursuit on his part.

Gabriel's gaze had yet to leave the girl. She was dressed much the same as the other, in a worn, muslin gown that might have once been green. The square bodice was cut low. She carried a heavily laden tray and had begun to serve frothy tankards of ale at the table across the room.

Gabriel couldn't help but note the way her hand fluttered to the low-cut neckline every so often; the merest hint of creamy roundness was revealed. He gave a cynical half-smile, for oddly enough, he found himself far more fascinated by what this lass humbly concealed than what the first barmaid brazenly displayed.

Small-boned and unearthly slender beneath that wretched gown, it slipped through his mind that she seemed strangely out of place here, like a frail pink blossom among thorns . . . He was abruptly irritated with himself. What nonsense was this?

Comparing the wench with roses? He was suddenly both angry and annoyed, yet buried beneath his self-derisive scorn was the realization that he could scarcely escape the reminder . . .

His mother had loved flowers.

Beside him there was a swish of skirts. The first maid sidled up between him and Christopher. "Hope you enjoyed your meal, gents." She glanced between them, her eyes dark and suggestive.

Ever the gentleman, Christopher proclaimed heartily, "Why, thank you, mistress. Indeed, you may pass our compliments on to the cook. The bread was fragrant and warm, the round of beef tender and well-seasoned."

She smiled and wet her lips. "My name's Nell," she offered. "Yer English, the two of you, aren't ye?"

"Aye, we certainly are." Christopher rose and gave a mock bow. "I am Sir Christopher Marley, and this is Gabriel Sinclair, the newly titled earl of Wakefield."

Nell's eyes widened. She dipped a curtsy—but not without another display of bountiful flesh— a calculated move, Gabriel thought, nodding in acknowledgement.

"Well, just so ye know, Nell here don't hold a grudge against ye Englishmen. We've had a few put up here at Black Jack's since the war ended. And real gents they were, not like some we get around here."

Gabriel smiled politely. He inclined his head toward the other barmaid. "Who is the other girl?"

Nell's smile faded. "Oh, that's Cassie. Her mum was one of the barmaids here years back." She winked. "All o' Charleston knew her mum was a lightskirt—and not one for the same man two nights in a row, if ye know what I mean. Wasn't long before she ran off and left her brat here. And still the girl's got the nerve to put on airs, she does!—just 'cause she talks better 'n me. But that's only 'cause Bess taught her. Bess was once a lady's maid, y'know."

Gabriel nodded. "I see. And who is Bess?"

"Was," Nell corrected. "Died a month past birthin' her babe, she did. Why, she and Cassie were tight as a babe on a mother's tit!"

Her mouth turned down when she saw Gabriel's eyes still fastened on the subject in question. She sniffed disdainfully. "Not enough arse to keep a man's backside warm. And not much topside either, if you ask me."

So saying, she tossed her head. Boldly she ran a fingertip along the collar of Christopher's waistcoat. "In case ye be wantin' anythin' else, just ask for Nell."

When she was gone, Christopher gave a dry laugh. "Dear Lord. Never say she is not eager."

Gabriel quirked a brow. "Or particular, it would seem." He nodded; Christopher turned his head just in time to see Nell snared about the waist by a heavy-jowled man near the entrance. He pulled her down hard onto his lap. Nell laughed and twined her arms about his neck. The man plunged his hand into her bodice, openly fondling her breast. Gabriel found the display unusually distasteful.

Just then the girl called Cassie emerged from the kitchen. Christopher's gaze flitted to her as well.

His smile faded. "Can you imagine? Her mother left her on her own? A child yet?" He shook his head, his expression suddenly very somber.

Gabriel stretched out his long legs beneath the rough-planked table. This part of Charleston was hardly a pretty place. There were cows and horses everywhere, even in the narrow alleys; the residents had no qualms about dumping garbage wherever they pleased. It was no wonder the streets were slimy and stinking. If what Nell had said was true, the girl was one of Charleston's own, the product of a hard life.

"Her plight is regrettable, aye," he agreed. "But we've children living in the streets of London, too, poor and starving with nowhere to go in the cold of winter or dead of night."

Christopher clapped him on the shoulder, saying lightly, "Why, Gabriel, I'd no idea you were even aware of such things. Perhaps there's hope for you yet."

Nearby there was a gust of laughter. Gabriel turned his head slightly. It appeared the men at the next table had decided to have a bit of fun with the girl Cassie, who was attempting to refill their tankards of ale while trying to avoid their groping hands.

"Aw, come on now, girlie. Let's have a look at what yer hidin' in there!"

Another snorted. "Why bother? 'Tis plain there's not nearly so much there as Nell—"

"But I vow what's there is a tad prettier than Nell. Aye, as round as a plump peach, with cherry-red nipples . . ." The man made squeezing motions with his fingers.

There was a burst of ribald laughter. Roving fingers plucked at the pointed thrust of her breast. "Aye, that's the way!" came a voice from still yet another table. "Give a little twist and see what she's got!" Someone slid a hand over the roundness of her buttocks, giving her a pinch. When she jumped, three of them roared while another leered in avid anticipation.

Gabriel started to lift his tankard to his lips, still a silent observer. Certainly he was not offended, for such bawdiness was commonplace in establishments such as this. Indeed, the banter was sometimes far worse at his club in London. As for the girl, certainly she was no stranger to it either. Aye, no doubt she liked it. Most of her kind did . . .

No. He was wrong. A burly sailor caught a fistful of her skirt. She yanked it away and whirled around. Though she said not a word, for an instant hate blazed keenly in her eyes. Hate? Slowly Gabriel lowered his tankard to the table. No. Surely not. Surely he'd been mistaken, he thought with a faint curl of his lip. Likely as not, the girl was a doxy just like the other . . .

Cassie McClellan slammed the tray down on the long work table in the kitchen. God, but she hated this! The smell of sweat and ale. Groping male hands and wet lips. She shuddered. It was disgusting, the way they pawed and grabbed. She'd far rather peel and chop onions, scald her fingers fetching hot kettles, even scrub the floors until her hands were raw and burning than return to that noisy hellhole. The very thought made her belly clench in dread.

But Black Jack was ever determined to please his customers—no matter their treatment of his barmaids. She shuddered, experiencing anew the feel of grasping hands and pinching fingers. Lord, but she hated those swine! They sought respite from their troubles in drink—and sport from those who served it.

And then, tonight there was *him*, the dark-haired one in the corner. Staring at her. Watching her.

Oddly, it was that she hated most. Knowing he watched while those awful men pinched and fondled her only deepened her shame and humiliation . . . and her anger. The soft line of her lips compressed. Had he been amused by it? Had he secretly laughed? Oh, but the nerve of the man!

Still, she could not help but wonder who he was, he and his friend. A wealthy captain and mate of a vessel berthed in the harbor? Low-country planters? Well-to-do merchants traveling through Charleston? Black Jack himself, in a rare moment, had seen to the supper preparations and served them their meal. That alone proclaimed them men of some stature.

Wiping her hands on a length of rag, she cast a furtive glance through the swinging double doors into the taproom. It was hard to see through the smoky haze, but sure enough, Black Jack was again at their table.

The double doors opened with a swish. Nell sauntered in, her braid askew, the shoulders of her dress rumpled and sagging from her shoulders. Cassie hastily averted her gaze. Nell looked as if she'd just crawled from someone's bed.

She gave a tittering laugh. "Sakes, can you imagine? An English earl stayin' here at Black Jack's! Ye saw him, didn't ye, girl, the two gents in the far corner? The black-haired one, 'e's the earl. Wickedly handsome, he is. Gives me shivers right down to me very toes, he does."

She dumped half a dozen dirty tankards into the washbasin. "I've never seen such hands on a man— so clean, even his nails, mind ye! And that coat he's wearin' . . . did you see it, Cassie? Made of velvet, it is! 'Course I don't know why I'm rattlin' on so about his clothes—it's what's beneath that interests me far more!" She let out a gusty laugh.

Cassie said nothing, but inside she winced. Nell was one such as her mother had been; she oft loved unwisely and too well. But while her mother had been far too free with her favors, Cassie had long ago vowed she'd not make the same mistake. Ducking the sides of ham and beef curing from the beam, she stepped before the pantry. With her back to Nell, she did her best to ignore her, placing several clean tankards back into the cupboard.

Nell paid no heed. "And the other one— Sir Christopher Marley, he called himself—why, he's almost as handsome as the earl! In fact, I'm feeling very generous tonight, Cassie. Sir Christopher Marley is yours!" She gave a cackling laugh. "Ah, but you wouldn't know what to do with a man such as he, would ye now, love?"

Cassie flushed, which made Nell laugh all the harder. Would she never get used to Nell making light of her? Oh, if only she could walk through the door and never return! And as for the earl, it mattered little to her whether he was the king of England, or master of a dung heap!

Black Jack hammered the doors open with beefy fists. Big, burly, and shaggy-haired as he was, Cassie had long ago decided his sour disposition had earned him his name. "What the blazes are the two of ye doin'?" he demanded. "Get yer lazy bums back where ye belong! We've customers waitin'!" His eyes lit on Cassie. "You," he growled. "Take a bottle of brandy to the two gents at the back table. Use the best crystal."

Nell wheeled about eagerly. "Oh, there's no need for Cassie to burden herself," she said brightly. "I'll serve it—"

"Not you, Nell. *Her*." He jerked his head toward Cassie.

Cassie had gone utterly still. A flash of alarm surged within her. Serve *him*? The one who stared so boldly? Cassie was well aware Nell had not made the offer out of any goodwill on her part— indeed, she was undoubtedly looking forward to warming the gent's bed tonight, which was just fine with Cassie.

Nervously she wet her lips. "It matters little to me if Nell—"

"Ah, but it does to me!" There was a long row of copper pans and utensils hanging from a beam. Cassie flinched when he grabbed a wooden spoon and shook it threateningly. "I said you, missy, not her! Now get to it 'fore I lose my patience. Smile and be nice to the gents—and stop trying to hide your bosom!"

Scalding tears burned Cassie's eyes. She damned Black Jack, even as she damned herself for her weakness. Blindly she reached for a bottle of brandy and Black Jack's best crystal goblets from the pantry. She tried to assure herself it was foolish to be so reluctant; after all, it wasn't as if she hadn't done this a thousand times before. And surely these two could be no worse than any of the others.

Mustering her courage, she pushed through the double doors and back out into the noisy taproom. Boisterous shouts hailed her return. Ignoring the coarse calls and snatching hands, she weaved her way through and around tables toward her destination.

Her steps slowed as she approached. She was but a few paces distant when the black-haired one, the earl, turned his head.

Their eyes locked.

For Cassie, it was as if a bolt of lightning zigzagged through her. Rampant in her mind was the urge to turn and run, as far and fast as she could. Why it was so, she did not know.

But for a timeless instant, she could not move. What was it Nell had said? *Wickedly handsome, he is.* But of the two, *wicked* was the one etched sharply in her brain.

Oh, there was no denying his handsomeness, by far and away. In all her days, Cassie had never seen a man's face so arrestingly pleasing to the eye. High cheekbones slanted above clean-shaven cheeks; his jaw was flawlessly chiseled, and all in perfect proportion. His hair was black as a crow's wing, and cropped rather short; dark, tousled curls fell across his forehead in a style unlike any Cassie had ever seen before. Yet for all its perfection, his was a face of supreme masculinity.

Yet she sensed a harshness within him, a harshness borne out by the unsmiling cast of his mouth. Set beneath winged black brows, his eyes were like pale frost, as cold and piercing as frozen glass.

Cassie was the first to look away. She swallowed, forcing her feet to do her bidding and close the remaining distance between them. All the while he stared at her through eyes of burning silver, as if he chose to see all that she would keep hidden. Nell was right, she thought on a note of panic. He gave her the shivers, but it was scarcely a pleasant sensation.

"Here you are, sirs." It was by no means an accident that she stationed herself next to the fair-haired gent Nell had called Christopher Marley. Quickly she set the crystal goblets before them.

Christopher Marley smiled up at her. "You are Cassie, are you not?"

Cassie reluctantly met his gaze, only to breathe a silent but profound sigh of relief. Instinct alone told her that his was a presence not nearly so threatening as his friend's. He had kind eyes, and a warm and gentle smile. "Yes, sir," she murmured. "Cassie McClellan."

"And is Cassie short for Cassandra?"

"Aye," she nodded. "But no one has ever called me anything but Cassie." Feeling more at ease, she ventured a faint smile.

His own deepened. "I must admit, Cassie does suit you." He leaned back in his chair, surveying her curiously. "Has Charleston always been your home, Cassie?"

Cassie's smile withered. Home? She had no home, for she scarcely considered the cramped, tiny room in the attic where she slept with Nell her home. In truth, it was the one great wish that preyed longingly on her mind. She and Bess had oft dreamed of saving their coin that they might buy a cottage of their own; there they would sew for fine ladies since they were both well skilled with a needle. It needn't matter if it were but a single room; what mattered was that they need not answer to anyone but themselves.

Bess, she thought with a pang. Dear, sweet Bess. Though not so very much older than herself, Bess had been far more mother to her than her own. She had taken her in, protected her, and watched out for her when no one else had cared.

A bitter darkness stole into her heart. No, she thought again. She had no home of her own, nor was it likely she ever would.

Her lashes dropped. She set her attention to removing the stopper from the bottle of brandy. "Aye," she said quietly. "I've lived in Charleston all my life." She smiled slightly. "Indeed, I've never been outside of the city."

He seemed to sense something was wrong. An awkward silence prevailed as she struggled with the bottle-stopper; uppermost in her mind was awareness that the earl still watched and had yet to say a word. Nervousness made her fingers clumsy. She plucked almost frantically at the stopper.

It was then that the earl finally spoke, a hint of barely restrained impatience in his voice. "Allow me." Cassie's eyes flew to his. Her lips parted. What she intended to say or do, she would never know. Strong fingers had already curled around the neck of the bottle. For the space of a heartbeat, the back of his knuckles lay cradled against the curve of her breast. It was all Cassie could do not to cry out, not from shock, but from the reaction his touch evoked. Like fire it was, clear through to the core of her body.

The stopper popped free. To Cassie, the loud *pop!* was like the blast of a gun.

She flushed as he proceeded to fill the two goblets. "Thank you, sir." The urge to flee was upon her again, but she'd caught a glimpse of Black Jack across the floor. He was looking her way, his expression as frigid as a sea wind in winter. Badly shaken and praying it did not show, she bobbed a curtsy, eyes downcast. "Will you be needing anything else, sirs?"

She had no desire to look at the earl, yet he drew her gaze with a force too powerful to resist. His eyes were cool and assessing. They wandered at will, over her neckline before settling, she was certain, with calculated deliberation on the swell of her flesh visible above the frayed lace trim of her bodice.

"Not at the present," he drawled at last.

Both angry and anxious at his brazenly thorough study, she gave a nod. "I'll just clear the table for you, then." Eager to be quit of the pair, no matter how pleasant his companion might be, she reached across the table for the tankards they'd set aside. But in her haste to replace them on her tray, she withdrew her elbow just a little too quickly.

The bottle of brandy tipped over with a crash. The dark red liquid inside pursued a straight and unerring path across the table and over the side. Both men leaped to their feet. By some miracle both emerged unscathed.

"By God, wench, I do believe you've no experience as a barmaid." The earl glared at her, his voice stripped free of any indulgence.

Cassie had already begun swiping at the sodden mess. She paused long enough to return his glare in full measure. " 'Tis hardly my first night—indeed I've been here nearly as long as Nell!"

"I wonder, then," came his grim response, "that Black Jack has any wine left in his cellars."

It was too much! Who was he to call her inept? She straightened indignantly. "And who are you to criticize me?" she cried. "Perhaps if you'd ever done an honest day's work in your life, you'd not be so quick to judge others who are but trying their best!"

Cassie did not see Black Jack approach. She gasped as her arm was suddenly seized in a grip she knew from experience would cause bruises. "How dare ye talk to 'is lordship that way! Tell 'im ye're sorry!"

Cassie's face was scarlet. A simmering resentment fired within her. It was bad enough to be chastised in front of the entire taproom, let alone knowing that *he* stood witness to her shame. Indeed, if it hadn't been for him staring at her, she wouldn't have been so careless in the first place.

Beefy fingers bit fiercely into her arm. "Tell 'im, missy!"

To Cassie's horror, her throat closed with the scalding threat of tears. She hated the earl for bringing her to this wretched point, almost as much as she hated herself for her lack of pride. The only thing that brought her chin up was the certainty that Black Jack would take immense pleasure in seeing her humbled.

"I am sorry." Her lips barely moved as she spoke.

Black Jack leveled a scowl at her and dropped her arm. He turned toward the other two men. "I'll see ye're brought another bottle," he began.

Christopher Marley held up a hand. "Not for me, thank you. I've had quite enough for the night." He turned and gave Cassie's shoulder a reassuring squeeze. "No harm done, lass. Do not worry your pretty head about it another minute."

"No, indeed," the earl echoed coldly. "We cannot have that, can we?"

The earl was forgotten as Black Jack began to drag her toward the kitchens. They were no sooner through the doors than he loosed the full force of his ire. "You've gone too far, girl! I've always held that a girl need not take to her bed a man she does not want, but no more will I put up with your airs and your unwillingness. Ye'll get away with it no longer, do ye hear? Aye, I've often thought if ye once had a man ye'd not be so damned skittish. Well, I think it's time we found out!"

The world around her seemed to spin and swirl. She shuddered. Dear God, surely he was not suggesting . . . She looked on numbly as he whirled and loaded another goblet and bottle of brandy onto a tray.

He turned to her and snarled, "Ye'll be making amends to 'is lordship—and to me, girl." He jammed his head toward the tray. "Take that up to the rose chamber. The earl is sleeping there. If a man pays more to spend a night here, by Gawd, he'll get more, and don't pretend ye don't know what I mean! If ye please him, ye please me. I'd keep that in mind if I were you. For if ye don't, I swear I'll see ye turned out in the streets by morning!"

Cassie's head jerked up. As awful as it was here, the streets were even worse. Only yesterday a young woman had been found in an alley, half-naked, her throat slit.

She waited no longer. His words were like a burr beneath her feet. She snatched up the tray and fled as if the hounds of hell snapped at her heels.

The rose chamber was the best in the inn. Black Jack always put the well-to-do guests there. A wide four-poster with a delicate, rose-embroidered coverlet dominated the large, spacious room. Matching brocade draperies trimmed the window.

When her mother had first started working for Black Jack, Cassie had often crept inside and let her fantasies take flight. She pretended she was a fine lady and mistress of a huge house with a dozen chambers such as this. She was never hungry and never cold.

Now her only thought was to escape—this horrid inn, the toil, the endless drudgery.

She deposited the tray on the pedestal table near the window. She pressed her cool hands against the fiery heat of her cheeks. Her heart cried out in weary despair. Was it wrong to want more? She didn't want much, just better than what little she had. A one-room cottage that was truly her own, where she need not worry she might end up on the streets. Enough coin to buy another dress, and maybe a new bonnet.

Dear God, she didn't want to die like Bess, in that stinking attic room that smelled of death and dust.

If only there was a way out. If only . . .

Gathering herself in hand, she straightened, wiping the dampness from her cheeks. Did Black Jack truly expect her to lay with the earl? Horror clutched her insides. How could she wait here, like a lamb on its way to the slaughterhouse?

She spun around. Her eyes lit on the chest of drawers just inside the doorway. Heaped in a small mound was a handful of silver. Oh, it was scarce a fortune, to be sure. But it was far more than she had seen in all her years.

She had only to reach out a hand, and it would be hers . . .

"A tempting sum, is it not? Ah, but if you want it, Yank, I'm afraid you'll have to earn it."

Chapter 2

It was him.

For a timeless moment it was as if she were without courage or wits—she could not move. A part of her longed to flee, like a tempest racing across the sea. But her feet seemed suddenly weighted with lead. Through some miracle she finally managed to turn and face him.

He was tall, she noted in some far distant corner of her mind, far taller than he had appeared downstairs. Oh, but no dandy, this one! His shoulders stretched the velvet of his jacket so taut there was nary a pucker or a wrinkle. Dark-colored breeches revealed every hard curve of bulging thighs, so tight they were almost like a second skin. He was all grace, all elegance as he approached.

A flurry of panic assailed her. If she tried to run, he could easily catch her. To her shock, he strode past her to the tray. He poured a generous portion of port into the goblet, then offered it to her. "Will you join me, Yank?"

Cassie blanched. Sharing a glass with him—placing her lips where his had been—was an intimacy she would take with no man, let alone this one!

She shook her head. "I've no taste for spirits," she managed to say.

"No? Well, then. To . . . Yankees." He tipped his glass to her and drank, his crystalline gaze never straying from hers.

She was scarcely as composed as she might have wished. "If you please, sir, I must return—"

"But it does not please me. I much prefer you remain here."

Cassie laced her hands together before her. She could not stay here for—Lord, she could not complete the thought, even to herself! Even Black Jack's threats could not make her do . . . that! Her mind churned frantically.

She had no recourse but to appeal to the earl's reason and hope he was an honorable man.

There was an unfamiliar dryness in her throat. "Sir, 'tis plain you have no liking for me. Indeed, I think you would not be here now were it not for Black Jack—"

"On the contrary, I am precisely where I wish to be. And more importantly, with *whom* I wish to be."

He toyed with her. Cassie sensed it with all that she possessed. Oh, but he was cruel to torment her so!

She gave a curt, jerky gesture with her hands. "Sir," she began. "I am sorry for my clumsiness. You cannot know how much. But I see no reason why I should be punished—"

"Punished! Why, you wound me sorely. 'Tis not punishment I have in mind, but pleasure."

Pleasure? Cassie shuddered. If there was pleasure to be had, it would not be hers, but his.

He smiled, as if he were privy to her very thoughts. "What!" he exclaimed. "Never tell me those oafs belowstairs do not know how to take care of a gem like you!"

Cassie's cheeks burned painfully. She surveyed him warily as he pulled something from his pocket—a watch, for she caught the glint of a fine gold chain as he dropped it next to the pile of silver.

He stepped forward.

Cassie inched back.

His laugh was both hearty—and heartless. "Come, Yank! Do I frighten you?"

Not in the way that he suggested, she thought with a shiver, but in a way that was utterly foreign to her.

"You dislike me, don't you, Yank?"

Yank. Cassie's spine stiffened. "I've a name, sir, and I'll thank you to use it."

"I think not. No, I do believe Christopher was wrong. 'Yank' suits much better, for you Yanks are often rowdy and unruly. Aye, 'Yank' it shall be. But back to my question. Why do you dislike me?"

"Indeed, milord, I believe 'tis you who dislikes me. Why else would you stare at me as you did?"

So she had noticed that, had she? Gabriel smiled dryly. She was shabbily dressed, her clothing little more than rags, and still it hid nothing of her beauty. He wondered vaguely if she had any idea how lovely she was. Her coloring was unusual, but striking nonetheless—hair like amber fire and eyes like clear topaz. And though she was young, she was years out of childhood. True, she was thinner than he would have liked, but the swell at breast and hip promised a bounty he suspected would scarcely disappoint him.

He frowned, rather irritated with himself. It wasn't like him to display such interest in a servant. Indeed, he preferred his women with far more sophistication than this uncivilized young lass. Still, the girl was scarcely untried. Indeed, he decided with more than a touch of cynicism, her experience might well equal his own.

And there was no denying she stirred his blood.

"Come, Yank. I've spent weeks at sea, without the company of women such as yourself. Can you not find it in your heart to be generous? Will you not cater to a weary soul who is in dire need of a soft, feminine body, a warm, soothing hand?"

A warm, soothing hand? Oh, but that was rich! Her hands were lobster-red, as rough as the scrub brush which rendered them so.

Her temper began to unravel. "Sir," she stated quietly, "I do believe you've not wanted for a single thing in your entire life."

On that score, she was right. Gabriel had not. He'd had everything . . . but a father's love.

His gaze flickered to the pile of silver. "That is a considerable amount of coin, Yank. If you are to earn it, I would expect much of you. You would have to stay with me . . . oh, not an hour, not even two—the night through, I think. And in the morning, why perhaps we might even share the bath together."

An icy jolt tore through her. Cassie had thought nothing could shock her, but . . . sweet heaven, bathe with a man? Surely people did not do such things!

He unnerved her, she realized, though he had yet to lay a hand on her. She was not ignorant. She knew what he wanted. Not long ago Bess had told her, "If a man's sweet and gentle, it's not so bad. But sometimes they're rough and quick and hard." Bess had turned her face aside. "Then it's awful," she'd said in a voice that sounded all tight and strangled.

Cassie knew whenever that happened. Bess would come to bed quietly weeping. Sometimes there were marks on her arms the next day, even on her breasts. Cassie remembered the last time. Not long after Bess had discovered she was with child—the child she'd died birthing. Cassie shuddered. She knew why Bess had done such things—for the money it brought. Indeed, it was that money which had saved Cassie from the same fate.

But Cassie was not yet ready to trade her virtue for a handful of silver.

Gabriel did not glimpse her distress. He saw only distaste.

Would she have been as reluctant if she were here with Christopher? The idea rankled. Gabriel recalled how sweetly she had smiled at his friend, while she would not even deign to look at him. A dark anger swept through him.

"Aye," he said softly. "A bath would prove quite delightful, I think."

Cassie's eyes flashed. "Black Jack pays me but a meager pittance to scrub floors and serve ale. Not for this!"

"Ah, but I'm not sure he sees it that way." His tone was slick as oil.

Her fingers curled against her palm. "I know your kind, sir. You take what you want, with no thought of anyone save yourself."

"Why, Yank, I do believe some man has wronged you! Loved you and left you, perhaps?"

Her chin came up. "I am merely angry, sir, that I have no say in the matter!"

He shrugged and glanced at the pile of coin. "I do believe you've already set your price."

"You do not understand, sir. What you want, I'll not give for any price!" Not to him or to any man.

It struck him then . . . he was goading her, and quite unmercifully. He'd not have done so, were it not for the defiance on her face. She looked at him as if she were his better . . . as if he was nothing.

And that was the one thing Gabriel could not tolerate.

Slowly he circled her. He sensed her nervous tension, just as he sensed her struggle not to reveal it. Her head was held regally high, the slender lines of her back as rigid as a soldier's. Gabriel was both amused and piqued by her resistance. It seemed the wench possessed not only beauty, but an abundance of pride, an odd combination for one of her station.

At length he halted before her, so close they stood but a breath apart. "I find this situation very much a novelty, Yank. You see, 'tis rare that a woman refuses me . . . therefore I must make certain I understand. 'Tis not I who spurn you, but you who spurn me."

Oh, but the conceit of the man! If she said yes, she risked not only his anger, but Black Jack's as well. Yet how could she disagree, for then he would assume she meant to lay with him!

Cassie battled a mounting panic. His nearness was disconcerting; a prickle of warning trickled up her nape.

It took every ounce of courage she had to meet the steely probe of his gaze, yet somehow she managed. "I cannot stop you if you choose to do this." Her tone was very low. "It would be foolish to pit my strength against yours, for I would be the loser. But I would have you know, sir, you have neither my consent, nor my willingness. Therefore, I ask that you let me leave."

In truth, it was not her plea, but the bitterness that lay biting in her tone which brought Gabriel up short.

Her gaze slid away, but not before he glimpsed the suspiciously bright sheen that glazed the breath-taking gold of her eyes. Tears? He scoffed. He was not one to let a woman's tears sway him. He'd discovered they were naught but a tool women used to get what they wanted.

"And if I let you leave, what then? There is no need for pretense between us, Yank. We both know why Black Jack sent you here. Most likely he does not expect you to leave this chamber until the night is well spent."

Cassie was certain her face was the color of fire. Her attention was confined to the intricate folds of his impeccable white cravat. "If you were to tell him that I . . . I pleased you," she whispered, "he need never know."

"But if we are to bargain, I should expect some kind of reward—at the very least, a trade."

"A trade!" Stung, Cassie bit back a dry, strangled sob. "Sir, would you take the very clothes upon my back? I have nothing to give."

"Save that which you *refuse* to give."

Her eyes squeezed shut. Oh, but she should have known better than to expect mercy from him! A wrenching despair rode heavy on her heart. Was this how it would be? Her virginity surrendered to one who cared only that his own pleasures of the flesh be satisfied?

Gabriel had already made up his mind he would not force her. Desirable though she was, there were too many other willing women in the world to trouble himself with one who wanted no part of him. But by God, the wench was a maddening little piece, and he would have none of it.

"A kiss," he said suddenly. "A kiss and you may go."

Her eyes flew open; his were hard as coal, glittering with a strange heat. Cassie went hot inside, then icy cold. His mouth, beautifully shaped though it was, was set in a thin, cruel line. There was no softness in him, none at all.

Strong hands shackled her about the wrists. Even now they drew her closer. Ever closer . . .

Her breath came fast, then slow. It was but a kiss. Was that so much to yield? She shivered. Far better that than the other . . .

His mouth met hers. A tiny little jolt went through her, but she kept her mouth tightly pinched together, her body instinctively resisting what she was certain would be another sloppy, slathering kiss like so many others pressed upon her unwilling lips.

Gabriel's head lifted. The grip upon her wrists tightened by a hair.

"Come, Yank, you must do better than that. I've no desire to kiss a wizened prune."

The bite in his words was sharp enough to wound. Cassie glared. "Sir," she began, "I would remind you—"

His arm was like an iron brace around her. Their bodies twisted together. A peculiar sensation of weightlessness assailed her. She felt the softness of the mattress at her back, the unexpected heaviness of the earl's chest atop her own.

His mouth closed over hers. The fleeting thought chased through her mind that this kiss was like none other, and then her mind seemed not her own. His lips were warm and compelling, starkly primitive yet oddly persuasive, draining her of strength and will. Cassie was dazed by the strange inner trembling that seized her. She felt absurdly lightheaded.

It took a moment to realize he had raised his head.

"Will you not change your mind, Yank?" A blunted fingertip traced the graceful arch of her throat. "I promise you a night you'll not soon forget."

She stared at him, shaky and confused. Sweet heaven, she was lying on the bed, and he was lying on *her*! Sanity returned with a galvanizing rush. She thumped his shoulders with her fists. "I'd just as soon forget *you*!"

Her blows might well have fallen on a pillar of stone. He studied her, turning his head first this way, then that. Finally a devilish brow rose high.

"This will not do—'twill not do at all, Yank. You lack the look of a woman well bedded ... Indeed, if Black Jack is not to guess the truth ..."

Cassie gasped as he proceeded to tug the pins from her hair; the silken strands tumbled over his hands, wild and dishevelled.

His head dipped again, but his target was not her lips. Cassie gave a small, stricken cry as his mouth settled on the side of her neck, nipping the tender skin with his teeth, gently sucking, then soothing the hurt with his tongue. Her fingers tangled in his hair. She tugged hard but he paid no heed. His mouth fastened greedily on its tender prey. Then all at once his mouth was on hers again, only this time demanding and ruthless, so raw and plundering that she could scarcely breathe.

Something exploded in her mind. Somehow she managed to tear her mouth free.

Small fists pummeled his shoulders. "You blue-blooded bastard! Let me go!"

Gabriel released her. Nell was right, he decided with vast amusement. The chit did put on airs.

"My dear, if you knew who my father was, you would hardly question my legitimacy."

Cassie scrambled to her feet. Her mouth felt swollen and bruised. The delicate skin around her lips still burned. "I don't care who your father is!" she cried. "That doesn't give you the right to touch me so!"

Gabriel shrugged. "My dear, I touched far less than those fellows belowstairs."

"What do you expect me to do?" She defended herself heatedly. "Black Jack watches my every move!"

He surveyed her a moment, his expression cool and disinterested, as if the exchange had never happened. "You may go, Yank. A wench who is unwilling is as much trouble as one who is untried. I've no taste for either."

She had been dismissed. He now stood at the window, hands behind his back, staring out in the stark blackness of the night. Hatred blazed within her, for it was very apparent he'd already forgotten her.

Slowly she began to back away. She swore, every vile curse she'd ever heard in the taproom, scarcely knowing what any of them even meant. But if he heard, there was no sign of it. He did not turn, nor did he speak, and that gave Cassie the very chance she needed . . .

She snatched his watch from the dresser and fled.

Chapter 3

In the attic, Cassie rushed to the crooked table in the corner to light the stub of candle there. Her hands were shaking so that she dropped the flint thrice before the task was completed. The flame flickered and wavered, casting an eerie reflection on the wall behind it.

Only then did she examine the prize clutched tight within her palm.

In all her days, Cassie had never seen such a finely crafted piece. The shell-shaped case was elaborately carved; it shone bright and golden as the sun on a warm spring day. There was writing on the back side, but Cassie paid no heed. With the ragged edge of her nail, she released the catch on the hinge. Opposite the face was a cleverly painted scene of a woman and a young boy, standing amongst a garden of flowers.

Her mind raced apace with the thunder of her heart. The watch was no doubt worth a great deal of money. Perhaps not a fortune, but enough to take her far, far away from Black Jack's Inn—and Charleston. Enough to see her settled in a decent boardinghouse. Enough to tide her over while she sought work, perhaps as a seamstress.

You can't, cried a voice inside. *What if the earl discovers it missing? He will know you stole it.*

You have nothing to lose, urged another voice. *You dare not trust the earl to keep his word. And you know what Black Jack said—he will turn you out when he finds out you refused to lay with the earl.*

Hours later she lay huddled on her pallet in the corner.

She was half-afraid the earl would appear at any moment, spewing anger and shouting for his watch, with Black Jack at his heels. The din from downstairs had long since died down. Nell did not come to seek her bed. Cassie was secretly glad she chose to warm someone else's rather than her own.

Gradually her fears began to recede. As the night grew darker, her hopes grew stronger. By now the earl was surely long since abed. Likely as not, he would not rise 'til the hour was well past noon. Lord or no, no doubt he was just like every other man—fond of cards and brandy and cigars—and women.

Daylight arrived at long last. A meager sliver of light sneaked through the dust-coated windows of the attic as Cassie eased down the stairs. She crept through the inn slowly, for fear of making some sound that might give away her presence. The quick hard pounding of her heart seemed to jolt her entire body as she inched past Gabriel's door, praying all the while that her luck would last . . . that he wouldn't notice the watch was missing until he had awakened, long into the day . . .

As was his habit, Gabriel opened his eyes to the first faint glimmer of dawn creeping through the draperies. He did not linger abed, but thrust off his covers and rose naked to his full, impressive height. A frugal smile touched the hardness of his mouth. He briefly entertained the notion of calling for a bath, that the girl Cassie might attend him. Would she resist, as she had last night? No matter. Her protests were a thin disguise for the response he'd tasted in lips that were startlingly sweet and warm.

His jaw hardened, then he forced a dry chuckle. It was really rather vastly amusing—a mere servant had spurned him—the future duke of Farleigh. He regretted that she'd not been willing. He'd have liked nothing more than to strip away those drab faded rags and discover the bounty of creamy pink flesh that lay beneath. Aye, the wench heated his blood—and his temper. Yet her very coolness merely made her all the more intriguing.

Perhaps he should have pressed the issue— warmed her ice to fire. Turned her fierce resistance into smoldering excitement. Indeed, he suspected lying with such a fiery wench as she might have proved quite satisfying . . . for both of them.

But there was much to be done this day. If all went as planned, the crew would finish loading the hold with indigo and tobacco to be taken back to England. With luck, they could set sail by noonday.

Five minutes later, he stood before the window, simply dressed in a loose white shirt, dark breeches, and shiny, high-topped boots. Fog lay over the harbor, a mysterious shroud of silver. The city was just beginning to stir. He glimpsed only a few trailing plumes of smoke curling from the chimneys.

He was just about to turn away when he saw it—there, in the street just outside the inn. From the murky shadows he picked out the slight figure of a woman, hurrying down the boardwalk. Her back was to him so he could not see her face. Her hair lay hidden beneath a scarf. In one hand she clutched a small pouch. Was it his imagination—or did her pace quicken? Gabriel's eyes narrowed. There was something almost furtive in her manner.

He whirled. His pile of coin still lay mounded on the dresser, untouched.

But there was no sign of his watch.

He swore, a vivid, blistering curse. Not only was the girl Cassie immensely desirable, maddening, and aloof . . .

She was also a thief.

Only when Cassie had stepped out into the damp morning chill did she dare to breathe again. She did not stop to say a tearful good-bye to the inn where she'd spent nearly half of her life. She had no regrets about leaving. She had only hopes that the future might hold far better than her wretched memories of Black Jack's Inn.

But she must hurry. There was a shopkeeper between the chandler and the baker. She'd heard Black Jack say the man dealt in used goods as well as new. She prayed he would purchase such a handsome watch for a goodly sum. And indeed, the winds of fortune seemed to be blowing her way. She hoped to catch him as soon as he opened his doors.

And then she would be free.

Shivering a little against the chill, she tugged her shawl from her head to her shoulders, pulling it tightly around her. She was scarcely upon the next row of buildings when she heard footsteps echo behind her. An eerie prickle tickled her nape. She glanced back, then froze.

Gabriel Sinclair's dark visage swam before her.

No, she thought numbly. It could not be him . . . it could not! Surely her mind played her false!

A choking panic climbed high in her throat. She turned and began to run. This time she knew she did not imagine the footsteps thundering behind her. Yet still she ran, her breath rasping and sobbing in her ears.

A hard arm snagged her by the waist. She felt herself borne free of the ground and caught against an unyielding muscular form. She struck out blindly. "Let me go!" she cried.

He whispered in her ear, his laugh a cold whisper. "We went through this only last night, Yank. Did you learn nothing from the outcome? I will free you when I am ready—and not before."

Cassie flung back her head and screamed at the top of her lungs. "Help! Help, I beg you! Please help me!"

The arm about her ribs tightened so that she could scarcely draw breath. Gabriel swore softly when a balding merchant poked his head through his doorway.

"Pay no mind to the lady," he called out. "She suffers from brain fever and fancies she is being persecuted."

Cassie gasped with outrage. Weak in the head, was she? She renewed her struggles but it was no use. He half-lifted, half-dragged her to a dingy alleyway, then backed her up against a hard brick wall. For one terrifying moment he held her there with the pressure of his body. His features displayed no emotion, though she knew instinctively he was fiercely angry. Her whole body jerked when he snatched her pouch from her hands. Withdrawing a step, he thrust his hand inside.

Cassie gaped, but only for an instant. "What do you think you're doing?" she cried. "That's mine! You have no right to touch it!"

He spared her not a glance as he pulled her threadbare nightgown from the pouch. "You have something of mine in your possession," he said coldly. "That gives me every right."

"Bloody hell it does!" With a cry she launched herself at him. But before she could do any damage, an unpleasantly strong arm wrapped around her once more. She was dragged frighteningly close to him once again.

"Yank, you seem determined to attract attention. Why, someone might be tempted to call the constable to see what is amiss."

The glitter in his eyes foretold the possibility only too well. Cassie went rigid but struggled no more. He let go of her, his countenance fierce and unsmiling.

"My watch, Yank," was all he said.

Cassie wet her lips. "You—you're too late. I-I sold it."

"Indeed," he stated calmly. "Forgive me for doubting you, but I fear I must find out for myself."

His smile was so pleasant, it was a moment before she realized what he was about. She tried to launch herself past him; he was too quick for her. With the back of his forearm he held her in place against the brick, barring her from any escape route she might take it in her head to find.

His gaze drilled into her like the point of a knife. He ran his fingers down her arms. And then that accursed hand slid deep inside her bodice, skimming the tops of her breasts, sliding over smooth, rounded flesh that no man had either seen or touched. Shocked beyond measure, Cassie gasped.

"Stop!" she cried.

He did not. Everything within her rebelled at his boldness, his intimacy. She drew a deep, fractured breath.

"Dear God, stop!" She gave a tearing, half-sob. "It—it's in my stocking! Turn around and I will give it to you!"

He released her, but he did not turn around. It was left to Cassie to shift awkwardly, aware that he surveyed her every move. Her hands were unsteady as she tugged down her right stocking. She straightened, his watch in her hand. She flung it into his outstretched palm.

"There! You have your watch back. Now let me be on my way!"

His features were grimly forbidding. "Not just yet, Yank. You cannot steal from me and think to get away with it." He hooked steely fingers into her elbow and began to pull her back the way she had come.

Cassie choked back a cry of bitter frustration. He was headed back to the inn! A hollow despair enshrouded her heart. Had she come so far, only to be wrenched back, like a dog upon a leash?

All too soon she was back inside the taproom. The door heaved shut behind them. Cassie cringed. Christopher Marley and Black Jack were there before the huge stone fireplace.

Black Jack spread his hands wide. "Yer lordship! I saw you leave . . . What goes on here?"

"The girl here is a thief. She stole my watch."

Cassie glimpsed the shock on Christopher Marley's face. Nell, she saw, had come to stand at the head of the stairs. Oh, but she should have known the earl would spare her nothing!

Black Jack's eyes bulged. "What! She stole it?"

"That she did. It seems she decided it was time to leave your employ. I should imagine she intended to use the proceeds from the watch as funding for her journey."

Christopher had moved to stand near Black Jack. His gaze rested on her neck; there was the faintest puzzlement etched upon his handsome features. His gaze flickered to the earl and back to Cassie again. She realized he had spied the moon-shaped purple mark the earl had put there.

Hot shame colored her cheeks. More than anything, she longed to shrivel up and die.

Nell sneered. "By God, you're a fine one to look down yer nose at me. Stealin' 'is lordship's watch—then runnin' off!"

Black Jack cursed. "I knew I should have shipped ye off to the orphan house when yer ma left ye behind! Yer trouble, missy, trouble!"

Cassie raised her head, undaunted. Her pride had wavered but was far from gone. "You think I've been better off here? I've scrubbed floors 'til my hands were raw and bleeding. I've emptied chamberpots and labored from dawn until midnight for as long as I can remember. You've begrudged me every bite of food I've ever taken. And all for a few pennies a year! Why, I'm hardly better off than the slaves in the fields!"

His face contorted. "Ye ungrateful little bitch! I think it's time I cured that smart, sassy mouth o' yours!"

Black Jack's fingers curled into a meaty fist. In some far distant corner of her mind, Cassie saw that Christopher looked appalled as Black Jack raised his fist high.

She braced herself inwardly. It wouldn't be the first time Black Jack had struck her. No doubt the earl would take great pleasure in seeing her thus defeated. But she wouldn't cry out, not while he watched . . .

The blow she expected never fell.

"If you strike the girl," the earl spoke with an almost deadly quiet, "you will answer to me. It was my watch she stole. 'Tis my right, and no one else's, to see to her punishment."

Black Jack appeared startled, yet even he dared not oppose the earl. He lowered his hand to his side and cleared his throat. "I meant no harm," he said gruffly. "But the girl needs a reminder o' her place now and then."

Gabriel's tone was frigid. "Sir, I believe you meant her every harm. But in this case, I shall decide what she needs." He curled his hand around Cassie's arm.

Cassie's insides knotted with sick dread. Perhaps it would have been better to suffer Black Jack's rage. At least she knew it was quickly spent. But the earl . . . The cold, controlled anger she sensed in him was frightening. Her mind churning, she moved along numbly as he pulled her up the stairs.

In his chamber, he pushed her down on the end of the rumpled bed. Cassie tipped her head back and eyed him warily, her fear masked in indignation.

"You have your watch back," she said stiffly. "What more do you want of me?"

He moved to pour himself a small glass of brandy from a decanter on the table. He did not look at her as he spoke. "I am curious as to why you took it, Yank. Indeed, I find myself wondering how many other men you have robbed."

Cassie's soft lips tightened. It seemed he meant to crucify her. Well, if that was what he was about, she'd be damned if she'd help him!

He turned. "Come, Yank." This time his tone was no less than a demand. "Am I the only one so honored?"

Her eyes flashed fire. "I took the watch because you are arrogant and bold, sir. *And* for the price it would bring."

"Why were you so determined to run away?"

Her eyes darkened. "Why, sir," she said with a mocking laugh. "I live a life of such ease. What possible reason could I have for wanting to forever leave this place?"

"And just where did you intend to go?"

She paused, but only for a moment. "I don't know—anywhere!—as long as it was far, far from here!"

Gabriel surveyed her over the rim of the glass. He wondered that he had even asked, for her bitter words to Black Jack had made her plight quite clear. Nor did he doubt that every word was true. His gaze swept over her ragged gown, the faded pouch she clutched so desperately still, to settle at last upon the cracked, dry skin of her hands.

Cassie flushed when she saw where his gaze dwelled. She swallowed, gathering her courage around her like a cloak. "I cannot stay here any longer." Her tone was low but fervent. "I *will* not. So if you intend to take me to the constable, just—just do it and be done with it."

Gabriel was unwillingly impressed. The girl had spirit—and courage as well. Oh, he knew she was terrified. He hadn't missed the desperation in her eyes. She was, he admitted, a worthy adversary. One perhaps even worthy of standing up against his father. Indeed, he wondered what his father would think of this upstart little Yank . . .

From out of nowhere, there was an echo in his mind, the words Christopher had spoken only last night.

No farmer's wife, this one, eh? No doubt she could aim far higher . . .

Slowly he lowered the glass from his lips. He stared at her intently, as if seeing her for the first time.

The girl was a thief. Fiery and unruly. Low-born and uncivilized . . .

An uncivilized *Yankee*.

It came to him then . . . an idea spawned by years of neglect, and a ragtag but beautiful wench.

Sweet heaven, that was it . . .

He was across the floor in an instant. Catching her by the arms, he pulled her from her perch at the end of the bed. He grabbed her chin and turned her face up for his inspection.

His gaze roved intently over her features. "How old are you, girl?"

When she said nothing, his hands fell to her shoulders. "Answer me, girl," he said sharply. "How old are you?"

Cassie wet her lips. "Eighteen, I believe," she said faintly. "Though I cannot be sure . . ."

"Nell said your mother deserted you when you were just a child. Have you no other relatives?"

Her eyes, trained on his face, were huge. Wordlessly, she shook her head.

"What if I told you I could rescue you? Save you from this wretched drudgery? What if I told you I could take you far, far away?"

She blinked. "Wh-where?"

"All the way across the sea—to England. Perhaps to Paris someday. Yes, you would like Paris, I think." He traced the back of his knuckle along the hollow of her throat. "I could give you jewels. Furs. How long since you've had a new dress, Yank? I could make certain you have a new dress for every day of the year."

Cassie shook her head slightly as if to clear it. "I-I cannot think why you should want to!" she blurted.

Gabriel smiled tightly. Oh, it wasn't out of the goodness of his heart, for indeed he wondered if he possessed such a thing. No, it had far less to do with generosity . . . and far more to do with revenge. And what sweet revenge it would be . . .

His father wanted him to marry. By God, so he would.

Cassie tensed visibly. "I-I thought you meant to punish me," she said, her voice shaking.

"Set your mind at ease, girl. I've no intention of turning you over to the constable—or to Black Jack."

"Sir, are you . . . unwell?" Cassie muttered.

He gave a short, harsh burst of laughter. "Indeed I've never been better." He paused. "So what do you say, Yank? You left this place this morning with little thought for your destination. I offer you the chance to see England—the entire continent. You have my word, you'll never again have to scrub floors."

Cassie bit her lip. "Such things do not come free," she said slowly. "And there is nothing I can give you in return . . ." He watched as deep color suffused her cheeks. "Dear lord," she gasped. "Never say you expect me to be your—your mistress—"

A grim smile lurked on his lips. " 'Tis not a mistress I want, Yank . . . but a wife."

Chapter 4

A *wife.*

Cassie's mind was racing. Oh, but the man was mad. Surely it was so! Or was it some monstrous jest? Or perhaps . . . sweet Lord, perhaps *she* was the one who was mad . . .

She could not tear her gaze from him. His posture exuded utter ease. But it was his eyes that chained her endlessly, for she knew she did not imagine the cold glitter of calculation in those strange silvery depths.

No, she was not mad. Nor was he.

Slowly she began to back away. She was scarcely aware when the mattress bumped the back of her knees. Dazedly she sank onto the rumpled covers, the powers of speech beyond her.

And still he smiled—a mocking smile. A taunting smile. A smile she could not fully comprehend . . .

At length she spoke, her tone very low. "You toy with me, sir. And 'tis monstrously cruel of you to do so."

"Monstrously cruel?" He laughed, a genuine mirthful laugh. "Yank, in truth I am being monstrously generous."

"And in truth I can think of no reason why a man like you would want to marry the likes of me." The words came out sharper than she intended.

"Ah, but I can." There was a fierce light in his eyes, a light that was somehow almost frightening.

"And I say again, sir, you toy with me!" Her chin lifted bravely. "I do not forget that you are an English lord—"

"Nor do I, Yank." She watched his slow-growing smile with mounting unease. "Why, you could soon be a countess . . . and the future duchess of Farleigh."

A countess? A duchess? *Her*? Why, the man had clearly decided she was a simpleton. Sheer anger propelled her to her feet. Cassie silently gauged the distance to the door. "I've no doubt marriage may well be on your mind—but not to me!" she cried, rushing forward.

He caught her mid-stride. Fingers like iron talons curled around her arm, thwarting her flight and whirling her around to face him. Cassie looked up at him with a gasp.

His smile turned chilling. "I assure you, my dear, I am deadly serious. I may be many things, but I am not a man to speak lightly about such matters. Marriage is most certainly on my mind, but make no mistake—'tis marriage to *you* that I am about."

Cassie could not help it. She blurted the first thing that came to mind. "But I-I do not know you . . . I'd be a fool to marry you!"

His smile vanished. "You'd be a fool not to," he said coldly. "You no longer have my watch, Yank.

Have you considered what your life will be like if you remain here?"

"I-I am skilled with a needle." She tried to speak defiantly and failed miserably. "I can find work as a seamstress—"

"And what if you do not? Who will hire you? You've no one to recommend you, no one who may testify as to your abilities. Indeed, what respectable dressmaker would hire a former tavern wench? And where will you live until you do find employment? In the streets? What if you chance to catch some man's fancy? Could you defend yourself if he decided to have his way with you and you did not wish it? Believe me, Yank, that is no way to live, in Charleston or any other place."

Cassie told herself he was trying to frighten her. She tried to shrink away, struggling to be free of his hold. He would not let her, but pulled her close—so close she could feel the heat of his breath on her cheeks.

"You could always go back to serving ale. Perhaps you don't mind the leering glances, the hands beneath your skirts . . ."

Cassie shuddered.

"You're fetching enough to earn your living with your body, I vow. Of course, if you've no aversion to spending the rest of your life on your back, exchanging one man for another, rutting between your thighs, night after night . . ."

Cassie's cheeks burned at his frankness, her expression reflecting her revulsion. Confusion roiled within her. Was this a nightmare—or a godsend? She knew, now more than ever, that she could never go back to the life she had been leading. She longed for nothing more than to leave it behind . . . forever.

She swallowed, forcing herself to look up into his hard, dark features.

"I do not understand," she said, very low. "What possible reason could you have for such an offer? You say you do not forget the differences in our station." Her voice caught. "So why—why me?"

Gabriel did not say it was those very differences that made him determined to wed her. To do so might jeopardize all that he sought.

A stab of black humor struck him. How ironic it was that all these years his father had had no use for his second son. But now that Stuart was gone, his father was determined to push his way into his life. Only now, the tables had been turned.

And at least the girl was passable to look upon. His gaze roved slowly over her upturned features, absorbing the smooth, creamy perfection of skin unadorned by powder or perfumes. Indeed, she was far more than passable . . .

His father was determined that he marry. Well, Gabriel decided with a grim feeling of triumph, he would be a dutiful son. He would give his father what he wanted, only it would not be quite as his father planned.

He would take as his wife this thieving, lowborn wench.

But he would offer her no more explanation than necessary. He realized he had snared her attention, if not her consent. He arched a brow, but did not flinch from the directness of her gaze.

"I see in your face that you do not delude yourself, Yank. I like that, for it would be a grave mistake to believe it's love which motivates me."

He released her, but his eyes commanded her
attention. He acknowledged, with grim satisfaction, the flush that flamed her face as he scruti-
nized her from head to toe.

"Nor," he added with a tight little smile, "is
it lust."

While Cassie smothered a sigh, he moved to stand
at the window, his back to her. Strong hands linked
behind him, he stared out at the harbor. After a
moment, he turned back to her.

"You ask why I should wish to marry you. Very
well, then, I shall be frank. My father is the duke
of Farleigh. I am the youngest of two sons. As the
eldest son, my brother Stuart was my father's heir.
Stuart died several months ago."

Not knowing what to say, Cassie remained silent.
Nor did he appear to expect anything from her;
his features, like his voice, reflected no hint of
emotion.

"Farleigh, my father's estate in Kent, borders
lands belonging to Reginald Latham, the duke
of Warrenton. Warrenton's only daughter, Lady
Evelyn, was betrothed to my brother Stuart at the
time of his death," he went on. "When Stuart died,
I inherited his title—earl of Wakefield—much to my
father's distaste, I suspect."

The subtle hardening of his tone did not go
unnoticed by Cassie. She could not help but
wonder why . . . "You do not seem to have much
liking for your father," she said slowly.

He gave a harsh laugh. "As much as he has for

me. You see, Yank, my father's wishes and mine seldom coincide."

Cassie frowned. "And what has this to do with marriage?" *And me*, she amended silently.

"Before I left on this voyage, my father informed me that he expects me to inherit Stuart's future bride as well as his title. I've no desire to marry Lady Evelyn, or any other woman for that matter, but my father feels it is my duty to marry." A brief spasm of fury crossed Gabriel's face. "My father is a strong-willed, powerful man who has seldom had his wishes turned aside. But I'll not let him lead me down a path that is not of my own choosing. If I let him control me in this, he will be convinced he can control me in all things. And yet I've no wish to turn my back on all that might someday be mine. Therefore, I shall fulfill my duty—only my marriage will *not* be to the bride of his choice."

There was a small pause. "As for why I've chosen you, by your own admission you have no relatives. There is no one to further interfere in my life. And I'll be blunt, Yank. I've no time to search for a bride, either here or in England. If the deed is done upon my return, there is nothing my father can do to change it." He was silent for a moment.

"We both wish to have control of our future," he said with a shrug. "Your future will be assured. And if I am already wed, there'll be no more simpering little misses eager to get their hands on my pocketbook. It seems a suitable match after all, does it not?"

An unlikely match is more like it, she nearly blurted. She managed to stop herself in time. Yet when she offered no reply, he arched a dark brow. "Well, Yank? I can be your salvation, if you will only let me. What do you say?"

Cassie could not help it. Bitterness spread through her like slow poison. As a child, she had often imagined that her father might someday appear, and take her away to a far-off place where there was no hunger, no smell of ale and sweat. But likelier than not, her mother herself had not known who her father was.

And she was neither blind nor foolish. No, she knew better than to expect salvation at the hands of a man. And this man was a stranger, a bold, irreverent one at that! Still, he could give her a far better life . . . She cared little about the furs and jewels he promised. But to Cassie, who had always dreamed of having a home of her own, a home that was not a hovel, such an offer was tempting. So tempting, indeed . . .

For a timeless instant she swung helplessly between heaven and hell. If she agreed, it meant traveling far across the ocean, day after day . . . She shivered inwardly, for she had been terrified of water since that horrible day she and her mother had arrived in Charleston . . . Could she stand such a journey?

She'd be mad to say yes. Dear God, just as daft to say no.

She struggled under the heat of Gabriel's anticipatory regard. "Think," he said softly. "This could be worth far more to you than the sum my watch would have brought you. I do believe you have it in you to be a lady of leisure, Yank. As my wife, you'll want for nothing."

Cassie drew a deep, ragged breath, summoning

her courage. "And what about later? A year from now? Ten years from now? Will you turn me out in the streets once I've served my purpose?"

He stepped toward her. Before she could stop him, he'd reached out and caught one of her hands in his. His expression impassive, he raised it between them to study her rough, work-roughened skin. More than anything, Cassie longed to snatch it back, bury her hands into her pockets, and hide them from sight. She tensed, but did not move though every instinct clamored within her to do just that.

His expression unreadable, he ran his thumb over the chafed, reddened skin of her knuckles.

"You will never again have to work a day in your life. Nor will you have to wait on anyone. Others will wait on you."

Cassie's palms had grown sticky. Her legs were not very steady.

"You would treat me well," she said slowly, "and not raise a hand against me?"

Gabriel's gaze sharpened. He pushed up the sleeve of her gown, revealing the purpled skin of her wrists. Cassie's gaze was riveted to his face. Something flared in his eyes; it was gone so quickly she could not identify it.

His lips barely moved as he spoke. "Black Jack?"

Her eyes slipped away. She nodded; there was no need to say more. Abruptly he released her hand.

"I was raised to be a gentleman, Yank, no matter that there are some who might claim otherwise. You will come to no harm at my hand."

Cassie stared at the toes of her shoes peeping

out from beneath her skirts. "And when would this marriage take place?" she asked quickly. "I'll not sail with you until it's done. I-I would know that you do not make promises you do not mean to keep."

A slow smile crept along his lips. "Why, Yank! Are you so eager then to be wed—or merely bedded?"

That was not it at all. Why, the very thought made Cassie cringe. Nell had brought customers to the attic on numerous occasions. Cassie had pretended to be asleep, but that was hardly the case. She'd heard groans and grunts, whispers and laughter. She shuddered. They'd sounded like animals!

He shrugged. "I'd intended to set sail no later than noon. But I suppose a cleric might be persuaded to marry us within the hour with the right amount of gold lining his pocket."

But she was not done.

Though the earl stood a few paces distant, Cassie was overwhelmingly conscious of the latent, masculine power hidden beneath his clothes. She recalled with nerve-shattering acuteness the heaviness of his body atop hers last night, the ruthless ferocity of his kiss.

She joined her hands to stop them from shaking. Her lips were trembling so that speech was impossible. "I do not want to share your bed. I've no desire to—to lie with you. And if you do not agree, I—I will not marry you." There! She'd said it.

He quirked a brow. "Why, I begin to think you ill-formed, Yank." He took a step forward. "Do you hide some deformity? You wish to bargain, but perhaps you are no bargain after all. Indeed, perhaps I should examine the goods."

Her head jerked up. She flung up her hands. "No!" she cried.

"I told you before, madam, 'tis not lust which draws me to you. I am a man of many appetites, but rest assured, I will pursue my pleasures elsewhere. There are other women who are perfectly willing to satisfy my needs." He gave a biting laugh. "And God knows the last thing I want is an heir." He met her gaze coolly. "So tell me, Yank. Do you travel with me back to England or will you remain here?"

It was with a vague sense of unreality that she heard herself whisper, "I will come with you."

He nodded, then moved to the door and opened it. Inclining his head, he silently indicated she was to precede him through it.

Cassie moved through in a daze. Her mind was whirling so that she could scarcely assimilate all that had happened. It seemed so incredible . . . impossible! Only moments ago she had entered this room expecting to be punished . . .

Instead it seemed she was about to be married.

Downstairs, Christopher Marley was pacing the length of the taproom. Black Jack had settled his bulk onto a bench in the far corner; he stared as if hypnotized into a stout glass of ale. Hearing the echo of steps on the stairway, Nell sauntered in from the kitchens, a scornful smirk tugging at her lips, her manner decidedly lofty. Clearly she thought Cassie would soon be getting all she deserved.

And indeed, so she would.

As they reached the bottom of the stairs, all eyes turned their way. Near the last step, Cassie found herself possessed of the desire to bolt wildly into the street and run for all she was worth. But the grip on her elbow tightened as if in warning. Cassie decided almost bitterly that he had no trouble guessing her intention.

Black Jack jumped up from the bench and hurried toward them. "Here, yer lordship, you needn't trouble yourself any further." He shot Cassie a dark glance. "I'll take her off yer hands. Oh, and you can be certain she'll never again steal from you or anyone else."

"Oh, I've no doubt of that. As my wife, there'll be no need to."

Black Jack's eyes bulged. His lips worked, but no sound came out.

Nell straightened with a strangled cry. "You cannot mean to marry the bitch!"

Gabriel paid no heed to either of them. "We shall be married within the hour," he went on smoothly. "There's a church near the docks. We'll stop there on the way to my ship."

Nell's face was purple. "Why? Why her?" she burst out. "The bitch just thinks she's better 'n me. But she won't please you in bed. Why, she don't know half what I know!"

Black Jack finally regained his powers of speech. "Yer lordship, you—you can't marry her! She's just a bar whore!"

A bar whore. Cassie cringed inside, and lowered her gaze to the floor. She could look at none of them.

So it was that she did not see Gabriel level on Black Jack a look of such blackness that the burly man fell back a step. "I will marry whom I please," the earl stated coldly. "Neither you nor any other man can stop me. Now if you don't mind, please have a carriage summoned. I'm anxious to be on my way."

Black Jack scurried to obey. Nell glared at Cassie's bowed head a few seconds longer, then flounced back into the kitchen, muttering under her breath.

Christopher had only now lost his expression of shock. He stepped up to Gabriel, tapped him on the shoulder, and jerked his head toward the entrance. "A word with you in private, if you please."

Only then did Cassie's head come up. She watched the two men leave with eyes both troubled and fearful. Outside on the boardwalk the two men faced each other.

It was Gabriel who spoke first, before Christopher even had a chance. " 'Tis my hope you will stand as witness to this wedding," he said calmly.

"Witness?" Both Christopher's tone and his features were unusually harsh. "Have you lost your mind, man? This marriage will be a mockery, and we both know it!"

Gabriel's smile held no mirth. "Tell me this, my friend. Would marriage to Lady Evelyn be any less of a mockery? At least this way my bride will be of my choosing."

Christopher's mouth opened, then closed. As dearly as it appeared he'd have liked to, it seemed he couldn't refute Gabriel's words.

"You may have fooled Cassie, but you don't fool

me. You marry her only to spite your father! He will be furious, and so will Warrenton when he discovers you unable to wed Lady Evelyn!"

Gabriel neither agreed nor disagreed. "I did not lie to her." *Perhaps you did not lie*, jeered a voice from within, *but certainly you did not reveal all . . .* "The girl is well aware of my reasons for this marriage—and knows all she needs to know."

"Do you mean to say you did not coerce her into it?"

Gabriel only narrowly held on to his temper. "I did not lay a hand on her," he said, his voice deadly calm. "And if you further imply that I did, you risk much, my friend, much indeed."

"I imply no such thing," Christopher said stiffly. "But she stole your watch and was caught with it. You could have used that against her."

Gabriel's eyes narrowed. "You do seem to have a great deal of sympathy for her," he said in deceptively dulcet tones. "Could it be that you have taken a fancy to her and envy me my choice of bride?"

"That's not it at all." Christopher defended himself hastily. "Gabriel, you know I have seldom judged you. But tell me this. Does the girl know what you will be dragging her into?"

"Christopher, I take her from a life of work and struggle and poverty. You know as well as I that her circumstances will be far, far better. Indeed," he gave a harsh laugh, " 'twould seem to me I am to be commended."

Christopher clearly did not agree, but he said nothing. Unfortunately, Gabriel had no trouble reading his mind.

"I will brook no interference from you or any other man," he said coolly. "My mind is made up. Now will you stand witness to this wedding or do I have to find myself another man?"

Christopher sighed heavily. "There is no need to search further," he said quietly. "I will stand as witness."

Moments later the three climbed in the coach. Christopher took a seat across from Cassie. The future bride sat huddled in the corner, as far distant from her husband-to-be as she could possibly get. Gabriel paid no heed, but stared out the window, no expression whatsoever marking his handsome features. The atmosphere was anything but jovial.

A short time later, they filed into a small church. Cassie could recall nothing of the conversation exchanged between Gabriel and the minister, a stout, pudgy man whose girth nearly exceeded his height. Over and over again, his eyes traveled between her ragged dress and the formidable, imposing man who proposed to wed her. He was clearly puzzled by such an unlikely union, yet he said nothing. Nor did Cassie wonder why—she did not miss the gold coins passed into his pudgy hands.

All too soon Cassie found herself standing next to Gabriel in front of the altar. The minister cleared his throat and began to speak, but his words were a blur.

Then it was over. Cassie swallowed, aware that the fingers clutching her pouch were trembling. Uncertain what was expected of her, slowly she lifted her eyes to the man who was now her husband . . . sweet heaven, *her husband*.

He was pleased. She could see it in the sly satisfaction of his smile. Dear Lord, she was married to this cold, hard man . . . and it was too late to change it. A shiver shook her form.

All at once she couldn't shake the feeling she'd just made a bargain with the devil.

Chapter 5

It was almost noon by the time the carriage delivered the trio to the waterfront.

Christopher was the first to alight from the carriage. Gabriel followed, landing lightly on booted feet. By then, Cassie had arisen from the seat as well. Gabriel turned, wordlessly extending his hand toward her.

Seeing him before her, his manner brisk and confident, she found herself caught in the grip of a fleeting uncertainty. Loath to touch him, though for the life of her she didn't know why, she made no move to oblige him. Eyes the color of slate hardened ever so slightly.

"If you please, madam, I'm hardly eager to remain here. I'd thought you felt the same."

Cassie flushed, then tentatively placed her hand in his and allowed him to assist her from the carriage. The instant she was out of the carriage, she quickly tugged her fingers free of his grasp. Gabriel's lips tightened slightly, but he said nothing. While he paid the driver, Christopher retrieved their bags.

Cassie remained where she was. Damp, moist air from a morning rain lay heavy and thick around

71

her, and mingled with the tang of salt, strong and pungent in her nostrils. Although the fog had lifted, the sky remained a pale, depthless shade of gray.

Beside her, Christopher cleared his throat. "The ship anchored there at the end—that's Gabriel's."

Cassie's gaze trailed his. There, where the wharf jutted into the bay, a sleek, three-masted vessel bobbed gently in tempo with the current.

She had no chance to reply. Gabriel was there again, a hand at her elbow, guiding her around numerous crates and barrels. Just ahead of them, a burly seaman heaved a square crate onto his shoulder, then marched up the gangplank onto the ship's deck.

Her heart sank. An awful feeling of dread wound its way around Cassie's spine. Was this the only way onto the vessel? *Silly fool*, chided a voice inside. *How else could you board?* Seeking to waylay her fear, she glanced down.

Below the gangplank, dark, choppy waters swirled in a furious eddy around and around the pilings supporting the dock.

She stood there, paralyzed. As if in a dream, a vision loomed in her mind. She saw her body tumbling in a slow arc, the dark green waters yawning wide, as if to swallow her whole. Her breath came jerkily. Her lungs burned like fire, for she knew what it was like to gasp desperately for air when there was only foul, fetid water filling her mouth, her lungs . . .

"Come, Yank. You may go first, and I will follow."

His words penetrated the haze surrounding her, widening her eyes. She shook her head and shuffled back a step. "No," she said faintly. "I cannot . . ."

"It's too late to change your mind, girl. We've already begun the first leg of our journey and soon will begin the next." His expression was as harshly forbidding as his tone.

Cassie swallowed a sick feeling in the pit of her belly. "I've not changed my mind." She faltered. "But I—I cannot swim, and if I should miss a step—"

"You will not."

Oh, if only she were as certain! But her knees had begun to quaver, along with her voice. "Please—" she began.

She got no further. Stifling an impatient oath, Gabriel swung her high in his arms. It was just as he'd said—they had come too far to turn back now.

Cassie had no choice but to cling to his neck. She squeezed her eyes shut as he strode with surefooted ease up the gangplank and onto the deck. He did not stop, but carried her down the companionway to a cabin below.

Only when she felt solid ground beneath her feet once again did Cassie open her eyes. For the space of a heartbeat, time was immeasurably still. Not until Gabriel cocked a brow did she realize her arms were still twined around his neck. She flushed furiously and withdrew them in all haste, anxious to put some distance between them.

"I suggest you make yourself comfortable. We will be weighing anchor shortly." He retreated, closing the door firmly behind him.

With that, Cassie was left alone. She glanced

around, taking belated note of her surroundings. She was in a generous-sized cabin—her husband's no doubt. The thought roused a shiver, but she willed her mind not to linger further on that troubling realization. Instead her gaze traveled slowly around the cabin.

A sea chest and wooden cabinet crowded one wall, both of which were framed in rich mahogany. There was a table bolted to the wall, while the center of the cabin was dominated by a desk covered with charts and maps. There was even a small, pot-bellied stove with a simple chair next to it. But it was the wide bed opposite the door that bound Cassie's attention the longest.

A sudden creaking accompanied the movement of the ship beneath her feet. It seemed to buck and heave and strain, but then they were off.

Both fear and excitement leaped high in her breast. The narrow seat set beneath the cabin's only window beckoned; it was there she directed her weaving steps. Scrambling up, she peered through the dingy glass.

The ship soon gathered speed, gliding through the waters of the bay. The forested coastline—and Charleston—grew further and further distant.

It struck her then . . . the enormity of all that had happened this past day. Never again would she see Charleston . . . or Black Jack. No longer was she bound to a life of servitude. There would be no more scrubbing floors, no more ducking eager hands, dodging pinching fingers, and evading lust-filled glances.

No, it was little wonder that she felt no sadness . . . yet neither was there joy—or the vivid relief she had expected to feel. There was only the familiar sense of being so very alone, as well as a gnawing unease of wondering what the fates held in store for her . . .

She could only hope the future brought better.

The feeling of being lost and alone persisted throughout the long day. Cassie did not dare to venture outside the cabin, and certainly no one ventured within. Soon the shadows began to lengthen, and a dark gloom invaded the cabin. She was given to wonder if she'd not been forgotten.

At that precise moment there was a knock on the door. Cassie had scarcely called a tentative "Come in" when the door was flung wide. A stocky young man wearing a scarlet wool cap jammed on russet brown curls appeared, whistling and pulling a small cart. The cart was barely inside before the formidable figure of the earl dominated the entryway.

"This is Ian, my dear. He will be tending to our meals and the cabin during our voyage. Ian . . . my wife."

Having already risen to her feet, Cassie smiled at the young man. He seemed a cheerful sort, and she could not help but respond to him. "Hello, Ian," she said softly.

"Milady." The young man swept the cap to his belly with a bow and a most engaging grin. He then set about transferring several dishes onto the table, along with service for two. Delicious smells assailed her nostrils, while ravening pangs of hunger began to gnaw at her belly. Cassie had not realized until then how very hungry she was. Ian finished his task, then quietly withdrew. The cabin door shut with a click.

She was left alone with her new husband.

He strode to the table and pulled out a chair, then glanced at her expectantly. It took a moment before Cassie gathered that he intended to seat her. She could not help the thought that rushed in at her . . . did he mock her? Or was he merely being polite? Feeling rather foolish, Cassie flushed and moved to oblige him.

He did not ask, but filled her plate for her—not that Cassie was inclined to be contrary. Perhaps it was silly, but the prospect of sharing a meal with this man made her distinctly nervous. She knew not what to say. She knew not what to *do*. Flustered, but determined not to show it, she turned her attention to the food. The fare was simple but filling—a rich, savory stew and warm, fragrant bread. Impossible though it had seemed just moments earlier, her hunger soon eclipsed all else, including her awareness of the man sitting across from her.

She had nearly finished her second helping when she chanced to glance up and find those crystalline gray eyes fixed upon her. There was an odd expression on his features, and hot shame colored her cheeks. No doubt to him she appeared half-starved and greedy.

She laid down her fork, lowering her lashes quickly. "I am sorry," she murmured. "I should not have—"

He shook his head. "You've done nothing to be sorry for, Yank. From the look of you, you've missed too many meals already." He paused, then added softly, "And I'd far rather see you eat your fill than see good food wasted." He did not mention that her enjoyment of the meal made him feel a trifle guilty for something he had always taken for granted.

When she flushed and clasped her hands in her lap, he allowed the merest of smiles to graze his mouth. "Only I must say, I am heartily glad you've not proven to be a poor sailor."

"Other than hunger, my stomach has not troubled me at all." Her smile was rather tremulous, but it served to dissolve some of her tension. Perhaps, she decided cautiously, he could be kind after all.

He would have refilled her wine glass, but she declined with a quick shake of her head. He studied her, then said suddenly, "I fear I must impose a few rules, Yank. There are many men on this ship, and as you are surely aware, sometimes seamen can be a rough lot. Bear in mind that it's not safe for you to be wandering about the decks alone."

Cassie thought of the dark and depthless seas that surrounded them. He need not worry on that score, she decided, barely suppressing a shiver of dread.

Ian entered and briskly cleared the remains of their meal. The earl rose and seated himself behind his desk. As he uncurled a rolled-up chart and spread it across the wide surface, Cassie retreated to the chair beside the potbellied stove.

The minutes passed. He seemed oblivious to her presence, engrossed in his papers, but Cassie did not mind. She could not help the way her eyes strayed to him again and again.

He had discarded his jacket and rolled up his shirtsleeves, baring tanned muscular forearms coated with a liberal covering of dark, silky-looking hair. The memory of being held tight in his arms as he carried her up the gangplank rose swiftly in her mind. They had been surprisingly strong and hard, those arms. Clearly he did not live a life of such ease as she had thought. His fingers were lean and brown, the nails square and clean. Wincing, she glanced at the rough, dry skin of her hands, then hid them in her skirts. Tucking her feet beneath her, she burrowed more deeply into the chair, as if to make herself disappear.

It wasn't long before her restless sleep the previous night claimed its due. She soon dozed. The next thing she was aware of was a strong hand shaking her awake. Eyes wide, she stared into the darkly handsome face of her husband.

He towered over her. "You're exhausted, Yank. I suggest you retire for the night."

Cassie sat up slowly, her mind still fuzzy. The remnants of sleep lent a strange huskiness to her voice. "Where am I to sleep?"

A mocking brow arose. "It should take no great surfeit of intelligence to figure out where, Yank—especially considering there is but one bunk in this cabin."

It was the coolness of his tone, far more than his words, which left Cassie in no doubt she'd just been insulted. Oh, but he was horrid—and to think she'd been foolish enough to believe he possessed even a shred of kindness!

Pierced by an angry hurt, her chin came up. She dropped her legs to the floor. "I've no wish to sleep in my gown," she said stiffly. "And I have no intention of removing it before you."

"What! Never say you expect me to leave. I think you forget this is my cabin, and just so there is no misunderstanding between us . . . I refuse to sleep on the floor during this voyage while you take my bunk. It's big enough for the both of us."

Cassie gasped. Why, the wretch—and to think he called himself a gentleman! "You led me to believe you had no desire to lie with me!"

He gave her a long, slow look. "Yank," he said in clipped, icy tones. "I see no need to repeat myself yet again, but I will. No one enjoys the pleasures of the flesh more than I. But you are not such a temptress, and I am not such a lecherous rogue that I cannot sleep next to a woman without ripping the very clothes from her back and ravishing her."

Each word struck home like a hooked barb. Her heart rebelled, though Cassie was wise enough to recognize when she'd been beaten. "Fine," she muttered. "But I'll thank you to at least turn your back!"

The taut line of his mouth did not ease. "You're hardly the first woman I've seen in her natural state."

"You have not seen me in my natural state—nor will you!"

He made a sound of disgust. "I hope you do not insist on maintaining this pretense of shy embarrassment. It's wasted on me, Yank."

More than anything, Cassie longed to cry that it was no pretense. Oh, she knew what he believed her to be—a bar whore. But what would he say if he knew it were not so? Would he be angry? Would he even care? She admitted she knew little of this man she had married—save that he was unpredictable! No, she would not take the chance he might turn the ship around and head back to Charleston, for then where would she be?

Back at Black Jack's, that's where, she acknowledged bitterly. And given the earl's present mood, she feared he needed little provocation.

But at least he had turned his back. Cassie hastily pulled off her boots and hose, then tugged her gown over her head. It would be just like the beast to change his mind before she'd finished! She felt meagerly attired indeed wearing only her chemise and a thin cotton petticoat. She scurried to the far side of the bunk and nestled beneath the covers, pulling them to her chin.

"All right," she said rather breathlessly. "You may turn around."

He obliged, but paid her no further heed. It gave her a start to see that his shirt was already unbuttoned. She surveyed him warily as he shrugged it from his shoulders. His chest and belly were brazenly masculine, matted with dense, dark hair. It took several heartbeats before she could fully catch her breath. When his hands went to the buttons of his breeches, it was shockingly apparent he had no intention of stopping.

She flounced to her side and presented him with her back. All went dark when he extinguished the lantern swinging from the beam. She squeezed her eyes shut and did not open them, even when she heard him climb into bed beside her.

She tried desperately to still the frantic throb of her heart. Their skin touched nowhere, but she couldn't rid herself of the fear that touch they most certainly would—and all she could think was that he was naked! Seeking not to draw undue attention, she eased this way and that, seeking to inch sideways, scooting as close to the edge of the bunk as she could possibly get.

A strong hand descended firmly on the curve of her hip.

His whisper, taut and furious, rushed past her ear. "Yank, I suggest you be still at once and go to sleep, or I will most assuredly see that you make your bed upon the floor!"

Cassie froze, afraid to move, to even breathe. The feel of his palm burned through the thin material of her chemise. Sleep? she thought wildly. With this man beside her? 'Twould be impossible!

Yet strangely enough, it was not long before the steady surge of the ship through the waves lulled her to drowsiness. Sleep she did . . . and quite soundly.

Chapter 6

C assie roused slowly the next morning. The mattress beneath her was downy and soft, and a hazy warmth enfolded her. She lay on her side, cuddled against a solid heat that made her feel cozy and safe; never before had she been more comfortable. For an instant she could not remember where she was, only that she was not in her pallet at the inn. It took another moment for her sleep-befuddled mind to register that she was not alone—and to recall the man against whom she lay curled so tightly.

Her eyes snapped open. Her cheek lay snug against the sleek hardness of his shoulder. Her hand, looking impossibly small and pale, rested in the midst of his bronzed and hairy chest. The contrast between their skin was riveting. It gave her a start to notice that the quilt lay haphazardly across the narrow ridge of his hips. Unbidden, her gaze wandered lower, skimming parts that were best left unnoticed and bringing a bright flush clear to the roots of her hair.

Swallowing an unfamiliar tightness in her throat, she jerked her eyes away only to find that his were open . . . and investigating her own lack of dress with far more boldness than her own had displayed.

"Good morning, Yank," he drawled. "I trust you found my bed quite to your liking?"

Cassie bit back the scathing retort that sprang to her lips. The next instant her eyes flew wide and she ducked her head when he shoved back the quilt and proceeded from the bunk. That he could be so casual about his nudity was quite beyond her comprehension.

The instant his back was turned, she rescued the quilt from about her ankles. Hearing water splash in the basin, she dared a peek at him. She was relieved to find he had donned his breeches, but he had caught her glance as well.

An arrogant half-smile dallied on his lips. "I've no objection to you looking, Yank, but it's only fair you accord me the same privilege."

She regarded him unsmilingly. "I cannot think why you should want to," she stated bluntly. "I am no temptress. You said so yourself."

He wiped his hands on a towel and returned to sit on the edge of the bunk. A blunted fingertip traced the graceful slope of one bare shoulder. "Ah, Yank, but perhaps I might be persuaded to change my mind."

She swatted his hand away. "I'll thank you *not* to!"

Gabriel watched the way her small fingers greedily clutched the quilt to her chin. Her eyes looked huge, like clear topaz. He was both mildly amused and slightly piqued that she chose to cling to this tack. Certainly he'd not expected a woman of her experience to be so discriminating in her modesty.

With a shrug he arose and returned to the basin.

He paid her no mind while he shaved. When he'd finished, he wiped the last traces of soap from his neck. He glanced at her, surprised to find her gaze still fixed upon him. Her expression was wary, yet he sensed something rather tentative in her manner.

He dropped the towel on the washstand and turned to her. "There is something on your mind, Yank. Come now. You may as well come out with it."

Cassie moistened her lips with the tip of her tongue. How could he know her so well already? She found the notion disturbing, and resolved to guard herself far better in the future.

"I merely wondered . . . what I am to call you."

Raising a devilishly arched brow, he reached for his shirt. "What would you like to call me, Yank?"

Yank. Why did he persist in calling her that? Already the address had begun to grate. Her eyes flashed and she flounced up unthinkingly, nearly losing the concealing protection of the quilt around her body.

"I can think of any number of fitting names to call you, sir, though I venture to say you'd not like a one of them!"

He pulled his shirt over the wide expanse of his shoulders. "Of that I have no doubt. But I do have a name, Yank."

"So do I, and it is not *Yank!*"

One corner of that hard mouth curled upward. "I see no reason why you should not call me Gabriel. As for yours, I told you the other night. 'Cassie' simply does not suit."

"*We* do not suit, yet here we are—and wed yet!" She snapped the comment before she thought better of it.

Gabriel's smile withered. Her spirit roused his temper—as well as an unwilling, but thoroughly male appreciation of her charms. Indignant or no, she presented a fetching picture, with her hair swirling in rich, thick waves over her shoulders, and invitingly so. But he found himself possessed of the urge to tumble her back upon the bunk, to show this haughty little vixen that were he so inclined, he might easily turn her sharpness to panting moans of rapture.

Blast! What nonsense was this! Perhaps it would have been better if he'd married a toad. Were she not so comely, he'd not be tempted to linger here and trade barbs with her . . . and perhaps a good deal more. He was vastly irritated that he had to remind himself he had more important things to do than wile away the morning with the wench he had taken to wife.

"You are right," he said coolly. "But I think neither of us would do well to dwell on that lamentable fact." He tugged on his boots and strode toward the doorway. There he turned to face her once more. "I'd get dressed if I were you. Ian will be down shortly with your breakfast."

His curtness hurt. Try though she might, Cassie couldn't banish the sensation she'd done something wrong . . . but what? Ian's smile was wide and friendly, but after he'd withdrawn, she felt cold and deserted.

She moved restlessly around the cabin, finally halting near a small bookcase behind the desk.

She stared morosely at the bound leather volumes housed there, wistfully wishing she'd had some schooling, even a little. Oh, she could write her name, but that was all. If she were able to read, perhaps the time would not drag so, as it did already.

Mid-afternoon, the cabin door was flung wide. Cassie looked up from where she was perched on the bed to find her husband's tall form filling the doorway.

"The seas are very calm this afternoon, Yank. I thought you might like to come topside for a while."

Topside? Oh, no. She much preferred her solitude to braving the watery world that existed all around them. Indeed, she thought with a shiver, she had tried hard throughout the day not to dwell on that very fact.

"There's no need to burden yourself on my account. I'm sure there are other more important matters demanding your attention." She managed to summon a smile. "Perhaps later."

Cassie held her breath. Several seconds passed while he stared at her, kindling a faint alarm. She prayed he would not insist . . . luckily, he did not. Finally he shrugged. "As you wish then, Yank. Let Ian know if you need anything." He turned and left her alone.

Three days hence, he was not nearly so obliging. When she politely declined, he did not move, but regarded her through narrowed eyes.

"You are remarkably stubborn, Yank."

"Hardly, sir." She tried to pass it off with a light laugh. "It's just as I told you, I've no wish to burden you further. And truly, there is no need—"

"There is every need, Yank." His countenance was grim and unsmiling. "You cannot stay below the entire journey. You need sunshine and fresh air, else you will sicken."

She drew herself up. "Of course I will not—"

"I'll not have you on my conscience, girl."

His approach was swift and unrepentant; the unyielding intent in his eyes promised little hope of refusal. There simply was no denying him. Clad wholly in black as he was, a long, dark cloak swirling about the tops of his boots, it passed through her mind that surely he resembled the devil himself.

And likelier than not, it was hardly concern over her welfare that prompted his insistence. No, it was probably simply that he must have his way!

But all her protests were to no avail. He pulled her to her feet, shackling her to his side with his hand about her waist.

She wrenched herself free and glared at him. "I've managed without assistance for a goodly number of years," she snapped.

He gave a mocking bow. "As you wish."

And so with him following but a step behind, she had no choice but to mount the companionway stairs before him. Once they were on deck, her heart began to thud painfully in her chest. She prayed she could somehow control her fear, for she had no wish to let this man glimpse her weakness. No doubt he would think her silly and foolish, and his scorn was the one thing she could not bear.

Her footsteps slowed; she halted, though she was scarcely aware of it. Though she tried not to look, she could not help it. Her gaze swept outward and away. Ominous gray waters filled

her vision as far as the eye could see. A jolt tore
through her as she realized she was standing near
the railing. Her gaze slipped inevitably downward.

A spasm of sheer fright tore through her. The
seas churned furiously as the ship plowed through
the waves. Yet Cassie felt as if the hungry waters
lapped at *her*, eager to take her within their watery
grasp and pull her deep within the icy embrace of
the sea.

"Please," she said in a voice she did not recognize as her own, "I—I cannot stay here."

Gabriel glanced at her sharply. Her face was
pasty white, making her eyes appear bigger and
brighter than ever. His mind slipped back to when
they had boarded in Charleston. He'd thought her
merely timid and uncertain, but only now did
he understand that she'd been terrified. It was
then Gabriel realized . . . he'd thought it was fear
of looking down, walking the narrow gangplank,
but such was not the case at all.

"Is this your first voyage?"

Her nod was jerky. "I pray it will be my last!"
She pressed close against his side, as if to meld
herself inside him. He was stunned to realize she
was trembling.

"Easy," he said quietly. "Take deep, calming
breaths and think of something pleasant."

"I can't!" Her cry was utterly stricken. She
squeezed her eyes shut.

He slid an arm about her shoulder. "Of course
you can, Yank. It just takes a bit of effort." His tone
was low and calm.

She shook her head wildly and turned her face

into his shoulder. His gaze fell to where she had latched onto his free hand. Her nails dug like spikes into his palm.

A dark brow arose. "If you please, Yank, I'd prefer to return to England with my hand still attached to my person."

On hearing his dry tone, Cassie's eyes popped open. Surely her ears deceived her, for there was neither mockery nor disdain on those handsome features. Her fingers relaxed somewhat but she would not loose her grip completely.

"Good. Now that your eyes are open, look high and yonder and tell me when you've seen the skies so blue and clear. I must admit, though, a clear day at sea is not quite so awesome as sailing at midnight when the moon is full and the heavens seem cast in silver. I vow you've never seen so many stars in all your life."

Even as he spoke, a self-derisive scorn burned deep in his chest. What nonsense was this that he spoke of beauty and color, when he'd known little of either for . . . oh, so long now. But her piteous cry had jarred loose some long dormant emotion inside him. Gabriel did not like it, but he could hardly dismiss her terror with callous regard.

Beside him, she shivered. "What is it, Yank? Still afraid?"

She shook her head. "I am just cold," she lied.

"Next time we must remember your cloak."

"I have none." She made the reply unthinkingly, then flushed when she found herself enduring the hard probe of his gaze. Gabriel cursed himself roundly. He should have known her wardrobe would be so sorely lacking such essentials. He tugged his own garment from his shoulders and swirled it around her. She glanced up at him in startled surprise, then slowly smiled her thanks. An odd sensation knotted the pit of his belly. So small was she that the rich dark folds dragged upon the deck, eclipsing all but the narrow oval of her face. It struck him that she looked very young and defenseless . . .

He was immediately irritated with himself. "Come, Yank," he said shortly. "You've yet to look as I asked."

Though his slight impatience was not lost on her, his hands had yet to leave her shoulders. The warmth of his touch oddly reassuring, Cassie obligingly raised her face. The sun was warm upon her cheeks, the scented breeze fresh and clean. Cassie glanced up at the endless stretch of billowing sails, where the clear blue skies opened wide. High above, the masts swayed with the movement of the seas, gently creaking.

"There. Is this so awful now?"

"No," she admitted cautiously, then paused. "Now may I return to the cabin?"

Gabriel felt a slight smile curl his lips. Her plea was full of childlike hope; he suspected she but catered to his whim.

"A moment longer. Then I'll take you back."

Strangely, his insistence did not distress her nearly so much as it should have. No, she decided hazily, it was most certainly not distress he roused in her. The scent of him clung to his cloak, clean and faintly spicy—a scent that was already familiar. She could feel the heat from his body, for he had moved to stand slightly behind her.

There was a shout from above. One of the crewmen stationed on the quarterdeck beckoned to Gabriel, who had raised his head.

"Damn!" he muttered with a grimace. "I am needed elsewhere." His gaze flitted back to Cassie, who quickly lowered her head. But Gabriel had already seen the brief rise of panic in her eyes.

Just then Christopher strode up from the companionway. Gabriel beckoned to him.

"Christopher! Would you do me the favor of staying with my wife while I attend to Simms?"

The other Englishman stepped up. "Not at all."

Cassie opened her mouth to say it was not necessary, but Gabriel's hands had already deserted her. The prospect of facing Christopher again made her wince. She could not help but recall how Christopher had stood slightly behind them, sober and unsmiling, when they'd been wed. She was very much afraid that Christopher disapproved of his friend's marriage—and of her. The thought pained her, for she sensed she might have liked him.

She tried to smile. "There's really no need for you to stay," she murmured.

He gave her a quick bow, his manner faultlessly polite. "It's no bother, I assure you."

They both fell silent, sharing the awkwardness of the moment.

Cassie pulled the cloak more tightly about her and stared down to where the toe of her boot peeped from beneath the cloak. "I'm sorry you don't like me," she said, her voice very small.

Christopher blinked. "I beg your pardon?"

Cassie swallowed. "I—I know you don't like me because I married your friend," she said, the words emerging with difficulty. "Because I—I am beneath him."

When no reply was forthcoming, she raised her head. She stared, both amazed and shocked to discover that he had broken into a wide smile.

"Cassie . . . I do hope you don't mind if I call you Cassie . . . moreover, I hope Gabriel does not take exception to it . . . but I'm delighted to inform you that you are very much mistaken. I most certainly am not angry with you. If anything, it's Gabriel I'd very much like to take to task."

"Why?" It was curiosity more than anything else that prompted the question. Cassie realized uneasily that she knew precious little about this man who was now her husband.

Christopher led her to an overturned crate where he seated her with a teasing flourish. He pulled up another next to her, and sat.

"You know that his brother Stuart is dead, which is why Gabriel is now the earl of Wakefield? That Stuart was to marry Lady Evelyn Latham, daughter of the duke of Warrenton?"

Cassie nodded. "He said his father expected him to marry her in his brother's place."

"Yes. It's easy to see why, of course. Warrenton's lineage goes back clear to the time of the Conquerer, and coupled with Farleigh's wealth . . . such a marriage would have been quite a coup, indeed . . ." He halted when he saw her confusion.

He smiled. "I'm sorry. I do tend to run on at times." His smile faded as he returned to his discourse.

"The situation between Gabriel and his father is complicated," he said at last. "Indeed, there is much even I do not understand—that he refuses to speak of. I assure you, Cassie, I am not such a snob that I am opposed to Gabriel marrying a woman not of his class. It's just that I'm not sure it was wise to bring you into this . . . situation."

Cassie was quiet for a time. "I have only just begun to realize," she said slowly, "that I am no longer Cassie McClellan. I am now . . . Mrs. Sinclair."

"No," Christopher corrected gently. "You are now the countess of Wakefield . . . *Lady* Wakefield."

Cassie sighed. "Countess," she said glumly. "Earl. Duke. I'm afraid I don't know one from the other!"

He chuckled. "Well, then, it will be my pleasure to acquaint you with the intricacies of the nobility . . ."

They were thusly engrossed when Gabriel returned. To Cassie's delight, she caught on quickly, and Christopher's warm praise brought a smile to her lips and a becoming rose flush to her cheeks. But her heart plummeted when she glanced up to find Gabriel towering over her. He wasted no time in escorting her back to the cabin. His image remained with her long after he'd retreated, leaving her alone once again. The cast of his profile was stern, almost forbidding. For a while he had seemed almost kind . . . but he was once again cool and remote.

She did not know that Gabriel was rather provoked that his friend seemed able to allay her fears quite admirably—and with far more enjoyment on her part!

The events of the day were still very much on Cassie's mind when she crawled into the bunk that night. She averted her eyes when Gabriel blew out the lantern and slid in beside her. Although the day had passed much more quickly than the others, she was not looking forward to another trip up on deck. She couldn't shake the flutter of dread that quivered in her belly; she tossed and turned just thinking about it.

An impatient exclamation split the air. Gabriel propped himself up on his elbow. "What is the matter with you?" he growled.

Cassie froze. Unfortunately, it was a mistake, for she ended up on her side, facing him fully. They lay so close she could feel the hair on his chest tickle the tips of her breasts when she chanced to take a breath. "This journey," she ventured finally. "How long will it last?"

"Six weeks," came the flat reply. "A little more, a little less, depending on the winds and the weather."

Cassie tried hard not to think about his naked chest. She did not know which was worse. Six weeks of being on the hated seas—or six weeks of sharing a bed with this man. But even while the latter prospect made her distinctly uneasy, she couldn't withhold a shudder at the thought of the former.

Slight though it was, Gabriel felt her quiver. He did not move, but remained where he was, stretched out beside her.

"Why are you so afraid of the sea, Yank?"

Cassie hesitated. Did he think her silly and weak to harbor such fear? She peered at him through the gloom. His eyes were glittering pinpoints of light, but the edge had left his tone.

When she said nothing, Gabriel decided to try a different tack. "You said the other day this was your first voyage."

She smiled faintly. "Indeed I've never lived anywhere other than Charleston."

"You lived with your mother? Never your father?"

Her smile withered. Stupid, foolish tears stung her eyes. "I never knew my father," she said very low. "He might have been any one of a number of men." Her tone grew unsteady. "My mother, you see, was a . . . a—"

"I know." Oddly enough, Gabriel did not want to hear the word *whore* cross her lips. "So what happened? Was there an accident, perhaps?" Gabriel was already more than half certain of her answer. He suspected it went much deeper than mere uncertainty of the unknown.

Cassie's memory stretched, yawning far back to that long-ago day. "I was very young," she heard herself say. "But I will never forget that day— no matter how much I would like to." She eased to her back, staring sightlessly at the ceiling. "It was early, and we stood on the end of the docks, watching the ships set sail. My mother was with a dark-haired, well-dressed man. I recall standing just ahead of her. She was laughing, hanging onto the man's arm. She thought I was not listening, but I was."

She shivered. Even after all these years, the memory made her cringe inside. She had buried it deep inside, wanting never to remember, yet it was as if she were there once again . . .

"What did she say?"

"I heard her whisper to the man, 'Just think. There is no one here. If she were gone, it would be just the two of us.' "

An awful sensation crowded Gabriel's chest. Sweet Christ! It could not be, he thought in horror. Surely the woman had not suggested . . .

"What happened then?"

Cassie bit her lip. "I felt a hand at my back, and then I was falling. There was darkness everywhere, and it was so cold . . . I remember screaming, and then choking . . . and I remember thinking that surely I was going to drown. But just when I was certain I would die, the man grabbed my arm and pulled me from the water."

"Wait," he said slowly. "I thought he was the one who pushed you."

It seemed an eternity before she spoke. There was a dull, empty tone to her voice.

"No," she said very quietly. "It was my mother."

Chapter 7

For the life of him, Gabriel wished he had never asked for the reasons behind her panic. For now that he understood her fear . . .

He wished he did not.

For indeed, this changed nothing. It was regrettable, but he could not allow the girl to soften his heart, for then it would all be for naught.

And Gabriel was determined that nothing would ruin his plan.

For Cassie, the weeks dragged by. It was always late when Gabriel came to bed; she was usually asleep both when he joined her and when he arose at dawn. During the day, she was left to her own devices much of the time. Being alone with him never failed to quicken her pulse. Somehow the cabin always seemed immensely smaller the moment he entered.

He still insisted she take an occasional turn about the deck. Cassie was not brave enough to venture out on her own, so either Gabriel or Christopher escorted her.

So it was that she found herself spending a goodly sum of time with Christopher. He was cheerful and kind, always with a winsome smile on his ruddy face. Cassie was fascinated by his tales of fashionable society, or the *ton* as she quickly learned it was called. She was wildly curious about London, the theater and gaming and clubs. Though she sometimes felt foolish, Christopher was endlessly patient and did not seem to mind her questions. Perhaps she did not quite realize it, but not only was she being entertained, she was also learning much about the ways of the peerage. And with Christopher she could relax.

With Gabriel that was *never* the case.

It was from Christopher that she learned the two had met when they were schoolboys. Cassie was not surprised to learn that Gabriel had scarcely been an obedient, dutiful student. According to Christopher, his boldness and daring had preceded him into manhood, but had not ended there.

"It was always a mystery to me why such a rakehell remained so popular with the ladies," Christopher chuckled early one evening as they sat on the deck after dinner. "I suspect many a miss will die of a broken heart when they learn he's already taken. But you need not despair," he added with a glimmer in his eye, "for I daresay many a young buck will most assuredly envy him his wife."

Though she knew he was teasing, Cassie blushed fiercely. She looped her hands around her knees and smiled. "I do not doubt anything you've told me about Gabriel. But I wonder, Christopher . . . are you as reckless and roguish?"

He winked. "Who do you think taught him his wild, wicked ways?"

Cassie laughed, but she knew better. She could not imagine Christopher being anything other than honorable and trustworthy.

Neither was aware of the dark and brooding scrutiny fixed upon them from the quarterdeck. Beneath the calm facade lurked some dark and seething emotion, well controlled but present nonetheless. Gabriel's gaze settled for long, uninterrupted seconds on the honey-haired head nestled so close to his friend's. Often he had seen the pair thusly over the past weeks—talking, sometimes laughing. It was not that he begrudged the girl her need for companionship; he trusted his friend implicitly or he would never have allowed it. But Cassie's face lost all its animation whenever he approached, as it did even now.

It was Christopher who saw him first. He jumped quickly to his feet. Burning silver eyes shifted to Cassie.

"I thought you'd have noticed by now that the winds are coming up." His tone was as sharp as a blade. "A storm approaches. You'd best get yourself below."

He started to walk away, then whirled when she made no move to obey.

"I suggest you be quick about it, Yank—unless you fancy going to a watery grave."

With that he spun around and departed. Cassie stared after him, still smarting from the sting of his rebuke. She was puzzled and confused, angry and hurt, for he had made her feel guilty—and she could think of no reason why she should feel so!

Christopher could have cheerfully throttled his friend just now. He gestured toward the skies.

"Alas," he murmured. "He's right. The skies are beginning to darken, and the wind begins to stir. You'll be safer below." He motioned toward the stairs with a faint smile. "Shall we?"

Cassie allowed him to take her arm, but not without a scathingly directed glance toward Gabriel's back. "I hardly think it's my safety he's concerned about," she muttered. "Indeed, I'm sure he scarce gives me a thought at all."

Christopher shook his head. "He does not mean to be unkind," he told her gently. "It's just his way sometimes, lass."

Her lips pressed together. "I do not understand him," she said bluntly.

Christopher hesitated. "Gabriel is not an easy man to know," he said slowly. "He's been surrounded by others most of his life, and yet he's spent most of his time alone—and lonely." There was a small pause before he added softly, "As you have."

Yet Cassie was not disposed to think of herself and Gabriel as kindred spirits. She turned and gave him a long, slow look. "If you are saying the two of us are alike," she stated quietly, "I'm afraid you are sadly mistaken." With that, she stepped inside the cabin.

But was he? Christopher stood before the door a moment, a faintly self-deprecating smile on his lips. He had the feeling he'd been wrong about the pair—perhaps the two of them belonged together after all. He hoped so.

For Cassie's sake . . . as well as Gabriel's.

But Cassie's mind was scarcely filled with wifely harmony. She paced back and forth across the cabin, her resentment fueled with every step. Everything within her rebelled against this fine-feathered lord and his lofty manner. He had treated her as if she were a simpleton! Poor she might be, but witless she was not! She possessed both pride and spirit aplenty to protest such treatment at the hands of the man she now called husband. And while it was true she was frightfully unschooled in the ways of the gentry, she was quite well acquainted with crusty men, the likes of which he exceeded by far!

She stopped before the small shaving mirror that hung above the cabinet. Two pink spots of color brightened her cheeks. Her eyes were flashing and vivid. Oh, but he was wrong if he thought she would quail here below like a coward. Bold and audacious she was not, yet neither was she meek and mild, and perhaps it was time he learned it.

She whirled and flung the cabin door wide. Bunching her skirts in her fists, she marched up the stairway.

She had completely forgotten his warning.

She had barely cleared the deck when she realized her mistake. The sails clapped like thunder, while towering masts lurched to and fro. The seas were gray and churning. She stood there, frozen in horrified fascination. From somewhere there was a shout, snatched away by the wind. Her head turned.

It was Gabriel. He was bearing down on her from the quarterdeck, as glowering and fierce as she'd yet to see him. He shouted again and gestured toward the companionway. This time Cassie did not pretend to misunderstand—he wanted her below. Nor was she inclined to linger.

But when she turned to retrace her steps, she found herself buffeted by a furious gust that sent her stumbling backwards. It robbed her of her breath and snatched away her strength. Around the ship, the churning waters of the sea swelled and broke in white-crested frenzy.

Then she saw it.

A tremendous wall of water, higher than the masthead, rushed at them like the sweeping hand of death. A frenzied scream ripped from her throat. It was headed right toward the ship! The thought bounded through her brain that she must run, and then that monstrous wave crashed against the hull. The impact sent her sprawling, her legs swept out from under her.

For an instant it was as if she'd been plunged into a black pit. Darkness was everywhere. Then she felt a tremendous surge of water, so frigidly cold it was beyond comprehension. Dimly she felt herself sliding. She was scarcely aware of the heavy weight that landed atop her, pinning her to the deck. Water crashed over and around her. She could not see. She could not breathe. Pure terror iced her veins as she felt the water sucking at her, trying to drag her deep within its embrace. She opened her mouth to scream. Seawater filled her mouth, nearly choking her.

The ship seemed to lean and moan, then slowly righted itself. With a muttered oath Gabriel jerked to his knees, already reaching for his wife. Her eyes were closed. Her body lay limp and unmoving. Her head lolled over his arm, her lips the color of wax.

Panic leaped high in his chest. "Yank," he muttered hoarsely. "*Yank!*"

There was a heaving cough, and a wheezing breath racked her body. Her lids fluttered open.

"Never tell me!" she gasped. "Am I dead then?"

Gabriel could no more withhold the rare smile that grazed his lips than he could the relief that rushed through his veins. His arms tightened their hold ever so slightly. "Why, Yank? Do you think you are in heaven?"

Cassie stared dumbly into the lean, craggy features that swam above her own. Awareness struck. She was most assuredly not in heaven! A pair of hard arms were wrapped snug around her body. She was being held tight against his chest. But then reality came back with a vengeance. She watched those beautifully masculine lips draw back with barely repressed anger.

"What the bloody *hell* did you think you were doing, Yank? I told you to stay below. You were very nearly killed!"

Cassie ducked her head, fighting to hold back the burning sting of tears. Her hair had fallen down, and streamed wetly about her face and shoulders. She prayed he wouldn't notice as a single tear escaped from beneath her tightly squeezed eyelids and mingled with the wetness on her cheeks. By the time he pulled her to her feet, she had recovered her composure, or what was left of it.

"Come along," he growled. "We'll both catch our death standing here in this wind."

He gestured for her to precede him. Cassie swayed dizzily. Whether from shock or cold, her legs were so stiff she could scarcely stand. With an impatient curse Gabriel turned and swept her into his arms.

In the cabin, he again set her on her feet. This time, though, his hands remained on her waist until she had steadied herself.

"I'm fine." Her voice was a trifle shaky. "You may—let go now."

There was a nearly imperceptible tightening of his features. His hands fell away. "Get out of those wet things," he ordered. "I'll not have your death on my conscience, Yank."

He was right. They were both soaked to the skin. Water dripped from them, pooling on the floor. Cassie turned away, shy and embarrassed about disrobing with him present. Always before she had been careful to guard her privacy, and though no mention had been made of it, he had respected that need.

But the lacings of her bodice were too sodden for her half-numbed fingers to manage. Again and again she tried, to no avail. Then all at once Gabriel was there before her. Strong fingers brushed hers aside. His chest was bare and he wore only his breeches. Droplets of water glistened like tiny diamonds amidst the dark forest on his chest.

Shivering, too miserable to protest, Cassie could only stand docile while he peeled her gown from her body. Cold as she was, detached and efficient as *he* was, her face was burning by the time he'd stripped her of even her underclothes. But it did not end there, for he grabbed a towel, squeezed the moisture from her hair, and ran the cloth briskly over her body.

Finally he gave her a light slap on the rump. "Into bed with you, Yank."

Cassie needed no further urging. Her teeth chattered uncontrollably. She crawled between the covers and dragged the enveloping quilts up to her chin. As Gabriel stripped off his breeches, she squeezed her eyes shut against the sight.

She heard wet cloth slapped against the floor. The light from the lantern was extinguished, and then Gabriel was sliding in beside her.

The silence was stifling. Cassie curled into a tight little ball and huddled there, trying desperately to erase the memory of what had just happened. She damned herself for her weakness, yet all she could picture in her mind's eye was that massive wave, like the gates of death yawning wide, waiting to swallow her whole. Sweet heaven, she'd thought she was going to die . . . she'd thought she was going to *drown*. Unbidden, a tiny little half-sob tore from her throat.

Instantly a firm hand closed around her bare thigh. "What is it, Yank? Are you ill?"

"No," she whispered.

"Are you cold then? Do you want me to fetch another blanket?"

Cold? She feared she would never again be warm! But had he spoken out of the goodness of his heart, she'd have gratefully accepted his offer. Hesitantly, she shook her head.

"Then I suggest we get some sleep." He released her, rolled over, and presented her with his back.

The minutes ticked by. She shivered and shivered.

"For pity's sake, Yank. You're safe and dry and warm now. Is it possible you could stop that damnable shivering?"

"I'm s-sorry." Blast! Even her voice was shaking. "I do not mean to be s-so much t-trouble."

He shifted; the mattress heaved. Through the darkness, she felt the touch of his eyes on her. After a moment, she heard his voice. "I must say, Yank, you chose a poor time to prove you no longer fear the ocean." His tone was dry.

"It wasn't that at all," she said with a shudder. "I was angry at the way you treated me," she went on, her voice very low. "If you wanted me to go below, you might have asked. Instead you made me feel as if I should be banished to the ends of the earth." Her chin came up. "I-I did nothing wrong and you had no right to treat me as if I had."

She was right. Though Gabriel knew it, some demon inside would not let him admit it to her. He'd been furious with both of them, both her and Christopher. A little voice inside taunted that at the root of his fury was jealousy. He dismissed the notion immediately, yet logic eluded him. He could think of no reason why the sight of Cassie and Christopher together should bother him in the slightest, yet he refused to analyze it further.

It was Cassie herself who saved him from making any further excuse. Her speech delivered, she flounced to her side and pointedly turned her back on him. It was not long, though, before her shivering began anew.

"You have a stubborn streak, Yank. You say you are not cold," he growled, "yet clearly you are. So come here, else you'll never be warm—and I will find no sleep this night."

He pulled her to him, molding her to his side and tucking her head against his chest. In some distant corner of his mind, he was stunned that she displayed no further inclination toward rebellion. Indeed, Gabriel was stunned at how willingly she accepted her fate, her form pliantly soft and yielding against his own. With a wispy little sigh, she curled against him, pillowing her head on his chest as if they'd slept just so for a lifetime.

Bristly dark hairs tickled her cheek, but Cassie did not mind—his arms proved a haven that was impossibly warm and safe—and just as impossible to resist. Little by little, the heat from his body seeped into hers. Her shivering ceased. Her muscles relaxed. Her breathing deepened. Soon she slept.

As always, Gabriel was the first to awaken the next morning. Dawn's golden, shimmering light was beginning to slant through the window, but he did not rise immediately as he usually did. Instead he let himself enjoy the feeling of the soft, feminine body curved against him.

Cassie had scarcely moved during the night. His lips tightened. He was reminded of the chemise he'd pulled from her last night, worn so thin it was almost sheer. A part of him was still appalled that she owned but two gowns, both of which deserved to be pitched into the nearest fire—and which he intended to do very soon.

Chiding himself for he knew he would regret it later, he pulled back the sheet to look at her, easing slightly away to see her better. His unhurried gaze slid slowly down the length of her body, taking in every detail at his leisure. He was, after all, but a mortal man, and the sweetness of her physical charms blunted the sharpness of the chit's tongue, which he had sorely underestimated.

Her hair was spread wildly on the pillow beneath her head, revealing all that he sought to see and enchantingly so. Her limbs were slim and delicate, her skin the color of smooth, pale cream. She had gained a little flesh since the voyage began, he noted with satisfaction. Yet she was still unearthly slender. He knew that were he to try, he could circle both her wrists in one hand, and effortlessly measure the width of her hips with the span of his fingers.

A simmering heat began to spread along his veins. No, he thought again, he was scarcely unappreciative of her feminine delights. His gaze lingered on cherry-rouge nipples which crowned breasts that were small but perfectly shaped. Reddish-gold down guarded her womanhood. The urge to tumble her back, to drive his shaft deep and hard and feel her tight, clinging heat surround his manhood bit deep.

He reminded himself this marriage was little more palatable than marriage to Evelyn. Though it was of his doing, it was not to his liking, and that part of him warned against the idea of making this a true marriage. Still another part, the male part of him, whispered it would be no hardship to make love to her . . . no hardship at all. But Gabriel was a man who had learned to master his passion as well as his emotions.

Still, a nagging notion persisted . . . a marriage was not truly binding until it was consummated.

He drew her against his length, his hands unconsciously measuring the narrowness of her waist.
She was soft and sleepy and warm, her lips parted
in drowsy invitation.

It was there his gaze settled. "Yank," he whispered, the sound but a wispy breath of air.

Cassie stirred. Her lashes fluttered slowly open.
Time stood still as she stared into the darkly handsome face that smiled with sardonic amusement just
above her own. Her eyes widened with the dawning
revelation that she lay snugly pressed against him
from breast to knee—and both of them naked yet!
She could feel the hairy roughness of his thighs
against hers. As for what lay between, why, she
dare not even think of such . . .

Her hands came up between them, as if to push
him away. But Gabriel allowed no retreat. His hold
about her tightened, bringing her into even closer
contact with his form.

"Why, Yank, what is this? You harbored no such
aversion to my touch at the inn." His fingers tangled in her hair. He turned her face up to his.
"Come now. What is a kiss between husband and
wife?"

" 'Tis not a kiss you want but much more!" She
pushed against his shoulders, to no avail. He merely held her in place with the heavy pressure of his
chest.

"Why, Yank, indeed it seems we make progress.
You know me so well already."

Cassie ceased her struggles and glared her displeasure. Oh, but she hated his sarcasm!

He bent lower still, a powerful, threatening presence. Cassie had never considered herself weak

or helpless, yet she felt so now, for there was no escaping him. A sickening dread assailed her, for she sensed a purpose in him that was somehow frightening. But just when she feared he would press home his advantage, he released her.

She scrambled back against the wall and clutched the covers to her breasts. He said nothing, but propped himself up on an elbow, still holding her in the vise of his gaze. Cassie's heart bounded wildly. She did not trust him, for his mind turned in ways she did not understand. And he made her nervous, lying there, watching her when she was so obviously naked.

"Our marriage," he said suddenly. "It has not been consummated. An annulment could still be had—by either of us. It occurs to me the matter should be rectified before we reach England."

Cassie blanched. Her mind churned, like the turbulent seas. Surely he did not mean to . . . Her lips parted. "But . . . you promised. You said we need not . . . you promised you would leave me be!"

"It occurs to me I spoke too rashly." His tone was iron-hard. "I will have no one question the validity of this marriage, Yank."

Her eyes were huge. "Your father, you mean?"

"Especially my father." His lips barely moved as he spoke.

Cassie's heart was pounding wildly. He stretched out a hand. She went utterly still, shocked when a brazen fingertip traced the thrust of her breast beneath its covering. "I am not an inattentive lover, Yank," he said softly.

"You'll be no lover of mine!" Blindly she struck out at him.

He snared her by the wrists. All at once this exchange was less a matter of consequence than it was a battle of wills. "My kiss gave you pleasure, Yank. Do you deny that I pleased you?"

Her chest was heaving as she sought to avoid further contact with his muscled chest. "I was neither pleased nor pleasured!"

But it was a lie, through and through. His kiss had wrought a peculiar sweetness, but she had no doubt that the eventual conclusion would prove disgusting and degrading.

A glint of anger crossed his features, yet his voice was smooth as fine brandy. "Forgive me, Yank, but I cannot believe I am truly such a beast. Why, there are women in London who would give a king's ransom to take your place in my bed."

Oh, the arrogant lout! "And I would gladly give them my place," she cried.

His expression tightened. "Unfortunately, that is not possible. And I fail to see why you cling to your stubbornness, for what am I but one more man?"

He pushed away the covers. Cassie trembled beneath his scrutiny as his eyes boldly evaluated all that lay revealed to him, feminine charms bare and unbridled.

"And I fail to see why you persist in taking what should be freely given," she choked out. "Have I no say in this? No choice?"

He merely shook his head and pressed her wrists down upon the side of her head. His nearness was overwhelming; his body lay heavy and hard upon hers. And there was an extra hardness, prodding the softness of her belly . . .

Her breath came in a desperate rush. "You said you had no wish for an heir! What if I should get with child?"

For one terrifying moment it was as if he had not heard. Then all at once, he rolled from her abruptly and rose from the bunk.

Still stunned by the encounter—but immensely grateful for his withdrawal—Cassie huddled in the bunk. She scarcely dared to breathe as he dressed. His movements were quick, almost savage. She sensed he was fiercely—violently—angry.

She knew it for certain when he turned. His jaw was clenched tight, his expression as frigid as his voice.

"This changes nothing, Yank. Should the question arise, you will confirm that our marriage has been consummated."

Cassie's head came up. Her breath wavered. "What?" she murmured. "You mean you would have me lie—"

His voice cut across hers. "I suggest you do exactly that, or else I will have no choice but to see the deed done. And make no mistake—your resistance will not stop me the next time. And do not think to defy me in this, Yank, to my father or anyone else. You must carefully guard the true state of our marriage. For it's all that keeps you safe," there was no escaping the determined glitter in his eyes, "—the *only* thing that keeps you safe."

Cassie shrank back against the wall, stunned and disbelieving. A cold knot of fear coiled hard in her belly. Sweet Lord, had he just threatened her virtue . . . or her life?

Chapter 8

A week later Gabriel announced they would dock in London within the hour.

Prodded into a jarring wakefulness, Cassie slid the quilts from the bed and arose. Her pulse beat a rapid tattoo of excitement as she hurried to pour fresh water into the basin. She scrubbed her face until it glowed, washed her body quickly, then brushed her hair and twisted it into a heavy knot on her nape. With a sigh she reached for her worn and tattered gown. Only yesterday she had mended one of the seams—yet again. But it was the low-cut bodice she hated even more than its ragged appearance. It had always made her feel cheap and tawdry, but never more so than now.

There was a knock on the door. "Cassie? I thought you might like to go above to watch as we approach London."

It was Christopher. She had scarcely ventured outside of the cabin this last week. The memory of being nearly swept overboard was still too painfully fresh in her mind to be forgotten easily. Oddly, Gabriel had not insisted. She opened the door a crack.

He smiled at her. "It would please me if you would. And we need not go near the railing, I promise."

Cassie bit her lip, then nodded. Christopher was kind and gentle and looked so hopeful she couldn't bear to disappoint him. Perhaps it wouldn't be so bad after all. "Let me just get my shawl," she murmured.

On deck the air was bracing but not overly chill. Christopher stood several feet away, near but not touching her. Cassie's heart began to thud. Now that the time was upon her, she didn't know if this was the moment she dreaded—or longed for with all of her being! Gabriel soon joined them, though he had little to say. She craned her neck to catch her first view of the city, unaware that both men watched her, one with an indulgent half-smile, the other with his thoughts carefully hidden from view.

Cassie stared out where warehouse after warehouse stretched along the shoreline. The port was teeming with the loading and unloading of ship after ship. Beyond, plumes of smoke drifted into the sky. The captain guided the ship into its berth; the anchor was dropped.

There was a hand at her elbow. Her husband's voice rushed past her ear. "Wait here while I see to the unloading of the cargo."

Christopher had gone below for his belongings. He returned, a portmanteau in his hand, his hat slanted jauntily atop his head. He stopped before her.

"It seems it's time to say good-bye," he said gently.

Uncaring that her husband might be watching, Cassie pressed a kiss upon his cheek. "Thank you for everything, Christopher. I—I shall miss you."

He gave a hearty chuckle and lowered his portmanteau to the deck. Reaching out, he clasped both her hands in his. "Oh, you've not seen the last of me, Cassie." Gently he squeezed her fingers. "I shall catch up to you and Gabriel very soon." With that he reclaimed his portmanteau, then turned to amble down the gangplank. At the bottom, he turned and waved briefly, then was gone. Try though she might, an endless weight of sadness pressed heavy on her breast. Besides Bess, Christopher had been her one true friend.

The unloading progressed quickly. It was not long before Gabriel was at her side once more, presenting his elbow. "Ready to greet England, Yank?"

With a bravado she was far from feeling, Cassie placed her fingers on his arm. With that first step upon the gangplank, she feared her heart would burst through her breast. Her nails dug into his arm, but she fixed her gaze on the figures scurrying to and fro on the wharf and concentrated on putting one foot before the other.

She was a trifle pale by the time she was on solid ground once more. The air was chill and damp, far cooler than Charleston. Only then did she note the carriage which awaited nearby. The driver jumped down and hurriedly swung open the door for her. Cassie hesitated, unsure how she was expected to proceed. Was she to enter on her own power, or wait for someone to assist her? Mercifully, the choice was taken from her. Gabriel handed her inside, then climbed in after her. He did not sit near but chose to sit opposite her. With a whinny and a word from the driver, they started forward.

Cassie peered curiously out the small window, eager to see London. She was silent as the carriage began to zigzag through cobblestone streets. From a distance came the sound of noisy vendors hawking their wares at every street corner. But it was not long before the man across from her claimed her attention once more. He remained as elegantly aloof, as distant as ever. None but the mere necessities of speech had passed between them of late. He sat across from her, a commanding—and disturbing—presence.

Nervously she smoothed her skirts. As anxious as she'd been to be rid of her past, she had scarcely dared to think of the future, for it still held so many uncertainties.

She broke the silence that had settled between them. "Do you have a house in London?"

Cool gray eyes slid to her. "I have a townhouse in the West End. But we will not be staying the night there."

Cassie folded her hands in her lap. She was not sure she liked the sound of that. "Then where will we be staying?" She hated the timidity of her voice, but she could not help it.

His regard was so piercingly intent she grew uneasy. "At Farleigh Hall, the family estate in Kent," he said at last. "But first we will make a slight detour," his brows rose when he glimpsed her uneasiness, "to visit a *modiste.*"

A dressmaker. So. He had not lied. Unfortunately, he read her mind far too accurately—and with far too much ease. A faint smile curled his mouth. "You need not look so surprised, Yank. I did promise to see you garbed appropriately, after all."

Lilliane Willison's creations were all the latest rage in London, though Cassie was hardly aware of it. A woman with sharp, dark eyes who had passed the first blush of womanhood, Lilliane was still very attractive.

"My wife is in need of an entire wardrobe, Lilliane—and I do mean everything. And Lilliane," his smile was breathtaking, "I'll certainly make it worth your while if you keep the extent of my wife's needs in strictest confidence."

Only through the most strenuous of efforts was Lilliane Willison able to conceal her shock. The handsome lord was a favored customer, for when choosing a gift for his paramours, he spared no expense. But . . . a wife! Of course she would honor his request, for one did not make an enemy of Gabriel Sinclair, but oh! the gossips would be abuzz when they heard of his marriage!

"You've come to the right place, milord." Cherry-red lips smiled demurely. Though her manner was quiet and dignified, Cassie had the immediate sensation that the woman was immensely clever and astute. Would she think it odd—the faultlessly dressed gentleman and his shabby wife? But then even that thought was lost as Lilliane ushered them into another room.

Bolts of muslin, silk, and velvets lined the walls, reaching nearly to the ceiling—in more colors than Cassie had dreamed possible.

The next few hours passed in a blur. Cassie's face flamed when Lilliane made her strip down.

Gabriel lounged in a chair and looked on; she did not dare to meet his eyes. Cassie found it rather disconcerting that he seemed so at home in these surroundings—and with every detail of a lady's wardrobe. But a niggling little voice reminded her that he was no doubt just as familiar with a lady's bedroom . . . and therefore all that was in it.

It was well into the afternoon before they finally departed. Lilliane had brought out several gowns which another customer had declined to purchase after all. Cassie was thrilled to find they were a perfect fit. Before they left, Gabriel asked that they be bundled into several large boxes. As Cassie watched them being stowed behind the driver's seat, she hid her disappointment, for she would have dearly loved to exchange her horrid gown for one of the others.

They made one more stop—at a jeweler's where Gabriel bought her a wedding ring. As he slid the shining gold band over her finger, Cassie could not halt the thought which vaulted through her mind. The ring somehow made their marriage all the more real . . . all the more binding.

As they left the city behind, Cassie did not know if she were more excited or apprehensive. Her mind was whirling. Gabriel seemed perfectly at ease, long legs stretched out before him. With a sigh, Cassie turned her attention to the countryside sliding by outside. It was so very different from all she had known, for seldom had she ventured outside of Charleston. As far as the eye could see was green, rolling hillside, patchworked with farms and dotted with sheep.

She must have dozed, for the next thing she knew, someone was calling her name. Her senses dulled by sleep, her first sensation was one of warmth and security. Her cheek resided on crisp broadcloth. The heartbeat beneath her ear was steady and soothing. Her lids drifted slowly open . . . she stared directly into piercing silver eyes.

She nearly sprang from his arms. Gabriel raised a sardonic brow and offered with a faint smile, "You looked most uncomfortable, Yank. I merely thought to save you from a crick in your neck."

Cassie folded her hands in her lap, willing her fingers not to tremble. Why was it she always seemed to find herself in his arms—the last place she wanted to be—the last place *he* wanted her?

Gabriel gestured toward the window. "We are nearly there, Yank."

Just then they passed through tall stately gates, flanked by a small brick gatehouse, down a long, pebbled lane. On either side, lush, landscaped lawns undulated gently. So stunned was she that she was only vaguely aware of the carriage rolling to a halt and Gabriel swinging her to the ground.

"The family estate, Yank." Gabriel's smile did not quite reach his eyes. "Farleigh Hall."

Cassie had never seen anything like it. Graceful pillars of stone dominated the center of the house. Massive wings stretched out from each side. She found herself overcome by awe, for never had she imagined such grandeur. But her husband allowed her no time to gawk. Quickly he ushered her up the wide stone steps.

The doors were swept open. A white-haired, stoop-shouldered butler ushered them inside. To the right, portrait after portrait lined the length of the gallery. To the left, a set of intricately carved double doors stood tall and imposing. Straight ahead rose a wide staircase, angling in either direction at the landing. Though the butler did not smile, his eyes were frankly warm. "My lord! 'Tis good to see you again."

"Thank you, Davis. Is my father in the drawing room?"

"No, my lord. He has gone out riding with the duke of Warrenton. I expect they will return shortly."

"Excellent," Gabriel murmured. He reached out to capture Cassie's arm. "Davis, I would like to present my wife."

Surprise flared, but the man was so well trained he recovered in a heartbeat. He bowed low, his manner formal but not stiff. "Madam, allow me to welcome you to Farleigh Hall."

"Thank you," she murmured. She summoned a tentative smile, feeling small and unimportant amidst such surroundings.

"Davis, would you see that our bags are brought in? Oh, and I'd like a chamber prepared for my wife. The yellow room, I think."

"Very good, milord."

His hands linked behind his back, Gabriel turned to his wife. "Well, Yank, I trust this meets with your approval?"

Her smile withered. He appeared rather pleased with himself, and there was a gleam in his eyes that made her distinctly wary. "Did you think I doubted you?" She posed the question very quietly.

His laughter was hearty—and false. "Ah, no, Yank, that I did not! Indeed, I suspect you'd never have consented to my proposal if you didn't stand to gain a great deal from it."

Cassie's nails cut into her palm. Must he make her sound so—so greedy? The man was ever ready to believe the worst of her. But she was saved from having to make a reply by the arrival of a maid.

"Milady, your room is ready," the girl said timidly. "I'll show you to it if you wish."

She leveled a burning glare at her husband, then pointedly turned her back on him. Her spine was rigid as she followed the girl up the grand staircase. Near the end of a long corridor on the second floor, the maid opened a door and paused. She smiled tentatively. "By the way, milady, I'm Gloria."

Cassie felt her anger drain from her. "Thank you, Gloria." It seemed so strange, to be called *milady*. She had to stop herself from looking around for someone else.

She stepped past the girl, then caught her breath in sheer delight. The room was huge, larger even than the taproom at Black Jack's. Pale yellow satin hangings draped an enormous four-poster. A delicately flowered washbasin topped the washstand. There was a wide dresser and spindle-legged dressing table with brush and comb and a silver-edged hand mirror spread across the top. Two low-backed chairs done in white velvet were drawn up before the fireplace.

She found herself tiptoeing across the floor, scarcely able to believe she was really here.

Gloria was looking at her anxiously. "I hope the room is to your liking, milady."

"It—it's lovely." It was all Cassie could think to say, so choked up was she. Filled with sunlight and warmth, the room was all she had ever dreamed of and more.

A sweet-scented breeze drifted in through the open window. Cassie pushed aside the frilly white curtain. Was it wrong to feel this giddy rush of happiness? All at once she felt immensely selfish. She thought achingly of Bess—sweet Bess, who would have cried for sheer joy at the privilege of having even a glimpse of such extravagance.

"Would you like me to help you change, milady?" She turned and saw that Gloria had laid out one of the dresses on the bed—an emerald-green evening dress, Lilliane had called it.

"Thank you, I—"

"That won't be necessary, Gloria." A familiar voice cut across hers. Gabriel strode into the room, as supremely masculine and arrogant as ever.

"Please ring for me when you need me, milady." Gloria dipped a curtsy and fled.

"Come, Yank. Your presence is required downstairs."

Cassie's hand fell from the curtain. Her gaze slid longingly toward the gown. "Please." Her voice was barely a whisper. "Is there no time to change—"

Gabriel girded himself against the pleading in her eyes. "There is not," he said curtly. "My father has arrived."

She faltered. Her fingers plucked at her dreadful gown. "But . . . this is what I wore at Black Jack's."

"So it is," he observed coolly. "For now it will simply have to do, I'm afraid."

Her lashes fell, but not before her eyes glazed over, suspiciously bright. Gabriel swore silently, damning them both. Perhaps it was cruel—perhaps it was cold. But he would not be swayed by her tears, for he was captive to his father's plans . . .

And she was captive to his.

She did not move, nor did she speak. Gabriel said nothing, but took her arm, his grip tightening when he encountered her silent resistance. But he was not to be dissuaded, and she must have realized it was futile to cross him in this.

Together they descended the stairs, a horrible coil of dread tightening her muscles with every step, her senses filled with a horrible expectancy.

The double doors off the entrance hall were now open. Cassie caught a glimpse of gilt-papered walls and window hangings of crimson and gold. Two men stood before the hearth, both dressed in riding clothes. One was heavy-jowled and balding. The other stood proud and straight as a youth of twenty, though his silvered hair proclaimed him far older. He turned, giving her a glimpse of hawklike features and frosty eyes. Recognition flashed through her brain. This could only be Gabriel's father . . .

The conversation ceased as they stepped into the drawing room. Gabriel halted just inside the doorway. He inclined his head slightly. "Father," he greeted. "Your Grace."

Gray eyes confronted gray. "Well, it's high time you returned, Gabriel. I began to wonder if you'd not decided to remain in that wretched country permanently."

A smile that Cassie was beginning to recognize as dangerous spread across his lips. "Why, Father, never fear. The notion never crossed my mind."

Edmund Sinclair's expression was rife with disapproval. "As usual," he stated coldly, "your disrespect knows no bounds. So if you don't mind, I suggest the three of us retire." His gaze flickered to Cassie. "We've important matters to discuss— such as your wedding."

That dangerous smile widened. "Actually, Father, my wedding is the very thing I wish to discuss as well . . ." He tugged Cassie forward. "My dear, allow me to present my father, Edmund Sinclair, duke of Farleigh, and Reginald Latham, duke of Warrenton. Gentlemen . . . this is Cassie, my beautiful American bride."

The silence that ensued was shattering. The very air seethed with a tension that seemed alive and pulsing. For the first time, Cassie wondered if she might not have been better off staying with Black Jack . . .

"Your bride!" It was Warrenton who spoke first, the veins in his temple standing out. "If this is some twisted form of amusement, I assure you, I am hardly entertained!"

"And I avow, Your Grace, I do not speak in jest. Cassie is my bride. We were married in Charleston, and surely you can see why I was smitten. Indeed, who could turn a blind eye to beauty such as this?" He touched her cheek, the gesture but a parody of tenderness. Cassie stood frozen, her limbs like ice.

Warrenton went livid. "You were to marry my daughter. My God, I should call you out for this!"

Gabriel's tone was deadly soft. "That is up to you, Your Grace. But I did ask that no formal announcement of the engagement be made until I'd returned from my voyage. I trust my wishes were followed?"

It was Edmund who answered at last. "We made no announcement."

"Then I fail to see why you would be so foolhardy as to call me out, Your Grace. I have neither dishonored nor disgraced Lady Evelyn. She will suffer no public embarrassment, for none but Evelyn and those in this room knew that such a marriage was even discussed. Indeed, who would have expected me to marry in my brother's place? You would be foolish to place your life in jeopardy, Your Grace. But that is up to you." There was no mistaking the threat implicit in his voice.

"He is right, Reginald. Were you to call him out, you chance bringing scandal down upon both our families." Edmund's tone was flat. "I've no wish for animosity between us. If it would ease your mind, perhaps we can come to some sort of . . . monetary arrangement."

Warrenton snatched his riding crop from the chair where he'd dropped it. Some of the red had left his face, but he was still very angry. "Of that you may be sure," he snapped. "I shall be in touch." He whirled and stalked from the room.

A seething tension took hold as he left. Cassie longed to run and hide, yet she stood rooted to the spot.

Edmund turned his head to stare at them, suddenly so angry he was almost shaking. "An American," he said tightly. "How could you, knowing

how I despise their very presence on this earth . . .
Even a bloody Frenchie would have been prefer-
able to an *American*!" He made the word sound
like something vile and rotten. "By God, I won't
stand for it. Do you hear, Gabriel? I'll not stand for
it!"

Gabriel's features were diamond-hard. "We have
been married before God and man, Father, for over
six weeks now. Christopher Marley stood as our
witness. Our marriage is indissoluble." His arm
slid around her. Lean fingers splayed across her
narrow belly. "You see before you the cradle of our
family, Father. Why, Cassie may well be carrying
your grandchild this very moment."

Cassie stood like a stone. He was enjoying this,
she realized, stunned. What kind of man was he—
to enjoy taunting his father so?

Edmund's eyes were focused on the expanse
of creamy flesh exposed by her neckline. His lip
curled. "At what dockside did you find her?"

"Actually, it was an alehouse." Gabriel's tone
was smooth as fine rum. "But I wonder that you
do not commend me for my generosity and compassion in rescuing this poor girl from the gutter.
I may well have saved her from an impoverished
existence for the rest of her life."

The duke's gaze hardened still further. "Please
leave us," he said abruptly. "I wish to speak to my
son alone."

Cassie needed no further urging. She picked up
her skirts and nearly ran from the room. She did
not fly up the stairs just yet, though she longed to
with all her heart. Some force much more power-

ful held her bound there, just outside the door, listening.

Inside, Edmund rounded on Gabriel. "A tavern wench! My God, how many beds has she lain in before yours?"

Gabriel shrugged. "I neither know nor care." He fell silent for a moment, watching the duke. "I find I am curious, Father. Which do you object to the most—that she is an American, or that she does not meet your standards of breeding?"

"Breeding?" The duke stiffened. "The girl has none!"

"It's true that her bloodlines are not so impeccable as yours. Her mother was a whore, and her father . . . well, in short, he might have been any of a number of men." Gabriel moved to stand before the mantel, hands behind his back. He no longer faced the duke, but he derived an immense satisfaction in picturing the duke's angry despair.

"A word of warning, Father—you need not threaten to disown me. I am still your son, though you may have wished otherwise countless times. And I know you will not let your precious Farleigh Hall fall into the hands of strangers. Oh, yes, your strong sense of duty will prevail in the end." He half-turned, slanting his father a mirthless smile. "After all, isn't that why you married my mother— because Stuart needed a mother?"

"What does it matter if I disown you?" Edmund said bitterly. "I shall be dead and gone!"

Gabriel's smile turned unpleasant. "Ah, but it matters very much indeed. I know you, you see, almost as well as I know myself."

Edmund was white with anger. "What do you want, Gabriel? What will it take to be rid of her?"

Outside, Cassie had gone utterly still. She pressed a hand against her chest, aware of a crushing pain. He had warned her, she thought vaguely, that love played no part in their bargain. Yet she had never dreamed that their marriage was forged out of *hatred* . . . but Cassie was suddenly heartbreakingly certain that had been Gabriel's only motivation . . .

For Gabriel must surely hate his father. Why else would he do what he had done?

His chilling laugh reached her ears. "Unlike Warrenton, money will not appease me, Father. You see, I want nothing from you—nothing at all. So do not think to entice her into leaving, to make her disappear."

Edmund's voice was thick with fury. "A change of gown will not make a lady of her. Think what the scandal will do to you!"

Cassie stumbled back; she could bear no more. She turned and ran up the stairs, fighting back a bitter sob.

"Ah, but the *ton* is used to seeing scandal associated with my name—not so with you, Father. Were I you, I'd make no attempt to be rid of my wife. Or I promise I'll see the scandal laid before you at your feet. And we both know the duke of Farleigh could not have that. So resign yourself to my wife, Father. She will be a part of your life . . . as well as mine."

The duke stood in the center of the carpet, his countenance as cold . . . as controlled as Gabriel had pictured it. Yet in his silence lay the triumph of victory.

He had been right to bring her here. Farleigh Hall was his father's pride and joy; it would annoy him mightily to have her installed here . . .

He inclined his head. "Good. I see we understand each other." Raising a dark brow, he continued, "Forgive me for not staying the night, Father. I shall be leaving soon for London. Oh, and Father," the merest hint of a smile crossed his lips, "it might be wise to put the silver under lock and key. My dear wife seems to have a penchant for thievery— why, she tried to steal my watch the first night in port."

Upstairs, a small lamp had been lit on a corner table, casting a welcoming yellow glow. But Cassie felt anything but welcome. She collapsed on the bed and pressed cool hands to her burning cheeks. All her pleasure in the room had fled. Gabriel had intended his common-born Yankee bride to be an embarrassment to his father. She felt cheap and terribly out of her element . . . as he had meant her to feel.

Exactly when she became aware that he had returned and surveyed her from the doorway, she did not know. As for why, she did not care.

She resented his presence in her room, in her very life! But she had just learned a valuable lesson, she told herself bitterly. How very much a pawn she had been! Oh, but never again would she allow him to use her—never!

Slowly she raised her head to stare at him. He did not flinch from her regard, as an honorable man might have, but boldly met her head-on.

"You hate him," she stated without preamble. "He is your father, yet you hate him. Why?"

His eyes flickered. "My feelings toward my father are justified, Yank—and none of your concern."

"You married me because I am an American. Because your father is a duke . . . and I am nothing, a—a nobody. Because you knew he would hate me! 'I shall be frank,' " she quoted. "Yet you were not. Damn you!" she cried. "Why did you lie to me?"

"Yank, I told you the truth—I simply chose not to reveal it all. My father expected me to marry Lady Evelyn in my brother's place. I had no intention of becoming his pawn, and this was the one sure way to ensure that did not happen."

Her face was pale, making her eyes stand out like jewels. "Then at least tell me why he hates Americans! Because he does, doesn't he?"

"Aye, Yank, that he does. You see, my elder brother Stuart and I did not share the same mother. The duke's first wife was Margaret. 'Tis said he loved her deeply."

It did not seem possible that the man in the drawing room was capable of love. Yet Cassie forced herself to listen quietly.

"Margaret had a sister in the colonies. When Stuart was a very small lad, the three of them sailed there, shortly after your Revolution ended, to visit Margaret's sister. Margaret's sister and her family had remained loyal to the Crown, but feelings against the Loyalists ran high. While the three of them were there, someone set fire to the house. My father and Stuart were gone, thus they were spared." There was a small pause. "Margaret and all those within the house perished. My father was furious. Her death fired in him a deep and abiding hatred for all Americans ... even before Stuart was killed in the Battle of New Orleans six months ago."

Cassie closed her eyes. Two young people in the prime of life—two tragic deaths laid on the doorstep of her country. And yet, it was so unfair, for *she* was not to blame.

She opened her eyes, sick at heart, sick to her very soul. Her hands locked tightly in her lap. "Dear God," she said numbly, "no wonder he hates me. And you—you knew he would!"

Gabriel did not deny it.

She swallowed painfully. "I do not pretend to understand your motives," she said, very low: "I know only that you sought to shame your father. But in so doing, you also shame me. And I—I hate you for that, for I cannot change who I am." A lone tear slipped from the corner of her eye. Determined he would not see her so defeated, she brushed it away. With a flick of her wrist, she indicated the wardrobe, where Gloria had neatly hung the gowns they'd brought. "No doubt you intended those to be my reward before you turn me out on the street!"

For an instant Gabriel said nothing. He ignored the voice that reminded him Christopher had predicted this would happen—that she would be hurt as much as his father.

He smiled grimly. "Oh, I've no intention of turning you out, Yank. You are my wife and will remain so. I am a wealthy man, and I will provide for you. You will never be poor again. So I promised, and so it will be."

Cassie's eyes were so dry they hurt. "You will provide for me always? Forever?" Her voice was but a thread of sound.

"Aye, Yank. A lifelong encumbrance." He could not disguise the mockery that entered his tone, for that is what he had been to his father. "Oh, I am well aware you feel deceived. Betrayed. Take comfort in knowing that this will be my penance." He bowed with exaggerated politeness. "For now, you need not suffer my presence a moment longer. I've come to take my leave of you."

"You are leaving?"

"Yes. I am returning to London."

Her eyes flew wide. She was on her feet before she knew it. "And you intend for me to stay here?"

"There are servants to attend to your every need. You have only to ask for whatever it is you wish. And Lilliane assured me your new wardrobe will be done within a fortnight."

"That is not what I meant! What about your—your father?"

His smile was tight-lipped. "This is a large estate. Your paths need never cross. Believe me, I know. Now come here, Yank. I would have a kiss to remind me of my dear, loving wife during the nights we are destined to spend apart."

Oh, the wretch! After all he had done, he expected her to be meek and willing? Her hurt was now blunted by outrage. "No!" she challenged. "And you cannot make me!"

The light caught the stubborn tilt of her delicate chin. Why was it he'd failed to see that in her? His eyes glittered.

He smiled. "Doubtless I could, Yank."

"Doubtless you would!" she snapped.

His lazy calm was deceiving, for doubtless he did. Three long strides brought him before her. Even as she sought to step back in protest, strong hands caught her shoulders.

She had one terrifying glimpse of fiercely glowing eyes and then that hard mouth came down on hers.

He did not beseech her willingness; he demanded it, as only a man could do . . . as only a man who knew much of women would do. Cassie's heart began to beat the pounding rhythm of a drum. There was no escaping the searing fusion of his lips upon hers; his hand anchored on the back of her head kept her mouth where he wanted it. His kiss was searing and blatantly bold, hotly persuasive, drawing from her a response she was helpless to withhold. She fell prey to a treacherous warmth, dark and sweet. Her breath caught, and a jolt shot through her as his tongue plied hers. Yet the sensation was scarcely unpleasant—no, not at all . . .

He pulled her against him, as if he would acquaint her with every muscle. Her breasts were crushed against the breadth of his chest. She could feel the sinewed length of his thighs hard against hers. A slow curl of heat unfurled deep in her belly.

Cassie was trembling when at last he let her go, awash with dizzying sensation. An arrogant smile touched his lips. He traced the outline of her mouth with the pad of his thumb, then stepped back. "Think of me, Yank," was all he said.

Sanity returned in a rush of self-loathing. She had fallen into his arms as if she were ripe for the taking—and ever so eager! No doubt he thought she was his to mold at his whim and leisure.

"Wait!" she cried.

He turned, already at the threshold, his expression one of idle indifference. In that instant, Cassie hated him as she had never hated anyone.

Reckless courage washed over her. "Do not expect me to be so trusting from now on," she stated clearly. "For tonight you have shown me what kind of man you really are."

His eyes were pure frost. "Indeed, Yank. And what might that be?"

Cassie took a deep breath. "You are heartless and cruel to do what you have done—and to your own father!"

He seemed to go utterly still. His reply, when at last it came, was as quiet as hers had been vehement. "Better that you see me for what I am, Yank, than for what I am not."

Chapter 9

A gentle knock on the door roused Cassie late the next morning. Opening her eyes to brilliant golden sunshine, it took a moment to recall she was at Farleigh Hall. The knock came again and she called a sleepy, "Come in."

A short, rotund woman with graying hair bustled in, a tray in her hands. "My lady? I'm Mrs. McGee, the housekeeper. I've brought your breakfast."

Cassie had already levered herself to a sitting position. She pushed at her hair, conscious of her tousled appearance. No doubt the household staff welcomed her shocking appearance here no more than their master. She was immediately on guard as Mrs. McGee placed the tray on her lap.

She lifted the silver pot. "I hope you don't mind, milady, but I took the liberty of bringing a pot of chocolate instead of tea." She poured a steaming brown liquid into a fine china cup and briskly whipped out a napkin.

With her cheery smile and plump red cheeks, Mrs. McGee's warmth was unmistakable. Cassie instinctively relaxed her guard, but she was half-afraid to pick up the fragile cup for fear of breaking it—never in her life had she seen anything so dainty and delicate! Carefully sliding her fingers around it, she raised it to her lips and took a cautious sip. She'd never had chocolate before and she detested coffee.

But the brew was warm and sweet, unlike anything she'd ever tasted. "Why, this is delicious!" she exclaimed, in startled surprise.

"Ah, I thought you'd like it. Now eat hearty, milady. Cook makes the best croissants this side of the Channel." So this was a croissant—Cassie took a bite of the crusty, crescent-shaped roll. It was as good as the chocolate, so light and airy it seemed to melt in her mouth. Mrs. McGee beamed. "As I told Cook when we saw you last night, there's a lass needs a spot of your cookin' to fatten her up."

The croissant suddenly tasted like ashes. Cassie was suddenly mortified. So they had seen her. What had they thought, she wondered, seeing such a scraggly waif with the master's son?

Mrs. McGee patted her hand. "There, now, milady. Don't look like that! His Grace told us how that dreadful uncle of yours worked your poor fingers to the bone—and refused to even spare the coin to buy you a decent dress! 'Tis a good thing Lord Gabriel married you and saw fit to bring you here to Farleigh Hall to recover your strength."

His Grace. The duke had made excuses for his son's shabby wife? Cassie had a difficult time disguising her shock. As for being here to recover her strength . . . oh, but that was rich! In truth, it was far more likely her husband had abandoned her . . .

Mrs. McGee had flitted to the windows, pushing apart pristine white curtains. "It's easy to see why such a bonny lass as you caught Lord Gabriel's eye." Mrs. McGee chuckled when she glanced back over her shoulder. Cassie's cheeks were burning, though not for the reason she suspected. "You must forgive me for callin' him Lord Gabriel . . . 'tis just that I've known him since he was a wee lad barely out of the cradle, and though he's an earl now,'tis hard to think of him as Lord Wakefield!"

Cassie found herself intensely curious, almost in spite of herself. "Did you also know his older brother Stuart?"

"Oh, yes, ma'am! I served as lady's maid to Lady Caroline—that's Gabriel's mum—in my younger days. That's how I came to be here."

"Was Stuart much older than Gabriel?" Try though she might, Cassie found it difficult to imagine Gabriel as a young boy.

"Four years, I believe. Oh, but they were very different—Gabriel and Stuart. The first duchess—Margaret—was Stuart's mum, y'know."

"Yes, I-I know." Cassie held her breath, hoping Mrs. McGee would go on. Though she hardly hoped that the woman might know why Gabriel so hated his father, perhaps she might gain some insight into this darkly brooding man she called husband. "Were they very much alike as children?"

Mrs. McGee pursed her lips. "His Grace was always ever so proud of Stuart. Gabriel was always inclined to stir things up a bit more." A faint shadow flitted across her features. "As I always tell my husband, Angus—he's the stablemaster—the loss of his mum was hard on the poor lad. He and his mum were always so close."

Cassie picked up the last crumb with a fingertip, hoping she did not appear too eager. "How old was he when she died?"

"Eighteen or nineteen, as I recall. Such a tragic death it was—she was still so young—and so sudden, to be sure! He changed after that, though. 'Course I never did believe all those stories about him running wild in London," she added hastily. "Oh, dear me, ma'am, I do run on!" She gave an approving nod as she retrieved the tray from Cassie's lap. "Would you like me to have Gloria start your bath now?"

Cassie's eyes lit up. "Oh, yes, please. And thank you, Mrs. McGee."

Mrs. McGee smiled broadly. "You're very welcome, milady."

Gloria entered almost as soon as the housekeeper departed. Although Cassie felt shy about disrobing with someone else present, she knew such things were done this way among people of quality. While she bathed, Gloria laid out a new chemise, petticoats, and stockings, all purchased from the dressmaker's. Cassie fingered the soft cambric of the chemise almost reverently—never in her life had she thought to wear anything so fine! Sliding a garter up to secure the white silk stocking she'd just donned, Cassie's heart squeezed. She could not help but be reminded of Bess, whose heart's yearning had been to own a pair of white silk stockings.

"Is this morning dress to your liking, ma'am?"

Cassie turned. Gloria was holding a dress of soft white muslin, the waist fashionably high. A series of buttons climbed demurely up the neckline. "That one will be fine," she murmured. While Gloria fastened the hooks and eyes at her back, Cassie battled the urge to cry. Yesterday she'd heard Lilliane murmuring softly about day dresses, morning gowns, walking gowns, ball gowns. She didn't know one from the other and she feared she never would.

Gloria twisted her hair in a neat coil at her crown, then quietly excused herself. Cassie remained motionless. She might have been a stranger, an imposter, for she scarcely recognized the wide-eyed girl staring back at her.

She had lain awake for a long time last night, her only thought being to flee before this masquerade progressed any further. She despised herself for her cowardice, her lack of bravery, yet where could she have gone? She was in a strange country, with no home, no money.

Gabriel had been right—she *had* felt betrayed. But as furious as she was with him, she was just as furious at herself. Perhaps it was her fault, for deep in her heart, she'd known he married her only to spite his father. She shivered, recalling that awful confrontation between the two men. Despite his promise otherwise, she'd been so afraid that now that she had served her purpose, Gabriel meant to turn her out on her own.

Slowly she slid around on the velvet-topped stool. Her gaze swept around the bedchamber. Lord, but this chamber—this house—was lovely, so much more than she'd ever hoped to have! Was it selfish or wrong to long for such comfort, to cling to all that had eluded her?

It would have been so grand, so perfect . . . if only she were not such an outsider! A hot ache filled her throat. Never had she felt so lost! She wanted to belong, she thought with a deep, tearing ache in her breast. Somewhere . . . to some*one*.

Yet Cassie was not inclined to wallow in self-pity, for she was well aware her fate could have been far worse. She might still be back at Black Jack's, serving ale.

And her body as well.

Gathering her courage around her like a cloak, she ventured downstairs. Davis appeared, as if from nowhere.

"I hope you don't mind, milady, but I thought you might like someone to show you the estate." He beckoned and a young man of perhaps fourteen appeared. "Willis here is done with his duties in the stable and would be happy to do so."

Cassie smiled at the boy. He was as likable as the rest of the staff she'd met thus far, with bright blue eyes and a smattering of freckles across the bridge of his nose. "Hello, Willis," she said softly. "Are you certain you don't mind?"

"Not at all, ma'am. 'Twould be a pleasure indeed." The youth swept his hat from his head and bowed low. In her youth and inexperience, Cassie did not realize the boy was convinced the new countess was by far the most fetching creature he'd ever seen.

Though Willis was clearly disappointed to learn she did not ride, nonetheless they spent the day exploring the house and grounds on foot. They hadn't gone far when Willis pointed out the crystal-blue glimmer of water, far beyond the rolling expanse of lawn; there in the distance was a lake she hadn't noticed before. A small dock jutted out into the waters. The boy went on to comment the lake was not visible from the house. Despite herself, Cassie experienced a sudden chill.

Still, the day had passed far more quickly, and far more pleasantly, than she had expected. Her feet were aching by the time she sent Willis off for his supper. She paused a moment, a tired smile on her lips. She had yet to encounter the duke, and for that she was heartily grateful.

As she passed the long line of heavy gilt-framed portraits in the gallery, curiosity got the better of her. Clearly these were ancestors of the present Sinclairs; many bore the same devilish slant to the brows, the same thin, arrogant nose. She paused, glancing at the painting of a bold and dashing dark-haired man from the last century, his hand curled around his sword handle, his hat beplumed and tipped at a rakish angle. His eyes were so full of life and laughter that she could not help but smile in return.

Not so with the next. This Sinclair was stern-lipped and distant, she observed with a sniff. There was no need to wonder where the present duke and his son had inherited their severity. Moving on, she stared upward. An elegantly dressed woman smiled down into the face of a very small boy she held in her lap. In the full bloom of youth and happiness, she radiated warmth and laughter. Her breath caught. Was this the duke's first wife—and their son Stuart? Tousled blond curls covered the boy's head; his features were angelic.

But it was the last portrait which held Cassie bound for a timeless span. This woman sat demurely on a chair before a marble fireplace, slender hands folded daintily in her lap. Her hair was dark and sleek—like Gabriel's. So this was the duke's second wife . . . Gabriel's mother. She felt a strange tugging on her heart, for unlike the portrait of Margaret, there was such sadness in her eyes, a world of it . . .

"You see before you Caroline, Gabriel's mother."

It was him—the duke. But the voice at her ear so startled her that she jumped. Recovering quickly, she spun around to face him. Her heart sank, for he surveyed her unsmilingly—and with ill-disguised hostility.

He made as if to turn away and leave. "Wait!" she cried before thinking better of it.

He glanced back, his spine so rigid she feared it might crack. Cassie squared her shoulders, feigning a bravado she was far from feeling. "I think you should know, sir, that I . . . I did not make my living as Gabriel suggested."

Commanding brows rose high. "Your name. It is short for Cassandra?"

Cassie nodded.

"Well, then, Cassandra. How then did you make your living?" His tone remained as frigid as ever. "My son said he found you in an alehouse."

It was a struggle not to drop her eyes before his imperiousness, for he was, she admitted, a highly intimidating figure. "That he did," she admitted, tipping her chin slightly. "But it was not as he said. I served ale and food, and scrubbed floors and worked in the kitchen—no more—and this I swear."

He made a faint sound low in his throat—disgust or disbelief, she thought with a sinking flutter in her stomach.

"He also said you were a thief."

Hot shame flooded her cheeks. "I will be honest, sir. I stole his watch in the hopes that I might sell it. I—I hoped to leave Charleston and make a living for myself as a seamstress."

She nodded at the portrait of Margaret.

"Gabriel told me how she died," she said quietly. She paused, then said slowly. "It must have been awful to lose her that way . . . I do not know what to say, except that . . . it's a terrible thing when such ugliness extends to innocent people."

"A terrible thing? You Yankees are a savage, ill-bred lot—every one of you!"

Cassie inhaled sharply. "I have done nothing wrong, sir, save to be born in a land you despise." By now her eyes were snapping. "If you brand me as guilty as those who killed your duchess when you know nothing about me, then it seems to me you are no better than they! And by the way, sir, it seems to me that you are hardly above reproach yourself, for I know you lied to the servants about me!"

Edmund was furious at her outburst, that this impudent little upstart dared to talk to him so. But alas, she was his son's wife . . .

And she riled his temper every bit as much as his son.

"You need not make excuses for yourself, young woman. I know exactly what you are, and you may rest assured, I have no desire to know more. And in future, do not presume to sit in judgment of me!"

He left Cassie standing in the middle of the hall, staring daggers into his back. Why, the pompous old man! He was even worse than his son!

Gabriel had been right. It was a large house, and easy for the two occupants to avoid one another, particularly when they had no desire to encounter the other. So it was that Cassie was surprised when Mrs. McGee breezed into her bedchamber one afternoon.

"You have a visitor, milady."

Cassie blinked. "Me?" she echoed blankly, then frowned. "You must be mistaken, Mrs. McGee. I'm afraid I don't know a soul—"

"Oh, there's no mistake, milady. She asked specifically for you. I asked her to wait in the drawing room."

She. Cassie was not certain she liked the sound of that. She rose, a cold lump of dread knotting her belly. It seemed she had no choice but to see who this visitor was. Her unease deepening with every step, she descended the stairs.

She did not have to wait long to find out. Perched on the edge of the divan sat the most stunningly beautiful girl Cassie had ever seen. Hair the color of ripe wheat swept high on her crown; her features were dainty and heart-shaped. She was dressed in a fashionable pale peach gown trimmed with white satin.

On seeing her standing in the doorway, the girl arose, the picture of grace and beauty. "Hello," she murmured. "You must be Gabriel's new bride." The voice was as sweetly pleasing as her features. She extended a gloved hand. "My name is Evelyn."

Evelyn. Cassie longed to curl up and die. Never had she been more aware of her shortcomings, her own humble beginnings. This girl, with her fair hair, petite and graceful figure, demure and soft-spoken voice, was the one Gabriel was to have married. She cringed inside, for this beautiful girl was everything she was *not* . . .

"Oh, dear . . . you are the duke of Warrenton's daughter." The instant the words were out, Cassie could have kicked herself.

But the girl merely smiled, a faint smile, but a smile nonetheless. "I see you know of me. Frankly, that makes this easier." She paused. "I'm afraid I don't know your name."

"I-I am Cassie."

"Well, then, Cassie," she swept an elegant hand toward the divan, "may we sit down?"

Cassie flushed. For the first time she realized how ill-equipped she was to handle the role of lady. "Of course," she murmured. They sat, Evelyn on one end, Cassie on the other.

A tiny smile curled Evelyn's lips. "Do you know," she said softly, "I've wanted to visit you for several days. But I was half-terrified of you, for I did not know what to expect."

Cassie hesitated. "Do you know . . . I-I feel the same!" The admission slipped out before she could stop it. But Evelyn merely laughed; miraculously, the tension cleared as if by some magic.

"I do not mean to be rude," Cassie said after a moment. "But I expected you to . . . to hate me."

A glimmer of understanding flashed in Evelyn's sky-blue eyes. "Because I was to have wed Gabriel—and he married you instead?"

Cassie nodded. "You must have been very upset when you learned what he had done."

Evelyn folded small, white-gloved hands in her lap. "Oh, dear me, not at all. My father was angry at first, for he was the one who wanted the two families united. But he will accept it; indeed, I believe he has begun to already. And I must be honest with you, Cassie. I am heartily relieved there is no need to marry Gabriel. He has always frightened me half to death." She gave a sad little smile. "And indeed, he still does. Stuart was always so charming and carefree. Gabriel is much more . . . oh, I don't know quite how to say it! . . . brooding almost."

Oh, yes, Cassie agreed with a shiver. That he was.

"Did you love Stuart?" Cassie flushed when she realized how bold she sounded. "Never mind," she said quickly. "It's none of my business—"

"Oh, I do not mind, really. I was fond of Stuart, but I did not love him. I believe we would have made a good match, and I genuinely mourn his death. But it was never my wish to be wed simply for who my grandfather's grandfather was, and his before that. Oh, I enjoy the London Season, the balls and *soirees* and routs, but I've always despised being put on display so! It would be grand to marry for love, though such things are most unfashionable. But I fear 'tis hardly likely. My mother might have understood, bless her dear, departed soul, but my father expects me to do my duty, and so I have resigned myself to my fate."

There was a lapse of several seconds before Evelyn spoke again. "I know I'm being dreadfully audacious, and so you need not tell me, but I confess I am frightfully curious. Did you and Gabriel marry . . . out of love?"

Love? No, not that, never that . . . Cassie might have laughed if she did not suddenly feel like weeping . . . Even now, her cheeks burned with hurt, shame, and fury as she thought of that arrogant pair—father and son. Unexpected though it was, she felt a surprising bond with this particular woman who was so different from herself . . . and yet not so different after all. Before she even knew it, the story of how she had come to marry Gabriel—how he had found her at Black Jack's, how Gabriel's sole intent was to spite his father—was pouring out.

Evelyn quickly hid her shock, sensing that it would distress Cassie even more. She patted Cassie's hand in sympathy, for she could not help but feel sorry for this poor girl whom life had treated so unfairly!

" 'Tis common knowledge Gabriel and his father are forever at cross-purposes." A disapproving frown furrowed Evelyn's white brow. "Why, it makes me furious that both could be so mean-spirited!"

"If it were within my power, I'd like nothing more than to show the two of them that they are wrong about me." Cassie's voice was a low murmur. Her hands clenched; she spoke as if to herself. "They are convinced I will fail, but I vow I will not . . . *I will not.*"

At that, Evelyn's eyes began to glow. "I say, Cassie, that's it." Excitement ripened. "That's it exactly!"

Cassie shook her head, not understanding.

"Don't you see? You are right. You cannot let these two best you. You must become the very thing they do not expect—a lady."

"How?" Cassie stared down at her reddened hands. "You forget, I am a—a tavern wench." Lord, but it hurt to say the words. "I would not even know a—a morning frock from an evening gown if it were not for the maid."

But it seemed she had found an ally in Evelyn. "But don't you see? I see you here now, a beautiful young woman, a match for any maid in London! Had you not told me, I would never have guessed you had such an unfortunate beginning. And it does not matter, for I could school you in proper manners and deportment. I could teach you how to be a hostess. How to run a household. And I do not think it would be so difficult, for I suspect you have a very good instinct for what is suitable already."

Beautiful. Did this lovely young miss really think she was beautiful? Oh, she could almost believe it. . . . Cassie warned herself it would be unwise to let her hopes gather. Yet the very thought of besting those two arrogant Sinclairs was so very tempting.

But most of all, this was a chance to become a lady, a *true* lady . . . Her heart beat faster.

"Why?" she asked quietly. "Why would you do this?"

"I've never had a proper friend, not since I was a child. After Mama died, for the most part Papa remained here in the country. I was left with a tutor and governess as my only companions." Evelyn reached out and gripped her hands. "And, oh, I don't know why, but I feel as if we've known each other forever!"

Cassie smiled mistily. "It is odd, isn't it? Because I feel the same."

Evelyn's eyes were shining. "Then let me do this, Cassie. Let me help you!"

Cassie squeezed her fingers. "Do you know," she said softly, "I think you are my friend already. And I gladly accept any help you care to give."

Evelyn laughed, a sweet, tinkling sound. "Excellent! Now, we really must do something about your hands . . . 'tis a good thing a lady always wears gloves, is it not? . . ."

Thus began the business of becoming a lady.

Chapter 10

Over the next weeks, Edmund Sinclair watched all unfold with no little amount of trepidation. Lady Evelyn was a frequent caller; she and Cassandra sat in the courtyard most every afternoon. For the life of him, Edmund could not fathom why Evelyn bothered with the chit. Although, he finally admitted grudgingly, without her wretched clothing, her appearance was at least presentable. Why, on first sight one might easily mistake her for a genteel young lady. Ah, but he knew better than to trust one such as she. She saw his son only as a lump of gold!

A hand like a vice seemed to squeeze his chest. God, but he missed Stuart! Losing Stuart had been like losing Margaret . . . a part of himself forever gone. And now Gabriel was all he had left.

If only things had been different! But he and Gabriel had never been close . . . they would *never* be close. And now it was too late, Edmund acknowledged wearily, for his youth was spent. Perhaps the future as well. Was it truly so wrong to ask that Gabriel marry and produce an heir? There was pride in the Sinclair name, though it seemed Gabriel wanted none of it.

It caused Edmund great sadness—and immense

frustration—to think his name might die out, that he might die without ever seeing his grandson, yet he could never confess such to Gabriel. There was so much distance between them, and he knew not how to breach it! Even as a lad, Gabriel had been ever willful, ever defiant.

A weary sigh escaped. Edmund made his way tiredly to the chair behind his desk, all at once feeling far older than even the heavens. Outside the drawing room, a gentle breeze carried with it the lilt of two feminine voices . . . and something else that made an odd little pain knot his heart, for it was something he had not heard in years . . .

The sound of laughter.

Gabriel climbed the entrance stairs to his elegant London townhouse. His steps were unerringly precise, his eyes unwaveringly clear despite the fact he was quite certain he'd never been more drunk in his life.

Yet still his drink-laden conscience allowed him no ease.

Hours later, he was still in his library, long legs sprawled out before him. In his hand was a glass. On the table beside him was a delicately-faceted crystal decanter of brandy. Gabriel stared into the golden liquid, his mind as clouded as his senses. Outside the streets of London lay still and silent as night turned to morn.

His return to England had gone exactly as planned. His father had been appalled to find his son forever tied to his Yankee bride . . .

But Gabriel's moment of triumph had been altogether brief—and infinitely less satisfying than he had anticipated. Nor did he understand this nagging feeling that plagued him—guilt of all things! He harshly reminded himself what Edmund Sinclair had done to his mother, the years of bittersweet hope, of crushing regret . . . of empty heartache.

He alone had known. He alone had cared. And that was something Gabriel could never forget. Nor could he forgive his father for the way she had died.

Yet thoughts of his father inevitably brought reminders of Farleigh.

He had missed Farleigh. He hadn't realized how much until he had returned! And still, there was a part of him that hated it.

No, whispered a voice. It wasn't Farleigh he hated. It was the memories which lurked there, the memories which refused to be shut away. That was why he had not stayed. There were too many memories there . . . of his mother . . . her death. He had vowed he could not stay—he *would* not. He had done what he'd set out to do—dumped Cassie in his father's lap and resumed his life in London.

But now he was tormented by still more memories . . . of warm lips and skin like fresh cream, as soft as swansdown. Of sweet-smelling hair. And the taste of revenge had not been nearly as sweet as the taste of those lips . . .

What madness was this! His mouth twisted. He was no besotted fool to take on like a lovesick youth. His mood grew even more black. Deliberately he hardened his heart against his poor but beautiful bride. He did not want a wife. Most certainly he did not *need* one. He had returned to

London with every intention of forgetting he had one . . .

Far easier in thought than in deed.

For Cassie, the days passed quickly. She learned to pour tea, what to say when exchanging niceties, what *not* to say. She was exhausted, her head spinning by the time she fell into bed at night, yet she was determined she would succeed in this.

Feeling emboldened one day, she entreated Evelyn to accompany her to tea with the duke in the drawing room that afternoon. Cassie hated knowing the duke watched her. He was not openly hostile, yet she sensed his disapproval. He was stiff and formal; Cassie's hand was trembling so fiercely she feared she would slosh tea all over the front of her gown. But Evelyn had clapped delightedly afterward.

"It's as though you've been born to it! Oh, Cassie, I knew you could do it!"

It was then that Cassie did something she had not dared to do only a month ago . . . she dared to dream. And she began to truly believe that despite the odds, she might find some measure of happiness that she could never have attained had she stayed in Charleston. She was well clothed, safe, and secure. Gabriel had promised she would always have a home—and she clung to that promise for she dared not do otherwise. Still, there were times she half-feared closing her eyes that it might all disappear.

Early one afternoon in late July, Davis announced Christopher Marley. Cassie's eyes lit up. "Please, Davis, show him in!" Christopher strode in seconds later, looking dashing in pale pantaloons and frock coat.

"Christopher, oh, I cannot tell you how pleased I am to see you again!" Cassie extended both hands. She had to restrain herself from hugging him; she'd have done exactly that if Evelyn were not at her side.

He laughed. "My lady, I had visions of you withering away in the country. I decided at last it was time to see for myself how you fared."

Cassie did not miss the silent query in his eyes. His concern warmed her heart. "I am well," she said softly, then smiled slightly. "And you need not bite your tongue. Lady Evelyn is well aware of the circumstances of our meeting . . . Are the two of you acquainted?"

Christopher hid his surprise. He'd certainly not expected to find such a scene as this, but for Cassie's sake, he was heartily glad. "My lady," he said warmly. "We met several times during the Season last year, though I hardly expect you to remember." He bent low over her hand and pressed his lips to Evelyn's fingers.

Evelyn dipped a curtsy. "I remember you quite well, sir."

"Then, milady, I consider myself quite privileged." As Evelyn's cheeks turned pink, he turned to Cassie. His eyes approved the visible changes in her—the stylish white flowered muslin day dress and chic upswept hairstyle. "I must say, you cut quite the figure."

It was Cassie's turn to flush. "I can be no less than honest, Christopher. The credit for the woman you see before you belongs to Evelyn."

Evelyn promptly shook her head. "Do not belittle your efforts, Cassie! I only offered suggestions. It was you who did all the work!"

Christopher chuckled. "Two humble women—a prize beyond price, I'd say. Though 'tis obvious you've both done a splendid job. I applaud your efforts."

Evelyn beamed, but her smile was rather short-lived. "Unfortunately," she sighed. "We have two small problems. We've not yet had time to see to her horsemanship. And though we've mastered the basics of most dances, I think 'twould be much easier for Cassie to learn if she had a gentleman for a partner!"

Christopher gave an exaggerated bow. " 'Tis a good thing then that I've booked a room at the village inn. Therefore, ladies, I am happy to place myself at your disposal."

The next week found the three of them together almost incessantly. Mornings were spent in the gardens or the drawing room. Afternoons were spent in the music room, where Evelyn and Christopher endeavored to teach her to dance, and they ended the day with a ride around the grounds. Cassie longed to ask if he had seen Gabriel; the question hovered on her lips a dozen times a day, yet she could never quite summon the courage to voice it.

To all appearances, it seemed Gabriel intended to stay in London forever—Cassie was not sure if she were relieved or piqued. The duke, as well, had gone to London on business for several days. But Christopher and Evelyn were charming and engaging, and she could not deny she enjoyed the time

spent in their company. Though she looked forward
to her riding lessons, it would be some time yet
before she would be comfortable in a sidesaddle.

But it was the hours spent in the music room
that Cassie truly relished. Under Evelyn and
Christopher's tutelage, she soon mastered the
minuet and country dance. On this particular sunny afternoon, the pair demonstrated what had been
a most scandalous dance—the waltz. When Evelyn
then played the tune she'd been humming on the
pianoforte, Cassie was entranced by the lilting
music and begged to learn the steps as well. Soon
her steps matched Christopher's. She began to swirl
and dip, feeling both light and light-hearted. Never
had she felt so carefree, carefree enough to forget
about everything, even her errant husband . . . She
was laughing, her senses spinning, when at last they
whirled to a halt. Still laughing, she gave a deep
curtsy and gracefully pulled herself upright . . .

She stared straight into blistering gray eyes.

Of the three, Christopher was the first to recover, though later he cursed himself for his startled
and inadequate greeting. "Gabriel! The last I knew
you were still in London. What brings you to
Farleigh?"

Gabriel's smile was a poor disguise for his displeasure. "I might ask you the same, my friend.
But it seems the answer is already very clear." His
gaze slid to Cassie and then back to his friend's
countenance.

But he had yet to say a word to her. To Cassie
it was like a slap in the face. She felt like a child
who'd been caught stealing and deserved a whip-
ping.

And there was no doubt that Gabriel was far from pleased. He had thought to retire his lovely wife to the country and forget about her. But she was forever on his mind, so much so that he'd been compelled to return to Farleigh. He had not, however, expected to find his wife in the arms of another man, let alone one who called himself friend!

Nor was his wife the ragged creature he'd left behind. Had he gone by her in passing, it might have taken a second glance to recognize her—but the faintly defiant blaze in those beautiful golden eyes was only too familiar.

Lady Evelyn had slipped around to Christopher's side. Gabriel accorded her a slight bow. "Lady Evelyn," he said smoothly, "always a pleasure to see you. Now if the two of you don't mind, I trust you will excuse us. I've been deprived of the pleasure of my wife's company for far too long. I should dearly like to have her to myself for a time."

"But of course," Evelyn said brightly, turning to Christopher. "Can I interest you in an early supper, sir? I confess, Cook makes the most delicious pigeon pie in the shire."

Christopher forced himself to relax. "An excellent idea, Lady Evelyn." His gaze was as chill as Gabriel's. "No need to see us out, old man. We can manage on our own quite nicely."

The instant they were gone Cassie rounded on him. Her spine was rigid. "That was rude!"

"Indeed." His lip curled. "What would you know about rude, my dear?"

"Far more than you, apparently!"

That bold, arrogant eye wandered over her, taking in every detail of her appearance. "I must say, Yank, you seem to have adapted to your role with consummate ease."

Cassie's jaw clamped tight. "And I'll wager that displeases you."

It did not, though it should have, Gabriel found himself admitting reluctantly. He made no reply. Instead his attention was drawn to the slender curve of her neck, where the ivory smoothness of her skin met the rich honey-gold of her hair.

"Do you have plans for the remainder of the afternoon, Yank?"

"As a matter of fact, I do. Christopher has very kindly consented to giving me riding lessons this past week."

The plane of his jaw hardened. "You need ask no other man to teach you, Yank. I am your husband."

"But my husband," she stated archly, "was nowhere to be found."

"And now he is, so let us leave it at that, Yank. In any case, since you appear to have your heart set on riding this afternoon, I would not dare disappoint you."

Disappoint her? Torment her, more like!

He turned her in the direction of the staircase. "Go change," he ordered. "I will meet you at the stables in fifteen minutes."

In her room, Cassie rang for Gloria. She dropped on the edge of the bed, the droop of her mouth mutinous. How dare he simply reappear, as if he'd not been gone these many weeks! She'd have dearly loved to leave him waiting there forever. Only the certainty that he would come and fetch her himself stopped her from playing that game.

With Gloria's assistance, she was soon snugly fashioned into a riding habit of deep green velvet. She was not surprised to discover Gabriel already at the stables. A groom stood by, holding two horses. Her heart gave a funny little leap at the sight of him. He looked every inch the aristocrat, from the tip of his well-shined boots to the folds of his snowy-white cravat. Skintight breeches clung devilishly to his thighs, outlining every sleek, hard muscle. Impressively wide shoulders stretched the dark material of his jacket so tightly there was nary a wrinkle. But his expression was one of leashed impatience.

"You are ready?"

She nodded and moved to mount Ariel, the docile little mare she'd been riding all week. Cassie, however, was not inclined to be so meek. "I wish I could ride astride like you," she muttered aloud. Though not, she decided hastily, on his mount. Black and powerful, his horse looked to be as fierce and contrary as his master.

Already up and in the saddle, Gabriel turned his head. "A lady does not ride astride," he said curtly.

"Ah, but I am no lady, am I?"

In truth, Cassie expected no reply; he made none. While Gabriel led the way, Cassie focused all her attention on maintaining her seat. She wouldn't have minded a tumble in the company of Evelyn or Christopher, but to suffer so before her husband was another matter entirely. But he kept a slow pace, and for that she was grateful.

But it appeared they were headed for the lake. That was the one place on the immediate grounds that Cassie had yet to explore. A trickle of apprehension slid up her spine. With Christopher and Evelyn, they had usually left the estate and gone out into the open country. Thankfully, Gabriel skirted the lake and directed his mount toward a grove of trees. Breathing a sigh of relief, Cassie began to look about with interest.

Gabriel did not halt until they reached a small clearing. Nestled within a ring of trees was a small white-trimmed gazebo. Cassie gave a gasp of delight when she saw it. "I didn't know this was here!" she exclaimed. "You can't see it from the house, can you?"

Gabriel shook his head as he helped her dismount. A genuine smile curved her lips, for this sheltered bower was a haven from the outside world. A noisy robin called to its mate. The smell of the forest was scented and fresh. But the gazebo was faded and peeling. A tangled overgrowth of weeds grew all around and climbed up the steps.

"This must have been very lovely once," she speculated aloud. "What a shame it's been so neglected." She bent, brushing away some of the dirt on the steps with her gloved fingertips. She straightened and glanced back over her shoulder, just in time to see an odd expression flit across his dark features.

Cassie's lips parted. "Wait," she said slowly. "This was your mother's, wasn't it?"

Gabriel was abruptly irritated with himself. Why had he brought her here? His mother had loved this place—he remembered she had told him she found its tranquility peaceful and soothing. And God knew she'd had little enough pleasure as it was . . .

"She came here often, yes."

Cassie longed to ask more, for she had often wondered about his mother. Why, she did not know, but it was almost as if some mystery surrounded her . . . But Gabriel's expression was closed and remote. She sensed that now was not the time.

He advanced toward her. "You have a natural ability for riding, Yank. But then, you seem to have many abilities."

Cassie wet her lips. Though his tone was easy, his mood was not.

"You might as well come out with it now, Yank. After seeing you again with Christopher, I am inclined to wonder . . . Have you given to him what belongs to me?"

Confused, she stared at him. "What?"

"Do not play the innocent with me. Have you lain with him?"

"Lain with him!" Her breath caught. "Why, you make me sound like a—"

"A dockside whore? You cannot leave behind your humble origins so quickly, Yank. But I give you fair warning. I will not be cuckolded. I will have no bastard as my heir."

He was shockingly crude—and hurtful. "Oh!" she cried. In that instant she hated him, hated him as she had never hated anyone. "You told your father you rescued me from the gutter, but it's there your mind dwells! Why couldn't you have stayed in London? Then there would be no need to tolerate your beastly mood!"

She was right. His mood was not tame. He was angry at her for drawing him back to Farleigh—and angry at himself for allowing her to invade this place that had belonged solely to the memory of his mother.

"My beastly mood might be much improved had I not found you in the arms of one Christopher Marley."

"Oh, stop!" she hissed. "You want me no more than I want you."

He caught her hands and stripped away her gloves, flinging them aside. She felt as if he stripped away her very soul.

He caught her up against him. His mouth hovered just above hers, its beautiful lines stark and sensual, as though etched from stone. "Ah, but there's the thing, Yank. I am *not* so unappreciative of your charms."

His head swooped down. His lips trapped hers. Again and again he plumbed the depths of her mouth, the rhythm of his tongue wildly erotic. Hard arms came tight around her body, pinning her against his unyielding breadth. Cassie pushed at his chest, the attempt pitifully weak, for God help her, something strange was happening. A fiery warmth stole through her limbs. His kiss blazed like fire all through her. His mouth opened wider, the pressure sweetly fierce, draining her of strength and will. She moaned, the sound wedged between their lips, aware of the urge to follow blindly wherever he would lead her.

Dimly she heard a low, triumphant laugh. His breath was hot on the side of her neck. "You've cost me a pretty sum indeed, Yank. So come, I wish to see what I have bought." Deliberately he brushed the velvet-covered peak of her breast. She gasped as her nipple grew all tight and tingly, and—Lord help her—the sensation was not unpleasant at all. And then she felt the brand of his fingers on the fastenings of her bodice, warm and adept.

Panic burst in her brain. She knew where play such as this would lead! She could not let him take her like this, so coldly determined—with no emotion save lust. Oh, if he loved her, if he cared for her, it might have been different. She might have surrendered what he now demanded . . .

She tried to wrench back. The binding circle of his arms caught and held her in place.

Slowly he raised his head. The merest hint of a smile graced those elegant lips. "I am, after all, only a man," he said softly. "Do you worry that I will succumb to desire?"

In truth, his shaft was rigid and full. A part of him longed to bury his swollen heat deep and hard in her body and the consequences be damned. Oh, no, he was not as unaffected by their kiss as he would pretend, or as he'd thought to be . . . which meant he must be careful, very careful indeed.

Her answer lay in the wide, wary distress of her eyes. Gabriel laughed curtly. "Do not worry, Yank. Tempt me not, and I will yield not." He released her.

Stung, Cassie spun away, further dismayed by her body's treacherous response to him. A horrible notion raced through her. Dear Lord, was she a wanton like her mother?

Suddenly there was a loud *pop*! The strong odor of something burning reached her nostrils. At almost the same instant, her left arm began to sting. She instinctively raised her fingers to the hurt.

They came away sticky and red. Bemused, Cassie stared at them. Blood, she realized dazedly, and suddenly it was very hard to think. A dull buzzing in her ears grew louder and louder. What on earth. . . . Belatedly her mind recognized the sound for what it was.

"Dear God," she heard herself say. "I've been shot."

She pitched forward into a dead faint.

Chapter 11

Gabriel reached her just as her knees began to buckle. A vile oath on his lips, he scooped her into his arms and ducked into the gazebo. Mindful of the need to keep his head low so he would not be seen, he ripped apart the torn sleeve of her riding dress. Snatching his handkerchief from his pocket, he pressed it to the wound. Gently he wiped away the oozing trail of blood and gunpowder.

The frantic fear left his heart. The shot had only grazed her, thank heaven. It was not even deep; even now the wound had begun to clot. No doubt it was shock, not injury, that prompted her collapse. He hesitated, torn by the urge to search for the scourge who had fired the shot but reluctant to leave her alone.

At length Cassie stirred. Remembrance of the shot flooded back with a vengeance. Her eyes flew open, but darkness swirled all around. She lurched upward with a stricken cry. "Sweet Lord! Do not tell me I am dea—"

A firm hand restrained her. "No, Yank," proclaimed a dry voice, "you are not. You are alive and unhurt, though clearly you fancy yourself in heaven once again." There was a brief pause. "You were lucky, Yank. The shot merely grazed your arm. The bleeding lasted scarcely a minute."

It was Gabriel. They were inside the gazebo, she realized vaguely. His back was propped against the wall. She was lying in his lap, cradled in his arms. Though it was not as dark as she had first thought, daylight was fading fast. As her eyes adjusted to the gloom, she saw the tattered edges of her sleeve.

A low choked sob caught in her throat. She gave no further thought to the danger they might still be in. It was suddenly all too much—the shot . . . the blood on her hands. "My beautiful riding dress . . ." She began to cry. "I've never had anything so grand . . . I loved it so . . . oh, God, and now it's ruined!" She turned her face into his shoulder and wept.

A strong hand smoothed her hair. "Cassie, hush now. *Hush.* I'll buy you another—I'll buy you a hundred if it pleases you."

Her breath caught on a half-sob. She sought dumbly to focus on the dark features that swam just above her own. She could not help it, for this man was a stranger. He had called her *Cassie*, with something that might have been tenderness softening his remonstrance. And his eyes . . . surely the glow of twilight was deceiving, for that could not possibly be *caring* she saw there . . .

She would have sat up but his arms closed around her more tightly. "Be still," he warned, the words but a breath. "The horses bolted when they heard the shot. In all likelihood it came from a poacher, but I'll take no chances. We'll remain here until it's dark and then return to Farleigh."

Cassie nodded, suppressing a shudder of fear.

She laid her cheek on his chest and huddled even closer, taking comfort in his strength, in the steady drumbeat of his heart beneath her ear.

It was well above an hour before they returned to Farleigh. Edmund was in the entrance hall with Davis when Gabriel flung the door wide.

"Confound it, Gabriel, what goes on here! Angus just informed me your horses—" Edmund stopped short on seeing the condition they were in. They were both filthy. Dust and dirt smudged Cassie's cheeks, a trail of tears clearly evident.

Edmund's jaw sagged. "Dear God, what happened?"

Gabriel's mouth turned grim. "We were at the gazebo when someone fired a pistol at us."

Edmund looked at her sharply. "Are you all right, Cassandra?"

Cassie. Cassandra. Cassie stifled the impulse to laugh wildly. Perhaps she'd gained some headway with these arrogant Sinclair men after all. She nodded, still too shaken to speak. She stood mutely while Davis was told to summon Gloria. Gabriel saw her safely delivered into the hands of the maid then turned to his father.

"A word with you in private, if you please, Father." He strode into the drawing room. Edmund followed, closing the wide oak portals behind them.

Gabriel poured himself a generous portion of port before turning. "I cannot help but wonder, Father . . . The events of the day seem to raise the notion that you might wish to see me a widower."

It took an instant before the full import of his

words sank in. When they did, Edmund's shoulders straightened. Fury ignited in his eyes. "I've thought you capable of many things, Gabriel. But to think that you would accuse me of trying to kill the girl . . ." Edmund only barely concealed his rage.

"I do not accuse you," Gabriel said calmly. The duke's shock had been genuine. And for all that his father's emotions ran cold, he was not inclined to violence.

"Perhaps no harm was meant for her at all," the duke said stiffly.

Gabriel frowned. "What do you mean?"

"Perhaps you've been plucking fruit in someone else's orchard."

His meaning was not lost on Gabriel, who smiled thinly. "I've always chosen women with care, Father. None are burdened by a husband, and none with male relatives who might be disposed to deprive me of my life for the sake of a mere dalliance."

"Likelier than not, then, it was a poacher. It might be wise to advise Cassandra to refrain from riding in the woods until we know for certain."

"Oh, you need not go to such trouble on her account. She will be returning to London with me."

Edmund's glance was no less than suspicious. "Whatever for?"

"The dowager duchess of Greensboro is having a *fête* tomorrow evening."

"I'm well aware of that. I'd thought to attend myself. But you cannot mean to take her!" Despite Lady Evelyn's attempts at grooming these past weeks, Edmund remained skeptical.

Gabriel merely raised his brows. "One does not refuse the dowager duchess. To my understanding it's to be a relatively small affair to begin the Little Season. And I do believe we've had this discussion before, Father. Is it your reputation which concerns you, or mine?"

Edmund resisted the urge to throw up his hands. "Do what you will," he muttered. "You will please yourself and no one else." He spun around and strode from the room.

Gabriel watched his retreat, his expression etched in stone. "That I will, Father," he said aloud. A faint bitterness laced his voice. "After all, I learned long ago there was little point in trying to please you."

Deliberately he turned his thoughts elsewhere, studying the amber liquid in his glass before taking a long, deep swallow. Perhaps his father was right. Yet one question led to another. Who had fired the shot? Was it intentional? Or an accident? And if not, who had been its intended victim? Cassie . . . or himself?

The line of his mouth grew thin. He could think of no one who would wish him dead. Yet why would Cassie be a target? Her circle of acquaintances was limited, both here and in Charleston. Likelier than not, the shooting was accidental. No, he could not leave her here in harm's way . . .

Upstairs in her room, Cassie sat at the dressing table while Gloria brushed her hair. Her expression was one of troubled thought but that quickly changed when Gabriel walked in.

"How is your wound?"

Cassie flushed, embarrassed beyond measure to think she had fallen apart in his arms. She lowered her gaze and stared at the gilt-framed mirror and matching brush. " 'Tis fine," she murmured. "A bit red, but that is all."

"Excellent. I will be able to return to London tomorrow as planned. Please have Gloria pack your things first thing in the morning."

Her head came up. She twisted around and stopped him when he would have left. "Wait!" she said breathlessly. "Does this mean . . . I am going with you?"

"It does indeed, Yank. Why, all of London is agog about the new countess of Wakefield. I am going to have to produce a wife else no one will believe I have one . . . And after all, you *are* my wife . . . where would you be but at my side?"

Did he mock her? Cassie did not know. At that moment, she did not care. She stared at the doorway long after he'd left, frightened, wary . . . and excited all at once.

It seemed she was going to see London after all.

Gabriel's townhouse was far from modest, at least in Cassie's eyes. Though it was not nearly so grand or vast as Farleigh Hall, it was still far beyond her realm of experience.

The domed ceiling of the entrance hall was a soft gold, carved with delicate scrollwork and cherubs. Just beyond, the staircase ascended dramatically between two tall, stately columns. The library was a smaller version of the one at Farleigh, paneled in rich mahogany. In the drawing room, the walls were hung with crimson silk; the carpet was deeply hued in golds, browns, and blues. Several chairs and a divan were drawn close to the warmth of the fire. All in all, Cassie found it most inviting.

She was also delighted to find her room every bit as lovely as the one she had occupied at Farleigh. Decorated in palest blue and yellow, she took one look at the canopied bed and immediately fell in love with it.

"If the furnishings do not suit you," her husband said formally, "you may make whatever changes you wish."

Even his dour mood could not dampen her spirits. Cassie fingered the frilled yellow skirt that trimmed the dressing table, then turned and graced him with a lovely smile. "It's lovely just as it is," she said softly. "I wouldn't dream of changing a thing." Just then she spied a door next to the dresser. Impulsively she opened it. "Where does this lead?"

But she had already discovered the answer. She caught a glimpse of sparse, masculine furnishings and an enormous four-poster.

Color stained her cheeks. "Your bedchamber, I take it?"

He nodded, his expression coolly remote, revealing no hint of his thoughts. But to Cassie, the atmosphere was suddenly stifling. No further comment was drawn from either of them.

And little wonder. They were both well aware the connecting door would see no use.

"By the way, Yank, we have an engagement early this evening."

"An engagement?"

"Yes. We've been invited to attend a *fête* given by the dowager duchess of Greensboro." He strode toward the door, then stopped and turned toward her. "I shall return shortly to oversee your choice of attire."

Cassie drew herself up proudly. "I'm quite capable of choosing my own gown," she said stiffly.

"Oh, no doubt you are, Yank. Nonetheless, I will be happy to lend my assistance."

Though she knew he considered the matter closed, Cassie opened her mouth, determined to argue. One glance from those icy gray eyes robbed her of the inclination. Still, it was not in her nature to accept such a commanding attitude with meek obedience. When he arrived in her room, she still wore her dressing gown, having recently bathed. Summoning all her bravado, she moved to the wardrobe and withdrew the gauzy white gown she had planned to wear. Turning, she drew it back across one shoulder and silently awaited his reaction.

A slow smile crept across his lips. "I think not," he drawled. "With you at my side in that gown, I would feel like a veritable wolf. Besides, you would look like an innocent—a virgin, young and untouched."

That's because I am! she longed to screech. Oh, but it would have given her great pleasure to disprove his arrogant high-handedness! But she was not certain how he would react, and so she held her silence. Her lips tightly compressed, she thrust the gown back into the wardrobe and withdrew another.

He disdained the choice as too girlish, still another as too simple, still another too formal. Cassie's anger began to stir. Blindly she reached into the wardrobe, yanking out the first one her fingers chanced to touch.

Gabriel paused, as if to consider the pale peach silk. " 'Tis a pretty enough color," he murmured, "but I would have you sparkle like the jewel you are. Something bright, I think."

He mocked her, and in that moment, she despised him for it. "I think black would prove far more appropriate!" she retorted hotly.

Devilish brows arose. "Black—to match your mood, sweet?"

"Black, to match your heart!"

By then Cassie's chin was tipped mutinously. He merely laughed. "You must learn to trust in me, Yank. I have much more experience in these matters." He strode forward and pulled out a gown of ruby-red silk gauze. "This one," he pronounced.

Cassie snatched it from his grasp. "You were not so concerned with my choice of gown when I met your father," she snapped. "I fail to see why you trouble yourself so now."

She had struck a nerve. Though his voice was mild, she could see it in the clench of his jaw. "Ah, but the eyes of the *ton* will be upon you now, Yank." He said nothing further, but left her alone.

At last she was ready. Gloria pushed her gently before the mirror, then stood back and clapped her hands together. "Oh, ma'am," she breathed, eyes shining, "you are truly a vision."

For a long time Cassie could only stare. Gloria had dressed her hair high and away from her face, setting off the vulnerable slope of her neck and shoulders. The gown's neckline formed a deep vee, both front and back. In Cassie's mind, it was scandalously low, but Gloria assured her it was the fashion. Beneath her breasts, the skirt fell in soft folds down to her slippers. Although she had been determined to dislike the gown, Gabriel had chosen well, for the overall effect was one of classic elegance.

She felt dainty and feminine . . . and beautiful. Tears started in her eyes, for this was a wholly new feeling for Cassie. But what would Gabriel think? All at once she was nervous and anxious.

It came as a shock to realize she wanted to please him. Why it was so, she did not know—nor did she care. But she wanted to please him so very much . . .

He waited in the entrance hall, pacing impatiently. Cassie descended the stairs as quickly as she dared, clinging tight to the ornately carved handrail. When she reached the last step, he finally glanced up.

Their eyes locked. Her heart thumping wildly, she stood still as a statue. His gaze raked her from head to toe and back again. Cassie endured his critical regard as best she could, but his inspection was so long and so thorough she feared she had done something terribly wrong.

At last he offered her his arm. "You will do," he announced.

Outside he handed her into a richly cushioned carriage pulled by two prancing steeds, but Cassie scarcely noticed as he took his place beside her. She turned her face away, feeling crushed inside. Never in her life had she thought to possess a dress such as this—to look as grand as this. And she had thought—hoped!—that Gabriel might think so, too. But neither approval nor condemnation had resided in his gaze. He was as cool, as remote, as ever.

In truth, it was hardly the case. His first sight of her, gliding down the stairs, stole the very breath from his lungs. It was all he could do not to haul her into his arms, rip off her dress, lovely though it was, to discover the sweetly curved treasures that lay beneath.

He could not give in to it. He could not give in to *her*.

He damned her, in that instant, for the way her eyes shone huge and eager and hopeful, just as he damned himself for being the coldhearted bastard that he was. And so he summoned an iron control, for he had learned to master his true emotions long ago.

His father had taught him that much, at least.

The Greensboro mansion was ablaze with lights, both inside and out. Cassie watched as the long line of carriages waiting to drop off guests slowly inched forward and realized theirs was next. Now that the time drew near, she was frightened half to death. What was it Gabriel had said? *The eyes of the ton will be upon you.*

All too soon they stopped before the front doors. A heavy knot of apprehension weighted her stomach. Placing her ice-cold hand in Gabriel's, she alighted from the carriage and allowed him to lead her inside.

Soon they paused at the entrance to a large ballroom. The scent of eau de cologne mingled with that of fresh flowers. Laughter and voices floated everywhere.

Panic swept over her at the crush of people. She began to quake, both inside and out. For the first time she realized what she was about to do—play the part of lady when she was anything *but* a lady. God, but it was almost laughable! Painfully conscious of her incompetence in such a role, she longed to be anywhere but where she was. And then, as she looked out across the sea of strangers, she spotted a familiar face. But it was scarcely a friendly face—no, not in the least . . .

It was Gabriel's father.

Just then the majordomo announced, "The earl and countess of Wakefield."

She was totally unaware that she pressed close to Gabriel's side, yet such was not the case with Gabriel. All at once he was angry with himself and with her. It had been in his mind to cut her cold, to reject her with callous disregard and leave her alone, knowing it would embarrass his father who watched them. Yet one look at Cassie's white face and terrified eyes and he knew he could not.

He tucked her hand gingerly into his elbow. "Smile, Yank," he said under his breath.

Cassie's face looked as if it would crack. "I—I cannot."

"Of course you can." Even as he spoke, he stepped forward. Later she decided it was the sheer force of his will that kept her upright.

A dozen introductions quickly followed. Cassie began to feel dizzy as one face blurred into another. She thought half-hysterically that Evelyn would have been proud; through some miracle, she managed to make the appropriate responses.

A handsome young man clapped Gabriel on the

back. "I can well understand your reason for keeping this jewel from envious eyes, which reminds me . . . How is it we've never before seen this beauty? I wonder that I should not avail myself of a quizzing glass, for by Jove, I could swear I've never set eyes upon her before. I'd have remembered a face such as this!"

Gabriel's smile was cool. "This is Viscount Rayburn, my dear."

Cassie inclined her head in greeting. "There is little to wonder about," she said softly. "I've never before visited London." Though the viscount's manner was somewhat brash, his smile was devilishly charming.

He raised a rakish brow high. "Never visited London! Why, the devil take you, Wakefield! You always did have the best of luck with a turn of the cards—and now in this, too! Wherever then did you find this lovely lass?"

Cool gray eyes rested upon the viscount. "All the way across an ocean, I fear."

Rayburn blinked. "What! Never say a Yankee!"

Gabriel merely shrugged, while Rayburn again turned his attention to Cassie.

"Thank heaven that wretched war is over," he announced, "that we might turn our attentions to far more pleasant matters. I confess, I cannot see Wakefield in the role of jealous husband. But, my dear, from now on, you must not let him keep you buried in the country . . ." When the earl of Harcastle stepped up to Gabriel, Rayburn skillfully guided her away.

So it was that Gabriel's subsequent absence from her side was not missed. But every so often, Cassie felt his eyes on her, and his father's as well. She hated being under their scrutiny, one so mocking and arrogant, one so cold and disapproving. But she need not have worried that she would be left alone. When Rayburn left to fetch a glass of wine for her, several eager young men stepped up to take his place.

It was not long before she heard a commanding female voice. "Move aside, yes, that's the way. I wish a word with the young lady there." One by one the crowd parted, like the sea before Moses.

Cassie's eyes widened. It was the dowager duchess and she was headed straight for her! For a split second all thought deserted her and she could not think what to do. Then, she recovered and dipped low in a curtsy just as the woman stepped before her. "Your Grace," she murmured.

The duchess was a stout, imposing-looking woman. She wore a gold turban topped with an ostrich feather. Well known for speaking her mind, she wasted no time looking Cassie up and down.

"Your husband's manners are atrocious," she pronounced. "Why, he did not even deign to introduce you." With a swish of her skirts, she settled herself on the bench and gazed expectantly at Cassie.

"Come now, dear. Sit and tell me everything about yourself."

Cassie's smile held a trace of wistfulness. "I'm afraid there is little to tell, Your Grace."

"Come now, don't be shy. Edmund mentioned how Gabriel found you working your fingers to the bone in Charleston."

Edmund. Cassie could not help it. She raised her chin and caught Edmund's gaze from across the crowded room, her own faintly challenging. Oh, but she would have liked to put the lie to his claim! But she did not, for if she had gleaned anything from Evelyn these past few weeks, it was that while a man could flirt with scandal and emerge relatively unscathed, for a woman it might mean instant ruin.

And Cassie had no wish to be cast aside. For once she wanted to feel she belonged . . . with all of her heart she yearned for it.

Still, it was not in her nature to lie. "I—I was made to work for my room and board, yes," she replied.

"Indeed! Well, work builds character, as the late duke used to say. And frankly, there is a shocking lack of such among young people today."

Cassie smiled slightly. "I fear you may be right."

"I must say, my dear, when I first heard Gabriel had wed you, I thought the match outrageous!" The duchess chuckled heartily. "Why, I can just imagine what Edmund had to say! Gabriel took everyone quite by surprise with this marriage. He was quite the libertine, you know, and 'tis quite obvious why he was so taken with you. You are *not* the usual, simpering London beauty."

Cassie shook her head. "I am hardly a beauty, Your Grace."

"You see, dear? I have watched you tonight, and you are totally unpretentious. My husband the duke would have found that a sterling quality indeed . . . as do I, and immensely refreshing as well!"

Gabriel chose that moment to glance across the room at them. The duchess beckoned to him, and seconds later he stood before them.

"Your Grace," he hailed, bowing low over her hand. "I see you have met my wife."

While Cassie looked on in wary apprehension, the duchess tipped her nose high. "I have, indeed, and I must say, I am most pleased with your choice of bride." She fixed him with a stern look. "I only hope that you are worthy of her."

Gabriel's polite smile froze. He was unable to believe his ears. It seemed the chit had just charmed the dowager duchess, and by so doing, the impossible had just occurred . . .

She had just assured her place in society.

Chapter 12

Nor was that the end of it.

Gabriel sat in his study the next afternoon, a pile of papers at his elbow, his tea untouched. The household had learned very quickly that the master's mood was anything but easy this morning. They hastened to do his bidding when summoned, but they knew from experience he was best left alone.

Nor was it difficult to detect the source of his ill temperament. Earlier, a messenger from the duchess of Greensboro had delivered an invitation to the new countess to take tea with her that afternoon. Since then, the bell had scarcely stopped ringing, and the stack of cards and invitations on the silver tray in the entrance hall was mounting.

Now, when the bell pealed once more, Gabriel shoved back his chair and stood. By Jove, he would remain here no longer. Surely even his shipping offices on the noisy docks would offer far more peace and quiet than could be achieved in his private study today.

He stopped short at the sight of his father in the entrance hall, handing Giles his hat and cane.

Edmund turned and spied him. "Gabriel, there

you are. A word with you, if you please."

Gabriel made no effort to disguise his irritability. "I am on my way out."

"I assure you," Edmund stated coolly, "this will not take long."

Gabriel scowled but turned and led the way back into his study.

Edmund closed the door behind them. "I thought we might discuss Cassandra's first public appearance."

Gabriel's eyes flickered. He said nothing.

"It went surprisingly well, don't you think?"

"Well enough, I suppose."

"Indeed," the duke said softly, "her speech is passable. Her name is not plebeian. Her conduct last night was not at all unseemly."

Gabriel's eyes narrowed. "What are you trying to say, Father?"

"Only this, Gabriel. The girl has possibilities I had not foreseen—or expected."

"And?" Every muscle in Gabriel's body had gone steely hard. His father was up to something, but what?

"Therefore, I've decided to give a ball two weeks hence in recognition of your marriage."

A hard smile edged Gabriel's lips. "Ah, now that's rich. Do you forget she is an American? Or have you decided to put aside your hatred and welcome her to your bosom?"

Edmund drew himself up proudly. "This changes nothing," he proclaimed with icy disdain. "Never will I forget what those wretched Yanks did to Margaret and Stuart—never!"

"As I recall, Father, 'twas you who claimed 'a

change of clothing will not make a lady of her.' "

"Lady Evelyn has taught her much, though I did not realize to what extent she'd met with success until now."

Gabriel was astounded. "Lady Evelyn!"

"Yes. She has been a frequent visitor at Farleigh of late. She and Cassandra seem quite fond of each other. An unlikely friendship, is it not? As unlikely a pair as the two of you, I might add."

Gabriel's smile had long since vanished. "You are mad," he said harshly. "She is not ready for this. She will make fools of us all."

Their eyes clashed fiercely. "I would remind you," Edmund said quietly, "I but play the game you began. 'Twas you who married her, Gabriel. And now you have no choice but to make the best of it."

Gabriel's eyes did not waver from his father's face. "Make the best of it," he repeated slowly. "Tell me, Father. Is that what you did with my mother?"

Edmund made no reply. He merely stood there, his posture wooden, as implacable as ever.

Possessed of a cold, biting fury, Gabriel's mouth twisted. "But I forget," he said derisively. "My mother was never of any consequence to you, was she? Nor was I."

His father did not deny it. He did not defend himself.

Gabriel made a sound of disgust and threw open the door. "Do whatever you will," he said furiously. "It matters little to me."

The front door slammed so hard the windows in the attic shook.

Slowly Edmund made his way to a straight-backed chair, his steps as heavy as his spirit. The venom in Gabriel's eyes had shaken him badly. God! his heart cried out. He buried his head in his hands. Dear Lord, he asked himself wearily, when had it all started—the hatred, the bitterness.

And when would this enmity cease?

Behind him there was a low cough. He did not look up, thinking it was one of the servants. "Close the door and leave me be," he muttered. "I shall see myself out shortly."

The door clicked shut. "Excuse me, sir," said a voice. "But are you unwell?"

Edmund's head jerked up. Cassandra stood before him. Her expression was tentative, her eyes mutely questioning. Embarrassed, but determined not to show it, Edmund got to his feet.

"I am fine," he said somewhat brusquely. "You need not concern yourself with me, girl."

Cassie's chin came up. "As I once told your son," she stated with calm dignity, "I have a name, sir, and I will thank you to use it."

For an instant the duke appeared quite taken aback at her boldness. "Very well then, Cassandra." He arose, once again every inch the noble lord, in command of himself and everyone around him. "Actually, your appearance is most fortuitous."

Fortuitous? Whatever it was, Cassie thought on a glimmer of panic, it sounded ominous. Somehow she managed to mask her turmoil, and even managed a faint smile. "How so, Your Grace?"

"I am planning a ball two weeks hence in acknowledgment of your marriage. I require your assistance."

"My assistance?" Her confidence, tenuous at best, fled like frost beneath a blazing sun. All at once, an awful feeling of dread crept through her.

"Yes. I have prepared a guest list." He withdrew a neatly folded paper from the pocket of his coat. "I've no doubt Gabriel will wish to add to it, but I could use your help to commence addressing the invitations."

Cassie blanched. "I'm afraid that is not possible." Her tone was scarcely audible.

"I beg your pardon?" His was clipped and abrupt.

Cassie stared at the rich carpet on the floor beneath her feet. Her hands twisted nervously in the folds of her skirt. "I . . . I fear I cannot help you."

Edmund's regard sharpened. "Cannot . . . or will not?"

His voice stabbed at her like the blade of a knife. Cassie stood mutely. To her horror, a burning ache closed her throat.

"I would like an answer, if you please, Cassandra."

The breath she drew was deep and frayed. "Cannot . . . will not . . . what does it matter? I would help you if I could, Your Grace, but I am afraid it simply is not possible."

"And I fail to see why not!"

Her voice was low and tear-choked. "Because I—I can write my name, but—but nothing else!"

There was a stunned silence, and then his voice came, almost deadly quiet. "Do you mean to say you cannot read? Or write?"

Cassie nodded miserably. Never in her life had

she felt so ashamed. The tears began to fall in earnest.

Edmund floundered for his handkerchief, then located it at last and thrust it into her hands. Though he'd have sworn the chit was not high-strung, weepy females made him nervous, they always had. Lord, all he needed was for her to fall victim to the vapors yet!

He stared at her shaking shoulders. "There now, Cassandra. There's no need to cry." He awkwardly patted her shoulder. " 'Tis a matter easily remedied."

"How?" she choked out.

"How else? The services of a tutor are easily obtained—"

"A tutor? For the earl of Wakefield's wife? Oh, but your precious *ton* will love that."

He pondered a moment. "You are right. That leaves us with only one choice then. I will teach you."

"You?" She was aghast.

"Of course. I assure you, Cassandra, I am quite capable."

That she did not doubt. She mopped her eyes and looked at him. "Why?" she whispered. "Why would you do this?"

He gazed down his nose at her, once again the imperious lord. "I'll not have it bandied about London that you cannot read. Lord knows the gossip mongers have more than enough to sustain them as is."

Cassie's eyes searched his. "Then I would ask a favor of you," she said slowly. "Will you not tell Gabriel?"

Edmund sighed. "If you wish it, I will not tell him."

Cassie did not delude herself. Edmund had not agreed to this task out of the goodness of his heart; his sole concern was that she not bring further shame upon his name.

Gently, she touched his arm. "Thank you," she said.

Edmund cleared his throat, embarrassed and something else, something she could not identify. "Now then," he said gruffly, "I believe Gabriel spends most afternoons at his shipping offices. Come to my townhouse promptly at one tomorrow afternoon."

Her lessons began the very next day. Cassie approached the first with mingled anxiety and delight. Though she had a hungry desire to read and write, Edmund had only to cast the most idle of glances at her and she longed to disappear forever. But as the week wore on, her apprehension began to lessen. His manner was stiff and formal, occasionally impatient, and always demanding. Like Gabriel, he seldom smiled. But she began to suspect he was not the ogre she had first believed.

She studied him covertly one afternoon. Wings of silver swept back from his temples. His mouth was thin and autocratic, his nose hawklike and arrogant. For a man of his years, he really was quite handsome. Indeed, she found herself speculating, no doubt Gabriel would resemble him as he aged . . .

Cassie could not help it. More and more often she was given to wonder afresh what had happened to alienate father and son. When they were together, the tension between them was thinly disguised. And Cassie could not help but note that while Edmund often mentioned Stuart, it was not so with Gabriel. Indeed, were it not for the strong resemblance between the two, Cassie might have been convinced that Gabriel was not Edmund's son at all . . .

Cassie returned home from her lessons one afternoon to find Giles opening the door to Lady Evelyn.

"Evelyn!" she cried. "Oh, you cannot know how good it is to see you again!"

Evelyn squeezed her fingers in return. "I convinced Papa it was time to return to London," Evelyn laughed. "Dear Papa! He never could refuse me anything, you know."

Cassie was thrilled, though deep in her heart, she found the duke of Warrenton almost as intimidating as Edmund Sinclair. There was no question that Reginald Latham's stern, unrelenting countenance was highly disturbing.

Were it not for Evelyn, Cassie would have refused any and every invitation that came 'round. She saw Gabriel only at dinner, whereupon he promptly bowed and informed her he would be spending the rest of the evening at his club. She was too unsure of herself to attend any evening engagements alone, though Evelyn assured her such things were not at all unusual. At Evelyn's insistence, she went to an afternoon tea with the dowager duchess of Greensboro, and attended a garden party given by Evelyn's cousin, the countess of Langston. Though Evelyn ecstatically assured her she had done splendidly,

Cassie was a bundle of nerves the rest of the night.

Finally the night of Edmund's ball arrived. Her gown was lovely, of soft emerald silk that brought out the gold of her eyes and the burnished highlights of her hair. The sleeves were tiny, gathered by shimmering silver thread. Soft, matching slippers had been laid out beside it on the bed, along with a dainty beaded reticule. Bathed and perfumed, Cassie sat before the dressing table while Gloria dressed her hair in a simple but elegant chignon swept high upon her crown.

Finally the last pin had been secured. Cassie smiled at the maid in the mirror. "Gloria, would you mind terribly fetching me a cup of chocolate? My stomach rebels at the thought of food, but a cup of hot chocolate would be wonderful."

"Not at all, mum."

Once the girl was gone, Cassie could sit still no longer. There was no point in dallying, so she decided to finish dressing. She went behind the screen and carefully stepped into the gown. She was struggling with the hooks and eyes when she heard the door open.

"Gloria," she called out. "My fingers are as much a muddle as my mind. I'm afraid I need help with these dratted fastenings."

There were several soft footfalls on the carpet. Cassie turned and presented her back, obligingly bending her head to allow the girl better access. Unfaltering fingers made quick work of the rest of the fastenings.

"Thank you," she said with a half-laugh, smoothing the folds of her skirt as she turned. "You're so much more efficient than I—"

Bold silver eyes gleamed down at her. Gabriel slanted her a lazy smile. "I will be happy to lend my services," he drawled, "now or any other time."

Cassie straightened her shoulders. "You might have knocked," she snapped.

"In my own house? I think not."

A suitable comeback failed her. Cassie could only glare her dissatisfaction, but her anger quickly waned at the distraction of his appearance. He wore a dark green velvet frock coat and brocade waistcoat. Skintight breeches showed off the beauty of his form. There was a froth of white lace at his throat and sleeves, yet never had he exuded a more intense masculinity.

Little did she realize Gabriel's thoughts followed much the same vein. While his fingers had been busily engaged, his eyes fixed hungrily on the naked expanse of her back. He'd fought an overwhelming urge to press his lips to the vulnerable sweep of her nape. Though the gown was admittedly magnificent, the wearer was by far the more stunning of the two. Her neck and shoulders were smooth and bare, devoid of any jewelry. And indeed, such loveliness needed no further adornment. Yet he could hardly have her looking like a beggar . . .

He pulled out a long slender case from his breast pocket. Aware of her gaze, he flicked the catch with his nail, offering her a glimpse of the contents. Cassie caught her breath, for inside lay a glittering diamond, vivid and bright, surrounded by a delicate, fragile chain of finest gold.

He lifted it from the case, saying, "This should go well with the gown, Yank." Cassie stood mutely, her head bowed low, while he fastened the chain about her neck. His hands on her shoulders, he guided her to the mirror.

"Well, Yank, do you approve?"

In all truth, Cassie was stunned. Never had she imagined he would lavish such a gift on her. Almost reverently she touched the pear-shaped stone. The diamond seemed to flash and gleam with a life all its own. Yet all she could think was how Gabriel's fingers were so very warm; they seemed to burn clear through her flesh.

"It's beautiful," she said softly. A tremulous smile curved her lips as she turned to him. "I don't know what to say, except . . . thank you. Thank you so very much."

"Remember I did promise you jewels, Yank." He paused. "Though I had in mind a more substantial means of repayment."

Her smile withered. "I thought this was a gift," she said unsteadily. "Is this . . . a favor to be bought then?"

"No doubt that is nothing new to you, Yank. And indeed, I might be interested in what you have to offer. What sane man would refuse a lusty tumble with a wench who looks like you?"

Cassie flinched as if he had struck her. God, but he was heartless! Shame, raw and scorching, spread all through her. So he still thought her a whore, did he? Fury rose like a tide within her.

In all her life, Cassie could not think when she'd been so fiercely angry.

Her hands were shaking, but somehow she managed to undo the necklace. Resisting the urge to fling it back at him, she grabbed his hand and dropped it in his grasp, determined to show no more emotion than he.

When she trusted herself to speak, she stated levelly, "I do not want this. I will never wear it, so you may as well return it."

"What is this? Would you have preferred emeralds instead?"

Outwardly she was calm, but inwardly she was raging. "I will not be bought," she said evenly. "And I would not lay with you for all the gold and jewels in this world. Furthermore, I wish to God I'd stayed behind at Black Jack's."

He laughed. Blast his arrogant hide, he laughed! "Oh, I know you better than that, Yank. You forget just how determined you were to flee that place."

"And had I known that you are such a detestable, loathsome creature—"

"Why, Yank," he drawled. "I do believe your speech is improving."

Cassie's nails dug into her hand. "You know nothing of me—nothing!" she said feelingly. "And I have forgotten nothing!"

His smile was unpleasant. "Oh, come now. You've made a far better bargain with me and we both know it. Or perhaps you have changed your mind. Perhaps the matter should be clarified once and for all. So tell me, Yank. Would you rather whore for all men—or just one?"

Her tenuous control snapped. Her hand shot

out, the movement prompted more by instinct than conscious thought. Before she knew what she was about, she delivered a stinging slap to his hard cheek.

It was a mistake. A hand like a vise caught her wrist and wrenched her close, so close she could feel the steely strength of his thighs against her own. Cassie's breath tumbled to a halt in her lungs. She was somehow almost terrified of all she sensed in him.

"I will allow you that once, Yank, *once*, for I admit I provoked you." His regard was as cutting as the slash of a sword. "But do not think *ever* to strike me again, for I promise you will rue the consequences."

He released her. His cheek still bore the white mark of her hand, but his features might have been etched in stone. Shaken, trying desperately not to show it, Cassie watched as he pulled out his pocket watch, the watch she had tried to steal, and glanced at the face.

"It's time to leave," he said coldly. "And since this ball is given in our honor," his tone turned mocking, "we dare not be late."

The evening was almost at an end. Though the dance floor was still filled, the guests were beginning to disperse.

How she had made it through until now, Cassie had no idea. She ate. She smiled. She chatted nonsense about the weather. For the first hour, Gabriel had kept her anchored to his side, to all appearances, the happy, loving couple.

Standing near the terrace doors, Cassie rubbed

her aching temples. She longed for the moment they would leave and she could seek her bed— and forget this night had ever happened.

"Alone at last. I've been trying to find my way through to you all evening, young lady."

She spun around to find Christopher standing before her. Only moments earlier he'd been dancing with Evelyn. His eyes wandered admiringly over her.

"You look beautiful, Cassie." He smiled gently. "But then I expect you know that."

All at once Cassie felt like weeping. Despite the horrible encounter in her room, it wouldn't have seemed so terrible . . . if only Gabriel had noticed her . . . if only he had given some indication that he saw her as something more than an unpleasant duty.

At some point tonight, her anger had fled, and in its place was a deep, despairing hurt.

Because she had wanted to please Gabriel. She had wanted so much to please him . . .

Her efforts to smile failed miserably. "A pity my husband has not noticed." It slipped out before she could stop it.

"Oh, believe me, Cassie, he has. He's always had an eye for a beauty, you know . . ."

Cassie made a faint choked sound. "Yes," she heard herself say. "He does indeed."

For the first time Christopher noted her distress. She was staring at someone across the width of the ballroom. He turned sharply, following her gaze.

Cassie could not tear her eyes from the couple across the room. A tall, dark-haired beauty stood next to Gabriel. Her figure was full, ripe and earthy. She was reminded how Evelyn had told her some women would dampen their chemise so their gowns might cling to their bodies. Still worse, some wore not a single stitch beneath their gowns. Clearly this woman chose the latter, for even from here, Cassie detected the deeply rouged outline of her nipples.

She wasn't prepared for the sheer, stark pain that gripped her heart. Their dark heads were nestled together intimately. Gabriel turned his ever so slightly, so that their lips almost brushed. He was smiling—smiling!—something he had never done with her. The woman laughed at something he said, and leaned forward, so close that Cassie had no doubt Gabriel was provided an unimpeded view clear to her waist.

What was it Gabriel had said that long-ago day in Charleston? *There are other women who are perfectly willing to satisfy my needs.* All at once Cassie had the awful sensation this was one of them.

"Christopher," she heard herself say, "who is that woman with Gabriel?"

Christopher hesitated. "Cassie—"

"Tell me," she said through lips that barely moved.

"Her name is Lady Sarah Jane Devon. She is the widow of the earl of Harcourt."

"She is his mistress, isn't she?" God, but it hurt to say the words. It hurt to think of Gabriel with another woman. And why it was so, she did not know . . .

"She was," Christopher allowed at last. "Though since his marriage to you, I've heard no rumors of their continued association."

Was he lying? Somehow Cassie found the courage to look at him. What she saw reflected in his face nearly frayed what little was left of her composure.

"Christopher," she whispered, "I'm beginning to think . . . what if I've made a terrible mistake by marrying him? He hates his father, and sometimes it's as if he sees us both as enemies . . ." To her horror, her voice began to wobble.

He took her hand in his. "Don't fret, lass," he murmured. "Gabriel is stubborn. And where his father is concerned . . . well, I suspect there's much that none of us even know about." He squeezed her fingers. "You can't give up. Not yet."

"Why should you care what I feel?" If she sounded bitter, she could not help it.

He chided her gently. "Oh, but I do, Cassie. Do you think because I am Gabriel's friend I cannot be yours?" Oh, but he suspected Gabriel did not know what a prize he possessed. Indeed, Christopher was suddenly very much convinced that the very thing Gabriel did not want . . . was the very thing he needed.

"Come now. Smile. A waltz is playing. And you would make me a happy man indeed if you would dance with me." He swung her lightly into his arms.

He was charming and winsome, and soon coaxed a reluctant smile from her. As they whirled across the polished floor, Cassie might even have been able to relax and enjoy herself had she not chanced to catch Gabriel's eye.

His mistress no longer clung to his arm. He stared directly at her, so long her cheeks grew warm and her heart began to race. And then he was lost from sight as another couple whirled in front of them, blocking her view across the room.

"If you don't mind, Christopher, I've yet to dance with my wife," Gabriel said sharply, appearing suddenly at their side. There was no give in his voice—he did not ask, he demanded.

"By all means, then."

With that her husband claimed her. Cassie took one glance at his shuttered features and confined her attention elsewhere.

But his nearness was overpowering. His arm was hard about her waist. Dancing with Christopher had been a pleasure. But dancing with Gabriel was an ordeal, for he was tense—so very tense. Was he still angry? Oh, foolish question, that! She need only look at him to find her answer.

"You are quite an accomplished dancer, Yank. Who is responsible? Christopher?"

That brought her head up in a flash. "And what if he is?" she snapped.

"Then I wonder what else he has taught you. Or perhaps it is the other way around . . . no doubt a woman with your background must have many tricks to please a man."

Oh, but he was cruel! "Christopher is a friend," she said, her voice very low. "No more. This I swear."

"A sworn oath from a thief!" His laugh held no mirth. "My lady, I humbly beg your pardon."

With an effort Cassie restrained her temper. "If you do not choose to believe me, so be it. But I know the truth, and to me that is all that matters."

Gabriel's mouth thinned. Oh, but she was so regal—so dignified! In some far distant corner of his mind, he marveled, for whoever would have thought it possible . . . She was trembling, he realized. He drew her close. Subtle though it was, he felt her stiffen. Damn her! he thought savagely. She was always resisting! He pulled her closer still.

Her tone was very low. "Gabriel, please. This is not proper."

"I care not, Yank."

"Please. People are watching."

"So let them watch." His fingers dug into her waist. "You are my wife, Yank."

Oh, yes, she thought bitterly. *Unwanted. Unloved.*

At last it was over. Gabriel released her. "I've ordered the carriage brought round. Wait for me in the entrance hall."

There was no need to tell her a second time. Cassie fled.

Gabriel did not have to look far to find his quarry. Christopher stood just outside the terrace doors.

"My wife seems to have found quite the champion in you, Christopher."

Christopher's eyes flickered. "Indeed," he said coolly.

"I will tell you what I told Cassie—that I will not be cuckolded, by you or any other man."

Christopher did not back down in the slightest. "And you insult her by implying she is less than what she is. I will tell you this only once, Gabriel, and if you value our friendship you will listen. Cassie has no claim over my affections other than friendship and concern. I was but trying to give her the comfort *you* should be giving her. Have you ever considered how she must feel? Alone in a strange land? A father-in-law who despises her? A husband who has used her as a pawn? I think not, for when you should have been with her at Farleigh, you were busy gadding about here in London."

An unpleasant smile rimmed Gabriel's mind. "For an unmarried man," he observed, "you presume to know much about the state of marriage."

"I know that were I married, I would give my wife the attention her status deserves. As for Cassie, she was most distressed at seeing you with your mistress."

"That was hardly my fault. My father no doubt invited her without knowing of our former relationship. And you know as well as I that Sarah Jane is a leech."

Christopher's regard sharpened. He did not miss his friend's irascibility. "I begin to understand your testiness," he said slowly. A grin crept along his mouth. He slapped Gabriel on the back, his spirits all at once much improved. "Go home, my friend. Give your wife the care she deserves—the attention she deserves. I predict you'll not regret it."

But Gabriel did not share his good humor. Back at his townhouse, Cassie immediately fled up the stairs. Gabriel retired to his study, his thoughts as black as his mood.

A generous portion of brandy in hand, he slumped in a velvet wing chair. His cravat was unwound and dropped to the floor; his jacket was flung aside as well. His mouth thinned as he thought of the hours just past—and his bride in particular. Oh, but she played the role of loving wife to perfection. When she was at his side, she was artlessly sweet, smiling and docile.

His mind turned to Lady Sarah. Sarah had satisfied his every need until this last voyage. He had gone to her one night, bent on relieving his masculine urges. Only her seductive wiles had left him cold. She had been so eager to please, while his wife was anything *but* eager. But now Lady Sarah seemed brazen and tawdry and almost cloying compared to his simple but elegant bride— Lord, whoever would have thought it?

He downed the fiery liquid in a single gulp. Was that what was behind this damnable attraction to Cassie? Simply that she was one of the few women who truly resisted his advances ... His thoughts turned mocking. She not only resisted him—she was downright repelled!

A dark shadow seemed to sweep over him. Though he willed it not, she plagued him night and day. She was forever on his mind—and only on his mind. Anger slammed through him as he recalled how the insolent chit had dared to scorn his diamonds—how she scorned *him*! Though her manner was shy and demure, she was a temptress, enchanting and inviting, smiling at every young buck who looked her way—and there were certainly enough of those!

His mood grew ever more vile as he thought of her laughing with Christopher. Dancing with him. He was not prepared for the way he'd felt on seeing her in the arms of another man, even his friend—*especially* his friend.

And he was tired of others feasting their eyes on what was his.

By God, she *was* his. She shared his home. His name. But she did not share his bed . . .

He slammed his glass down. The chair scraped across the carpet. Prodded by drink, driven by desire, he took the stairs two at a time. He did not knock to gain entry to her bedchamber; he merely flung the door wide.

Clad in a white lawn nightgown, she was standing near the bed, preparing to blow out the lamp. Her head came around and she spied him.

"What is it?" Her tone was breathless. "Was there something you wanted?"

You, he nearly said, but didn't. He smiled thinly. "The night has not yet ended, Yank. Indeed, it only begins."

Her heart ceased to beat. A slender hand came up to her throat. "What do you mean?" she whispered.

Very deliberately he closed the door.

"I've already made you my wife," he said softly. "It's time I made you mine."

Chapter 13

He began to advance. "It occurs to me I have neglected you, Yank. It's time I fulfilled the requirements of a husband."

She blanched, her eyes wild and panicked. Her insides twisted in sickening dread.

Her lips parted. She could barely find the breath to form his name. "Gabriel . . ."

Her heart beat in a wild frenzy. She could not move. She could scarcely even breathe. The room seemed to seethe with the power of his presence. His shirt was open halfway to his waist, revealing a strong, hair-roughened wall of muscle.

"You play the role of lady far better than I dreamed possible, Yank. Will you play the role of wife and lover as well, I wonder?"

Their eyes collided, hers nervous and uncertain, his hard and relentlessly piercing. The message she glimpsed in his brought a surge of blood to her cheeks.

She had to force her lips to move. "You cannot be serious," she said faintly.

"Oh, but I am. If you play the role of wife to all the *ton,* you will also play it here—in private."

Cassie felt as if she were strangling. "But we had a bargain!"

"I've changed my mind, Yank."

"And I have not!"

She stared into eyes that held no gentleness, eyes as cold as the northern seas.

"Come now. You're well schooled in the drawing room. Shall we see how well skilled in the bedroom you are?"

"No!" she cried. "I-I'd not lay with you if you were the last man on earth!"

Her eyes were huge and stricken, glistening with tears. Gabriel was both furious and confused. What game was this that she played? Had he not known better, he'd have thought she was frightened. But he shunned the mantle of innocence which clung to her, for she was anything but innocent.

"You would not lay with me if I were the last man in the world, eh? Well, for you, Yank, I am the *only* man."

He stopped, a mere two paces distant. "Come here."

Cassie did not move. She had known his kiss . . . but not the touch of his hand. Only now that was about to change . . .

His tone took on a note of icy menace. "Yank, you are not dull-witted."

Cassie's eyes darted to the door. Silently she gauged the distance. If she hurried . . .

"It will do you no good to run, Yank."

For all the fierceness of his expression, his voice was almost whimsically soft. Cassie drew a deep, uneven breath, trying to banish her rising panic. Then all at once he was there before her, so close she could feel the burning heat of his body, the rush of his breath on her cheek.

Cassie drew a sharp breath, wanting desperately to retreat yet not certain she dared. She stiffened as a blunted fingertip came out, tracing a flaming line over her jaw, down the arch of her throat, across her shoulder.

Cassie froze, aware that something had changed . . . His touch was disturbingly warm, yet light as a feather, almost absurdly gentle, as if he meant to soothe and seduce . . .

"Why do you fight this, Yank? Why do you fight *me*?"

Cassie said nothing. Indeed, she could barely think. The pad of his thumb swept across her collarbone, back and forth. Fiery shivers played over her skin. Never had Cassie been so quiveringly aware of Gabriel as a man . . . and herself as a woman.

His fingers slid down her throat. Then his hands were on her bare shoulders, drawing her close. "I've not forgotten how it was between us that first night in Charleston. You played the unwilling maid then, too. But you did not fool me, Yank. You felt something—"

She shook her head wildly. "I felt nothing! I was there only because Black Jack demanded it!"

For the space of a heartbeat, anger leaped in his eyes. But it was gone in an instant, replaced by a dark, sultry promise that was somehow all the more frightening.

He smiled slowly. "Black Jack was not there in that room with us, Yank. And though I have tried, I've not forgotten what passed between us." Even as he spoke, his hands laid claim to her waist. His head began to lower.

Cassie opened her mouth to deny it—to deny him. "Why are you doing this?" The words were torn from deep inside. "It's hardly ardor that prompts you to—to take me. I am merely a possession to you, a pawn! You—you said the day we made our bargain that you did not want me!"

His hand twisted in her hair, bringing her face up to his. "You underestimate yourself," he muttered just before his mouth closed over hers.

But his kiss was not the brutal assault she expected. Oh, at first she kept her lips clamped tightly shut. But he was endlessly patient . . . endlessly seductive.

"That's the way, sweet . . . open your mouth, love, just a little more . . ."

Their breath mingled deep in the back of her throat. Cassie was helpless against his masculine persuasion. A dark, sweet thrill ran through her. She could feel all of him against her—the indomitable breadth of his chest, the burning brand of his thighs against her own, the swelling potency of all that lay between.

She gasped as his tongue traced the pouting fullness of her lips, and then that daring invader trespassed deep within to breach the honeyed sweetness and claim it for his own . . .

As he would soon claim her.

With but a touch her flimsy nightgown was whisked down her shoulders, pooling around her ankles. Instinct alone compelled her to protect her modesty at all costs. Her arms came up to shield herself but he did not allow it. With a husky laugh he clamped her arms tight to her sides.

"Don't do this." She despised the pleading in her voice yet there was no help for it.

"Why?" His voice was muffled against the arch of her throat. "God knows I am paying dearly enough for the privilege."

And Gabriel could no more have stayed his desire than he could have stilled the beat of his heart. She was as glorious as he remembered. Her hair fell in rich, deep ripples over her shoulders and down her back, an invitation no sane man could resist. Her breasts, small but perfectly formed and tipped with rose-hued nipples, peeped insolently between silken strands of gold. The golden thicket at the juncture of her thighs paved the way to the treasure beneath.

His blood was pounding almost violently. His manhood, already hard and near to bursting beneath the restraining confines of his breeches, swelled still further.

He freed her, but only for an instant. His hands closed possessively over both breasts. With his thumbs he traced tiny circles around and around her nipples, leaving them tight and aching. He brushed his thumbs across the tips; alive to an aching sensitivity for the very first time, a jolt of sheer pleasure shot through her.

She moaned into his mouth. The sound only inflamed him further. Without releasing the delicious fusion of their lips, he swept her into his arms and laid her on the bed.

Still dazed by the riotous sensations pouring through her, Cassie opened her eyes just as his boots hit the floor. She could not tear her gaze from him as he ripped off his shirt. Flickering lamplight played across the contours of his shoulders, the knotted muscles of his arms. Her throat grew dry and parched. In awe she stared at his chest and abdomen, densely matted with hair. Her gaze strayed helplessly lower, just as he stripped off his breeches.

She had seen him naked before . . . naked . . .

But never aroused.

Her eyes widened. She was unable to stifle a gasp, for never had she imagined the proof of a man's desire would be so brazenly blatant and bold. To Cassie's untutored eyes, his staff was huge, swollen and irrefutably erect. And suddenly she understood so very much more . . . Sweet heaven, how could he take her? He would tear her in two!

She would have bolted then, but he was already there. Arms like twin bands of iron came around her. He dragged her close—closer still, as if he sought to fuse their bodies together . . .

As indeed he would. Oh, she knew what he intended. Etched into her mind were memories of Bess crawling into bed, quietly weeping, her body sore and bruised. He would vent his lust in her body, defeat her in that age-old way that man dominates woman.

"Stop," she cried. "Stop!"

His laughter was a terrible sound. "Cease this game, Yank, for I know you want me. Oh, you would try to hide it from me, but I see it in your eyes. I've felt you tremble beneath me, your lips soft and yielding. You want me as much as I want you."

She flung out her hands as if such feeble resistance could keep him at bay. "If I tremble, 'tis because I can hardly stand the thought of laying with the likes of you! I do not want you—do you hear? I do not want you!"

Cool gray eyes glittered down at her. With the weight of his chest he pinned her beneath him. "A pity you feel this way, sweet, for I've decided to claim my rights as a husband—and I will claim them now."

His usual cool control had vanished. She sensed within him all that she feared. Oh, but she should never have been so rash with her words, for now he meant to punish her!

Dark and dangerous, he loomed above her. His eyes were no longer cold, but heated and searing. In some distant part of her being, Cassie knew he was right. There would be no escaping this night. There was no escaping *him*.

"No!" She twisted beneath him, but there was no denying him. On some far distant plane, she knew he was not a violent man—hard and ruthless perhaps, but not unspeakably cruel. Her mind recounted that not-so-distant day at Farleigh when they had been shot at. His features had not lied—his icy remoteness had vanished. She remembered him bending over her, his expression anxious, almost frantic. And when she had nearly been swept from his ship, he had held her tight to his warmth when he might easily have left her alone. Though she might never view him as kind and considerate, she could be no less than honest. Whether he knew it or not, whether he willed it or not, he *could* be gentle . . .

But there was no softness in him now. There was only a stark, unyielding purpose that somehow frightened her.

His mouth captured hers, hot and consuming. A tremor coursed through her. She could scarcely tell when one kiss ended and the next began. There was nowhere their bodies did not touch. She could feel the iron-taut shaft of his manhood rigid and thick against her belly.

His hands were on her breasts again. She gasped as his fingers again circled her nipples, as if to taunt and tease. She clutched at the hardness of his shoulders. An odd, melting sensation fanned low in her belly. Then, even as she watched, his mouth fastened on that turgid, aching peak. His tongue curled slowly around her nipple. In shock she felt his mouth close fully around it. Tugging, suckling, the contact blatantly erotic . . . She tossed her head, whimpering. Tiny needles of sensation were centered there, on the throbbing point of her breast. But just as she abandoned herself to a swirling pleasure, his hand strayed still further.

With no hesitation his fingers slid boldly through her golden fleece. He touched her there between her thighs. Deliberately. Boldly. Neither realized he moved far too fast for a woman of her inexperience.

Cassie stiffened, instinctively closing her thighs against his shamefully invading encroachment, shocked to the core. Surely it was wrong— surely it was wicked. Surely no gentleman would touch a lady so! And then she remembered . . .

He thought her a harlot.

He thought her no better than her mother. That bitter truth tore through her—the one thing that Cassie could not endure.

She tore her mouth free. "No," she cried. "Damn you, stop—stop!" She shoved at his shoulders, this time no pitiable effort, but with all her strength.

He was as immovable as stone. His head came up. His eyes were pure frost, his mouth a grim slash. "Why do you fight me?" he said furiously. "Why do you deny me, your husband, what you've given so freely to others?"

She had no chance to answer. His mouth came down on hers, fiercely devouring. Her fingers were caught and laced within his, borne down to the mattress alongside her head. With his knees he pried her thighs apart.

With one burning, stretching stroke of fire he claimed her, clear to the depths of her womb.

How tight she was . . . impossibly tight. Even as the thought ripped through his mind, a strangled cry of pain broke from her throat.

Confronted with the truth, Gabriel froze. Though reason compelled retreat, his body ruled otherwise. He could not battle the blind, driving passion which seized him, the fire that had not abated since the day he'd set eyes on her. The red-hot desire in his body clamored for release. With a groan of defeat, he began to move, slowly at first, then faster, until he was lunging mindlessly again and again. He shuddered, his scalding seed erupting deep inside her.

Gabriel was the first to recover. He rolled from her, reaching for his breeches.

"How can this be?" he demanded. "Black Jack offered you to me that first night—how can it be that you were a virgin?"

Her eyes opened slowly, wounded and bruised, as if he'd run her to ground . . . and perhaps he had. His mouth twisted. The taste of self-disgust was like dust in his mouth.

He saw her reach for the sheet that lay tangled about her ankles. He saw the way she trembled; with one swift movement, he wrenched it over her nakedness. He damned himself for his weakness— and damned her for hers.

Cassie would not look at him. "Black Jack did not make us lie with the customers if we did not wish to. Nor was there any need for me to . . ." She faltered. "Nell was only too willing," she went on, her voice barely audible. "My friend Bess did it for the money it would bring. But she died birthing her babe only a few days before you arrived. I— I did not want to end up like her."

"So why didn't you tell me the truth—that you were a virgin? All this time you let me believe you were well experienced when it came to the ways of men!"

At last Cassie braved a glance at him. She was blind to all but the tense line of his jaw. She sat up slowly, clutching the sheet to her naked breasts. "I *let* you?" Her eyes darkened. "You've made no secret what you thought of me, milord. You called me thief. You thought me a . . . a whore." God, but it hurt to say the word aloud! "Had I told you the truth you would never have believed me." Her tone was as scathing as her eyes. "You believed what you wanted to believe."

She was right, Gabriel conceded silently. And now that he had discovered it for himself, it was too late.

"Nonetheless," he said tightly, "this might never have happened if you had been honest with me from the outset—"

All at once Cassie's eyes were blazing. "To what purpose? Would that have stopped you? Would you have *cared*?" She lashed out at him bitterly. "I think not, for I've learned that you are a man who will have his way and mine matters little. I hate you, do you hear? I hate you!" At last her voice broke. "So just leave me be . . . leave me be!"

Gabriel's dark features froze. "You are right, Yank." When at last he spoke, his voice was as frigidly empty as his expression. "This should never have happened. Rest assured, it will not happen again."

Chapter 14

The day dawned dark and ominous. Cassie stirred, her subconscious rebelling against wakefulness yet jarred to such by the very events she longed to forget. Oh, but the hand of fate was cruel! Her eyes snapped open, only to confront the damnable reminder of all that transpired here in this very bed.

On the floor in front of the chair lay her nightgown, wadded in a heap.

Quickly she moved to retrieve it. Even as she dropped the gown over her head, her entire body grew hot. She remembered how Gabriel had swept it from her. She tried to close her mind to what came next, but it was no use. He had seen all of her—sweet Lord, he had *touched* all of her. Most of all she recalled the way his burning shaft stretched her virgin flesh wide . . . the way he had plunged himself deep—ever deeper—to the core of her being.

Within her, a tempest of emotion blustered and raged. She was obsessed with the events of the previous night and couldn't shake the memory from her mind. She stared up at the pale blue satin bed hangings; her throat tightened oddly. In the cold light of day, she regretted the words she had flung so rashly. Despite all, she did not hate Gabriel. She had begun to hate his wretched plan to hurt his father, but she did not hate *him*.

Inexperienced though she was, Cassie knew instinctively that it wouldn't have been so—so awful . . . if only he had stayed with her . . . and held her, tight against his warmth. If only he had shown her a tender regard, comforted her with his strength . . .

Tears scalded her eyelids. Instead he had left her alone . . . alone as always.

There was a tap on the door. Gloria entered, bearing a tray of pastries and a silver pot of chocolate. Cassie brushed away the foolish, bitter tears and reached for her robe. Gloria glanced at her anxiously when she left her roll untouched. The brew she had come to savor did little to sway her from her melancholy mood. The hot bath she emerged from an hour later scarcely soothed the ache from her weary limbs . . .

But nothing eased the ache in her heart.

She was vastly relieved when she arrived downstairs and Giles informed her Gabriel had left already for his shipping offices and most likely would not return until late that afternoon. Though she did not know what the duke's reaction might be, she arrived at his residence earlier than usual for her lesson. Though he had yet to admit such, Cassie sensed he was pleased with the progress she was making in her lessons. She had quickly mastered the alphabet and already had begun to string small words together in sentences.

Not so today. Cassie found herself scarcely able

to concentrate. Her mind was all atumble with images and feelings, doubts and fears. Would Gabriel return to her bed again? She had no faith in his promises—she had learned that painful truth last night. She shuddered, besieged by the memory of his hard, thrusting body, the rending pain. She had no wish to repeat such a vile act, but what choice did she have? Refusal would accomplish little, she acknowledged bitterly. All at once she remembered the tales Nell had so delighted in telling her—if Nell was to be believed, a man might take a woman more than once a night. To Cassie's horrified mind, such a possibility was not to be endured.

Her frame of mind was as unsettled as the weather outside. One minute she felt like crying; the next she was snapping at the duke when he pointed out a minor error in her lettering. He closed the heavy volume before him and pushed back his chair. "I see little point in continuing our lessons today," he said with a glower. "Your attentions are clearly elsewhere. Come back tomorrow. By then I would hope you will be more inclined to reap the benefits of our efforts."

Feeling small and ashamed of her pettiness, Cassie made no reply. She gathered up her things and bid him farewell. In the carriage she rested her forehead against the velvet-lined wall, feeling utterly defeated. Lord, would this day never end? She longed for the moment she could crawl into bed, close her eyes, and blot out the rest of the world.

All at once the carriage swerved and jolted to a halt, sending her sprawling to the floor. Mystified, she scrambled up and opened the window to see what was amiss.

"Thomas," she called. "What is wrong? Why have we stopped?"

Thomas had just leaped down from his perch atop the coach. A man surged around the front of the coach, dressed in shabby black clothing, his face thin and pockmarked. Before either she or Thomas could say a word, the man brought up his arm. Cassie glimpsed the dull glint of metal—sweet heaven, a pistol! Even as the realization rampaged through her mind, the man brought up the butt of the weapon and dealt Thomas a stunning blow to the temple. The coachman crumpled to the cobbled street without a sound.

With a cry Cassie fumbled for the door latch. But she had no chance to wrench it shut, for the man was there, a malevolent smile on his lips.

"Well, what have we here?"

Her heart skipped a beat. Her tongue felt as if it were glued to the roof of her mouth. She'd seen his kind before, many a time in Charleston. The man was a footpad, a thief, perhaps even a murderer, for there were those who had no mercy, no scruples whatsoever.

"Please, sir." Her voice betrayed her. "I have no money, no jewels." Oh, but that wasn't quite right. She was reminded of the plain gold band encircling her middle finger. Though her marriage was but a mockery, she hid her hand in her skirts, for the very idea of handing over her wedding ring did not even bear thinking about.

He grinned, displaying a blackened gap between his front teeth. "Oh, don't you worry, missy, I'll be

taking what I please." His gaze roved down and
back up. "Ah, but you're a tasty little piece, ain't
you now? Well, we're goin' to have a bit of fun,
you and I,'fore we get down to business."

Cassie shrank back, even before he thrust the
door closed, shutting her securely inside. The next
moment she heard the lash of a whip. The horses
bolted. The ensuing motion flung her back with
such force she cracked her head.

She scarcely noticed the pain. Icy terror clogged
her veins. Dear God, was the man mad? What did
he hope to accomplish by carrying her off like this?
He would soon discover she spoke the truth—that
she had nothing of value in her possession save the
clothes on her back and her wedding ring! What
then?

The answer sent fear winging through her anew.

Faster and faster, they rumbled through the
streets, the coach gathering speed with every
second. Outside there were shouts and curses
and screams. All too soon they broke free of
the city and onto an open roadway. The coach
careened around a curve and it was then Cassie
made a split-second decision. She could not stay
and meekly accept what awaited her in this robber's
hands. With luck, the robber would not notice until
it was too late . . .

She flung open the door and leaped out.

She landed hard upon the shoulder of the road.
A painful cry escaped her, for the impact jolted her
entire body. Tiny stones jabbed her palms like a
thousand daggers. Precious seconds passed while
she labored for breath, struggling upright. She ran
blindly into a small copse of trees.

But providence had forsaken her. Behind her there was a curse; she heard the carriage stop and tried to quicken her pace. But both her skirts and the damp, uneven ground hampered her efforts. Branches slapped across her cheeks. She stumbled and fell, bruising her knees and scraping her hands again. Thrashing footsteps sounded just behind her. She bit back a sob of despair and lurched upright.

The robber lunged at her. His fingers latched onto her sleeve; there was a rending tear. Yet still there was no escape, for he grabbed her by the other arm, wrenching her around with such force that she cried out in pain.

Filthy hands dug into her arms. "You bitch!" he spat. "Think you can get away, eh?"

He swung her around and began to drag her back toward the carriage. Though she pummeled and kicked and struggled, there was no escaping his vicious hold. Desperate and despairing, Cassie opened her mouth and gave a bloodcurdling scream, though she knew it was useless.

The robber jerked her around. He struck her hard across the cheek. Cassie fell to her knees. She could taste blood in her mouth.

Twisted lips drew back over his rotted teeth. Evil radiated from him, as foul and fetid as his scent. "I was going to save it for after I'd had some fun with ye," he hissed. "But I might as well kill ye now and be done with it." He raised a huge fist high. Cassie closed her eyes and waited for the blow.

All at once came the sound of running footsteps. "Hold there!" came the authoritative command.

"Release the girl, do you hear? Release her at once!"

Cassie sagged with relief. It was the most heavenly sound she'd ever heard.

It was early evening when Gabriel came through the front door of his townhouse. Inside the entrance hall he paused, looking for a long moment up the stairway. His features were carefully guarded, betraying no hint of the turmoil beneath his calm exterior.

He did not relish the prospect of facing his wife again . . . and little wonder.

Throughout the day, his conscience had given him no respite. There was simply no evading the immensity of his actions or his blind foolishness. He could not forget the way she had looked last night—the way he had left her! He kept seeing her, her bewildered shock in that split second when he'd thrust deep inside her. God, but she'd been so small, so tight around his swollen flesh. And over and over her stricken cry of pain tolled through his mind . . .

Self-contempt roiled in his belly. Despite everything, he should have known she was innocent. A better man would have, he acknowledged bitterly. For indeed, all the signs had been there . . . her sweet shyness whenever he'd kissed her, her tremulous response . . . her wide-eyed shock at seeing him naked.

And to think he had boasted what a great lover he was! Oh, but that was rich! He had neither relished nor revered her. He had all but ripped her clothes off. He had shown her no melting caresses, no lingering tenderness. He had taken her coldly. Callously.

He had taken her like a whore. And she was his wife—regardless of how or why, she was his *wife* . . .

Gabriel was not a man accustomed to losing control. He cursed himself fiercely for allowing his angry desire to sway his good judgment. It was just as he'd said—it should never have happened . . .

He swore beneath his breath. But none of this was turning out as he'd planned, and he hadn't fully realized it until last night. He had taken Cassie to his bed once . . . *once*.

It could not happen again. It *would* not.

"Good evening, milord."

Gabriel glanced up to find Giles before him. "Good evening, Giles. Is my wife in her bedchamber?"

"No, milord. She has not yet returned."

The tight knot in his stomach began to ease. For a time, he'd thought he might have broken her spirit—thank God he had not.

"I see. Is she out with Lady Evelyn?"

"I do not know, sir. 'Tis not her ladyship's habit to inform us of her whereabouts on her afternoon jaunt."

Gabriel's eyes narrowed. "Her afternoon jaunt? Is this a daily occurrence then?"

A thin sheen of perspiration appeared on the man's lip. "Yes, milord."

"And you mean to tell me she's been disappearing every afternoon and no one knows where she goes?"

Giles cleared his throat. "Well, sir, I would assume Thomas—the coachman—is aware of her whereabouts. But certainly I have made no inquiries, for 'twas my feeling that if her ladyship deemed it my concern, she would have informed me—"

"Yes, Giles, I am quite aware of what you are trying to say!" Gabriel was suddenly furious. The chit charmed all she encountered! Was he the only one immune to her wiles?

"Milord," Giles coughed slightly, "if I may be so bold, I am beginning to be quite worried about her. She has always been quite punctual in her return—until today, that is."

Gabriel's mouth was a grim slash in his face. "What time did she leave?"

"She left shortly before one o'clock, milord, as she has these past few weeks."

"And you're certain she made no mention of her plans?"

"No, milord, only that she would return as usual before the dinner hour." Giles's tone was a trifle stiff.

Gabriel's eyes narrowed. It would be just like a woman to spend her afternoons shopping, yet he suspected that was not the case. She'd not made mention of any purchases, nor had he received any bills . . . so where on earth had she been?

Perhaps the better question was . . . with *whom* had she been?

But there was no time for further speculation, for at that precise instant the bell at the front door rang. Giles moved to open it to find a burly police sergeant on the doorstep.

A small, slight figure stood next to him.

A muffled imprecation broke from Gabriel's lips. "Good God—Cassie!"

Something was very, very wrong. Her gown was mud-spattered and torn. She clutched the tattered edges together where the seam had been ripped at the neckline. Her face was chalk white and tear-streaked. Her hair was falling down around her shoulders.

She took a single step forward. But she was so shaky, her knees almost buckled under her weight. Impulsively, he slid an arm reassuringly about her waist and brought her close.

Her body turned into his. One small hand clutched the lapels of his jacket. She sagged against his length and buried her face against the side of his neck. He both felt and heard the deep, racking breath she took.

He tightened his hold ever so slightly. "Are you all right?"

Her hair tickled his chin as she nodded.

The policeman cleared his throat. "I'm afraid there's been an unfortunate incident, milord. Your wife was returning home when your coachman was accosted by a footpad. The man was struck down—and your wife abducted."

"Abducted!" Gabriel was stunned. He glanced down at her. Where the devil had she been? he wondered furiously. And with *whom* had she been spending her afternoons? He decided to save his questions for later.

His gaze slid to the butler. "Giles, would you please escort milady to her chamber? And please see that a hot bath is prepared."

"Very good, milord." The butler stepped forward and offered his elbow, his eyes unusually soft. "Milady?"

Once they were out of earshot, Gabriel turned to the sergeant, his features cast in stone. "Now then, Sergeant. You say my wife was abducted?"

"Yes, milord. After the driver was struck down, the scoundrel leaped on the box and left straightaway with your wife inside, and God help anyone in his path—oh, but these thieves are a treacherous lot! 'Twas sheer luck that I happened to see the rogue and took off after him. Your wife managed to leap out of the coach but the rascal saw her and stopped. That was when I caught up with them."

"She came to no harm at his hands?"

"No, milord, she assured me she did not, though he frightened her half out of her wits, poor lady." The man's chest swelled with self-importance. "I doubt that would have been the case had my arrival not been so fortuitous. I've no doubt 'twas thievery he had in mind—that and who knows what else."

"And I am thankful for your intervention, Sergeant." Gabriel paused. "I trust that you were able to apprehend the rogue?"

A little of the starch went out of the sergeant's posture. "Unfortunately, milord, while I assisted your wife, he escaped." He shook his head. "By now I'm afraid there's little chance of ever catching up to him."

"I see." Gabriel paused. "Sergeant," he said slowly, "is there any sign the abduction might have been planned?"

The man looked startled. "Planned? You mean that your wife was *meant* to be taken?"

"Exactly."

The sergeant scratched his chin, considering. "Oh, I doubt it, milord," he said heartily. "Your man Thomas should be along shortly—he was not injured seriously—but he gave no indication it might be so. As I'm sure you are aware, milord, the gentry—and in particular, the ladies—are a prime target for such riff-raff."

Gabriel nodded and led him to the door. "I thank you again, Sergeant. And it would be greatly appreciated if you would notify me should this brigand be caught."

The sergeant tipped his hat. "You have my word on it, milord."

Once he was gone Gabriel headed straight for Cassie's bedchamber. He stopped at the threshold, his shoulders filling the doorway. Gloria had just poured the last bucketful of hot water into the hip bath. Slow curls of steam drifted toward the ceiling.

Cassie stood near the window. Gabriel had the uneasy sensation she had neither moved nor spoken since entering the room. Her head was bowed low. One hand still clutched the tattered edges of her gown together over her shoulder.

"Cassie."

Both she and the maid turned. Gloria dropped a curtsy but Cassie still said nothing.

He crossed to her. "You must be hungry," he said quietly. "Would you like a tray in your room?"

She averted her gaze. "No," she whispered. "I— I'm not hungry."

Gloria spoke up then. "If you please, sir, p'rhaps

milady would like a bit of hot chocolate. She's very fond of it, y'know. She has it every morning."

It was Gabriel who answered, though his eyes did not waver from Cassie's profile. "Thank you, Gloria. Would you see to it, please?"

The little maid bobbed. "Most certainly, sir." Gabriel stopped her before she left, whispering something in her ear.

He returned to Cassie, laying his fingers atop hers where they rested on the slope of her shoulder. Hers were ice-cold.

"Your bath is ready, Cassie."

That brought her eyes skipping back to his in a flash. Gabriel smiled almost in spite of himself. "I did promise we would one day bathe together, did I not?"

Her wide-eyed dismay did not go unnoticed. His smile withered. His gaze dropped to her lips—they were soft and slightly parted. The urge to part them beneath the demanding pressure of his took hold, but he swiftly quelled the impulse.

"You have nothing to fear," he said very quietly. "I am not such a cad as you think."

He gave her no time to reject him but set to work on the hooks at the back of her gown. She offered no resistance but a faint pink flush crept beneath her skin. That she gave herself over to him was a sign of just how shaken she really was—such unconditional surrender was the last thing Gabriel had expected. His mood turned grim by the time he'd finished, however. The ivory smoothness of her skin was marred by dozens of scratches and bruises.

Cassie flushed as he helped her into the tub,

acutely aware that there was no evading the critical regard that saw so much of her and revealed so
little of himself. She sank below the waterline as
far as she could, desperate to hide her nakedness.

She started nervously when she felt his touch.
The back of his knuckles brushed her cheek, then
firm fingers grasped her jaw and turned her face
to the lamplight glowing from the corner.

His thumb brushed the puffy skin on the right
side of her lip. "Did he do this, too?"

Her lashes fell in answer. She drew her knees up
to her breasts and said nothing, for indeed there
was no need to.

Gabriel didn't understand the blind, irrational
anger that swept through him. He told himself it
was only because she'd been taken advantage of
by one who was stronger than she—not because
he cared . . . never that. But a muscle in his cheek
betrayed the depth of his fury. Never had he known
a rage as encompassing as that which possessed
him now.

"Would you recognize him if you saw him
again?"

Cassie shuddered. The heat of the water had
seeped through to her muscles, warm and soothing. But all at once it was as if she'd been plunged
into a sea of ice.

"Yes . . . no." She faltered, suddenly feeling wholly inadequate. "I . . . I just don't know."

Gabriel made no reply. He handed her a sponge
and turned his back, allowing her the privacy he
knew she craved. Cassie washed hurriedly, beset
by the notion he would turn back around at any
second. An inner voice chided her, for what did it

matter anyway? He had seen what no other man had ever seen. And he had *touched* her in ways she had never dreamed a man might touch a woman . . . The hand holding the sponge stilled, directly above her heart. Her throat tightened oddly.

A part of her wished desperately that he would leave. Another part of her longed just as fervently for him to stay, for she did not want to be alone. Yet his nearness was an unsettling reminder of all that had passed between them only the night before—Lord, but it seemed a lifetime had gone by since then!

Gabriel's nerves were keenly attuned to her every move. Eventually the splash of the water ceased. He glanced over his shoulder to find her eyes fixed upon him, wide and faintly distressed.

He beat down the heated rush that ignited in his veins, pooling hot and heavy in his loins. Her shoulders were bare and glistening. Never before had he been so sharply aware of one woman— and his own hungry, masculine desires to possess her. Yet the very nakedness that so sorely tested his willpower was the very thing that saved her, for her vulnerability pierced him as nothing else could have.

He raised his brow with an elegant sweep. "Finished?" he murmured.

She nodded. Bracing her slender arms against the side of the tub, she rose, turning immediately into the length of toweling that awaited her in his hands.

The downy softness engulfed her first, and then his arms, as he lifted her from the tub. Cassie stood docilely as he proceeded to dry her. His touch was light and impersonal, and he was carefully considerate of the bruised, tender areas that marked her flesh. But her fiery blush proclaimed the depth of her embarrassment by the time he pulled a soft white nightgown over her head and twitched it into place.

There was a knock at the door. Gabriel answered it, taking a small tray from Gloria into his hands. Cassie hugged herself, feeling naked and exposed despite the fact she was now covered from head to foot. Gabriel inclined his head toward the chair before the fireplace, indicating she should sit. Once she was seated, he held out a delicate china cup and saucer. The sweet, enticing odor of chocolate teased her nostrils.

Cassie sipped the hot, sweet liquid, grateful for the opportunity to busy her hands. She was not aware of the piercing gray eyes that watched as she drank every last drop of the brew. Not until she had finished did she chance to look up and find his intense gaze upon her.

He had removed his jacket and rolled up his shirtsleeves, baring strong, muscular forearms. The muscles of her stomach clenched. His elbow was propped against the mantel. His pose was casual, yet purely masculine; it appeared as if nothing— or no one—could ever hurt him.

It was he who broke the silence. "Giles told me you have been gone every afternoon the past few weeks." His eyes sheared directly into hers. "How is it you failed to mention this to me?" Despite the quiet of his tone, his words were no less than a demand.

Cassie swallowed bravely. It was difficult not

to retreat from his frown. "I was not aware you cared to know my whereabouts at every moment of the day."

Gabriel's scrutiny sharpened. "That is hardly an answer," he said curtly. "Now if you please, I would like to know where you were today—and all those other days."

Panic flared. She could not tell him where she had been without telling him *why*, and that was the one thing she wanted to avoid at all costs. He thought little enough of her now—he would think even less of her if he were aware of the truth.

In this, at least, her dignity served her well. She stared at the rim of the cup she held in her hands, determined to reveal no more than necessary.

He swore under his breath. "Why must you be so stubborn? Dammit, Yank, I am concerned for your safety! 'Tis not safe to be wandering the streets of London alone."

Still she avoided his gaze. "You need not trouble yourself. I was not wandering the streets, as you call it. I was in no danger"—she faltered—"at least not until tonight."

"Then why will you not tell me where you were?" Two white lines of anger appeared alongside his mouth when she shook her head. Three strides brought him before her. He set aside the cup and saucer, caught her shoulders, and pulled her up before him.

"Were you meeting someone?" He knew the way she started that she had. "Christopher? Is that the reason for your reluctance? Was this a lover's tryst?"

"No!" she cried. "Christopher is my friend—no

more, and I will swear to it on the Cross if that is
what it takes to convince you!"

"Who then?"

His patience was clearly at an end. There was
a tempest alive and brewing in his eyes. Cassie
fought a scalding rush of tears, the muscles in her
throat locked tight.

"I was with . . . your father," she whispered. "I—
I have been spending the afternoons . . . at his townhouse."

Gabriel was astounded. "What! You and my
father—surely you jest!"

Wrenched with shame, she stammered, " 'Tis
because I—I cannot read . . . I cannot read!"

There was a stunned silence. "Good God. Do not
tell me that *he* has been teaching you."

"Yes . . . yes!" Was he truly so heartless as to
make her say it again? "He-he teaches me himself
so no one else will know—so no further disgrace
will befall the family."

Gabriel's frustrated anger fled, as if it had never been. He sighed wearily. "Why didn't you tell
me?"

"Why?" She gave a bitter half-sob. "Am I to be
spared no humiliation? It would have pleased you
to no end to know that I could not read—it would
have been just one more thing to flaunt to your
father . . . the poor little Yankee you dragged from
the gutter, who possesses neither money nor title
nor even the slightest scrap of knowledge!"

He scowled. "Now it's you who wounds *me*—"

"No! It's true—you would have." To her horror,
a tear beaded down her cheek. Then another, and
another. "You know it's true!" Above all, Cassie

did not want him to see her like this. So foolish. So confused. But all at once her tenuous control was gone. She buried her face in her hands and began to cry. Helplessly. Pitifully.

Her shoulders were shaking uncontrollably. Slowly, with an almost painstaking hesitance, his arms came around her. Small hands wound into the front of his shirt. He bent and folded her into his embrace, then sat in the chair, cradling her in his lap.

He could feel her trying to hold back the anguish that rent her body. It was no use. "I'm sorry," she cried on a watery sob. "It's just as you said it would be. I am a burden . . . an encumbrance. You must wish that—that horrible man had killed me. I-I thought he was going to . . . Oh, God, I-I wish I *were* dead . . ."

Gabriel went utterly still, both inside and out. "Don't say that." His whisper was numb and strained. "Don't even think it!"

He stroked her hair, the shallow groove of her spine. Gradually the laudanum began to take hold. She stirred. "Something's wrong." Drowsy and confused, she struggled to keep her lids from closing. "I feel so strange."

With his fingertips he brushed tear-damp strands of honey-gold from her cheeks. "It's all right. I asked Gloria to put several drops of laudanum in your chocolate to help you sleep. Just relax and don't fight it."

His explanation seemed to satisfy her. Her lashes, dark and spiked with tears, began to droop. Soon she quieted until she lay limply against him, asleep at last.

He lifted her, bearing her to the bed and laying her carefully on the mattress, then pulled the covers up over her. But when he would have straightened, she flung out a hand, groping blindly for his.

"Don't leave me, Gabriel. Don't leave me." Her eyes snapped open. Even as he watched, glistening tears brimmed and overflowed. "Why—why do you hate me?" she cried brokenly. "Will you always hate me?"

Gabriel felt he'd been slammed in the gut with an iron fist. Guilt burned a searing hole deep in his breast. He stood, his entire body stiff, an awful tightening squeezing his heart.

Never had he been so torn.

He stared at the small hand so desperately gripping his own. A pain ripped through him, so searing it drove the very breath from his lungs. Christ, what was she doing to him?

Christopher had fallen under her spell. So had the dowager duchess of Greensboro. Giles. Lord, even his father! What magic did she possess that she so easily wove a spell around all those with whom she came in contact?

If he were wise, he'd let her go now. Before things progressed any further. Before she was hurt . . . *Fool*, taunted a scathing voice in his mind, *she's already been hurt*.

Something bitterly dark and ominous crept over him. He despised the emotion she roused in him— for years he'd felt his heart encased in ice—and he resented her fiercely for all he felt, for all she had made him feel . . . all he did not *want* to feel.

Yet he could not turn his back on her.

He sighed, a sound borne of weary resignation.

After tugging off his boots, he stretched out beside her and drew her into his arms. He stared at the shadows dancing on the ceiling, a lean hand absently stroking the tangled length of her hair, the other measuring the slender nip of her waist.

It was she, he thought blackly, who had every reason to distrust him—every reason to hate him. How could she possibly think he hated her? That he would wish her dead? But all at once Gabriel's blood ran cold.

God knew *he* did not . . . but what if someone else did?

Chapter 15

Several days later they returned to Farleigh.
Gabriel made the decision the morning after
Cassie was accosted. For the life of him, he
couldn't rid himself of the unsettling notion that
her kidnapping had, perhaps, not been a random
incident, as the police believed. It made his blood
boil every time he thought of it. By God, but he'd
have liked to get his hands on the scoundrel—he'd
take him apart piece by piece!

But Gabriel had long since outgrown his reckless,
careless youth. He would make no accusations—
no assumptions—without just cause. Perhaps his
suspicions were unfounded—more the better. But
he offered a reward should her assailant be found,
and he hired an investigator to return to Charleston.
He did not doubt Cassie's claim that her mother
did not know the identity of her father, or that the
vile woman had abandoned her. But if there was
someone from her past who might be responsible,
Gabriel intended to find out. Perhaps there was
some connection between the shooting and her
kidnapping—perhaps there was not. But Gabriel
had decided it would be easier to keep her safe
at Farleigh rather than in London. He said nothing

to Cassie, though. He did not want her to worry herself lest his suspicions were unfounded.

While another might have deemed his behavior toward his wife fiercely possessive—and even more protective—Gabriel did not acknowledge such a thing, even to himself . . . *especially* to himself.

The days flowed into weeks. Though he struggled to maintain a cool distance from the beauty who was his wife, his feelings were far from indifferent . . . indifferent?! Gabriel was discovering she was far too tempting for his peace of mind. He had not bargained on the hungry desire she aroused in him. It was torture, having her forever at hand, so near and yet unable to touch her.

She had only to enter a room and all she stirred in him rushed to the fore. He was vastly irritated with himself, for where Cassie was concerned, he was no longer in control of his emotions. Her slightest accidental touch, the merest scent of her perfume, sent sharp needles of desire raking along his spine.

Hardest of all was sleeping with but a single wall between them. Even in his sleep his mind plunged backward. He yearned for lips as tender and dewy as moist summer berries. He could almost feel her beneath him once more, her skin sleek and soft beneath his lips and hands, her woman's flesh clasped hot and tight around his rigid hardness. Countless times he woke marble-hard and throbbing, his shaft ready to burst the bonds of his skin . . . No, indeed, Gabriel had not forgotten the shattering night they had shared.

Nor had she.

In truth, Cassie was heartily relieved when they left London. The whirlwind pace of the city still left her in awe. So many of the parties she had attended were boring, the people shallow with the exception of a handful. And though she tried to brush it aside, that horrible encounter with the footpad had left her wary of every shadow and stranger.

She loved the peace and quiet at Farleigh, the smell of the fresh, country air, the lush greenery. As often as she could, she indulged her newfound love of riding. She often rode with Evelyn, who had returned to Warrenton with her father. But when she did not, Gabriel had been most insistent that a groom accompany her.

But all was not as it had been before. Oh, there had always been a tingling current of awareness whenever she and Gabriel had chanced to lock gazes. But there was a difference now—a sizzling tension that made Cassie heartstoppingly aware that everything had changed. Her heart set up a wild hammering whenever he was near. And he was forever on her mind, though she tried her very best to put him *out* of it.

But he kept her ever off-guard, for she never knew what to expect from him. He could be charming and ever so pleasant when he wished. At other times he was so distant and aloof she wanted to cry. She found herself wondering if he would visit her bed again. The very thought made her tremble— but with excitement or fear she was not certain!

Only the night before, he had walked her to her room. At the door, she shyly bid him good night. But he did not move on to his door, as she expected. He stood there, his eyes night-dark and burning.

Her heart had skipped a beat. The heated blaze she saw—was it desire—or anger? Her confidence

in herself was tenuous at best. Did he still find
her humble beginnings distasteful? Oh, if only she
were like Evelyn—delicate and blond, sweet and
refined. For she was very much afraid that was the
kind of woman Gabriel preferred . . .

A lady. A pang swept through her. God above
knew she would never truly be a lady, not like
Evelyn. For no matter what the rest of the world
thought, Gabriel would never see her as one . . .

"Was there something else?" She could not hide
her nervousness, nor could she look away from
him. Her mind was all awhirl. He smelled of soap
and crisp starch. She fought the strangest urge to
lay her palm against his lean cheek, to feel the
slight roughness of his jaw against her fingertips.

His gaze was fastened on her lips. It shocked her
to realize just how badly she longed to feel his lips
upon hers, taking command of her senses, arousing
her with devastating persuasion. But the very idea
spawned heated images in her mind that were best
left undisturbed.

Later she chided herself, knowing she should
have been glad he had merely bid her good night
and moved on to his room. But Cassie, unable to
deny it, felt her disappointment like a weighted
stone on her breast, for God help her, she had
wanted him to kiss her . . .

On this particular evening, he stared at her all
through dinner in a way that made her grow hot
all over. She and Edmund then sat at a rosewood
table playing whist. Edmund had only recently
taught her the game, and to her delight, she was
fully capable of besting him. Gabriel sat in the

corner, his long, elegant legs stretched out before him, nursing a brandy.

The hour was still early when Cassie began to yawn. She had been feeling dreadfully tired of late and rarely seemed to get enough sleep. To her embarrassment, usually everyone in the household was up and bustling about long before she arose.

She sent a slight smile across the shiny parquet-topped table toward Edmund. "You, sir," she said lightly, "are very fond of winning. Therefore I believe I will cry off, and plead my excuses."

Edmund frowned. "But 'tis still early yet."

Cassie glanced across at Gabriel. "Perhaps Gabriel will join you."

The corners of the duke's mouth turned down. "I know better than to ask such a thing of him. Gabriel is nothing like Stuart—why, Stuart could have played the night through! But Gabriel was never one to play whist for the sheer sport of it. I have it on good authority that he is not fond of cards unless there is a wager involved and the stakes are high."

The subject of their discussion rose and ambled toward them. Those beautifully masculine lips smiled, but as always, his regard was distinctly cool as it rested upon his father. "I've not seen the inside of a gaming hall for quite some time, Father. And I daresay in a game of chance you and I are evenly matched." That wickedly beguiling smile widened. "But in a game of skill and wits, well, you may have noticed, my love, that neither of us likes to lose."

My love. Cassie felt her face grow hot. She darted a glance at Edmund. Though his expression was not precisely disapproving, she sensed his displeasure. And though Gabriel's tone was deceptively pleasant, she had the distinct impression he was deliberately taunting his father.

Smoothing her skirts, she got to her feet, doing her best to summon a smile. "I fear I must say good night, for I simply cannot stay awake another minute."

"I will escort you to your room then." Gabriel set aside his glass and took her elbow. Neither was aware of the speculative gaze that trailed them as they left.

At her door, she tilted her head back to regard her husband. "If you do not mind," she stated evenly, "I would like a word with you in private."

A mocking brow climbed high. "Why, Yank," he drawled. "Are you inviting me in to your chamber? This is an unexpected surprise."

Cassie colored, yet somehow she managed to retain her calm. Turning, she entered her room. Gabriel said nothing but followed her inside.

The quiet was all-encompassing. She crossed to stand before the fireplace, feeling the need to put some distance between them. As always, Gabriel's presence was unnerving. Though he did not touch her, she felt as if he did.

She folded her hands together before her and gathered all her courage. "In all the time we have been married," she said quietly, "I have asked you for nothing."

He gave a short laugh. "True enough, Yank. Though you've cost me a pretty sum indeed, you have asked for nothing—and no doubt you've acquired far more in the bargain."

Cassie's lips tightened ever so slightly. Oh, but it was just like him to make her sound mercenary and greedy! " 'Tis not your money I speak of, nor anything money can buy," she said sharply.

He slipped long fingers into his pockets. "I admit, Yank, I am intrigued. But I suspect that is about to be remedied, so let us not mince words. What is it you would ask of me?"

"Very well, then, I will tell you. There are times you look at your father as if you hate him." She delivered her statement not as a question, but as a challenge. "I suspect there is far more to your reasons than the little you have told me, and . . . I would like to know why."

Surprise flitted across Gabriel's handsome features. Clearly this was not what he'd expected. His lips twisted in something that only remotely resembled a smile. "Believe me, Yank, the feelings between my father and myself are mutual."

"Are they? I think not."

It was his turn for his mouth to tighten. "I have known my father far longer than you, Yank. I know him far *better*."

"I think you know him not at all. You hold him at a distance." The way you hold me, she wanted to cry. "Oh, I know he is like you, for I have watched you both. He tries to hide his feelings from everyone around him. And when he looks at you, there is sadness and pain—"

"You are mistaken," he said flatly.

Cassie persisted. "I have watched him. Regardless of what has existed between you in the past, I could almost swear he is hurt—"

"What you see is outrage, outrage that I have replaced his precious Stuart as his heir."

"Perhaps he has changed—"

"He has not. He *will* not."

Cassie shook her head. "You cannot say that for certain! Oh, I know he can be hard and difficult—no one knows that more than I. But so can you—"

"He may have fooled you, Yank, but he has never fooled me. My father, you see, is a bit like Stuart. Upright and noble and very much the gentleman—so much the gentleman that he would not dare let anyone glimpse his true feelings. He's too supremely decorous ever to admit it, but I know if I were to walk out of his life and never return, my father would sing praises to the heavens."

His tone was no less than bitter. Cassie stared at the stiff, unyielding lines of his back as he moved to the window. There he remained, staring broodingly out into the night. Quiet descended, thick and unbearable.

It was Cassie who broke it. She swallowed painfully. "You are trying to punish him. I know that's why you married me. But even after all this time, I've yet to understand your reasons."

He whirled on her, his dark features so intensely fierce Cassie instinctively fell back a step. "You think I have no cause? You're wrong, Yank, and here is why—here is what you want to know. Oh, I've no doubt you've envied me my childhood. You grew up with so little, while I grew up swaddled in luxury and riches. And indeed I wanted for nothing as a child, nor did my mother. We were well fed and well clothed. But neither of us ever forgot . . . Stuart was Margaret's son, the son of the woman he loved. I was merely the son of the woman he later married." His tone was bitter.

Cassie's lips parted. She remembered what Gabriel had said that horrible night he had brought her home to his father, while she stood outside the door of the drawing room ... "He married her," she whispered, "because he wanted a mother for Stuart."

"Precisely. Make no mistake, I loved my brother Stuart. But I was too young to realize that Stuart alone claimed my father's affections. Never did my father have any regard for me."

Cassie's insides twisted in sick dread. Surely no man could treat his own child so abominably. Yet she had only to think what her own mother had done to her to realize that such was the nature of life ... and such was the nature of love.

She heard his harsh laugh. "Foolish child that I was, I wanted my father to notice me, to love me just a measure of the way he loved Stuart. But Stuart was ever dutiful and obedient. He could do no wrong, while I could do no right. I used to stand near Stuart, praying that my father would notice me, that just once he would smile—and look at me the way he looked at Stuart. I remember once ... my father had been to London. He presented Stuart a pony upon his return. I remember wanting to cry, for he'd brought nothing for me, again ..."

Again. There was a wealth of meaning in that single word. Her chest began to ache, for she suddenly began to gain a very clear picture of all that Gabriel had endured.

"Condemn me if you will, but I was jealous—and so very angry with both of them. If I could not have a pony, then neither should Stuart. That night I snuck into the stables and led Stuart's pony from his stall, and released him into the night. I wanted the pony to run away—and he did. One of the grooms found him the next day. He'd stumbled and broke his foreleg. He had to be killed. I'd never seen my father so furious. I remember him shouting how cruel I was to ruin things for Stuart, how greedy and selfish."

Cassie's hand unknowingly rested just above her heart. She did not condemn Gabriel. Dear Lord, how could she? She had no trouble envisioning him as a young boy, clamoring to be heard, to be seen . . . to be loved. Oh, what he must have suffered, being forever overlooked in favor of his brother.

Cassie's chest was aching. "You did not mean to be cruel," she cried. "You were just a child! He was the one who was cruel, to so favor Stuart over you!"

"My father would not agree, Yank. Yet despite everything, I still longed for nothing more than his approval. But there was never a kind word for me. I was naught but a troublesome nuisance. My mother tried to hide it from me, but I was not fooled. He did not love me. He did not love her. We were both just an encumbrance."

An encumbrance. Cassie cringed inside. Lord, but she was coming to hate that word!

Gabriel's mouth twisted. "She married him thinking he would come to love her, you know. But it was as if he were blind. He could not see her for his memories of his beloved Margaret."

He said it as if it were a curse. Cassie was half-afraid to speak. "Your mother loved him then?"

His voice grew ever more brittle. "Yes. But she loved him from a distance, for he did not want her love. She thought I did not know, but I saw the yearning in her eyes that spoke of all she felt— all she could not withhold. But there was never a tender word for her from my father, never a tender touch. He tolerated her presence in his life as a necessity, no more. He cared nothing for her. Nothing!"

Cassie's heart began to bleed, for all he had lost, for all he had witnessed, watching his mother in torment all those years. She thought of the portrait that hung in the gallery; now she understood the air of sadness that dwelled in the eyes of Caroline Sinclair.

"But she would not allow a single word to be said against him. She was sweet and kind and good. She would have done anything for him. I used to hear her weeping at night, but in the morning she greeted me as if naught were amiss. Day after day, year after year she went on loving him." His mouth thinned. "And in the end, it was that very love which killed her."

Cassie frowned. There was something rather vague about his statement, but before she could question him further, she heard his voice again.

"My father broke her heart," he said harshly, moving toward her dresser. "He broke her spirit. For myself, I could have forgiven him the wrongs done me as a boy, but never will I forgive what he did to my mother. I am no longer the naive, adoring young boy I once was, so do not ask me to be merciful or lenient. He spared none for my mother, and I will spare none for him. I have learned to live with his indifference—we do well to endure each other's presence, but there can never be more. *He* cannot forget . . . nor can I."

With that he left her, the lines of his back rigid and proud as he strode through the connecting door that led to his bedchamber.

Cassie's eyes remained fixed on the door long after he had passed through it. Her heart ached for the lonely little boy he had once been. It ached just as much for the bitter man he had become. Though she no longer wondered what demons drove him, it saddened her to think that Gabriel and his father might remain forever distant and alienated—that there could never be a true measure of peace and forgiveness between them. She prayed that he was wrong—that it was not so. For if it was, then all was lost.

Perhaps it was already.

There was no sleep to be found that night. Though her body was weary, Cassie's mind refused the balm of rest. She tossed and turned for what seemed like hours. But all at once a splintering sound rent the night. Her eyes flew wide. She bolted upright.

The sound had come from Gabriel's room.

Slipping from her bed, she snatched up her dressing gown and pulled it on, already halfway across the floor. With no hesitation, she flung open the connecting door and rushed into his suite.

The room was lit by the yellow glow of a lamp in the corner. The full-length mirror mounted on the wall next to the tallboy had been shattered. Shards of shiny glass lay scattered on the thick Aubusson carpet. Cassie instinctively started toward the mess.

"What do you want, Yank?" His voice sliced the air as sharply as a knife blade.

Cassie froze. From the corner of her eye she saw Gabriel prop himself up on an elbow from where he'd been reclining on his bed. There was a glass in one hand.

The hold of his gaze was utterly commanding—and utterly relentless. Cassie was almost tempted to flee beneath the fierceness of his glare—almost, but not quite.

She moistened her lips. Her pose reflected her uncertainty, one small hand at the neck of her dressing gown. "I heard something . . . I thought perhaps you were hurt."

"As you can see I am fine. I suggest you go back to bed." He swung his legs to the floor. His shirt was unbuttoned and gaped wide, revealing the hair-matted roughness of his chest. Cassie's mouth went dry, but she did not look away.

He paid her no heed, but strode toward the dresser—and a half-empty decanter of brandy.

Cassie had no recollection of moving until she found herself at his side. Gabriel continued to ignore her, but when he would have tipped the neck of the decanter into the glass, she thrust her palm over the rim. "Gabriel, please." Her tone was breathless. "Don't you think you've had enough?"

He whirled on her, eyes afire with temper. "Have I, Yank? But you are right, there are other ways for a man to seek ease from his troubles. So tell me, would you offer more comfort?"

His gaze seared hotly into hers. Deliberately, boldly, he laid his hand on the upward thrust of her breast. Cassie could not still her instinctive leap of fear.

His lip curled. "You see? I thought not." He removed his hand and turned back to the decanter.

Cassie was quaking inside but determined not to show it. She laid beseeching fingers on his arm.

"Gabriel, please. You accomplish nothing by drinking yourself into oblivion."

"Why, Yank, I do believe you have no idea of the surcease to be found in a bottle of fine brandy. Amazing, to be sure, particularly for a former barmaid."

Cassie had to stop herself from flinching. His mockery cut deep and she suspected he knew it.

"Since you will not join me in my bed, then perhaps you wish to join me in a drink?"

"No!"

His eyes narrowed. His features grew blacker by the heartbeat.

"Then I recommend, once more, that you return to your own bed."

She shook her head. Cursing beneath his breath, Gabriel reached out to forcibly displace her touch. But Cassie's other hand joined the first. She clung to his forearm; the muscles beneath her fingertips grew rock-hard and tense.

His jaw clenched. "Why are you here? Do you enjoy seeing me like this?"

"Of course not!" The words were a fervent denial.

He stared at her as if to lay bare all that she was. A part of her longed to flee as he demanded, for a heated blaze had begun to glow deep in the pure silver of his eyes—anger, frustration, and something else—something that frightened her. But she knew, in some strange, unfathomable way she could not explain, that Gabriel was only a heartbeat away from losing control. And yet she felt compelled beyond reason to remain where she was, for she could not banish the strangest sense that if she turned from him now, he would remain beyond her reach forever.

"I was glad we left London," he said suddenly. "I hated all those young bucks watching you, wondering if your lips are as soft and sweet as they look."

Her lips formed a wordless sound of surprise.

"Oh, come now, Yank." His laugh was harsh. "Surely you knew. Surely you are not so green as all that. All the while they pretended to be gay and merry, ever the gentlemen, they were dying for a taste of you, stripping away your clothing with their eyes and imagining what lay beneath . . . Viscount Rayburn—he was the worst."

Surprise widened her eyes. "But . . . I am a married woman—"

"That matters little to men like Rayburn. Surely you saw enough of London to know that gambling and lustful pursuits are the order of the day. Believe me, had you given him any sign you were willing, he would have been under your skirts in a thrice." Gabriel's eyes were hard and glittering.

Without warning he caught her against him, the movement so sudden she nearly cried out.

"Be glad that he did not, Yank, for I do not think your tender heart could withstand his death on your conscience."

His possessiveness thrilled her, yet there was an aura of danger about him that sent a prickle of unease through her limbs. "Gabriel," she said shakily. "You should not say such things—"

A mask of icy coldness descended over his features. "Why not? It's true. So make no mistake. I'll kill any man who dares to claim what is mine."

Her breath caught halfway up her throat. "Gabriel, please, you—you don't know what you're saying. You've had too much brandy—"

"And what if I have?" His tone was fierce. "You drive me to drink, Yank. You drive me to madness. You drive me to *this*."

Chapter 16

His mouth crushed hers, a searing brand. There was no tenderness in his shackling embrace. There was nothing but sheer, male mastery as with his tongue he ruthlessly plundered the honeyed interior of her mouth, slick and warm. She twisted beneath his hands but his grip was relentless, his kiss rampant with the thunder of emotions gone wild and unchecked and wholly out of control. Whether he was goaded by drink or desire, she did not know. She knew only that there was no escaping him.

To Cassie it was just like before. She sensed no mercy in him, no softness. She did not know he was blind and deaf to her struggles, to all but the driving pulsebeat of desire pounding through his veins. Only when a low whimper broke from her throat did the punishing ferocity of his kiss lessen. The crimson haze of lusty passion which surrounded him began to subside. Gradually he became aware of the fragile span of her shoulders beneath his hands.

He broke away from her mouth and stared down at her. Her lashes were dark and damp, spiked with tears. She appeared dazed, her lips red and damp and swollen. The faintest glimmer of wounded vulnerability shone in her beautiful golden eyes.

Gabriel stepped back, his breathing ragged and scraping. "Go," he said roughly. "Just go." He retreated to stand at the window, his back to her as he stared out at the moon-drenched sky.

Cassie remained where she was. Something painful caught at her heart. She could not identify the force which kept her there. It was as frail and fragile as a gossamer thread of hope . . . as powerful and potent as a blazing noonday sun.

Time stretched, dark and endless. Hearing no rustle of movement behind him, he turned. His mouth grew ominously thin as he beheld her standing there.

The set of his shoulders was rigid. "You need not look at me like that, Yank. My father taught me well, you see—I am undeserving of your compassion. And I most certainly do not need your pity."

There was a stark, wrenching pain in the region of her heart. Oh, yes, she thought. He was too proud to accept pity. Too bitter to accept compassion. But like her, he knew what it was to feel truly alone . . . truly unworthy. A shattering realization washed over her then.

She could love him . . . if only he would let her.

"Dammit," he growled, "didn't you hear? Leave me alone!"

Slowly she raised her head. His regard was so blistering she was half-afraid to speak. "Is that what you want?" she asked faintly. "For me to leave?"

His eyes glittered. "You know what I want, Yank."

Still she stood there, marveling that she had not the good sense to do as he commanded. Fear dragged at her insides, a fear that surpassed all other. If he rejected her now, her humiliation would be complete.

She shook her head, the muscles in her throat aching so that it hurt to speak. "No," she whispered. "I am not certain that I do." Something blazed across his features, something swiftly suppressed.

Deliberately he said, "I want you in my bed, Yank. Beneath me. Your legs wrapped tight around mine as I lay buried deep and hard inside you." He watched as her face flamed crimson. He did not mean to be crude, just brutally frank, for he would have no misunderstandings between them this time.

Still she did not move. She stood before him, her gaze shying away, her hands clasped in a white-knuckled grip before her. Both betrayed her. Doubt? he wondered. Or fear?

With his eyes he pinioned her. His scouring gaze swept her from head to foot, lingering on the gentle upthrust of her breasts beneath her dressing gown. By the time his gaze returned to hers, Cassie was stunned to find his expression raw with undisguised passion. Her pulse was suddenly throbbing.

"Come here, Yank."

She went, on legs that weren't entirely steady. Only when she stood before him, so near he could feel the flutter of her breath, did she falter. Her lashes fanned dark and thick upon her cheeks; her gaze climbed no higher than the hollow of his throat.

Warm hands descended to her shoulders. He pushed aside her dressing gown, leaving her clad only in a nightgown that revealed far more than it concealed. Her nipples thrust pink and round against sheer white lawn. Further down the triangle of her womanhood shown dark and dusky.

He stroked her body with naught but the touch of his eyes.

"You're beautiful, Yank."

Her embarrassment at standing nearly naked in front of him fled as if it had never been. Cassie's heart surely stopped in that moment. She held herself perfectly still, wishing it would last forever. She had never dared hope he would say such a thing—never. The words were like music to her heart, a healing balm to her soul.

A lean hand slid beneath the fall of her hair, cupping her nape. He pulled her head back slowly, so that she could not look away from the searing intensity of his gaze.

"I am tired of pretending I do not want you, Yank, when I have wanted you from the start—when I suddenly find that is *all* I want. Oh, I know I told myself I wanted revenge. I told myself I could handle it, that I could accept a marriage in name only—that you were beautiful but I've lain with other women just as beautiful. But I was wrong. For you are ever on my mind, ever and always."

His eyes darkened. "But know this. If you come to me tonight, then that door will remain forever open. I will not be barred from your bed. If you cannot accept that, then I suggest you leave now. Either way, the choice is yours."

Her eyes clung to his. The tension spun out endlessly. Just when he thought he could bear it no longer, first one small fist crept up to rest on his chest, and then the other.

It was all the encouragement he needed. He reached for her, eager to claim what she so temptingly offered. "So be it," he muttered, "for I can wait no longer."

He kissed her then, a wordless entreaty that spoke of desire long denied. Her lips quivered beneath his, then parted. He felt her response, sweet, warm, and clinging. The reins of control snapped within him.

With a groan he crushed her against him, lifting her full off her feet. The pressure of his mouth was no less fierce than before, yet there was a difference. He kissed her as a starving man consumed the most bounteous of feasts. The taste of brandy was heady on his tongue . . . but so was the tormented hunger, and Cassie exalted in it. She twined her arms around him and shamelessly pressed her body against his.

Her nightgown met the same fate as her dressing gown. Their lips still ardently fused in a long, unbroken kiss, he swung her up into his arms and laid her on the counterpane. Only then did he reluctantly release her mouth, shrugging his shirt from his shoulders. He straightened, his hands at the buttons of his breeches.

Though she could feel a heated tide of embarrassment coloring her entire body, Cassie could not tear her gaze away. As each straining button was released, hair that was darker and coarser than the wiry mat on his chest filled the ever-widening gap.

His manhood sprang taut and free. Deep inside her, it spun through her mind that she had been hoping—praying—that her imagination had played havoc with her memory of the night she had lost her virginity . . .

It had not.

He bent and freed his legs of his breeches, kicking them aside and turning to face her. Oh, she could not deny there was a wild, primitive beauty to his body. His shoulders were wide and sleek, his arms and legs long and lean, spare and tight. She tried to mask it, but her pulse skittered madly in alarm. Though she knew it was not so, it flashed through her mind that what he intended was not possible . . . between the corded stretch of muscled thighs his manhood stood stiffly, rigidly erect.

She turned her gaze to safer territory, focusing on the chiseled beauty of his mouth as he stretched out beside her. But Gabriel had heard the deep, shuddering breath she drew.

He spoke, his tone dangerously low and tense with frustration. "We've come too far for you to change your mind, Yank."

Through some miracle, she whispered, "I have not."

"What, then? Are you afraid of me?"

She shook her head, but her expression told him otherwise. Her eyes were wild and panicked.

He turned her in his arms, his hold loose but all-encompassing. His nearness was overwhelming. The scent of man and musk swirled all around, mingled with the cologne he used. His mouth hovered just above hers, so close her very breath seemed not her own.

Lean fingers brushed stray strands of honey-gold from her flaming cheeks. "If you are not," he said softly, "then why do you tremble like a frightened bird?"

Her fingers curled and uncurled in the furry darkness on his chest. Her breath tumbled out in a shaky rush. "Because I . . . I want to please you . . . and . . . oh, 'tis not you . . . so much as—as what you will do . . . and what you will do it with . . ." She buried her head on his chest in abject shame.

Gabriel sucked in a harsh breath. Had she known what effect her confession would provoke, he felt certain she would never have made it. Though he'd have sworn it was not possible, his straining rod swelled to even greater proportions. The pulse in his shaft raced apace with the thudding of his heart.

With his thumb he traced the vein throbbing wildly in her throat. "I'll not hurt you again," he muttered. "That pain when I first took you . . . a woman has it but once, Cassie."

She did not believe him. Though she did not outwardly deny it, her lips were tremulous, her struggle vivid in her eyes. Yet she did not tear herself away, as he suspected she wanted to. Some emotion that was almost painfully intense caught at his heart, knowing that despite her apprehensions, she would give herself over to him so completely. In an instant, his decision was made. He'd never been pretty with words, not really.

He could show her far better.

The suddenness of his movement wrung a gasp from her. His hand engulfed hers and dragged it down over the grid of his belly . . . still further.

With unyielding pressure he guided her, filling her palm with himself, curling cool fingers around his burning shaft.

Her innocent touch inflamed him almost past bearing. He gritted his teeth against the urge to tighten her grip and pump his hips—she clasped but half of him—to take his satisfaction in this way and spare her the invasion of her body. Yet he sensed that, too, would shock his untutored young bride to her very core.

Nor were his motives entirely unselfish. He wanted to possess her, to fill her with his pounding essence, for she was his . . .

His and no other's.

"Feel," he said thickly. "Feel how my body craves yours. But do not forget I am but flesh and blood. *This* is but flesh and blood—and more desire than my body can contain." His words were heated and shattering, raw and undisguised. "Oh, yes, you please me, Yank. You please me more than you can know." His eyes sheared into hers. "Now let me please you."

His mouth captured hers. With a low moan, she caught his head in her hands and surrendered to her passion . . . and to his. God, but it felt so good to be held . . . to be touched. Her mouth was as sweetly clinging as his was greedy.

A shudder rippled through him as her tongue sparred tentatively with his. She reveled in it—and in the way his thumbs traced slow, maddening circles around the pouting tips of her breasts, teasing, skimming lightly back and forth. They seemed to peak and swell, springing tight and engorged.

She longed to clamp his hand there that she might capture that elusive pleasure.

Slowly he raised his head, his gaze dark and brilliant. She was irresistibly beautiful, her breasts round and delectably full, her nipples deep coral centers against pale, unblemished flesh. He kissed her there now, an odd little laugh escaping as her breathing hastened.

"You're very sensitive there, aren't you, sweet?"

He shifted suddenly, gently squeezing and filling his hands with ripe, jutting flesh. His tongue came out to touch the very tip of one deep rouge circle, leaving it shiny and wet and aching. A stab of sheer pleasure bolted through her.

She couldn't look, and she gasped at the shocking sensation as he took the whole of her nipple deep in his mouth. The wanton lashing of his tongue was wild and erotic . . . an exquisite delight. Her head fell back as he licked and sucked first one dark nipple and then the other. She gave a breathless little cry of ecstasy.

His mouth came back to hers, devouring and consuming, his tongue plunging hotly between her lips in a blatantly evocative rhythm. Tormenting fingers skimmed a nerve-shattering path across the sensitive skin of her belly. But she gasped when those same fingertips embedded themselves in the tight gold curls at the apex of her thighs. Cassie cried out and sought to clamp her thighs tightly together. But his hand was already firmly entrenched there, undaunting as he staked his claim.

"Don't fight me, Yank." His whisper was low and strained. "I promise I'll not fail you now." He kissed her with slow, seductive persuasion, letting her adjust to this intimacy until at last he felt her tension subside.

With the tips of his fingers he taunted and teased, lightly brushing, retreating, then returning ever bolder. She shuddered both inside and out as those devilish fingers parted tender pink folds of flesh, sliding sleek and bold and sure along each side of her furrowed cleft.

Blistering flames licked through her as his thumb joined the foray, brushing an achingly sensitive bud of flesh she had not known she possessed. Her body seemed to swell and throb and weep. She cried out softly as one long, strong finger flexed deep inside her, again and again. And all the while his thumb now worked its magic, circling and rubbing until there was a raging inferno blazing inside her.

Eyes closed as if to shut out the delicious torture, she began to whimper and writhe. He tore his mouth from hers and stared down at the tears her body wept, glistening and damp against his hand and her flesh. He groaned. His finger sank deeper, clear to his palm.

"Gabriel!" His name was a shivering cry. In it he heard all that he sought—all he had waited for. He levered himself up over her, scarcely able to breathe.

Her eyes were glazed, her expression dazed. The hardness of his belly pressed hers. With his knees he nudged her thighs apart. The sleek round crown of his shaft probed damp, dark curls, forcing her open, wider still. She clutched at him, certain she would be torn asunder by his straining entry.

He felt the bite of her nails in his back. "Look at me, Cassie." His tone was ragged. That he could yet speak he deemed a miracle.

Helplessly she obeyed. There was no help for it. His shoulders gleamed like oiled walnut. She sensed the iron control he was exerting over himself; his features were taut with the strain of holding back.

He lowered his head so that their lips almost touched but not quite. "Do I hurt you?" His words were but a breath of air.

Her deep shuddering breath only made her aware of his massive rod buried deep inside her, swollen and thick. But there was no pain, she realized with blinding relief, there was only the mindless excitement of being filled as never before.

Her lips formed a tremulous smile. "I—am fine," she said faintly. And then her smile faded. Their eyes clung as she guided his head down, so their mouths were clinging too.

Slowly he began to move. She nearly cried out when he withdrew almost completely. The muscles of his buttocks tightened, and again his swollen shaft pierced deep within her. Pleasure swirled all around her, dark and heady.

Her eyes half-closed. Her back arched. Her hips caught his rhythm. Lifting. Circling. Heat shot through her like molten fire. A low moan broke from her throat. It was a plea, a wanton cry for more. She wanted him deep, deeper than she ever thought possible.

At the sound, Gabriel raised himself above her, his eyes burning like embers, the muscles of his arm corded and bulging. Every nerve in his body

was centered *there*, where her velvet sheath impris-
oned him, hot and sleek and tight. His mouth took
hers with frantic urgency.

"I don't want to hurt you," he groaned. "But . . .
God help me . . . I cannot be slow and easy . . . I
want you too much . . ."

Something gave way inside her, a rush of emotion that melted her insides. "Oh, Gabriel," she
cried. "I want you, too. *I want you, too.*"

His control splintered. A powerful lunge took
him deep, clear to her womb, clear to the center
of her heart. Again and again he plunged, torrid
and intense, driving and wild. Cassie wrapped her
arms and legs around his limbs and clung, caught
up in the same burning frenzy. Then suddenly the
world exploded, white-hot and dazzling, spread-
ing out from that secret place he possessed so fully.
She did not recognize the keening cries of rapture that tore from her throat, but Gabriel did.
Her spasms spurred his own release. He plunged
as if he would rend her in two. His body stiffened and throbbed, flooding her with his spewing
wet heat.

His head was buried in the hollow of her shoulder. Above her, she felt his body slowly relax.
Her fingers curled into the dark hair that grew
low on his nape, an unconscious caress. He did
not leave her, as she thought he might—as she
feared he would. Instead he propped himself up
on his elbows and gently—lingeringly—kissed her,
a caress so unbearably sweet it brought tears to
her eyes.

No words came to mind, and none to her lips.
It was then that she knew . . . this was what she

had longed for all her life. This breathless feeling of closeness, of belonging, so much a part of another . . .

In that moment, she could ask for no more.

Chapter 17

~~~~∽∾∾⌢~~~~

Cassie awoke to blazing sunlight streaming brightly through the windows. For a moment she stared, puzzled at the stark masculine furnishings that surrounded her. Vivid remembrance scorched her mind as she recalled she was not in her own bed ... and why. But along with that came a warm fuzziness that sent her gaze peeping shyly to the other side of the bed. She frowned, admitting to a sliver of disappointment at finding herself alone.

Just then the connecting door opened a crack. Gloria peeped through. "Milady?"

Aware she was still naked, Cassie slid down beneath the covers. "Good morning, Gloria."

"Morning?" The little maid giggled. "It's nearly noon, mum."

"Noon?" Her state of undress was all that kept Cassie from leaping up. "My heavens, why didn't you wake me?"

Her round cheeks wreathed in a smile. "His lordship made it very clear I was to let you sleep as long as you wanted." Gloria couldn't have been more pleased at finding her mistress's bed empty this morning. She was ever so kind and tender-hearted, and the earl so darkly handsome, for all that he was so stern and sober, a bit like his father . . . She sighed her approval. If anyone deserved happiness, it was those two. Oh, but she couldn't wait to tell Mrs. McGee!

Cassie blushed as her dressing gown was laid within reach. "Is my husband downstairs?"

"Yes, mum. He went out for a morning ride, but I believe he's returned."

Cassie hurried through her toilette, anxious to see him again. After the intimacies they had shared last night, it was her most fervent hope that Gabriel's icy remoteness was a thing of the past—if the hours spent in his arms were any indication, surely it was so!

Her heart was pounding riotously as she descended the stairs. Though she told herself she had no reason to be, she was just a trifle nervous. Her slipper was on the last stair when a sudden wave of dizziness rolled over her. She paused, flattening her palm against the wall and inhaling deeply. This was not the first time she'd had such a spell of late. Mercifully, it passed as quickly as the others. But just as she would have moved forward again, she heard the spiral of angry voices just around the corner in the entrance hall.

Gabriel and his father.

She froze. Though she did not mean to eavesdrop, she could not help but overhear.

"I cannot," Gabriel was saying flatly. "I have an appointment in London this afternoon."

"But I've already made arrangements for you to meet with the vicar this afternoon to discuss our yearly donation to support the parish charities." Edmund was clearly vexed.

"I suggest you make it another day."

"I cannot. I told him you would be there!"

"Then handle it yourself!"

"Blast it, Gabriel, I would remind you such responsibility will someday be yours alone! Nor will I be on hand to step in for you when you decide such matters are inconvenient with your wishes. You will ultimately take my place as the duke of Farleigh. You cannot shirk your obligations then, and you cannot do so now. You have a duty to uphold!"

Cassie held her breath. There was every indication this had taken on the proportions of a major row.

"Father, I have made myself available to you these last weeks though you seldom had the courtesy to ask if I were. I admit no one was more surprised than I by your decision to involve me in estate affairs. Indeed, it occurs to me that perhaps you have been merely waiting for me to fail. So if this is your way of testing me, so be it. But I draw the line at having you make my plans *for* me. In future, consult me first."

Footsteps echoed. A door opened.

"Stuart would not have walked away as you do, Gabriel. Never would he have been so careless of his duty." Edmund's fury boiled over. "If one of my sons had to be taken from me, why couldn't it have been you? God, but I wish you had never been born!"

Cassie reeled as if she'd been struck. Oh, sweet Lord, surely her ears had played her false. Surely he had not said . . .

"Do you think I do not know that, Father?" In comparison to Edmund's rage, Gabriel's voice was whimsically soft. "I've always known you did not want me—you *never* wanted me."

The door closed quietly. Cassie clamped a hand to her mouth, her eyes tortured. Her knees refused to hold her. She sank to the stairs, utterly sick inside.

She swept into the study scant seconds later, her posture regal, her demeanor one of sheer, calm conviction.

Edmund was seated behind a polished mahogany secretaire. He glanced up at her entrance. "If you don't mind," he said curtly, "I prefer to be alone right now."

"Oh, but I do mind." The wide double doors swung closed. Four steps placed her squarely before him.

The duke's eyes narrowed. "I would like those doors kept open, if you please."

Cassie gazed at him steadily. For the first time she did not feel as if she were beneath him. Lord or no, duke or no, he was as human as she . . . and at this moment, he was beyond contempt.

"I suggest we keep them closed, Your Grace. Unless you do not care if the servants hear what I have to say—and I do believe they've heard quite enough. I know I certainly have."

He jumped to his feet, as haughty as ever. "You go too far, Cassandra. I will not brook such impudence—"

"And you, sir, will not bully me. You will not browbeat me into silence. I will have my say and I will have it *now*." Her gaze was as icy as his.

"Were I you, I do not know how I could live with myself," she went on. "To wish your son dead . . .

to wish him never born . . . Were I you, I would be on my knees asking God's forgiveness that I could be so cruel, so very heartless!"

Edmund went a trifle pale. There was no doubt the chit had heard the whole unfortunate exchange with Gabriel. Pride compelled him to defend himself.

"You do not know of what you speak, Cassandra—"

"Oh, I know far more than you think! Gabriel told me of his childhood. How you always placed Stuart before him, in all things, how you favored Stuart."

Edmund threw up his hands. "You see? He's *always* been jealous of Stuart!"

Cassie's eyes began to blaze. She confronted him boldly, though her body trembled with the force of her emotions. "And what if he was? He was just a little boy! Oh, I've no doubt you will choose not to believe it, but Gabriel loved Stuart, and I have it from his own lips! But you gave all of what he so desperately wanted from you to his brother! He felt all alone!"

"Alone! Why, the boy was hardly alone! The servants doted on him! And he had his mother—"

"His mother was *all* he had!" she accused. "Gabriel looked up to you. He worshipped you. Yet you spared him not a look, not a touch, never a hint of warmth. He told me how you gifted Stuart once with a pony, and brought nothing—*nothing*—for him! What kind of man are you to do such a thing to a child, to slight him so, to be so cold and heedless of your own son? You talk of duty. But where was your duty to *both* your sons?"

"You are mistaken. Gabriel wanted for nothing as a child. And make no mistake, Cassandra. As a child he was troublesome and willful and head-strong. As a youth he was even more rebellious and defiant, but it was never so with Stuart!"

" 'Tis not hard to reason why! A child knows when he is not wanted, no one knows more than I! Gabriel was wounded that his father shunned him so, and his hurt turned to anger—to rebellion. And must you forever compare him to Stuart? You said last night that Gabriel was nothing like Stuart and you are right. Gabriel can never replace Stuart and 'tis unfair of you to expect such of him! Nor is he a child any longer, and you cannot order him about as if he were."

Edmund stared at her dumbly. An awful band of tightness crept around his chest. He was not selfish, not in the way she thought. He had put Farleigh first, for it was his birthright, as it had been for generations before him and as it would become Gabriel's. But Cassandra made him sound like a monster.

"You are blind," she charged, her voice shaking with quiet outrage. "Blind to all but your own self-ishness. You think yourself so much better than I. But you give not a thought to the feelings of those around you. Gabriel told me you never loved him, or his mother. Yet still in my heart, I was con-vinced he was wrong, that he had misunderstood you. Yet now I find it hard to believe you were ever kind, that you are even capable of love!

"My mother wished me dead," she went on. "My mother tried to *see* me dead. God alone knows who my father was. But I used to dream that he would someday return for me, that he would take me away and we would be happy. But perhaps I was luckier than Gabriel after all. Perhaps it was better to grow up with no father at all than to have been like Gabriel—with a father like you!"

Hot tears slid down her cheeks. She wiped them away. "You may chastise me however you wish. Beat me. Banish me to the streets, for all I care. But I will never recant a single word—never!"

With a swirl of skirts he was left alone.

Slowly Edmund sank to his chair, his face bleached of all color. Did the girl truly think that he would find some way to *punish* her? No, he thought. He would do nothing, for she had *done* nothing.

Nothing but speak the truth.

If one of my sons had to be taken from me, why couldn't it have been you? God, but I wish you had never been born!

Inside he cringed. His carelessly flung remark speared clear to his heart. Dear God, he thought numbly, she was right. He *was* a monster . . .

How could he have said such a thing to Gabriel? Sweet heaven—*how*?

He had made a terrible mistake, he realized numbly. A mistake that might never be rectified.

For the very first time, Edmund Sinclair, duke of Farleigh, saw himself as Cassandra saw him . . . Cold. Harsh. Arrogant and unfeeling.

He saw himself for the man he really was.

His shoulders sagged. There was no pride. Only a despair that dragged upon his very soul . . . a world of regret. It was only now that he gained even a glimmer of Gabriel's feelings. Whatever his son had felt for him had surely turned to hatred. He had killed any love or respect through his own neglect. He began to understand, now . . . when it was too late.

He had thought he still had one son left . . . Now it seemed he'd lost them both.

Cassie was too angry and restless to remain at Farleigh. Feeling the need to be alone and clear her head, she changed into her riding habit and went out to the stables. She gave the little mare she rode her head, and soon she was trotting up the drive to the Warrenton manor house. Though the house itself was grand and sprawling, the grounds were not as faultlessly sculpted and immaculate as those of the Farleigh estate.

Cassie idly brushed away a spot of dust from her clothes as she rang the bell. As the housekeeper admitted her, it belatedly flitted through her mind that perhaps she should not have come calling without an invitation. But Evelyn greeted her with both hands extended, her manner warm and welcoming as always. Still, Cassie was secretly glad when Evelyn let it slip that her father was not at home. Despite the fact that the duke of Warrenton was always polite and civil, his haughty manner had thawed but little over the past months.

She and Evelyn spent the afternoon drinking tea and talking. But when Cassie began to tease her about the beaus she had surely left behind in London, a faint distress crept into her lovely features.

Cassie frowned. "What is it?" she murmured.

Evelyn smoothed the folds in her gown before meeting her gently encouraging gaze. " 'Tis just that . . . oh, I wish Father were not so intent upon seeing me wed." She shook her head and added glumly, "I know 'tis but my imagination, but it seems 'tis all he thinks of. He's already begun plans for a grand ball the next Season—nearly half a year away yet!"

Cassie studied her for a moment. "Has he received any offers?"

Evelyn nodded. "From Viscount Ashton."

"He did not accept it, did he?"

Evelyn shuddered. "No. Ashton is an impertinent lech, and a fortune hunter to boot!" She sighed. "I suppose I should be glad Father is not so set upon seeing me married that he will accept just anyone's suit. He is determined I shall not marry below an earl."

She paused, staring down at the half-cold tea in her cup. Cassie could have sworn her lovely eyes were marred with a wistful sadness but it was gone so quickly she could not be certain. The next instant Evelyn had raised her face and flashed a smile.

"Enough of me. I would much rather talk about you."

Cassie could not help it. The memory of all that Gabriel had done to her only last night—all that she had *let* him do—vaulted into her mind. Her cheeks flushed a delicate pink.

Evelyn laughed delightedly and patted her hand. "You need not say more, love. I shall take that as a good sign."

A pang bit deep. It was Cassie's turn to smile wistfully. " 'Tis not wise to nurture hope where none exists," she murmured.

"Nonsense," Evelyn declared with such conviction that Cassie looked at her in surprise. "Gabriel cares for you, I'm certain of it. Oh, he may not know it yet—men can be such obtuse creatures you know! But I have watched him, Cassie, and when you are in the room he can scarce take his eyes from you—and if his eyes and mind are thus entranced, his heart is sure to follow."

Cassie did not argue. Evelyn's outlook was always so rosy and bright, she could not bear to disappoint her. She set aside her cup and saucer, then said slowly, "Evelyn, if you don't mind, I'd like to ask you about Gabriel's mother."

"Of course I don't mind. But I'm afraid my memories of her are very vague. It's been quite some time since she died."

"I know," Cassie said quickly. "But her death is what I'd like to talk about . . . and it's so difficult for Gabriel, I hate to pry further. Mrs. McGee mentioned once how tragic her death was, so I thought, perhaps Gabriel was with her at the end . . . Had she been ill before she died?"

"Oh, no. Her death was tragic, to be sure. But it was an accident—a terrible accident. The lake at Farleigh is where it happened, you know."

The lake. Her heart began to thud with thick, painful strokes. "No," Cassie said faintly. "I didn't know."

Evelyn's brow knitted as she sought to remember. "I believe she was quite alone, though. She had a little craft she often took out—but one summer day they found the craft floating in the middle of the lake." She paused. "Her body was found several days later."

Cassie fought a light-headed sensation that made it difficult to breathe. "Good Lord." Her voice was half-stifled. "Do not tell me that she . . . that she—"

"Yes," Evelyn said quietly. "She drowned."

Chapter 18

Though she tried to disguise it, Cassie's mood was troubled as she left Warrenton. It made her shudder to think how Caroline Sinclair had died. At the same time, an elusive hurt tugged at her heart. Why hadn't Gabriel told her his mother had drowned? That he offered to share so little of himself made her ache inside.

Foolish girl, chided a silent voice. *He is well acquainted with your deathly fear of water . . . Perhaps he wished to spare you.*

But there was little point in dwelling on it, she realized. Regardless of his reasons, she would say nothing, for such memories of his mother were best left undisturbed.

The soft line of her mouth pressed together as she ducked a low-hanging branch. Thoughts of Gabriel inevitably turned to his father . . . She dreaded returning to Farleigh, for she fully expected to face Edmund's wrath. For whatever reason he had chosen to hold his tongue while she had so busily engaged hers, she was certain that such restraint would not last long.

It was then she felt it . . . a sensation so strong, the hair on the back of her neck prickled . . . as if secret eyes watched . . . and waited . . .

She was not far from the gazebo, she noted with a shiver. Lovely as it was, Cassie had not returned there since that awful day she and Gabriel had been shot at.

She reined Ariel to a halt and called out sharply. "Who's there?"

There was no answer. All around her, the ground lay brushed with orange-gold leaves. Dappled sunlight poured through twisting tree branches. Though the autumn day was clear and sunny, a shaft of icy terror constricted her breath.

She dug her heels into Ariel's flanks, nearly losing her seat as the mare leaped forward. Bending low, she clung to her mane all the way back to Farleigh. She was still rather shaken when she slipped off the saddle and handed the reins to a groom.

It was then she noted Edmund's black and gold carriage was gone. Encountering Mrs. McGee in the entrance hall, Cassie waylaid her.

"Will His Grace be returning soon?"

"He's gone to his house in Bath, milady. I gather he plans to stay for at least a month." Mrs. McGee shrugged, then smiled. "A bit sudden, his decision to leave. But then he usually spends this time of year in Bath."

Cassie bit her lip. She harbored no illusions. The duke had left because of her—and Gabriel. Though she was vastly relieved that she need not face him so soon again after her outburst, all at once she was beset by a niggling feeling of shame.

At dinner she felt woefully alone sitting at the immense dining table by herself.

She was exhausted by the time she climbed the stairs to her bedchamber. Long after she had dismissed Gloria, she paced the length of her room, her ears straining for some sound that Gabriel had returned from London. It was long after midnight when exhaustion gave way to despair, and then a weary resignation; finally she slipped beneath the counterpane.

But too much had happened that day for rest to come easily. Her sleep was fitful and restless . . .

She was back in the woods again, only this time without Ariel. She was running. Alone. Desperate. Her heart pounding in sheer terror.

An air of menace hung dark and thick, like heavy fog. Phantom shadows darted all around, pursuing her, faster and faster. Frantic to evade them, she ran faster. Branches whipped her face, stinging her cheeks. Her muscles burned. She stumbled and fell.

All at once the lake was there, its turquoise waters pristine and serene. She could see herself, as if she were floating outside of her body. She was standing on the dock, her expression one of stricken horror. Even as she tried to cry out a warning, a hand came out and pushed . . .

Then she was back in her body again. Icy water closed over her head. She gasped, straining to breathe, to survive. Surrounded by a dark, murky underworld, she clawed for the surface. But something was dragging her, pulling her down, ever down . . . She tried to scream. Water filled her mouth, choking her, scalding her lungs. How odd, she thought. For she could hear herself scream, a shrill of pure terror . . .

"Cassie! Open your eyes. It's just a dream, sweet, just a dream."

The command penetrated her haze of consciousness. Her eyes opened. The golden glow of a candle lit the darkness. Gabriel's face, grim and unrelenting, swam above her. His arms were strong and hard about her back. With a moan, she sagged against him, curling her fingers in the front of his shirt. She inhaled deeply, a long, ragged breath; he smelled of crisp, starched linen, and he felt so good, all warm, heated strength.

"I did not know you were back," she whispered after a moment.

"I've only just arrived. You scared the devil out of me—I thought some madman was in here with you." Warm fingers traced soothingly up and down her spine. "What were you dreaming of?"

She suppressed a shudder. She could not tell him. All at once she felt silly and childish. " 'Tis nothing." She raised her head and tried to pass it off with a tremulous smile. "I was at Warrenton this afternoon, and when I rode back, I had the strangest sensation that someone was watching me—"

"You were alone?"

She frowned, for she had felt the brittleness that invaded his hold. "Yes," she whispered into his shoulder.

With a muttered imprecation he drew back. He stared down at her, his mouth a tight white line. "Dammit, Cassie, I don't want you out riding without a groom. I thought I made myself clear."

Her smile wavered. He was tense, so very tense . . . "Evelyn does not ride with a groom."

"Evelyn has not had a precipitous number of so-called accidents of late."

Cassie's breath stilled, along with the beat of her heart. An eerie foreboding trickled along her spine. She searched his face. "You do not think they were accidents?"

Gabriel cursed himself roundly. He had said too much—revealed too much—while knowing far too little. Still, perhaps this was best.

"In all likelihood they were, both the shooting and the attack in London." He did not want to alarm her, yet perhaps now she would take more caution. "I hired an investigator to try to find the man who accosted you. I met with him this afternoon in London. Unfortunately, the rogue has slipped from our grasp."

"I thought you were convinced he was just a footpad."

"Oh, of that I have no doubt. Nevertheless, I wish the man caught." He paused. "Cassie, I do not want to frighten you needlessly. But I want you to think. Is there anyone back in Charleston who might wish you harm? Someone connected with your family, perhaps."

She hesitated. "I told you before, there's no one. My father, whoever he is, does not even know I exist." The briefest spasm of pain passed over her face. "And I doubt my mother remembers." She shook her head, then murmured, "I'm afraid the only person I know of who might wish me ill is your father."

Gabriel's regard sharpened. Cassie bit her lip, obviously disconcerted. "Your father left for Bath this afternoon."

"Bath! But I saw his calendar only this morning. He had no such plans."

"I know." Cassie's eyes avoided his. "I'm afraid I am responsible."

"You?" His short laugh affirmed his disbelief. "Yank, I doubt there is a soul on this earth who could make my father do something he did not wish to."

She hesitated, yet she knew she had no choice but to come out with the truth. "I heard the two of you this morning," she said quietly. "I heard the terrible things he said to you. I was furious— furious that he could be so callous. And I fear I simply could not help myself . . . I gave him quite a dressing down."

"I see." The muscles of his face seemed to freeze. He put her from him. Cassie felt cold and bereft.

And he was angry. She could see it in the set of his jaw, as inflexible as iron.

"You need not defend me, Yank. I assure you, I am quite capable of fighting my own battles."

He had retreated from her, wholly and utterly, in spirit and in body. How could he be so warm and comforting one minute, so cold and patronizing the next? Hurt and outrage brought her chin high.

"Let us not mince words, my lord." The coolness of her tone matched his. "Do you mean to say I have no right to intrude in your life?"

"Why, Yank," he paused, his smile flashing white against his dark features, "it seems we understand each other perfectly."

Small hands fisted at her sides, Cassie rose to her feet. A curious tightness settled around her heart.

"Oh, yes, I understand, Gabriel. I understand all that you do not. Oh, but you are so very much your father's son, just as blind and stubborn! You think yourself so much above him, don't you? You judge him for his mistakes. You despise your father for neglecting your mother, for doing to her . . . what you would do to me . . . and for what, I ask? To spite him, to punish him! Oh, but you are no different than your father—no *better* than him."

She spun around and strode to the connecting door between their rooms. "I will thank you to leave me alone." Her tone was as cutting as her glare.

Gabriel's eyes flickered. He did not move a muscle.

By now Cassie was too incensed to be afraid. A scalding rush of anger poured through her. "Didn't you hear me? Get out." She stamped her foot. "Get out!"

A dangerous half-smile curled his lips. He faced her, his booted feet braced wide apart, his thumbs hooked into his breechess, revealing his jade embroidered waistcoat; his posture was one of unswerving masculinity despite his handsome elegance.

"I think not, madam," was all he said. But deep inside he was bitterly stung that she compared him to his father—his father! And he dared not give in to the rage that simmered just beneath the surface.

Slowly his gaze raked over her, trespassing at will. The candle behind her caught her in its glow—and rendered the frail covering of lawn she wore useless. The shape of her body was clearly discernible. Her breasts were soft and full, her nipples dark, pink enticements, the down fuzz of her womanhood a deeper shadow.

And now a fire of a different sort had kindled.

Cassie realized too late the vulnerability rendered by her state of undress. She recognized the glitter in his eyes only too well. Her fingers curled more tightly around the doorknob as he began to close the distance between them. Though she clung to it with all her strength, the knob was wrenched from her grasp as he thrust the door shut with the heel of his hand.

Sparks of rebellion burst inside her. "Damn you!" she swore. "You will not lay a hand on me!"

There was the sound of husky, masculine laughter. "Oh, but I will, sweet. I daresay you will know much more than just the touch of my hand tonight."

She drew herself up proudly, for now he blocked her way. "I will not!" she cried. "You cannot keep me at arm's length and expect submission whenever the whim strikes you."

He took a step forward. Cassie paled, retreating in tandem as he advanced. But soon he had her backed against the door.

His forearms came up on either side of her body, effectively pinning her in place. Panic engulfed her. He was so close her breasts brushed his shirt with every breath.

His fury was ill-disguised; it glimmered in his eyes like quicksilver. "You are wrong, Yank, for there is a very great difference between my father and I indeed. I used to marvel that I was ever born, for he felt nothing for my mother, not even a man's passion for a woman. And I must confess, sweet, you have only to come near and my body reminds me quite insistently of my desire for you."

"Desire?" Inwardly she trembled; outwardly she scoffed. "I know what drives you. You've been stuck here in the country with me—and without your mistress. So go back to London—back to the welcoming arms of your mistress!"

"My mistress!"

"Yes! Lady Sarah, I believe."

"I've not seen her in weeks, Yank. Nor did I wish to. Besides, what need have I of her when I find such welcome in *your* arms?"

"You'll find no such welcome again!" She shoved at his chest. He merely leaned closer, barring any further movement on her part with the pressure of his body.

"It is pointless to resist me, Yank. We both know that."

"Oh!" she cried. "So now you tout your charms? Do you think I am a fool that I find you so irresistible? If that's what you think, perhaps it's you who are the fool!"

"Perhaps I am," he said, his voice low and intense. "And I do not 'tout my charms,' as you choose to put it. Indeed, Yank, 'tis you who charm me, you who bewitched me the moment I set eyes on you, you who are irresistible. You stir me past bearing. Beyond all reason . . . beyond endurance."

He bent his head and pressed his lips to the place where her neck sloped into her shoulder. The touch of his lips went through her like a bolt of lightning. "And it's not submission I want. I want you naked and twisting and eager in my arms as you were last night."

Oh, but he was a wretch to remind her! His words shattered her composure like broken crystal. All at once she was quivering. No, not with fear, or even anger, but with the intoxicating effect of his nearness.

But when she would have argued, his mouth, demanding and devouring, captured hers. Her gown was swept from her shoulders. His hands came out to play with the tips of her breasts. A shock of sensation curled deep in her belly.

Caught in a maze of conflicting emotions, her hands clenched and unclenched against his chest. Her fingertips were achingly sensitized; she could feel the raspiness of his body hair beneath the fabric of his shirt. A wave of longing swept her in its tide. She yearned to tug aside the barrier of his shirt, to feel the intimate slide of skin against skin. And when he did exactly that, tearing off his jacket, ripping his shirt over his head and burying her nipples in the furred darkness on his chest, she thought she would die of sheer bliss. She had to fight from wrapping her arms around his neck in reckless surrender.

Only the tangle of heart and mind and body stopped her. She wanted him desperately, yet knowing he thought so little of her hurt unbearably!

Somehow she managed to tear her mouth free. "Gabriel, please." Her plea was a ragged cry. "You do this only because I dared to defy you."

He raised his head. His eyes rained silver fire upon her upturned face. "No," he said fiercely. "I told you last night that door would not be closed against me and I meant it. And I do this because it's what we both want."

With that he bore her to the bed and stripped off his boots and breeches. When he was as naked as she, he stretched out beside her.

God help her, he was right. She did want him. Heat and dampness gathered there between her thighs, just thinking what he would do to her—what she *wanted* him to do.

His tongue entwined with hers, a purely erotic mating that primed them both for the one soon to follow. His fingers toyed with her nipples until they stood taut and tingling, aching for the hot brand of his mouth, the lashing glide of his tongue. And then his chest slid slowly down her breasts, the tormenting friction making her gasp for air. Once again he gauged her every desire better than she herself.

But there was still much she did not know . . . much she had yet to learn . . .

He was about to teach her.

For Gabriel there was no conscious thought. There was only the pounding need to pleasure her. To possess her. To please her, for he wanted her as he had never wanted another woman . . . all of her, in the age-old way, in every way . . .

In *this* way.

He slid down her body, his tongue blazing a swirling path across the satin plane of her belly. "Gabriel," she gasped. "Dear God . . . what . . ."

He pressed with the breadth of his shoulders until he felt her thighs give way. Her hands fluttered helplessly against the corded tightness of his arms. But he was persistent. Determined.

He tasted her, his breath a heated rush, a scorching lick of wildly erotic fire against flesh that was already damp and dewy. He groaned. She was hot and tangy-sweet.

Her head jerked up off the pillows. Again and again he teased sleek, wet recesses, elusive and circling, tormenting and exploring. Her fingers knotted in his hair. Soft, breathless panting filled the air, driving him to a frenzy. She whimpered, her hips unconsciously seeking. His blood pounding with a primitive heat, he gave her what she so artlessly sought.

He touched her then, her swollen core, the press of his tongue laid high and full and tight against the very pearl of sensation. A convulsive shudder wracked her. Feeling his manhood near to bursting, he levered himself over her.

Her eyes opened, smoky and dazed. Lean fingers separated soft, springy fleece, then pink, dewy folds. With a groan he plunged deep, embedded tight within her heat. He pulled himself out, all hard and glistening and glorious. Neither could look away as he came inside her, driving and powerful, again and again, with mounting frenzy.

His seed was rising, burning him from the inside out. He was only a heartbeat away from spilling himself. But he ached for her to know the full measure of her pleasure and so he held back.

Her nails sank into his shoulder. "Gabriel." She gasped out his name. "Oh, please . . ."

Her cry echoed in his throat. He claimed her mouth in a kiss that was raw and hungry and unbridled. He thrust harder, deeper, faster and faster in answer to her plea. Did he possess her? . . . Or did she possess him? He no longer knew. He no longer cared, for then he felt it— the pulsing spasms of her tight, clinging sheath around his throbbing member. With a muffled cry he reaped his joy from hers, exploding inside her again and again, his own release no less scalding— no less splendid—than hers.

Chapter 19

Autumn came full upon the land. The country-side brightened to vivid shades of russet and gold. The days grew short, the nights brisk and cool. But with the chill upon the land came a chill upon her heart.

She was distinctly unsettled over the next few weeks. She simply could not help it, for the seed of doubt had been planted and sown. What if Gabriel was right? What if someone were after her? She hated herself for the thought which always sprang to mind. Edmund hated Americans with a passion. What if he had decided to try to be rid of her—permanently?

He had yet to return from Bath, and for that Cassie was thankful. A part of her scoffed at the possibility Edmund might be responsible for the "accidents" which had befallen her. Gabriel seemed convinced his father would do her no harm, yet Cassie could think of no one who could possibly want to hurt her.

Nor was that the only matter which preyed on her mind.

No longer did she and Gabriel deny themselves the sensual pleasures to be found in one another.

When he made love to her, he demanded all she would give—and more. At first the stormy passion he aroused in her was frightening. It frightened her even more that Gabriel commanded such surrender with only a kiss—the merest caress! Yet she could withhold nothing, and soon did not want to. His lovemaking was sometimes fierce and possessive, sometimes tender and protective and achingly sweet. But while her nights were spent discovering the enchantment of the flesh, lying snug in Gabriel's arms, her days were filled with anguish and confusion.

Oh, he gave his body wholly to her. Only last night, in stark, wanton whispers, he told her over and over how she pleased him, how he delighted in her shy exploration of his hard nakedness. But when morning came, his warmth was gone, his passion checked.

In truth, she was secretly shattered, for he kept his emotions shielded from her, ever distant, as though he wore a cloak of iron. He would not let her close . . . and that was where she longed to be.

She yearned for all she had disdained—for all she had never dreamed she might want from him.

It had never been wealth or possessions that she coveted, though she thought bitterly Gabriel might well dispute that fact. In truth, she had thought to be satisfied with a home, a safe and secure future, free from a life of poverty and struggle. But Cassie could not lie to herself any longer. Hidden deep in the furthest reaches of her heart, she longed for a true and happy marriage, a husband who cherished her with all his soul, and children who would never doubt they were loved and wanted by *both* parents.

Heavy was the burden carried by her treacherous heart. She prayed nightly that Gabriel might someday come to love her, but she was afraid that was the one thing that would forever elude her. Yet even as that hope grew ever more dim, another certainty loomed stronger with each passing day.

She was to bear his child.

And she knew not how to tell him.

Little did she realize the matter was already out of her hands.

Gabriel was working in the study one drizzly afternoon in late November. A timid rap echoed on the door. He paused, his quill still in hand. "Enter," he called.

A frown creased his brow when Gloria slipped inside. She stood for a moment on the threshold, her demeanor mousy and tentative.

"Could I have a word with you, sir?" She posed the question timidly.

"By all means, Gloria." He gestured her forward, but he was faintly puzzled. He could think of no reason why Gloria would approach him rather than Cassie.

Gloria wrung her hands nervously and decided that, having come this far, she might as well simply come out with it. "I know 'tis not my place to say so," she blurted, "but I'm fair worried about my lady."

Gabriel tapped the quill against the ledger he'd been writing in. "Indeed," he said slowly. "Tell me why, Gloria, and please be frank."

"Well, milord, to my mind, she's been feeling poorly this last month. Oh, I know she tries to let on that nothing is amiss, but more than once these past weeks she's gone pale as snow—why, I had to help her to a chair. Indeed, I feared she would faint dead away!"

Gabriel frowned. Cassie was no willy-nilly young miss to suffer an attack of the vapors at every silly little thing. She had no shortage of either pluck or pride.

"So you believe she is ill?"

"That's the funny thing, milord. Some days she's right as rain. Others she's so fagged out I can see it's all she can do to drag herself from bed." Gloria warmed to the matter. "Forgive me for being so bold, sir. I've tried to get milady to see a physician, but she insists 'tis nothing and will pass."

Gabriel rose. "I appreciate your concern, Gloria—and you were right to bring this to my attention. Rest assured, I shall see that your mistress neglects her health no longer."

Gloria bobbed a curtsy and left, vastly relieved yet feeling a trifle guilty. Though she had a very good idea what ailed her mistress, Gloria was worried about her and was convinced the lady should be examined by a physician. But had she managed to convince the earl of that? Unfortunately, not a single one of the servants could ever predict where lord and lady stood with the other. Of course, they all had their hopes—and doubts as well. But Gloria smiled happily when she peered around the corner scant seconds later. The earl was striding up the staircase two at a time.

Upstairs in her bedchamber, Cassie sat in a wing

chair near the window, her embroidery in her lap. Though her fingers lay idle, her thoughts were far busier . . . She glanced up at Gabriel's entrance. His face was bronzed against the whiteness of his cravat, so very handsome he took her breath away. The makings of a smile creased her lips.

He folded his arms across his chest and glared. "Gloria tells me you've been ill," he stated without preamble.

Cassie blinked. She did not know what it was she'd expected him to say, but this was not it. With a shake of her head, she laid her embroidery on the table.

"Gloria," she said lightly, "worries far more than need be."

An arrogant brow climbed high. "She tells me she was certain several times you were about to faint dead away."

"Ah, but I did not. So you see, there is no need for either of you to concern yourself—"

"I do not agree, Yank. Nor do I believe you should dismiss these episodes as if they were nothing. Furthermore, I do not understand why you chose not to inform me."

Cassie's smile wavered. She could not help the faint bitterness that seeped through her. What would his reaction be were she to tell him she chose to say nothing because there was simply no point—she was well aware he cared nothing for her.

But already her heart had begun to pound hard and fast. What would Gabriel say if he knew the truth? She dreaded what his reaction might be . . . she feared what it would *not* be . . .

That alone was reason enough to hold her silence for as long as she deemed possible. God knew it would not be long before she could hide her condition no longer.

"I have had a few dizzy spells," she murmured cautiously. "I said nothing because they were over as quickly as they came."

"Nonetheless, you should have told me, for it seems this ailment persists and should not be discounted so easily. Therefore, I shall summon a physician. No doubt he can prescribe some cure."

Panic rose, swift and sure. Cassie was on her feet in an instant. "No!" she cried. "I don't need a physician, I'm certain of it! These spells will pass, I swear—this illness will pass, I assure you!"

"You cannot know that, Yank—"

"Oh, but I do. I swear, I do! I am fine, truly I am!"

Gabriel's eyes narrowed. "By your own admission you have not been feeling well. If you wish to explain yourself, please do. But do so now, for your stubbornness tries my patience."

Cassie stared down at the toes of her slippers. Oh, but she had been backed into a corner and there was no way out of it!

Slowly she raised her head. "I am not ill," she said again. She swallowed bravely, but her mouth was bone dry. " I am . . . with child."

Shock and disbelief flitted across his features, swiftly replaced by unshuttered anger. His gaze scraped over her, as if to prove her words a lie. He spoke through lips that barely moved. "You are certain?"

She nodded miserably.

"How far along?"

She hesitated. When at last she spoke, her voice was no more than a breath of air. "I'm not certain. Nearly four months, I think."

Gabriel said nothing. His very silence was condemning. Tears glistened in her eyes. It demanded every bit of courage she possessed to whisper, "You are not pleased, are you?"

In two strides he was before her. "What! Did you think I would be?" He wrenched her chin up to the light and stared at the tears which even now began to overflow. "Your tears tell the tale only too well, Yank. You are no more pleased about it than I!"

The ache in Cassie's breast was nearly unbearable. Oh, he thought he knew her so well. But he knew her not at all!

Tears scalded the back of her throat. She stretched out an imploring hand. "Please, Gabriel." Her voice was thick with the effort it took not to burst into tears. "Please do not be angry."

"Do not be angry, she says!" His fists clenched and unclenched. To Cassie it was as if the very fires of hell leaped in his eyes. "Have you any idea what this means? I've fallen right into my father's hands—and you may be certain that *he* will be pleased! Now he will have the grandchild he was so determined I give him!"

He spun around and stalked into his bedchamber. Cassie trailed behind him, standing on the threshold between their rooms as he threw a portmanteau onto his bed and began throwing clothing into it.

He did not speak to her, nor did he deign to even look at her. Yet she knew he was seething. The very air around him was charged with his burning rage. Not until he strode to the door was she able to summon the strength to break the horrible silence.

"Gabriel . . . you are leaving?"

He stopped. The cold, biting fury in his eyes was like a blow. "I shall go to London where the sight of you need not forever remind me of my folly."

Cassie could not help it. "Where?" A smothered cry tore from her chest. "To your mistress?"

"Now there's a thought, Yank, an appealing one at that!" His jaw was tense. His gaze raked over her. "Christ," he ground out tightly, "if I had to be burdened with a wife, why did I have to choose you? Why couldn't you have been barren?" He whirled. The door slammed so hard the walls shook.

Heartbroken, Cassie began to sob. Nothing could have wounded her more . . . *nothing*. Everything inside her—her very soul—seemed to wither up and die. His reaction was all she had known it would be . . . all she had feared.

Her feeble strength deserted her. She collapsed on the floor, her heart in shreds.

Oh, but she had been foolish, so foolish and mistaken! Even worse, she had deliberately blinded herself . . . Gabriel had felt no tenderness for her. No warmth. No protectiveness. Yet in that shattering instant, Cassie could hide from the truth no longer.

She loved him. Through his anger. His indifference. *She loved him*.

She always would.

Chapter 20

Though the night was near spent, the crush of people in Lord Chesterfield's gilded, elegant ballroom had only recently begun to disperse. Gabriel was among those who had arrived hours ago. He drank. He talked. He laughed.

He whirled Lady Sarah around the floor and stared into smiling, upturned features. He listened idly to her chatter, but his mind was miles away. And indeed, it was not Lady Sarah he saw at all, but the image of another . . . of hair like a golden sunrise, of eyes as clear and bright as topaz, of lips as soft and sweet as ripe, juicy fruit.

And all the while a seething tempest of emotion squalled and churned inside him. Confusion. Pain. Resentment. And something else . . .

Regret.

With a start he realized the dance had ended. Lady Sarah touched his forearm. "I grow weary of so much company, my lord. Perhaps we might depart for my townhouse and more quiet surroundings."

Dark, sultry invitation gleamed boldly in the lady's eyes. The seductive slant of her smile proclaimed her invitation more clearly than words themselves. But Gabriel was neither seduced nor bewitched, beckoned nor persuaded.

"I'm afraid the time is too late, my lady," he murmured, holding her gaze. "Therefore, I must refuse your kind offer." He knew by her indrawn breath she understood his silent message—just as he knew she had not pined his loss these many months. He kissed her fingertips in last farewell, then glanced toward the sidelines. "I do believe Lord Waverly awaits this next dance." He bowed, made his excuses to his host, and departed.

A nagging restlessness persisted as he descended the wide stone steps. He shunned the cab the footman would have procured for him and decided to walk instead.

Wispy tendrils of fog curled all around him. The London streets were damp and deserted. The caped layers of his greatcoat swirled around his legs. His footsteps echoed on the cobblestones.

If I had to be burdened with a wife, why did I have to choose you?

Christ! Had he really said that? What demon had possessed him?

Why couldn't you have been barren?

Each word sank into his brain like a hooked barb. Over and over again, his reckless taunts pounded through him, haunting him, tormenting him. A voice in his soul cried out. How could he have been so cruel? No . . . not just cruel. *Deliberately* cruel.

For the life of him he could not explain what provoked him. He knew only that it was as if he'd been seized by the throat. Spurred by the helpless fury that heated his blood. He'd felt as if he'd been . . . tricked. Trapped. Betrayed by this beauty he now called wife . . .

His steps came to a halt. He ground his fingertips into his forehead, as if to drive out the devils that possessed him.

A shuffle of sound nearby roused him. He raised his head. It was then that he saw her—a woman leaning against the corner of a crumbling brick building.

She was poor—and with child—soon to deliver from the look of her. She was young, far younger than he, yet the sorrows of the ancients dwelled in her eyes. A heavy mist had begun to fall, but she wore no cloak to protect her from the elements; her clothing was little more than rags.

But it was on her tremendous belly, heavy and swollen with her burden, that his gaze lingered endlessly.

Cassie, too, he thought numbly, would soon be cradling a babe in her arms. But no, that was not right . . . Not just a babe. *His* babe.

For an instant Gabriel could not breathe. His breath burned like fire in his lungs. The enormity of that realization washed through him, humbling him, nearly bringing him to his knees.

Why couldn't you have been barren . . . barren . . .

Self-disgust ate into his stomach like acid. He had treated her as if she had done something wrong—as if this were all her fault! But if the blame were to be placed on anyone, it belonged squarely on his shoulders.

His lips twisted. He'd made precious little effort to restrain his desire. Night after night he had wanted her. Night after night he had taken her.

Selfishly. Uncaring of the consequences—refusing to even *consider* those consequences.

Yet he'd hated himself for making love to her. Because every time, he'd felt as though he had lost a part of himself . . .

He fumbled beneath the layers of his greatcoat. The woman watched him warily, retreating a step as though she did not trust his motives. But when he pulled out a small pouch stuffed full of coins, her eyes widened.

He extended it toward her. "Here," he said with a nod. "Take it."

Her cracked lips parted. She gaped openly. "But, sir . . . 'tis surely a fortune."

The merest hint of a smile creased his mouth. She reminded him just a little of Cassie, that very first night at Black Jack's. She, too, had been struck dumb by the pile of silver coin on the dresser.

He shook his head. "Hardly a fortune," he corrected. "But if you guard it wisely, 'tis enough to tide you over for many months, you and your babe." He dropped it into her palm.

The woman looked up at him, both awed and moved beyond measure. "Oh, bless you, sir." She clutched the pouch to her breast and looked up at him. Tears sparkled in her eyes. "You are a saint, truly a saint. And I will never forget you—never!"

He watched as she ran off around the corner, then continued on his way. But when he arrived at his townhouse, it was not his own bedchamber that he sought, but that of his coachman.

Thomas rubbed his eyes sleepily. "My lord! What is it? Is something amiss?"

Gabriel shook his head. "I've decided to return to Farleigh, Thomas."

The young man blinked. Through the narrow window at the foot of his bed, he saw that streaks of dawn pinkened the eastern sky. "Now, my lord?"

Gabriel nodded. Thomas dallied no longer but reached for his clothes.

A short time later, Gabriel closed the carriage door. No doubt Thomas thought him mad—returning to Farleigh when they'd scarce been in London half a day. A self-deprecating smile rimmed his lips. And perhaps he *was* just a little mad . . .

It was mid-morning when they finally passed through the iron gates of Farleigh Hall.

He had no more than stepped into the entrance hall than he knew something was terribly, terribly wrong.

A dozen servants milled near the other end of the gallery. It was the little maid Gloria he spied first. Her eyes were red-rimmed and swollen, as if she'd been weeping for hours. Mrs. McGee was patting her shoulder, only slightly less teary-eyed.

So distracted were they that not a one of them heard his entrance.

"What the devil goes on here?"

An odd pall seemed to fall over the assembly. It was Davis who stepped forth, his expression harried as Gabriel had never seen it.

The old man cleared his throat. "My lord, I fear we have dreadful news to impart."

"Do not mince words, Davis." Gabriel's tone came out sharper than he intended. "Just come out with it."

"Very well, then, my lord. Her ladyship was not

in her bed this morning . . . to all appearances it was not even slept in. Our first thought was that she had gone to London to be with you. Yet she asked no one to drive her, and her horse was in the stables. Therefore, we thought it best to continue searching." He faltered, a faint distress flitting across his face. "My lord, she is nowhere to be found."

"What! But, that is impossible."

Davis's features were very grave. "No, my lord. We have searched the house from top to bottom. And we've every hand out combing the grounds this very instant." He hesitated. "There has been no sign of her, my lord. We know nothing except . . . a number of her gowns are missing. And Gloria believes a small bag as well."

Gabriel's blood froze. All conscious thought fled his mind. His skin was ashen.

"My lord, 'tis possible her ladyship found some other way to London—"

"She did not," he said in an odd, strained voice. A sick sensation knotted his belly, mounting until he felt he could not breathe.

"My lord—"

Before their horrified eyes, he bolted up the stairs. There was a mighty crash as Cassie's door banged open. To anyone who might have looked on, he must have appeared crazed. But there was no one to see, no one who might know how truly alone he was.

Alone . . . as never before.

A dainty lace handkerchief lay near her wardrobe. He picked it up, staring at the delicate scrap of fabric.

There was an awful tearing in his chest. Her

image played again and again through his mind. He saw her as she had been when last he'd seen her, shocked and stricken, pale and ashen, her expression bruised and wounded and pleading.

"Cassie," he cried. His fingers crushed the handkerchief in his palm. *"Cassie."*

Edmund returned home three days later. In the entrance hall, Davis swept the doors wide and bowed low. "Your Grace,'tis good that you have returned."

" 'Tis good to be back, Davis." He handed the butler his hat and cane. "Is Gabriel at home?"

It was a moment before Davis replied. To Edmund's surprise, the butler appeared discomfited. "He is upstairs in his chamber, Your Grace."

Edmund frowned, for it was unusual for the man to display anything but aplomb. "Is something wrong, Davis?"

"All has not been well in your absence, Your Grace. But I do believe you will wish to hear it from his lordship—"

Edmund had already started up the stairs. "Your Grace," the butler called, "you should know . . . his lordship is not himself . . ."

An understatement, to be sure.

The drapes had been drawn and closed tight. Only a wintry trickle of light seeped through. Standing on the threshold of his son's room, it was several seconds before Edmund's eyes adjusted to the gloom.

Then he could only stare. He had seen his son angry. Fighting mad. Defiant and rebellious and unafraid of anyone.

Never in his life had he seen Gabriel like this.

He was sprawled in the chair near the window. He wore no jacket. His shirt was half-in, half-out of his breeches; wrinkled and untidy, it looked as if it had been slept in for days. His jaw and cheeks were dark with stubble. The air reeked with the unmistakable odor of stale brandy.

"Gabriel . . . Gabriel, my God, you're foxed!"

Slowly Gabriel raised his head. Bleary, bloodshot eyes sought to focus. To his brandy-laden mind, it seemed only fitting that his father be here to witness his misery.

A hard smile twisted his lips. "That I am, Father. And that I shall stay."

Edmund's gaze narrowed. "What's the meaning of this? And where is Cassandra? In London?"

Cassie. The very mention of her name sent knife-like pains shooting through Gabriel's heart. When he shook his head, his father persisted. "Where then?"

Gabriel's lips drew back over his teeth. His arm came out in a wide arc, sending empty bottles and glasses crashing to the floor from the table next to him.

"Christ," he shouted, a furious rage suddenly exploding inside him. "Do you have to hear me say it? She left me. Goddammit, she left me!"

Edmund jerked, as if a giant fist had plowed into his belly. "Dear God," he said faintly.

Gabriel turned blistering eyes upon him. "There's no need to pretend," he sneered. "Isn't that what you wanted all along?"

Not anymore, Edmund thought dazedly. God in heaven, not anymore.

Lord, but he'd been so very stubborn . . . Too proud to readily admit his heart was softening. For the life of him, Edmund did not know precisely when it had happened . . . But there was no denying the truth. The country of her birth was no longer of any consequence, nor was her former station in life. Somewhere along the line, the chit had sneaked her way into his heart. He had opened it just a crack and she had slipped inside . . .

Shame poured through him like boiling oil. He deserved his son's scorn. He deserved his condemnation, and so much more . . .

Gabriel's anger drained as suddenly as it had erupted. "She's with child," he said heavily. "That's what started it all."

Edmund inhaled sharply. "Gabriel, you must think. Where would she go?"

"I don't know. Christ, I-I just don't know! Lady Evelyn has heard nothing. Neither has Christopher." Leaning forward, he braced his forehead in his hands. His voice dropped, so low Edmund had to strain to hear. "She took only a few of her belongings. All I can think is that she's out there somewhere. Cold. Hungry. With no money. Nowhere to stay."

"Gabriel, we will find her. Never doubt it."

"We won't," he said hoarsely. "I deserve this, don't you see? She didn't want to marry me." His mouth twisted. "She thought she wasn't good enough to marry a lord. She thought she wasn't worthy. But she fooled us all . . . she fooled us all."

Slowly he raised his head. "She was crying when I left. I did not care. Heartless bastard that I am, I did not care." There was a heavy pause. "I can still hear her crying," he whispered.

Edmund's skin prickled eerily, for Gabriel looked not at him, but through him, his features etched with a tortured despair.

"When she told me she was with child . . . I was so angry. I didn't spare a thought for her—or even myself. The only thing going through my mind was how you'd said you wanted a grandchild . . ."

Edmund had gone very still. He had begun to form a very clear picture of all that had transpired, a very clear picture indeed.

"I said . . . such terrible things. Things I did not truly mean." His voice grew raw. "Things that should never have been said . . ."

Edmund sighed. He had crossed the floor before he knew it, and dropped his hand on Gabriel's shoulder. "So do we all, boy," he said quietly. "So do we all."

Gabriel said nothing. Edmund's face was lined and grim as he looked down at his son's dark head. "God knows I am the last one to offer words of wisdom. You can only hope she will forgive you, Gabriel. But first," his tone was grim, "first you must find her."

Chapter 21

On this particular night in late March, the Hare's Den was packed to the rafters. As usual when a fishing vessel returned to port, there was scarcely a seat left in the common room. Coarse male shouts and ribald laughter filled the air, filtering all the way back to where Cassie stood in the kitchen.

She rubbed the small of her back, which ached almost constantly now. The thin slippers she wore were unlaced to accommodate her swollen feet. Though she'd have liked nothing more than to beg Avery's indulgence and creep off early to her cubbyhole in the attic, she did not. Avery ran his establishment with an iron fist, and he did not hesitate to use it on the help.

When she had left Farleigh, her only objective was to get away. She had eventually made her way to London, where she hoped to find employment working for a modiste. One look at her shabby, wrinkled appearance and she was turned away time and time again. And even while the babe within her rounded and swelled, her hopes were gnashed to bits. She was forced to sell off what few possessions she had been able to take with her in order to simply put food in her mouth.

London had been as terrifying as she remembered—and far less friendly than she recalled. Though Cassie would have joyously accepted even the most menial of jobs, one scornful glance at her expanding middle and the door was slammed in her face. She had spent the first weeks in January begging on the streets.

Then came the day she thought she spied Gabriel near the riverfront. Once again, she fled. It was only later she realized how foolish it was to think he would even care should he chance to see her.

No doubt he thought he was well rid of her.

It was at a local inn in a fishing village near Brighton that her journey ended. The cook's assistant had quit to join the crew of a cargo ship bound for India. Though she would not have thought it possible, Avery was far worse than Black Jack had ever been. The wage he paid her was but a pittance. Still, he allowed her to sleep in the attic, and he allotted her a meal a day, to be taken after her work was done.

A sudden tightening of her belly made her draw a deep breath. Her hands gripped the edge of the wooden table; she smiled slightly as the spasm eased.

He moved often now, this child beneath her heart. She carried a boy, of that she was convinced. But her smile was altogether fleeting. Gabriel would never see his son. He would never know his son.

He did not *want* his son.

Unwittingly, her mind spanned the weeks, back to her last days at Farleigh. Oh, what a fool she had been! She had thought that Gabriel had begun to care for her, perhaps even love her a little. And she had so hoped the baby might be a new beginning for them, that they might truly begin to build a life together, and at last put vengeance and mistrust behind them.

Someday, she told herself, this bittersweet pain in her soul would lessen. But when . . . *when*?

As for the future, Cassie dared not speculate. She was well aware that Avery would not let her stay once the baby was born. His greed would not allow him to tolerate an idle pair of hands for even a few days. He would thrust her back out into the streets, and then where would she be, for who would hire a woman with a babe in her arms? So while her body ached from hour upon hour of exhausting toil, fear and worry preyed upon her endlessly.

Her mind thus occupied, she did not notice Avery's entrance into the kitchen.

"Did you not hear me, girl?" He pinched the side of her breast cruelly. "We need help out in the common room, so stop your dallying! Some well-breeched young gent's decided he wants brandy, not ale—the table in the far corner. See to it and be quick about it!"

Cassie hastened to obey. As she placed a bottle of brandy onto a tray, she caught sight of her hands. Between the winter's cold and the hours spent scrubbing the floor, they were chafed and reddened, as badly as they'd been at Black Jack's. She smiled rather sadly. Definitely not the hands of a lady. Evelyn would have been horrified.

Seconds later she walked across the floor of the common room, her gait careful as she headed toward the table in the corner. Though the memory made her ache inside, Cassie could not help but recall another time when she had taken a bottle of brandy to another rich, well-dressed gentleman . . .

Across the crowded room, she spotted him. He was alone, his back to her. All at once a staggering dread gripped her chest. Her breath caught halfway up her throat. The tilt of his head was so very familiar, the set of his shoulders wide and proud. Her heart lurched. Oh, but her mind was playing cruel tricks on her. And surely her eyes played her false . . .

He turned his head then, providing her a clear view of his profile, flawlessly chiseled and wickedly handsome.

Her heart began to pound. She felt the blood drain from her face. The tray slipped from trembling fingers. "No," she whispered faintly. "Oh, no . . ."

In the weeks after Cassie's disappearance, Gabriel knew fear as never before.

He despised himself for lashing her with his tongue as he had. All along, he had thought only of himself—and getting even with his father. He had used her with a callous disregard for her feelings and how all this would affect her. Yet for all her starch and spirit, she was scarcely invincible . . .

He had hurt her, hurt her immeasurably.

Though he fought it with all he possessed, there were times he could not control the wandering of his mind. Times when his thoughts veered straight to his mother. It was despair which had killed his mother . . . what if he'd driven Cassie to the same fate?

It was enough to make him break out in a cold sweat. Surely the hand of Providence could not be so cruel as to deal him such a blow *twice* . . .

Gabriel was not a man to pray, but he prayed as never before.

Four months later, he had begun to despair of ever finding her.

In the hope that it would give him more time to devote to finding her, he had decided to sell a portion of his shipping business. It was this which brought him to this small village near Brighton. The owner of a fishing fleet there had inherited a goodly sum from an uncle, and had expressed an interest in purchasing several of his vessels. An hour of dickering and they had finally settled on a price and terms. His solicitor would visit as soon as the papers were drawn up.

Now, his dealings concluded, Gabriel sat alone, feeling morose and detached and totally unmindful of his boisterous surroundings. Thomas had gone back outside to await him in the carriage, yet Gabriel could not find the energy to move.

It was then that his ears picked out a crash, and the splintering sound of glass . . . He glanced around in idle curiosity.

Suddenly he couldn't breathe.

Oddly, it was the shape of her that registered first—round, full, heavy with child.

In a heartbeat, he was on his feet, the movement so sudden his chair banged to the floor behind him. "Cassie . . . *Cassie!*"

Sheer horror flooded her eyes. She whirled, her intention plainly to put as much distance between them as possible. But she hadn't gone more than a few steps before she found herself jerked around.

It was Avery. His fingers bit cruelly into her flesh. He shoved her back against the end of a table. Had Cassie not flung her hand behind her to reach for the edge, she would have lost her balance.

He drew back his fist. "You clumsy bitch!" he snarled. "You'll pay for that, by Gawd!"

Before he could make good his threat, his arm was wrenched behind his back. "Lay a hand on her," said a voice from behind him, "and I promise you'll never see the dawn of another day." For all that his tone was deadly calm, Gabriel's face was a mask of lethal fury—and unrelenting purpose.

"All right, all right—just let me be!" Avery whirled, his thick lips curled. He had backed off but he was hardly subdued. "What's it to you if I give the wench the clubbing she deserves? It just so happens I pay 'er wages—"

"And it just so happens she's carrying my babe, so you'd be wise to find yourself another barmaid. She's leaving with me, and I'll kill any man who thinks to try and stop me." It was not a threat, but a mere statement of fact. The atmosphere had gone utterly quiet—and utterly sober.

Glittering and dangerous, Gabriel's gaze encompassed the room. "No? A wise choice, gentlemen." He flipped a gold coin toward Avery. It struck the floor, landing between his feet. "Here. That should more than cover the cost of the brandy." With that he caught Cassie's hand.

Struck dumb by his presence, Cassie was scarcely aware as he tugged her toward the door. Her head was still spinning, her heart pounding madly as he nudged her into the carriage and slammed the door. A signal to Thomas and they were off.

She shivered, whether from cold or reaction she did not know. Gabriel was here . . . *here*. A dozen different emotions blustered and squalled within her. Anger. Frustration. Strongest of all was a soul-deep humiliation.

"I think you owe me an explanation. What the *devil* were you doing in that place?"

He sat across from her, silently accusing. Harshly condemning. Her gaze dropped. She began to tremble. Oh, why did he have to find her—why did it have to be *here*? Her face burned with shame and embarrassment. Nor did she want him to see her like this—oh, she knew how terrible she looked. Her hair had lost its luster. Her skin was pale, stretched tautly over her cheekbones. She felt so ugly and cumbersome . . . A pang rent her breast. Oh, but how fitting that was! Hadn't Gabriel told her that long-ago day she would forever be an encumbrance?

She could not stand to be an obligation. A duty. Didn't he know that was why she'd left?

"Answer me, Cassie. What the hell are you doing here?"

She stared at her hands, clasped in her lap as she sought to still their shaking. Her lips began to quiver. She could not summon the courage to meet his gaze.

"Dammit, *look* at me!"

She did. It proved her downfall. Her mouth was tremulous. Tears stung the back of her throat. Her chest hurt with the effort it took not to break down. "Why did you have to find me?" she said brokenly. "Why?"

His jaw locked hard and tight. "What! Do you mean to tell me you would prefer to remain here? You were so anxious to escape the life you knew at Black Jack's—but that place is no better than all you left behind in Charleston! I still can't believe you left me—and for this yet!"

"Did you think that was what I wanted? I tried to find a position as a seamstress in London . . . And then I thought I saw you there . . . I knew I must flee . . ."

In jagged bursts her story came out. Gabriel went white as he listened. Guilt and shame forged a searing blot on his soul. He had no one to blame but himself. To think of her alone on the streets of London, with no money, nowhere to stay . . . She could have been robbed, beaten, killed!

His hands came down on her shoulders. He dragged her onto the seat next to him. His fingers curled into her arms. "God," he cried. "Did you really think I wouldn't look for you? How could you think that—how?"

Tears welled in her beautiful golden eyes. "How could I not?" A million layers of hurt bled through her tremulous whisper.

Gabriel shook his head, his tone as anguished as hers. "I was a fool, Cassie. I was wrong to say what

I did, for I did not mean it, I swear! I came back to Farleigh that same night, only to find you gone . . . I know I hurt you and I would take it back if only I could. But I have suffered, too . . . My God, did you ever think how I would feel when I discovered you gone? All these weeks of searching, wondering where you were, if you were all right . . . I nearly went out of my mind! And you could have come home, Cassie. You *should* have!"

She hugged herself, trying hard not to tremble and failing miserably. "To what? Your scorn? Your disdain? You did not want me," she cried with heartbreaking candor. "I could not stay knowing how you felt . . . I had to leave . . . don't you see, I had to!"

Her despair was his undoing. It wrenched at everything inside him. She resisted as he began to pull her close, but she was no match for either his strength or his resolve. His embrace engulfed her; with his arms he encircled her tight and close, wrapping his greatcoat around them both.

At his touch, something inside her seemed to break loose. Suddenly it was all pouring out. Her heartache and grief. Her shame and fear.

"All I ever wanted was to please you. I wanted to be the lady . . . you thought I could never be." Her fingers clenched and unclenched on his chest. "I should have known better than to hope . . . My mother did not want me. Your father did not want me. *You* did not want me." She began to sob. Helplessly. Uncontrollably. "What's wrong with me, Gabriel? What's wrong with me?"

His hold tightened. His heart twisted as he held her, her arms so brittle he thought they might break. "There's nothing wrong with you, love." His whisper brushed the baby-soft skin of her temple. He kissed away the tears cascading from her eyes. "You're sweet and lovely. Beautiful and desirable. All a man could want. All *I* want."

If she heard, there was no sign of it. She lay against him and cried her heart out until she was limp and exhausted, her emotions bled dry. Gabriel held her, his own throat achingly tight. At last strain and fatigue took their toll; she fell asleep curled against his chest.

It was very late when the carriage rolled down the long curving lane toward Farleigh Hall. Gabriel's expression was bleak as he carried her up the staircase to her room. He tugged off her gown and slippers, laid her on the bed, and tucked the counterpane beneath her chin.

She stirred, uttering a low moan. Gabriel was beside her in an instant. "Hush, love," he soothed. With his fingertips he swept a tangle of golden strands from the curve of her cheek. "It's all right. You're safe now."

She quieted, turning her cheek into his palm. She seemed so pale and fragile, he thought with a knifelike pang. With a sigh of weariness, he straightened. In the darkness he stripped off his clothes and slipped in beside her. Carefully, so as not to wake her, he reached for her, drawing her loosely into his arms. She nestled against him, unconsciously seeking his warmth.

He watched her as she slept, feeling the rise and fall of her breasts against him. His fingertips light and immeasurably gentle, he traced the outline of her tear-ravaged face, the curve of her cheek. She was so trusting, so innocent.

All I wanted was to please you. I wanted to be the lady you thought I could never be.

His heart squeezed.

What's wrong with me, Gabriel? What's wrong with me?

He thought of how she had cried, her spirit broken, her pride in tatters. He cursed himself again and again. Christ, but he had been so blind, so careless and hard. She had been so starved for love, for affection. Yet what had he given her?

Cassie, he thought. *Oh, Cassie, what have I done to you?*

It was then he felt it, a slight stirring there, where her belly pressed his side.

There was a life growing in her. A part of her . . . a part of *him*. How could he turn his back on that? On her? A wrenching pain ripped his insides. How could he do to his own child what his father had done to him?

Yet he knew how deeply he had hurt her. All along he had done nothing but hurt her! So what was he to do? Thrust her from his life? No. He could not. He *would* not.

Easing back just a bit, he spread his fingers wide on the mound of her belly. Holding his breath, he waited. His reward came scant seconds later—his unborn child rolled beneath his hand, as awake as his sire. The ghost of a smile touched his lips. He was glad that Cassie slept, for he knew if she awoke, she would no doubt slap his hands away.

He stayed that way for a long time, his hand on her belly, his palm conforming to her tummy, solid and warm. Feeling and discovering. Stroking and marveling. Pondering . . .

And praying.

Eventually the babe's movements quieted. Cassie slept on, unaware. Gabriel turned her in his arms, cradling her—cradling their child. Very gently he kissed the swell of her belly, her closed eyelids, the softness of her lips, then he lay back and closed his eyes.

It was a long, long time before he joined her in slumber.

Chapter 22

Weary beyond measure, Cassie slept through the morning and well into the afternoon. When at last she awoke, tepid sunlight slanted in through the curtains. The hour was indecently late. A fire crackled in the hearth, casting out its golden glow. The room was warm and cozy, yet she felt curiously tired and reluctant to move. And there was a nagging ache in her back.

Just then the door opened. "My lady?" whispered a voice.

It was Gloria. Cassie turned her head to find the little maid peeping through the crack of the door. When she saw that her mistress was finally awake, she rushed across the floor.

"Oh, my lady," she cried. "You are home! Oh, I cannot tell you how glad I am that you have returned!" She dropped to her knees beside the bed, tears flowing freely.

Cassie smiled sadly and laid her hand on the girl's head. If only for Gloria's sake, she wished she could say it was good to *be* back. Yet she felt neither joy nor regret; indeed, it seemed rather strange to be at Farleigh once again.

Within minutes a tray of food was whisked onto her lap, including her favorite pot of chocolate. She had little appetite, but she forced herself to eat. While she ate, her bath was prepared, strategically placed before the hearth to take full advantage of its warmth. She soaked for a luxuriously long time while Gloria chattered on, straightening the bed and dusting as if her mistress had never been gone.

At last Cassie rose from the tub, giving herself over to Gloria's capable hands. But she sighed when Gloria moved to the wardrobe. "I'm afraid my choices will be a bit limited," she murmured. Her hand fluttered self-consciously to her middle. "I daresay not a one of those gowns will fit."

Gloria plucked a voluminous flannel nightgown from the shelf. "No matter," the girl said briskly. "His lordship gave strict instructions you're to stay in bed and lift nary a finger." She dropped the nightgown over her mistress's head and twitched it into place. Then she brushed Cassie's hair and left the tresses loose and flowing around her shoulders. The task completed, Gloria urged her mistress back into bed.

Though it was in her mind to protest such cosseting as silly and wholly unnecessary, Cassie leaned back against the plumpness of her pillow, telling herself she would rest for just a few minutes. Her body gauged its needs far better, however. Though she'd have sworn it nigh impossible, soon her eyelids began to droop. She dozed.

The blue-gray haze of twilight seeped within the room when she woke again. Stung by the sense that she was being watched, her eyes snapped open.

Gabriel stood on the threshold. Apparently he'd just come in from riding. Her heart gave an odd little catch. She'd forgotten how devastatingly handsome he was! His cravat was impeccably wound around his throat, spotless as always. He wore knee-high boots and tight breeches that shamelessly displayed his muscular thighs like a second skin.

Seeing that she was awake, he closed the door and strode toward her. Cassie braced her hands on the mattress and pushed herself up to a sitting position, feeling acutely clumsy and awkward, and keenly at a disadvantage—definitely not a desirable state when dealing with her husband! She pushed at the tousled length of her hair, wishing there had been time to run a comb through it.

He did not stand or take the chair at her bedside, as she expected. Instead he sat on the bed, so close she felt the steely hardness of his thigh against the softness of her own, even through the thickness of the quilt.

Anxiety gnawed at her. The memory of how she'd wept in his arms last night soared high in her mind. Did he despise her for her weakness? Was he disgusted for her lack of control? Her hands knotted atop the counterpane. She knew not what to say. She knew not what to do.

He caught at her hand. Strong, warm fingers curled around her own. She quivered slightly at his touch. That, too, she had not expected.

"Better today, Yank?"

She swallowed; her nod was jerky. The cast of his mouth was unsmiling, yet not so very grim. How much better prepared she was for his rancor—his kindness made her come all undone!

Gabriel's gaze searched her features. She looked very young and vulnerable, her hair tumbling artlessly over her shoulders and down her back. But she was so thin! He could feel the fragility of her bones within his grasp. Her skin was like parchment, so pale and almost transparent. Despite her thickened waist, she seemed so frail she would break in half.

"Thank God I found you." His voice was low and intense. "I shudder to think what might have happened had I not."

Cassie stiffened.

His grip on her fingers tightened, not hurting her, but not relenting either. "No," he commanded softly when she tried to free herself, "do not draw away."

She said nothing. Her eyes, wide and anxious, grazed his.

"I meant what I said last night," he said quietly. "I deeply regret the pain I have caused you." He paused, and his voice grew softer still. " 'Tis my hope we can put the past behind us and start anew."

She trembled. This was a side of Gabriel she had yet to see revealed to her. Humble. Contrite. And she could have sworn tenderness lingered in the eyes that dwelled upon her. Tenderness and caring.

No . . . *no*. She dared not believe it. She *did* not believe it.

"I cannot think why you should want to." Her tone was stiff. She could neither hide her bitterness nor deny it. Even now, she could still feel the sting of his anger when they had last parted.

"I bear your name but we have nothing else in common."

A glint of anger flashed in eyes. "I disagree, Cassie. We have *this* in common." In one swift movement he shoved aside the covers. Deliberately he laid both hands on the hard mound of her belly, splaying his fingers possessively wide. "You will soon bear my child. That changes everything."

"That changes nothing!" She tried to push his hands aside but she should have known it was useless. When he was determined, there was no stopping him. And so in the end, she glared her indignant outrage.

"You made your feelings very clear, my lord earl, very clear indeed. You said you did not want a child, an heir. But in truth, you did not want a child of *me*." A hot ache constricted her throat. Lord, but it hurt to say it aloud! "It's just as I once told you, Gabriel. We are no different than your father and your mother!"

His jaw hardened. "You're wrong, Cassie. You are my wife. I want this child. I want *you*."

"Oh, stop!" she cried. "If there can be nothing else between us, then let there be truth, at least. I am nothing but the club you wield to hurt your father. I can think of only one reason you have decided you want this babe—'tis only because you see him as another weapon to use against your father!"

A dull red flush crept beneath Gabriel's cheekbones. "I am trying to rectify matters as best I am able."

"What! Do you tell me now that it's guilt which prompts your concern? Oh, but I forget you will someday be the duke of Farleigh. You must think of your duty, your obligations. And a wife and heir are among them, are they not?"

He snatched his hands from her belly. "I hardly think it's wrong for a man to want to take care of his wife and child."

Something twisted within her. If only it were so simple! She was suddenly overwhelmed, uncertain of her feelings, but most of all, so uncertain of his.

"You talk of what you want. But what of what *I* want? Were you thinking of me when you brought me back here?"

"That was my only thought!" He stood, towering over her, both irritated and frustrated. "My God, Cassie, have you looked in the mirror? You look like a wraith!"

She caught her breath—coming from him, such insult was unbearable. All at once she felt as if her world were splintering apart, but she would not let him glimpse her pain. And it was so much easier to seek refuge in anger.

"Oh, but I—I wish you had never found me. And I won't stay here, do you hear? I won't!"

"You would rather be back where I found you?"

"Yes . . . yes! I hate you . . . do you hear? I hate you!"

The muscles in Gabriel's face seemed to freeze. "I refuse to let you go back to the life you were leading," he stated through clenched teeth. "And you *will* stay here, Cassie, if I have to lock you in your room! For now, you are clearly overwrought and I see no point in continuing this conversation. I will return when you are feeling more rational."

He spun around and strode across the floor.

Cassie shoved aside the blankets and swung her feet to the floor. "Oh, but 'tis just like you to walk away! But I won't be pushed aside again. Do you hear? I won't!"

He strode into the hall. His gait never faltered.

"Damn you, Gabriel . . . *Gabriel!*"

His name was a scream at the last, but mingled within was a note of desperation that sent ice running through his veins. He bolted back into her chamber. She stood at the side of the bed, one thin hand around the poster at the end of the bed, the other splayed upon her belly. Below her waist, her nightgown was soaked.

She raised huge, tear-bright eyes to his. "The water has broken," she gasped. "Oh, God, the babe is coming . . ."

He bent. His arms came around her with almost painstaking gentleness. Very carefully he lifted her and laid her back down upon the bed. Looking up at him, Cassie spied on his face the one thing she had not expected to see . . . Fear.

It dawned on her then . . . She began to sob. "Oh, it can't be now . . . it's too soon. It's too soon!"

He tried to straighten. She clutched at his hands. "Don't leave me. Gabriel, please don't leave me!"

Her piteous cry tore at him. "It's all right, sweet." He squeezed her fingers, then bent to kiss her quivering lips. "I must send Thomas for the physician. But I'll be back within minutes, love, I promise."

Love. It was as if a giant pair of hands squeezed her heart. Gabriel didn't love her—he would never love her. Yet his touch was so tender, his words so sweet. She could almost have believed he cared, at least just a little . . .

Gloria soon rushed inside. "My lady!" she cried. "The earl said the babe comes!"

Cassie struggled for a calm she was far from feeling. Even while she longed for her body to be rid of its burden, she was terrified of the ordeal ahead. She tried to smile. "I'm sure it will be hours yet. First births are always longer, I believe."

With Gloria's assistance, her sodden gown was exchanged for a fresh one. She had just leaned back against the pillows when she experienced a sudden tautening of her middle. She gasped and let out her breath slowly. It was then that Gabriel reappeared. He displayed not the slightest hesitation whatsoever, but drew up a chair next to the head of the bed, bold as you please, and took his wife's hands.

It was some time before the physician arrived. Dr. Hampton was a stout, pot-bellied old man with a kindly demeanor. Cassie had begun to pant softly at each gathering of her womb, for each such occurrence was longer and stronger in intensity. Gabriel, whose temper was simmering over the physician's delay, took swift and vehement exception when he was politely but firmly advised to vacate his chair and wait downstairs.

"I will not be banished from this room. I was present when this child was conceived. I see no reason why I should not be present when he is born."

Dr. Hampton rolled his eyes and shook his shaggy head. Most expectant fathers proved themselves a veritable nuisance and he fully expected the same of this one. Yet as the hours wore on, it was clear the earl was the exception. His presence seemed to ease his wife's fears as well.

As her labor progressed, Cassie tried to stifle her cries. As one especially strong contraction gripped her belly, a low moan escaped.

"I'm sorry," she whispered when she was able to catch her breath. "I'm such a coward, I know."

Gabriel's heart contracted. Her eyes were two glassy pools of endless pain. With his fingers he brushed the damp strands from her brow. "A coward?" He chided her gently. "I think not, Yank. You're a woman like no other—brave and strong— the strongest woman I know."

Tenderly he wiped the beads of sweat from her brow, but his face was ashen as he watched over his wife and whispered encouragement. Had she spent these last months coddled and well-fed, he'd not have been quite so worried. But she was so thin, so weak, and it was as if he could see her struggle draining away her strength. And she possessed so little in reserve to begin with . . .

Another spasm knotted her womb, harder and longer than the rest. A tremendous pressure began to build, there between her thighs. Though she tried to mask her suffering, a cry of anguish tore from her lips.

Her nails dug into Gabriel's palm, slicing his skin. When it was over, her head fell back upon the pillow, her beautiful hair matted and tangled. With a gasp she went limp—so limp that for an instant sheer panic leaped in his breast.

Deep down he was shaken to his very soul. He hated himself for his helplessness, yet there was nothing he could do to help her. Icy tingles of fear ran along his spine. He alternately cursed and prayed. Christ! How much more of this could she stand?

But with the next contraction the physician's voice rapped out sharply. "There, I can see the crown! When the urge comes, you must push and not fight it . . . yes, yes! That's the way . . . I have his head . . . once more and then you may rest a bit . . ."

A thin, bleating cry filled the air. Gabriel did not see the tiny, wriggling body in the physician's hands. His every sense, his entire being, was focused on the slight figure that lay prone in the bed. He bent and kissed her full on the lips. " 'Tis done, sweet. I knew you could do it, I knew it."

Gabriel rose to his feet. He was only half-aware as Dr. Hampton passed the infant to Gloria, then turned to deliver the afterbirth. He was still standing there numbly when he felt a tug on his sleeve. Gloria stood before him, her round face beaming. Shyly she placed a small bundle into his arms.

Slowly he pushed away the flannel covering, revealing the tiny new creature. He beheld a miniature little face with little dark brows screwed up in a frown. He swallowed, and saw pink, healthy skin, naked, flailing limbs . . . He stared in mingled awe and disbelief. A tremor of emotion rushed through him, weakening his knees, even as humble pride swelled his chest. He wanted to shout, to fall to his knees in prayer and thanksgiving.

Instead he whispered, "We have a son, Cassie. *We have a son.*"

Cassie's eyes fluttered open. She turned her head, her vision clouded by a dull gray film. Hovering on the fringes of unconsciousness, she battled to keep her eyes open. She was so tired, but she so desperately wanted just a glimpse of her baby.

Gabriel glanced up just as she tried to raise herself on an elbow, shaking with the effort. Tears glazed her eyes as she collapsed weakly, tears that reached out and caught hold of his heart. He was there in an instant, easing his precious bundle down beside her and parting the blanket with one big hand so she could see.

"Is he . . . all right?" Gabriel had to strain to hear, so feeble was her voice.

"I see ten fingers, ten toes . . . There is certainly no surfeit of flesh—or hair either!—but he looks to be a fine little lad."

The merest smile grazed her lips. Her fears extinguished, her strength at last depleted, she closed her eyes and slept.

When Cassie woke again, afternoon sunshine trickled through the windows. She stirred, wincing a little as she turned to her side. Gloria scurried in just then, a tray in her hands.

"Ah, you're awake and just in time! Are you hungry, milady?"

"Do you know, I—I'm starving." Cassie was startled to find that she was indeed ravenous. She ate every bite of the steaming lamb stew and fragrant, yeasty bread. Afterwards, Gloria brought a warm basin of water with which she was able to wash. Once her nightgown had been changed, her hair brushed and braided, she felt distinctly more presentable.

She cleared her throat as Gloria carried her toilet articles back to the dressing table. "Is my husband home?"

"I believe he's in the study." The maid gave a hearty chuckle. "Oh, but you should have seen him last night, milady. He'll be a proud, strutting papa to be sure—why, it was all the doctor could do to pry the little one away from him so he could examine him proper."

So Gabriel had been well pleased with his son . . . a little of her anxious dread departed. Perhaps it was silly of her, but somewhere deep inside she'd been half-afraid he might reject him. She glanced longingly toward the corner, where a cradle had been placed. Peeping out from the end of the blankets was the top of a tiny dark head.

Just then, there was the faintest movement from within the heap of flannel. A woeful little cry emanated forth. Gloria laughed when she spied the leap of joy in her mistress's eyes. Cassie leaned up on an elbow and looked on eagerly as the maid plucked the infant from his nest and changed his napkin. She had nearly finished when a tall form appeared in the doorway.

It was Gabriel, freshly bathed and shaven from the look of him. Cassie's pulse leaped and skittered. His hair gleamed dark and damp and she could smell the faint scent of the cologne he used. Gloria had straightened, lifting the fretful infant to her shoulder. Gabriel wordlessly beckoned with a finger, and the maid passed the child to him.

Miraculously, the babe quieted the instant he was snug in his father's arms. The maid bobbed a curtsy and quietly retreated. Cassie did not notice, for her attention was utterly commanded by the pair which even now came near.

His lips quirked as he addressed the babe. "I think your mother feels it's time the two of you met properly, my little lord." An unmistakable tenderness lurked in those silvery eyes as he bent to lower their son into her waiting arms.

Cassie scarcely felt the brush of his hands as he passed the bundle to her. Gabriel was forgotten—everything was forgotten as she felt the slight weight of her baby nestled in the curve of her elbow for the very first time. A rush of delight poured through her, sweet and pure.

Her babe regarded her with his father's usual severity, tiny little brows drawn over a nubbin nose. His eyes were a deep, murky blue. A fine dark fuzz covered his head. But even Cassie, with her limited knowledge of infants, knew he was smaller than most newborns.

A tremor went through her. She cradled his head in her palm. "He's so tiny," she whispered. "Oh, Gabriel, what if—"

Gabriel laid the back of his knuckles against her flushed cheek. "The physician said he appears to be in exceedingly fine health despite his early arrival in the world," he said gently.

Cassie squeezed her eyes shut, for a moment too choked up to speak. She was lucky, she realized, shaken to her very soul. If anything had happened to him, she'd have felt guilty for the rest of her days.

After a moment, she poked curiously at the faded white gown he wore.

Gabriel had perched himself on the side of the bed. "I'm afraid we were rather ill-equipped for an infant in the house quite so soon," he said with a crooked smile. "We borrowed several items from the cook's daughter until Father and Mrs. McGee get back from London. They left very early this morning to see to his needs."

A vague memory surfaced, of Edmund standing beside the bed, a smile creasing his face. Edmund . . . smiling? Surely it was her imagination!

Her quizzical gaze had traveled to the cradle in the corner, fashioned of dark, polished mahogany.

"The cradle, too, is an old one, I'm afraid—mine and Stuart's. My father sent Davis to the attic to retrieve it." Gabriel paused. "But we can certainly purchase a new one if you'd like."

His father again. Cassie resisted the urge to glance at him sharply. Usually when he spoke of Edmund there was a decided edge in his tone. Yet curiously, such was not the case now. Could it be that in the time she'd been gone, the two had mended their differences?

The notion progressed no further, for the baby decided he'd been patient long enough. He was impatient for his dinner, and it appeared he was determined both his parents should know it.

Cassie started at his sudden loud squall. Gabriel sighed and reluctantly reached for his son. "We've engaged a wet nurse from the village," he murmured. "I'll bring him back as soon as he's done, I promise—"

But Cassie was not about to relinquish her precious bundle. "A wet nurse!" she cried. "There is no need for one! I can feed him myself!"

Gabriel hesitated. "The physician said he must be nursed every two hours until he begins to gain some flesh," he said slowly. "And ladies do not usually nurse their own—"

"I fail to see what difference that makes," she said, her chin tipped high. "We both know I am no lady."

Gabriel's lips tightened. "I have no objection to your nursing him, Cassie. I am concerned over your health and I merely thought you might find such a demand taxing." His arrogance returned in full measure. "But I do not care for the implication you are less than a lady—less than what you are. You are the countess of Wakefield and the mother of my son, and as such, I will hear no slander against you, even when it comes from your own lips."

Cassie ducked her head. The babe was wailing in earnest now. She was suddenly ashamed of her pettiness. Gabriel showed no signs of leaving to allow her privacy to feed the baby, and after making such an issue over it she realized she had no choice but to see the deed done.

Gabriel's unceasing regard made her nervous. Her fingers tugged at the drawstring at her neckline. The material gave way, sliding down her arm and exposing the round, rosy-tipped fullness of her breast. Feeling acutely clumsy and awkward, she turned her son's body ever so slightly. Quite by accident he latched onto her nipple and began to suck.

The quiet which followed was somehow more strident than the babe's cries. She took a deep, shuddering breath. "Please don't be angry with me." Her voice was low and choked.

He touched her then, stroking the curve of her cheek with the pad of his thumb. He leaned close, so close she could feel the warmth of body and breath, and for a heartstopping second she thought he might kiss her. She wanted him to, she realized. She wanted it with a yearning that made her feel all hot and shivery inside.

"I am not angry," he said very softly. "I am only very very glad that you are back where you belong." Pinned by the raw emotion in his eyes, Cassie could not look away. But his thumb merely brushed the fullness of her lower lip, then was gone.

His gaze fell to their son. "Have you given any thought to what we might name him?"

Feeling bereft but determined not to show it, Cassie bit her lip. "Actually," she said very low, "I do have a name in mind." She did not confess that she had never doubted she would bear him a son. "I have always liked the name Jonathan . . . and I thought perhaps Stuart for a second name . . ." She held her breath and waited. For the life of her, she was not certain what Gabriel's reaction might be.

"Jonathan Stuart." He murmured the name experimentally, and then his expression grew incredibly warm. "I like that, sweet. Jonathan Stuart he shall be."

Her heart brimmed. In all her days, she did not know when she'd known such happiness, such contentment. Perhaps Gabriel had been right to bring her back. He loved his son—of that she had no doubt. And the knowledge filled her with a joyous peacefulness. Even if he never came to love her, pride in their son was something they would share forever . . .

She could ask for no more.

Chapter 23

It was a week before Cassie was allowed to leave her bed. She protested her confinement heartily, but either Gabriel or Gloria made certain it was enforced. In truth, she did little more than eat, sleep, and nurse Jonathan. Soon she began to regain her strength and color.

Deep in her heart, she knew Gabriel had been right to bring her back to Farleigh, for now that she had held her child in her arms, she wanted everything for him. On her own, she could never have provided for him as Gabriel could. Nightly she gave thanks to the Lord, for Jonathan would have so much that she had never had. He would never be hungry. Never lack for a roof over his head. But she was determined that he would also grow up knowing he was loved and wanted . . .

She had resisted at first when Gabriel suggested hiring a nurse, but falling to Gabriel and Evelyn's persuasive arguments, Cassie relented. She did insist, however, that the choice of help remain solely in her hands.

Although both women Cassie interviewed, at the recommendation of Edmund's reliable sources, were no doubt eminently capable, in Cassie's mind, they were both stiff and crusty and decidedly glacial. She wanted someone warm and vibrant, who was unafraid to laugh—someone Jonathan could trust as well as love. In the end, she chose a big raw-boned girl from the village. Alice had sparkling brown eyes and a warm, ready smile. With eight younger brothers and sisters, she also had a wealth of experience with babies. Even Jonathan appeared to like her. He had cooed and promptly fallen asleep in the crook of her arm, quite content as his mother conducted the interview. Cassie suspected that Edmund did not particularly care for her choice, but she was confident she had chosen well.

But where Gabriel was concerned, there was still so much unresolved tension between them. Though his manner was not precisely cold, and he was always faultlessly polite, Cassie was tormented. She loved him so! And she craved some outward sign that he cared for her, at least a little . . .

But time only ripened the distance between them.

As the days turned to weeks, Cassie's heart cried out in anguish. She wavered between hurt and indignation, hope and yearning. Not once had he returned to her bed, though Dr. Hampton had tactfully made it clear to both of them there was no need to abstain any longer.

But Gabriel had made no sign that he wanted her in that regard. Cassie was secretly devastated. Had the sight of her misshapen, pregnant body killed his passion? She was newly slim, with the exception of her breasts, which were noticeably fuller. But perhaps Gabriel no longer desired her. She ached to think she had lost even that!

In the midst of her agitation, Christopher came to call one bright afternoon in late June. Gabriel was not there, but was out tending to estate business. Cassie invited him to stay in the hopes that Gabriel would return. While they took tea in the drawing room, Christopher tickled Jonathan beneath the chin and exclaimed how he'd grown since he'd last visited several weeks earlier. After Alice took the baby upstairs, Christopher glanced at his watch, then arose.

"It's time I took my leave. I've lingered long enough and it appears Gabriel may be some time yet."

Cassie walked with him outside. They stood at the top of the wide stone stairway and waited for a groom to bring his horse. Christopher slipped his hands into his pockets, then turned to Cassie, his expression faintly sheepish.

"Actually, Cassie, I have some exciting news I thought to share with you and Gabriel."

"Well," Cassie said lightly. "Since Gabriel did not have the good grace to appear, you shall just have to tell me."

Christopher chuckled. "Very well, then. Do you know the old manor house along the lane north of here?"

"I do indeed! I pass it when I ride to Warrenton. 'Tis truly a shame no one lives there! Why, it would be quite lovely if only it had the proper care and were not so neglected."

"I am quite inclined to agree, though I daresay that will very soon be rectified."

Cassie blinked. "What! Do you mean that you . . . why, Christopher . . ."

He laughed at her astonishment. "Yes, Cassie, 'tis true. You see before you the new owner. In fact, I will spend this very night there."

"Oh, Christopher, I'm so pleased!" She exclaimed her delight, but couldn't resist teasing him. "Hmmm. Does this mean you have given up your wild, wicked ways in order to become a gentleman of leisure?"

His grin was infectious. "I must say, with Gabriel settling down so admirably which only a year ago no one would have considered even remotely possible, I suppose anything could happen!"

Cassie's heart beat a little faster. Was it true, then, that Gabriel was content? Oh, if only she dared hope . . . "Now that you have acquired a country house, Christopher, you lack only one thing."

"And what might that be?"

"A wife to tame you!"

To her surprise, his smile withered. "I would like nothing more," he said, and it was almost as if he spoke to himself. "But that is the one thing that will never be."

His ruddy features were somber. A wistful, almost melancholy sadness had entered his eyes. Cassie frowned.

"Why do you say that, Christopher? You are young. You are handsome. I cannot imagine why a young lady would refuse if you chose to pay court to her."

He was silent for a moment. " 'Tis not in the refusal of the lady in question that the problem lies." With that cryptic statement, his gaze flitted north, to his newly acquired manor house . . . and Warrenton.

Cassie caught her breath. Comprehension dawned with a rush. "Why, it's Evelyn, isn't it?" She answered her own question. Of course it was. She recalled how often she'd seen them together in London—dancing. Sometimes just talking . . . perhaps it had started even then.

"Christopher, you and Evelyn!" She laughed her delight. "Why, that's wonderful!"

A twinge of pain flitted across his face. "No, Cassie. 'Tis impossible."

"But why? Doesn't she love you?"

He hesitated. "She does," he admitted finally. "I bought the manor house so that I could be near her, at least until she marries."

Cassie was horrified. "If you love her, you cannot let her marry someone else! Why don't you simply declare yourself?"

He sighed. "Her father is pompous and of the old guard, Cassie. 'Tis common knowledge he will not be satisfied unless she marries both a fortune *and* a title—an earl at the very least. I am only a lowly baronet, unworthy of his recognition. Were I to declare myself, Warrenton would make certain I *never* saw her again."

Cassie's heart went out to him. "Oh, Christopher, how sad for you both. But you cannot give up hope, not yet. Evelyn still has no serious suitors, nor does she desire any."

"She will not forsake her duty, Cassie. She will not dishonor her father's wishes by going against him." He paused. "And I will not dishonor her by asking such a thing of her."

Cassie bit her lip. A part of her whispered he was right, yet she dared not admit it to him. Instead she touched his sleeve.

"Do not give up," she said softly. "Perhaps there is still some way the two of you can be together. Perhaps a solution can still be found." On impulse she reached out and laid her hands on his shoulders, kissing his cheek before she bid him goodbye.

The memory of Christopher's visit still dwelled in her mind as she made her way upstairs. She peeked into the newly decorated nursery where Jonathan lay sound asleep in his cradle. Her gaze was troubled as she moved further down the hall to her room.

She stood at the windows for a long time, a slender hand parting the curtains. Beyond the rolling expanse of lawn, the purple haze of twilight clung to the treetops. She sighed, seeking to come up with some way to help her friends, to ease their plight. Christopher and Evelyn were both so dear to her heart. If only something could be done to sway the duke of Warrenton, so he might not ruin his daughter's only chance at happiness!

Perhaps Gabriel could persuade his father to talk to Warrenton. The two still rode and hunted together often. She seized on the possibility, determined to put it to him at the first opportunity. Her mind so engrossed, she turned.

She gave an abrupt start, for suddenly there he was, standing not three feet before her.

"Gabriel!" Her laugh was rather shaky. "My word, you startled me! I did not hear you come in."

Apparently he had just returned from his errands. He had not yet changed, and still wore boots and riding clothes. The width of his shoulders completely eclipsed her view of the door, and all at once the room seemed absurdly small. The fact that he was dressed all in black, coupled with the riding crop held between gloved fingers at his side, lent a curious air of menace to his demeanor.

Perhaps not so curious after all.

The cast of his jaw was grim and forbidding. He spoke no words of greeting, nor did he smile. Instead he fixed her with an unwavering gaze of piercing intensity.

"Gabriel?" A faint alarm began to pound along her veins. "Is something wrong?"

"I saw you, Yank. I saw the two of you before he rode off."

Cassie gaped. "Who? Christopher?"

"The very same. So tell me, sweet. Do the two of you deceive me under this very roof?"

Though his tone was mild, his eyes were blistering. Cassie shivered. It spun through her mind that he was jealous. And while a part of her fairly reeled with elation, she was furious that he could think so little of her—and of his friend!

She squared her shoulders, striving for as much dignity as she could muster. "Nothing has changed, Gabriel. *You* have not changed, for I have done nothing to deserve this. You insult me by implying that I have—and you insult Christopher as well."

Across the hall, Jonathan began to cry. Gabriel spun around, his intent clear. Cassie was only half a pace behind.

They were in the nursery now. Cassie spoke up quickly, just as Gabriel reached the cradle. "Here, let me—"

"I'm quite capable, I assure you." He was curtly dismissive.

Cassie stood back as Gabriel's dark hands slid gently beneath Jonathan's small body. Though she had once been convinced such a thing would be impossible, Gabriel's love for his son was unquestionable. A pang twisted her heart. Why couldn't he spare even a measure of it for her?

As always, Jonathan quieted the instant he was picked up. Tucked in the crook of Gabriel's elbow, he gazed at his father with complete and utter trust. Gabriel traced a dark finger down the front of his muslin gown. He chuckled softly when Jonathan seized his finger, carried it to his mouth, and sucked strongly. But the infant voiced his annoyance quite loudly when he realized no food supply was forthcoming. He began to wiggle and squirm, turning his head toward Gabriel's chest.

An elegant brow arched high. "I'm afraid this is something I cannot do for you, Jonathan." Hard gray eyes swiveled to capture hers. Without a word he laid him in her arms.

Cassie settled herself in the chair that overlooked the courtyard. Jonathan's cries had begun to gain in pitch and volume. He rooted frantically against her, anxious and demanding. She rocked him in her arms, trying to soothe him. Her breasts tingled as her milk began to come in. Oh, damn . . . damn!

Gabriel spoke the obvious. "He's hungry, Yank."

The soft line of her lips compressed as she glanced up at him. She wished he would leave her alone to feed her son, and to that end, she let her glare speak for her.

He merely smiled—oh, a demon's smile!—she thought indignantly as he stepped behind her. His hands flashed into her line of vision. She stiffened in shock when he sought out the drawstring of her bodice. A deft, sure tug from those long, strong fingers and her breasts spilled free.

For a mind-splitting instant, his fingers lay hard and warm on the curve of her naked flesh. Then Jonathan latched onto her nipple with eager greed.

Cassie bowed her head low and sought to confine her attention to Jonathan. He was a good, sweet-natured baby who cried only when he was hungry or wet. Nor was he sickly, as she had feared he might be. His belly had grown round and firm, his little cheeks plump. But the peace and contentment that usually slipped over her as she sat and nursed him was glaringly absent.

The disquiet was stifling. Jonathan suckled noisily, the sound loud to Cassie's overwrought nerves. Gabriel stood behind her, stark and remote. Cassie was achingly aware of him. He had been present numerous times before when she'd fed Jonathan, yet now his regard made her feel vulnerable and exposed as never before. He was an expert at bridling his feelings, while suddenly it seemed hers were strewn in every direction! When she switched Jonathan to her other breast, she discreetly tried to tug a blanket up over her exposed flesh and Jonathan's head. Gabriel's hand closed over hers, stopping her cold.

The battle began in earnest.

At length he moved to where she could see him. His eyes were glittering. "Such a devoted mother," he observed mockingly. "A shame you are not such a devoted wife."

"Oh, for pity's sake!" Jonathan had begun to fall asleep at her breast. She had to settle for a heated whisper when she longed to storm at him furiously. "Christopher came to see you, to tell you he bought the manor house near Warrenton!"

"So now he will be our neighbor—how convenient for the two of you."

Now that Jonathan had finished, it appeared there was to be no reprieve. When Alice appeared, Gabriel plucked his son from Cassie's arms and handed him to his nurse. At the door, he stood and awaited her. Cassie smoothed her skirts and tipped her chin high as he took her arm, knowing she had no choice but to accompany him.

In the hall, she tried to free herself of his hold. His grip on her arm merely tightened.

Only after he'd guided her into her room did he release her. He closed the door and crossed his arms over his chest, then continued as if there'd been nary a pause in their conversation.

"I saw you kiss him, Yank. A touching scene, I must say."

Cassie drew a deep, jagged breath. "On the cheek, Gabriel . . . that is all, I swear. It was a kiss meant to comfort—no more!"

Gabriel could not withhold the doubts that crowded his mind. They were bound, by more than just the son they shared. And he could not forget the fervor with which she had claimed she hated him. No matter how sweetly she smiled at him, the knowledge was always there, like a needle beneath his skin.

"Indeed. Tell me, sweet. Are you still so unhappy that I made you return to Farleigh?"

Gabriel did not miss the fleeting shadow that crossed her lovely features. A vile anger swept through him, dark and brooding.

Very deliberately he began to shed his clothes. His jacket was tossed across the arm of a chair. "You comfort Christopher. You tend Jonathan. Well, I am your husband and I fail to see why I am not accorded the same consideration."

Oh, what arrogance! She felt giddy and hot, yet her hands were ice-cold. She pressed them together before her, shaken and uncertain by the tempest she sensed in him.

His shirt landed atop his jacket. "I would disrobe if I were you, Yank. If you do not, it will be my very great pleasure to do it for you."

The sight of his naked, hair-roughened chest made her mouth go dry. "Gabriel," she cried, "you must believe me! It was a kiss on the cheek between friends. Nothing compared to what we have shared!"

By now he was naked. "No? Show me the difference then."

Cassie swallowed. Her chest was so tight she could hardly breathe. She shook her head lest she give in to her weakness, to him.

His hands were on her bare arms now, warm and disturbing. Far more disturbing was his arousal—proudly, rigidly erect. Though she tried not to look she could not help it.

"I repeat, sweet, if I am to believe you, then you must persuade me."

"No!" She drew a deep, burning breath. "Not like this—not when you're so cold and angry!"

Within seconds her clothing was cast aside, leaving her as naked as he. "Stop!" she cried. "I—I will not come to you willingly!" She pounded his chest as he tumbled her down on the bed. "Do you hear me, I will not!" And yet her arms came around him, whether to push him away, or pull him close, she did not know . . .

Furious that she would refuse him, something snapped inside Gabriel then. A crimson mist swam before him that obliterated all thought, all reason. He drove home in one fiercely burning thrust, an iron blade of steel . . . through dry, tender tissue unprepared for his thrusting invasion.

Her body jerked with the power of his entry. Though she tried to choke it back, her cry of hurt rent the air.

Imbedded to the hilt inside her, Gabriel went utterly still.

The stricken sound ripped into him like the tip of a lance. He levered himself up on his elbows to stare at her. Her eyes were wet and swimming with tears. Even as he watched, they brimmed and overflowed.

She began to sob. "Christopher means nothing to me, I swear. Oh, don't you see? It's Evelyn he loves, not me. He only wanted to be close to her—to her, Gabriel, not me!"

His eyes squeezed shut, his features contorted with anguish and desire unchecked. "Cassie," he whispered. "Oh, God . . . Cassie . . ." His blinding fury had vanished, replaced by a deep, abiding shame. He tried to withdraw, his only intent being to spare her.

She wouldn't let him. She wrapped her arms around his neck and clung. She hated what he had just done—his anger. His bitterness. But she did not hate *him*. And she could not stand the thought that he would hate himself if they did not change the memory of this encounter from something painful and grim ... to something wonderful.

"No," she pleaded. "*No*."

"I can't. Cassie, I *can't*." His voice was low and tight. "I am a brute to treat you so."

"You can. Just love me, Gabriel. Just," her voice broke then, "just love me." Her palms framed the rugged plane of his cheeks, the brutal clench of his jaw. She kissed him, with all the shy, sweet longing held deep in her breast, the salty warmth of her tears trapped between their lips.

At first his mouth was closed tight against her ... as closed as his heart, she thought with a wrench of despair. But then his eyes flicked open; they sheared directly into hers. She glimpsed his pain and guilt anew, and with a breathless little cry, shaped her mouth against the heat and hardness of his.

All at once his arms clamped around her body, his hold almost convulsive. And this time when eager, trembling lips lifted to his, he took hot, searing possession of the honeyed interior of her mouth, taking the sweetness she offered so ardently and giving back in full measure.

"Don't leave me again, Cassie." His voice was tinged with a dark desperation, a hoarse mutter against her lips. "Promise me you won't leave me again."

Cassie's heart gave a wild leap. She could have wept for the joy that surged in her veins. He *did* care. Oh, sweet heaven, he did! With a smothered sob of gladness, she locked her arms tight around his neck and shamelessly pressed her lithe young curves tight against his hardness.

She could feel the hunger in his kiss, the thickness of his shaft still incredibly full and snug within her. His withdrawal left her empty and aching and clutching the tightness of his hips, but he shook his head and pressed his lips to the ivory swell of her breast.

Time ceased to exist. He kissed her endlessly, greedy and tender and urgent all at once. Fever rose inside her, for all the while he toyed with her nipples, first one and then the other, until they grew tight and hard and aching for the touch of his lips. There he lingered until she lay gasping and breathless.

His lips journeyed lower, across the silken plane of her belly. With brazen intimacy he pried her thighs wide. Cassie swallowed, eyes wide and glazed, as for one mind-splitting moment he hovered there. The moist heat of his breath grazed her first, and then the lashing glide of his tongue played over sleek feminine folds, again and again, until she lay writhing and panting, pleading for him to end his exquisite torment.

When he finally moved over her, beads of sweat dotted his upper lip, testimony to his rigid restraint. Though he was hard and throbbing, his penetration of the flesh he'd earlier ravaged was unendurably slow, and stunningly thorough.

At last he lay buried deep within her. He tightened his jaw, for the feel of her velvet heat clamped hot and tight around his swollen member nearly pushed him over the edge. He rolled suddenly so that she lay atop him, still filled with the rigid thickness of his staff.

Her eyes flew wide. With one small hand she braced herself against his chest. The deep, uneven breath she drew only made her all the more aware of his size and breadth within her.

"Gabriel—"

His eyes were dark and burning. "Take me," he said thickly. His hands swept down to her hips. He lifted her, bringing her down on his pulsing erectness. Stretching. Guiding. Seeking.

"That's it, sweet . . . yes, *yes!*" He groaned as the storm of passion caught them in a raging tempest, sweeping them high, ever higher. Somehow he held back until he felt her clinging spasms of release tighten around his turgid flesh. He gritted his teeth as his own came, flooding again and again at the gates of her womb. With a cry she collapsed against his chest.

He eased to his side; a corded arm cradled her close. Hands that were immensely gentle brushed honey-gold tendrils from her cheeks. He smiled a little at her dazed expression. A finger beneath her chin, he tipped her face to his. His kiss was long and slow, meltingly sweet. Together they fell asleep, wrapped in each other's arms.

Chapter 24

The creak of the door opening the next morning prodded Cassie from a sound sleep. From across the room came a faint gasp. Cassie smothered a half-smile. It appeared Gloria had just discerned her mistress was not alone in her bed. She propped herself up on an elbow as Gloria slid the tray she carried onto the table near the door.

"Gloria." The maid turned at the sound of the low, masculine voice.

A warm hand cupped Cassie's bare arm. Until then she hadn't realized that Gabriel was awake as well.

"Would you have Cook add a pot of tea to her ladyship's morning tray from now on?"

"Of course, milord." With a hasty curtsy Gloria fled.

There was a wealth of meaning in Gabriel's request—and they both knew it.

Cassie turned into his arms. He trailed a fingertip down the length of her nose. "Do you object, Countess?"

His mouth carried a crooked half-smile that made her heart turn over. His dark, unshaven jaw and hair-matted naked chest fairly shouted his stark masculinity, but his sleep-tousled hair and his eyes of pure and shining silver, made him look younger and far less harsh than she'd ever seen him.

Cassie shook her head in answer to his question. A sense of delirious happiness bubbled within her like a wellspring. For perhaps the very first time, she truly felt she played the role of wife and lady.

Slowly he lowered his head, grazing his lips lightly across hers. When he drew back, she saw that although his lips still smiled, his eyes did not.

"I hope you can forgive me for being such a fool last night," he said quietly. "Once again I judged both you and Christopher so unfairly." He shook his head in self-disgust. "I should have known about Christopher and Evelyn."

She pressed her fingers against his lips. "How could you?" she admonished gently. "I did not, yet now I, too, realize how blind I was. When I think back on all the times I saw the two of them together . . ." A troubled frown creased the smoothness of her forehead. "Christopher is convinced Evelyn's father would not consider him a fit husband. He will not even try to make his suit known for fear Warrenton will not allow him to see her at all."

Gabriel hesitated. "I know how fond you are of Evelyn," he said slowly. "But I must be honest, sweet. Christopher may well be right. Like my father, Warrenton values his title above all else. I suspect he would allow no hint of scandal to besmirch his name."

Cassie said nothing. It saddened her greatly to think her friend might never know such happiness as she had found. After a moment, Gabriel pressed his lips against her temple. Warm breath feathered across her skin.

"Sometimes," he said, his tone very low, "there comes a time to forget—a time to start anew." A finger beneath her chin, he tilted her face to his. "I would like very much for us to start this marriage anew, sweet."

To her surprise, there was an unusual uncertainty in his manner. Her tongue came out to moisten her lips. "A new beginning?" she whispered.

"Exactly. A new beginning."

Her face was suddenly radiant. "I would like that very much." She twined her arms around his neck, unable to contain her joy. "I would like that very much indeed!"

"Ah, but I've proven to be a jealous husband. I should think you are sorely vexed with me."

She bit her lip. "How could I be? I fear I—I've also proven to be a jealous wife."

His gaze roved over her face. "You've nothing to be jealous of, sweet."

"No? Not even Lady Sarah?"

His eyes darkened; his arms tightened. "Listen to me, sweet. I've lain with no other since the moment we met. I've *wanted* no other."

Her eyes clung to his. "Truly?"

"Truly."

His husky tone sent fiery shivers playing over her naked skin. She thrilled to the hotly possessive flare in his eyes. She wanted desperately to say more, for their emotions lay open and unguarded between them as never before. She loved him. She loved him desperately, her heart so full she thought it would burst. What would he say if he knew? Her lips parted; she trembled on the verge of confession.

But before she could say a word, Gabriel claimed her lips, his kiss one of infinite tenderness. Cassie's arms around his neck tightened. She melted against him in sweet surrender.

Outside in the hall there was a loud wail. A knock followed, and then the door opened. Alice stood there, her arms full of a squirming, fretting infant.

"He's a bit impatient this morning," the girl announced cheerfully.

Gabriel reluctantly released her mouth. A rare note of laughter in his tone, he whispered in her ear, "Our son has rather ghastly timing, does he not?"

He laughed softly as Cassie's cheeks flooded crimson.

When Alice had gone, he teased her unmercifully when she insisted on donning her nightgown before she sat up to nurse Jonathan. Clearly Gabriel had no such inhibitions. He strolled naked through the connecting door to his own room, and returned in that very same state, stopping for his cup of tea which sat on the table by the door. He had just begun to pour Cassie's chocolate for her when there was yet another knock on the door. She burst into laughter when he fairly dove for the bed.

"My lady," came Gloria's voice, "Lady Evelyn is downstairs and wishes to know if you will join her for a ride this morning."

Cassie bit her lip and glanced over at Gabriel. *Do you mind?* she mouthed. He shook his head.

"Please tell Lady Evelyn I'd love to," Cassie called. "And tell her I shall be down shortly."

When Jonathan had finished, she handed him over to Gabriel, who leisurely enjoyed the view from the bed while she hurriedly washed. With his assistance she was finally hooked into her riding habit. Before the mirror she adjusted a jaunty little riding cap atop her head. It was then she saw that Mittens, one of the cats Mrs. McGee kept, had apparently slipped into the room earlier. The furry little creature had leaped onto the small table where Gabriel had left her cup of chocolate. Now he sat greedily lapping at the rich brew inside the cup.

She whirled. "Oh, stop. Stop!" The creature paid no heed, but lapped every last drop from the cup. Without so much as a glance at the horrified woman, it daintily licked its paw then leaped to the floor.

This time it was Gabriel who burst into laughter. Cassie tried to summon a severe glare and failed miserably. She was still chuckling when she entered the morning room downstairs.

Evelyn sat on the plump gold cushions of the settee, basking in the brilliant yellow sunshine that flooded through the windows. So preoccupied was she that Cassie had to clear her throat twice before Evelyn twisted around and spied her.

"Well," Cassie teased, "I would dearly love to know what is on your mind that you are so distracted this morning—or perhaps I should ask *who* so engages your attention."

Evelyn blushed fiercely.

Cassie lowered her voice to a whisper. "Let me guess. Is his name Christopher?"

Evelyn's huge blue eyes widened in alarm. "Oh, no! Is it so obvious then?"

"Not at all!" she hastened to reassure her friend. Cassie sighed, some of the light fading from her eyes. Reaching out, she patted Evelyn's hand. "You need not worry," she said softly. "I will keep your secret, though I wish you and Christopher would go to your father. Perhaps he would not be so opposed to Christopher's suit as you think."

Evelyn spoke with painful truth. "No, Cassie. I am heartily glad that Christopher bought the manor house, but I fear it is for naught. My father is more committed than ever to seeing that I marry both a title and a fortune."

Seeing how the matter distressed her friend, Cassie declined to say more. After a moment Evelyn summoned a tiny smile.

"My father rode over with me this morning. He and Edmund planned to go out hunting. Just before you came down, Edmund asked if we wished to join them. I hope you don't mind, but I declined."

"I'm glad you did," Cassie said dryly. "I could never keep up with the three of you in a hunt." They had just arisen when all at once there was a sharp cry from outside the room.

Evelyn's startled gaze met Cassie's. "What on earth—"

"It sounds like Mrs. McGee!" Cassie was already dashing through the door.

The scream had indeed come from Mrs. McGee. The housekeeper was on her knees in the entrance hall. Mittens, her little cat, lay in a heap before her.

"Oh, the poor thing," she cried. "I started to shoo him outside, but he was walking as if—as if he were foxed. Then all at once he just stopped cold! He looked at me—rather puzzled like—and then the poor mite just fell over!" She wrung her hands. "I—I think he's dead!"

By then Edmund, Evelyn's father, and Gabriel had stepped up as well. Gabriel knelt down beside Mrs. McGee. With gentle fingers he examined the limp body of the cat. Finally he glanced over at the housekeeper.

"From what you described," he murmured, "it almost sounds as if he *were* drunk." He shook his head and laid a hand on Mrs. McGee's shoulder. "In either case, I'm sorry, Mrs. McGee. It appears he's passed on."

Davis had joined the group as well. "Sir, perhaps the creature might have got into some spirits in the kitchen."

Cassie swayed. *It almost sounds as if he were drunk.* No, she thought faintly. Not drunk . . .

Drugged.

A terrible light-headedness assailed her. A hideous, awful possibility leaped through her mind.

Slowly she began to back away. "No," she whispered, her gaze fixed solely on Gabriel. "Dear God, no . . ." She whirled and bolted up the stairs.

Gabriel leaped to his feet, an expression of consternation darkening his brow. "Cassie! What the devil . . ." He strode after his wife.

Upstairs in her room, she tried to close the door in his face. He flung it open with a fist and stepped within, his face like a thundercloud.

"Cassie! Whatever the blazes has come over you?" He was concerned. Angry. Most of all puzzled, for her eyes were huge, her skin pasty-white. Damn! If he didn't know better, he would swear she was terrified of him . . .

He curbed his frustration and extended a hand toward her. "Come, sweet, tell me what's wrong."

She stood in the center of the room, hugging herself. Terror iced her veins. She was shaking from head to toe. "As if you didn't know!" she choked out.

"Cassie, I swear I do not! Please, tell me what has come over you for you to act this way!"

Her mind would not stop working. Was this why Gabriel's mood had been so very fine this morning? She thought piercingly that perhaps he hadn't meant today to be the beginning of their marriage at all . . .

Perhaps it was meant to be the end.

"The cat drank my chocolate!" she cried. "And now he is dead . . . he drank the chocolate meant for me, and now he is *dead*!"

Gabriel sucked in a harsh breath. "Sweet Lord! Surely you do not think that I—"

"You put laudanum in my chocolate once before," she screamed. "Do you deny it?"

"No, but that was only to help you sleep—"

"I am the only one in this house who drinks chocolate, Gabriel. And now perhaps I was meant to sleep forever!"

She was not herself. He could hear the frenzy in her voice, see the wildness in her eyes. He reached for her. She shrank back and eluded his grasp. Dragging a bag from the wardrobe, she threw it on the bed along with several gowns. Blindly she began stuffing them inside. Her hands were shaking so that she could hardly manage.

With a grim expression on his face, he raised his hands to her shoulders. He spun her around and dragged her close. "Cassie, look at me," he demanded, giving her a little shake. Though his voice was harsh, his eyes mutely pleaded. "Look at me and tell me you truly believe I would ever hurt you, much less plot to see you dead!"

Tears slid down her cheeks. "I've been shot," she cried. "Accosted. And now this! What am I to think? And you truly did not want a wife, Gabriel, you know you did not!"

"All that has changed, Cassie." His voice was gritty with emotion. "My God, you are the mother of my son! As God is my witness, I would sooner cut off my arm than harm you—in any way— ever!"

"And what about your father? Gabriel, we have gone over this before! He despised me when you brought me here. I was not his choice of bride—I was an American! Perhaps he would see me dead for no other reason than that!" She put a hand to her head. "I don't know what to think. I-I just don't know!"

It was then she spied Evelyn hovering at the door. She broke free and flung out her hands. "Oh, Evelyn, please, help me!" She was weeping, half-hysterical. "I-I cannot stay here. Will you help me?"

"Oh, Cassie, of course I'll do whatever I can to help . . . but . . ." Evelyn's gaze met Gabriel's over her shoulder. He gave a silent nod of assent.

She grasped Cassie's hands. They were ice-cold. "Calm yourself, love. I'll tell you what. You and Jonathan may stay at Warrenton with Father and I until all this is sorted out . . . Father won't mind, I'm certain of it . . ."

An hour later, Gabriel stood atop the wide graceful steps before Farleigh Hall. His posture wooden, he watched the carriage pass through the tall, ivy-clad gates, toward Warrenton—watched until the last swirl of dust had settled on the ground.

Inside were his wife and son.

Edmund stood just inside one ornately carved double door. "Good Christ, boy! I cannot believe you allowed her to go!"

Gabriel's jaw clenched so hard his teeth hurt. He stepped past his father, pointedly ignoring him as he strode toward the drawing room.

Edmund dogged him every step of the way. "Gabriel!" He frowned his disapproval as his son went straight to the crystal decanter of brandy. "Have you nothing to say?"

Gabriel slammed the glass he was holding onto the tray so hard the glass shattered. "No," he bit out furiously, "but apparently you do, since it appears I have once again failed to live up to your expectations!"

Edmund was undaunted. "Oh, come now! Her charges are outrageous. The cat no doubt died of natural causes—not because it drank chocolate laced with a lethal dose of laudanum. Why, 'tis common knowledge women who have just given birth are inclined to emotional outbursts. Oh, I can see where you feel you must humor her. But by allowing her to leave, you must be aware you merely encourage her fears—and surely they are totally unfounded!"

"Are they? I might remind you, Cassie has been shot at, kidnapped, and now someone may very well have tried to kill her yet again! I brought her back from London believing I could keep her safe here. Clearly I cannot, for it appears someone is very well acquainted with her likes and dislikes. Can you honestly blame her if she is frightened half out of her wits? Someone is trying to kill her, perhaps someone in this house! 'Tis not me, and I highly doubt any of the servants capable of such a thing. So tell me, Father, who does that leave?"

Edmund stood stiff as an iron rod. "I will ignore that, Gabriel, but were you not my son, I believe I would call you out for daring to suggest such a thing! Under no circumstances would I harm someone weaker than I—and my own daughter-in-law yet!"

"Your daughter-in-law is also an American, Father. And your dislike of Yankees is known far and wide."

Edmund glared his outrage. "Nonetheless, I would never harm Cassandra. And I still fail to see why she found it necessary to leave Farleigh!"

Gabriel's mouth twisted. "Come now, Father. Maybe it's better that she does not stay. My mother did not leave and look what happened to her."

"Your mother!" Edmund was startled. "I fail to see what she has to do with this discussion."

"No, but then I am not surprised. I meant only that I do not think I could watch Cassie live here—

miserable and unhappy, as my mother was. You see, Father, I won't do to her what you did to my mother."

"What I did to your . . . I did nothing!"

"That's right. You did not care for her. You did not love her. You scarcely knew she existed . . . what do you think *killed* her?"

Edmund blanched. "What do you mean, Gabriel? She—she drowned in the lake . . . a horrible accident, to be sure, but an accident nonetheless . . ."

"No, Father. Her death was no accident. She drowned because she wanted to die . . . she *killed* herself!"

Stricken, Edmund stared at his son. He had turned a sickly shade of gray. "How do you know this?" he whispered. "How?"

"I know because she left a note for me, Father. She knew I would understand, just as she knew you would not *care*." His tone was fierce. "She loved you, you know. She loved you in spite of everything . . . Would you like to know what the note said? She wrote that she could no longer stand to be *in* your life, and not a part of it. And so she chose to end her own!"

Edmund cried out. "I did not know, Gabriel . . . dear Lord, I did not know . . . I thought it was an accident! Why did you never tell me?"

Gabriel's eyes were glittering shards of ice. "You did not care when she was alive. Why should you care when she was dead?" He spun about and left, slamming the door so hard the windows shook.

Edmund's knees were suddenly too weak to hold him. Slowly he made his way to a chair. Everything, he realized with shattering clarity, was suddenly so very clear. His son's distance. His resentment . . .

He buried his hands and wept. For all he had done. For all he had lost.

For all that would never be.

Chapter 25

Gabriel came to call the very next day, both
morning and afternoon.

Both times Cassie refused to see him.

He came the next day, and the next.

Still she refused.

For the life of her, she could not put her finger on what held her back. She knew only that
to see him would add to her turmoil. Her days
were spent wavering between hope and fear, misery and outrage, anger and longing. Her nights
were spent crying herself to sleep. In the morning,
she woke with aching head, puffy eyes . . . and bat-
tered heart.

And always—*always*—she was confused.

Gabriel . . . or Edmund? Father . . . or son?

At times she was convinced she had taken leave
of her senses. Surely it was madness to even *think*
Gabriel or Edmund capable of murder. And then
there came the slightest sliver of doubt, and she
was convinced it had to be one or the other, for
though she wracked her brain, she could think of
no one else who might want her dead.

One week later she stood upstairs in the room
she and Jonathan shared, gazing out at the vivid

green landscape. Brilliant sunlight danced across the land, but her mood was dark and melancholy.

Aware that she had not been sleeping well, Evelyn had insisted these past few days that she rest in the afternoon. To that end, Evelyn had taken Jonathan downstairs so she could nap undisturbed. But today, Cassie was restive and impatient. She could not stop the workings of her mind long enough to relax. Finally she turned away from the window. There was no point in remaining here in her room. She might as well join Jonathan and Evelyn downstairs.

She peered into the drawing room, but there was no sign of them. She scarcely noticed that the terrace doors were ajar. But as she turned to leave, the sound of soft feminine laughter caught her ear. Quickly she retraced her steps.

On the terrace outside, Evelyn sat on a wooden bench. Opposite her was Gabriel, the muscled length of his legs stretched out before him. Jonathan was perched on his thighs, staring avidly at his father, tiny hands curled around Gabriel's thumbs.

Evelyn saw her first. She started guiltily, rising from the wooden bench where she'd been sitting. Cassie bristled. She could not help but feel thoroughly betrayed—and by her friend yet!

"Do let me guess," she stated coolly. She glanced between Evelyn and her husband, only barely disguising her outrage. "Is this visit the reason I've been urged to rest each afternoon?"

Gabriel rose to his feet, lifting Jonathan to his shoulder, careful to support his head and neck. Evelyn appeared most distressed while Gabriel's features were tightly drawn and guarded.

"Well," Evelyn said brightly. "I can see the two of you wish to be alone." She glanced at Gabriel. "Would you like me to take Jonathan?"

Gabriel nodded. He pressed his lips to the babe's dark scalp then handed him to Evelyn, who hurried inside.

He did not speak until they were alone. His gaze flickered. "You may be angry at me, Cassie, but there is no need to blame Evelyn. It was I who persisted in this."

Cassie's small chin jutted forward. "Oh, but I should have known!"

Gabriel's gaze had grown diamond-hard. "When you refused to see me, I accepted it. But what right have you to refuse me the chance to see Jonathan? I would remind you, he is my son as well as yours."

"The son you did not want—by the wife you did not want!"

His face tightened to a mask of stone. "I suggest you watch your tongue, Yank. I was cruel to strike out at you once—to say hurtful things I truly did not mean, and I have regretted it ever since. But are you any less cruel at this moment? I think not."

He had stepped close, so very close she could feel the raw, sheer power of his presence, so close the familiar scent of him swirled all around her. Her thoughts were a mad jumble. She prayed he wouldn't see how her pulse leaped at his nearness. With him so near she could not think clearly, for her senses were besieged by feelings . . . and memories. Piercingly she recalled how it felt to be in his arms, his lips warm and persuasive upon hers, his arms strong and protective and safe.

Her hands were suddenly trembling. She hid them in her skirts. "What would you have me do, Gabriel? Or was I wrong about the cat? Was I wrong about my chocolate being drugged?"

The tension spun out endlessly. At last he broke the silence. "No," he said finally. "In all likelihood, you were right. The physician examined the cat, and he, too, felt the animal was drugged. And an empty bottle of laudanum was found outside the kitchen. Gloria said the tray sat in the kitchen for several minutes before she took it upstairs. I have questioned the servants over and over again, but other than that, no one knows anything of value."

He had not wanted to tell her. Cassie had glimpsed the indecision warring keenly on his face. "The servants are loyal," she pointed out. "Both to you *and* your father! And you would stand to gain the freedom to marry where you choose if I were dead!"

He made a sound of disgust. "If you recall, I had no desire to marry in the first place! And for all that you may believe otherwise, my father is a man of honor and integrity. And surely you know that I, of all people, would not come to his defense unless I was certain it was true."

He paced in a tight circle before her. "Believe me, Cassie, I understand why you fear for your safety." He could not disguise his impatience. "What I find difficult to accept is that you still think I may be responsible! You forget, I was with you at the time you were shot!"

"And you might easily have hired someone to see the deed done—and the same with that—that awful man in London! And if not you, Gabriel, then who? *Who*, I ask you?"

"I have no idea!" he exploded, his eyes a silver blaze. "I have had investigators searching for months. I've had men watching you *here*, though I've no doubt you won't believe me. I grow tired of defending myself, Cassie, for I have no way of proving my innocence other than to find the perpetrator!"

"And where does that leave me?" she cried in a tear-choked voice. "I fear I shall not be so lucky the next time!"

He reached for her. But chaos and confusion roiled in her breast. How could she love a man who might want her dead? she asked herself desperately. She could not let him touch her, not now. If he did, she felt certain she would splinter into a million pieces. "Don't!" she cried, wrenching away. "Don't touch me! Don't touch me ever again!"

Gabriel stepped back. The muscles in his face were rigid. The taste of defeat was bitter on his tongue. "This marriage was doomed from the very beginning," he said in a terrible voice she knew would haunt her 'til her dying days. "Perhaps you're right. Perhaps we should end it now."

The blood drained from her face. She stared at him, her face colorless. "What do you mean?"

His lips were ominously thin. "Oh, you need not worry. I promised you I would provide for you, and so I shall. But we need not tolerate each other's presence anymore. We need not endure this unfortunate mistake we call a marriage. You have only to decide where it is you wish to live and I will see that you are installed in a house there." His mouth twisted. "God knows I am the last man to play at nobility. But perhaps it's better if you leave. If you desire, I'll even send you back to Charleston."

A burning ache closed her throat. For a timeless moment Cassie could not speak. She felt as if the very ground on which she stood was crumbling beneath her feet. She could hardly force enough air past her lips to speak.

"What of Jonathan?"

"Jonathan is my heir, as I am now my father's heir." His tone was as unyielding as his spine. "He must be raised as such. He *will* be raised as such."

Stunned, she could only stare at him. Rampant through her mind was the realization that the man before her was a stranger. She sensed no compassion in him, none at all.

"You would have me leave him here? To be raised by you—and your father? To end up like you?" Sheer fury flamed in her eyes. "No. *No!*"

She saw only a stony determination in the look he flashed her. "You may deny *me*, Cassie. But you will not deny me my son."

Her heart was beating wildly. "You would take my baby from me," she whispered, still unable to believe it. "God, and you dare to call *me* cruel!"

The jutting thrust of his jaw bespoke his utter relentlessness. "It would appear you have made your choice. You doubt my word. You do not trust me. So be it, for by God, I will beg no longer." With that he stalked from the terrace.

Minutes passed. Perhaps hours. Cassie had no way of knowing. Her arms crept around her body. She huddled there, her heart like a stone within her breast, shattered beyond measure. The pain that ripped through her was like a knife twisting over and over.

There was a dry cough behind her. She whirled to find Reginald Latham standing behind her.

"Your Grace," she muttered. "I-I am sorry. I did not realize you were here."

He inclined his head. "Cassandra." He stood with his hands linked behind his back, gazing down at her. "Forgive me for being blunt, but I could not help but overhear your discussion with Gabriel."

He had heard! Embarrassment flooded her. For the life of her, Cassie did not know how to respond. Reginald was not smiling but, Cassie noted, he was not so grim-visaged as usual.

"Then I must apologize," she murmured at last. "When I came here, it was not my desire to upset your household."

"There is no need to distress yourself needlessly. Indeed,'twould seem you have far more serious matters to consider, such as your husband's determination to wrest your child from your grasp."

Cassie swallowed painfully. "I know." The words emerged with difficulty. "I thought I knew him far better . . ." She shook her head. "I—I just do not understand how he could do such a thing!"

Reginald sighed. "I've known him since he was a boy, you know. He can be . . . willful, to say the least. Some might even say . . . vengeful."

Vengeful. A clamp seemed to close around her heart. Wasn't that why he'd married her? Oh, Reginald was right. She was well acquainted with

Gabriel's ruthlessness. She shivered. And he had been so cold, so heartless!

"My dear, I fear I must warn you . . . Gabriel is not a man to make threats lightly. You must not underestimate him."

Her breath quickened. Eyes wide, she fixed her attention intently on his face. "What—what do you mean?"

"Only this. His father is my greatest friend, but I cannot condone Gabriel's intentions. 'Tis my belief a child needs his mother."

Cassie began to tremble. She sank down onto the bench. "I can't let him take Jonathan away from me—I can't!" She buried her face in her hands. "What am I to do?"

"There, there, now, do not fret. 'Tis not so bad as all that." He pressed a fine linen handkerchief into her hands. "Come now, dry your eyes and listen."

Cassie dabbed at her tears. When she was able, she raised her head.

"Here is what I think, Cassandra. If you remain here, you stand every chance that Gabriel will indeed snatch Jonathan away from you. He can be very unforgiving, you know—why, you have only to consider his father to know it!"

Cassie cried out. "I can't let him do that! Jonathan is all I have—he is *everything* I have."

"Oh, I quite understand, child. That is why you must flee while you still have that chance."

"Flee! But where would I go?" She moaned her distress. "Gabriel would be sure to find me in London. I've no doubt he would search the whole of England until he found us!"

Reginald rubbed his heavy jowls. "On your own, you would have little chance of eluding him. But I've a sister in Ireland—never has there been a woman more kind and generous! I could help you find passage on a ship out. And with my letter in your possession, I know she will let you stay with her until you are established on your own."

Cassie shuddered. "A ship?" She spoke unthinkingly. "I hated the voyage here. I-I have a deathly fear of water and I—I cannot swim."

"The choice is yours, of course. Only you can decide which is more important."

Cassie bit her lip. Another voyage. It seemed a small enough price to pay, for she could not bear to even think about losing her son.

Her mind was racing. Reginald was right. Gabriel would make a dangerous enemy. He had power and wealth at his disposal. Her only hope, she thought with bleak despair, was to escape now, while there was still a chance . . .

"You are right." She spoke haltingly. She swallowed, her eyes lifting to his. "And I gratefully accept your help, Your Grace, as long as you are willing to give it."

"Excellent, my dear! Oh, I think you'll not regret it. Now, here is what we shall do . . . Pack only a small bag for you and the child. I will send along the rest of your things before the ship departs. Now then, meet me at the stables in an hour."

Cassie frowned. "What about Evelyn? What am I to tell her?"

"Do not trouble yourself with Evelyn. I shall tell her I am taking you and Jonathan for an evening ride about the countryside in the curricle. That way there will be no room should she wish to join us. Do not worry, she will not question it. And later, I will tell her the truth. For now,'tis too risky."

So it was that Cassie left the Warrenton estate an hour later. Jonathan, angel that he was, lay asleep in the crook of her arm. For a time, as she had hurriedly prepared for her journey, a blessed numbness had settled over her. But they had not gone far before her heart, her soul, her very being began to ache. Her chest was like a vast, hollow drum. Guilt dragged at her like an oppressive weight.

She could not leave Gabriel, not like this—not like a thief in the night. They had come so far, and gone through too much to give up so easily. Now that the future was in her hands, she found herself searching the depths of her heart for the truth.

Unbidden, her mind filled with memories. In the space of a heartbeat, she relived every word, every sweeping touch—every tender caress—that passed between them. With her palm, she cradled the soft down of Jonathan's head. A loving fingertip traced the shape of his brows, brows that even now resembled his father's arrogant slant.

Her heart squeezed. Gabriel was right. Jonathan was *his* child, too . . . and she loved him all the more because he was so much his father's son . . .

Just as she loved Gabriel. With every breath, every beat of her heart. And the thought of living without him was far more terrifying than anything else could possibly be.

Don't leave me again, Cassie. Promise me you won't leave me again.

The words were a burning echo in her brain.

I would sooner cut off my arm than harm you.

She believed him, she realized, feeling the emotion rise inside her like a surging tide, powerful and endless. She believed *in* him.

And now, having found the answers that had so eluded her, she could not continue this course she had so rashly pursued.

They were not far from Farleigh. Another ten minutes and they would pass the gates. Raising her chin, she tugged on Reginald's sleeve.

"Please stop," she said when she had gained his attention.

With a jerk of the reins, he brought the curricle to a halt.

"What is it, girl?"

Cassie shook her head, "I'm sorry," she said levelly. "But I cannot do this. I cannot leave Gabriel like this. It . . . it is not right."

"What! Do you mean to tell me you wish to return to Warrenton?"

"No, Your Grace," she said softly. "I would like to go home. To Farleigh Hall." She paused. "To my husband."

Something raced across his florid features, something that she could have sworn was rage . . .

Instinct pressed her spine against the leather-backed seat. Very slowly he turned his head to look at her. She stared into gleaming dark eyes alight with the frenzy of madness.

"Perhaps you are right . . ." He threw back his head and laughed then. A grating, horrible laugh. A menacing laugh.

A laugh that chilled her to the very marrow of her bones.

"You wish to return to Farleigh, eh? Well, so you shall, girl. So you shall."

Gabriel did not return to Farleigh. Instead he rode to Christopher's manor. There he paced the length of the drawing room, past white-sheeted furniture, until Christopher grew dizzy simply watching him.

Gabriel was angry. Angry at himself, angry at Cassie for provoking him into saying something he had never intended to say—certainly something he did not mean.

But he was far more furious over his helplessness, his inability to trace the source of Cassie's tormentor. He smote his fist against his palm. All this time and still no answers! Was he blind . . . or merely a fool? Throughout the day, he'd had the nagging feeling there was something he had overlooked, something right beneath his nose . . .

"Gabriel, this pacing will gain you nothing," Christopher observed dryly, "while I, on the other hand, may have to replace my carpet far sooner than I care to." When his friend did not slow his pace, he sighed. "You made the right choice. After what happened at Farleigh, Cassie is safer at Warrenton right now."

Gabriel ground to a halt. "You are right." He dragged a hand down his face. "If the past is any indication, she is far more likely to encounter foul play at Farleigh than at Warrenton. If there had been even the slightest possibility of her encountering danger there, I would never have allowed her to go. And yet I cannot rid myself of this feeling that . . ."

All at once he stopped. Christopher straightened abruptly in his chair. Gabriel was staring vaguely into space; for the life of him, he looked as if he'd seen a ghost.

"What?" Christopher demanded. "What is it?"

Gabriel shook his head, as if he were stunned. "Cassie said the oddest thing today. She said that I would stand to gain the freedom to marry where I chose if she were gone."

"A morbid thought, that." Christopher grimaced. "This cannot be easy on her, Gabriel. She will come to her senses, surely—"

" 'Tis not that," he said numbly. "Christopher, don't you see? She was right. If she were gone, I would be a widower—it would almost be," his voice fell to a whisper, "as if I'd never been married at all."

Christopher's gaze narrowed. "I'm not quite sure I follow you. Do you mean to say that you would be free to marry Evelyn once again?"

"Yes . . . yes!" Both fear and excitement gathered in his voice.

Christopher lurched to his feet, swearing hotly. "By God, Gabriel, you go too far! How dare you suggest Evelyn would try to kill Cassie simply so the two of you could marry! Why, Evelyn could hurt no one, let alone Cassie—"

Gabriel gripped his arms. "No," he said grimly. "But can you say the same of the duke of Warrenton?"

Christopher was stunned. "My God," he breathed. "Her father . . ."

"Think, Christopher, *think*! The duke was in residence at Warrenton when Cassie was shot. He was in London with Evelyn when she was abducted."

"And he was at Farleigh when her chocolate was drugged." Christopher went as pale as his friend. "Gabriel, we must do something."

Both set out at a dead run for the stable.

At Warrenton, Evelyn had no sooner come down the stairs than Gabriel was before her. "I have come for Cassie, Evelyn. Where is she?"

Evelyn's smile wavered. "My father took her and Jonathan out for a drive in the curricle. They've been gone . . . oh, perhaps a quarter-hour."

"No . . . oh, God, no!" Gabriel's face turned ashen. "We must find them. We must find them before it's too late!"

Evelyn glanced to Christopher. "Something is wrong," she said slowly. "Oh, please tell me what has happened!"

Christopher took her elbow, his expression pained. "Evelyn," he began. "For your sake, I hope we are wrong . . ."

She was much stronger than he had realized . . . for she was with them when they left Warrenton moments later at a breakneck pace. And it was she whose sharp gaze first spied the curricle sitting by the side of the rutted roadway . . .

Empty, but for a screaming infant.

Chapter 26

⌒‿◯◯‿⌒

Jonathan was plucked from his mother's arms. Warrenton leaped heavily to the ground. "Get out!" he snarled.

Her pulse pounding violently, Cassie climbed from the curricle. She stretched out her arms. "Please," she pleaded. "My baby . . ."

Warrenton's eyes were glittering. He thrust Jonathan onto the floor of the curricle. Jarred awake, Jonathan began to whimper and squirm. Cassie darted forward but Warrenton grabbed her arm and yanked her to him.

"No!" she screamed. "Oh, God, are you mad? My baby!"

Warrenton paid no heed. Pudgy fingers gouged into her soft flesh, cutting off her circulation. He dragged her through the trees alongside the road. Though she resisted mightily, her struggles were no match for his bulk and strength. Through the haze of trunks and branches there was a glimmer of water. An icy foreboding shot through her. A soundless scream echoed in her brain. The lake! Oh, sweet heaven, not there, not the lake! In an attempt to thwart him, she stumbled and dropped to her knees. Warrenton yanked her to her feet so viciously she feared her arm would be wrenched from its socket.

He did not halt until they reached the end of the small dock that jutted into the waters.

He retreated a step. "So you do not swim, eh, girl? Very fortuitous of you to enlighten me." With a grinning leer he taunted her.

It was all she could do not to break down. He meant to kill her. She could see the deadly intent in the gleam of his eyes.

"It was you who shot at me, wasn't it? And that man in London . . . did you hire him to kill me? I remember one day riding back to Farleigh—you watched me, didn't you? And the chocolate—you put something in my chocolate that morning!"

"Yes, my dear, and you were right. It was laudanum. And my aim was deplorable that day, to be sure. And that fool in London!" He cursed foully. "You put me to a great deal of trouble, you know. I wanted to have done with it, but when the first two attempts were botched, I had to bide my time. It was my intent to make it appear an accident, you see. And those months when you disappeared—I prayed you'd be found dead in some alley. But then you had to return!" His features contorted into an evil mask.

She could hardly speak for the awful constriction in her throat. "Why? Why do you hate me so? I have done nothing to you!"

"Nothing! Why, were it not for you, Gabriel would even now be wed to Evelyn!"

"Evelyn was relieved at finding Gabriel already married! She did not want to be his wife!"

He shook his head. " 'Tis not a case of Evelyn's

wants. No, 'tis more a case of needs must. You see, my dear, 'tis my fondest wish to restore Warrenton to its former grandeur . . . you've noticed 'tis in a rather disreputable state of late? I've other estates which must be maintained as well. And I fear I've grown fond of gambling these last years . . . a pity my luck is not what it once was! Indeed, my dear, my debts at this moment are monstrous! Can you imagine—the duke of Warrenton in the poorhouse? Why, my ancestors would surely turn over in their graves if they knew! My only hope is to see Evelyn married to a wealthy suitor."

Her lips parted. "So that is why you sought a marriage between her and Stuart—and urged marriage between her and Gabriel."

"Clever girl. But I have my family honor to uphold, you know. I could scarcely marry off my daughter to a nobody in the merchant class. Ah, but once you are dead, all can be as before. Evelyn and Gabriel will be free to wed."

He glanced from Cassie's face to the glimmering surface of the lake, and back again.

"I must say, 'tis altogether fitting that you should die like Caroline—and so fortunate that the lake is so distant from Farleigh Hall. Oh, yes, m'dear, I fear you will be the victim of an accident, just like poor Caroline." He gave a dramatic sigh. "And I, alas, was simply unable to rescue you before you succumbed! A tragic loss, I fear—but in your death lies my salvation."

Terror twisted Cassie's insides. He was right. There was no one to see. No one to hear. The story he would concoct would sound entirely plausible, so plausible no one would ever guess he had murdered her . . .

Warrenton drew a small but deadly-looking pistol from his pocket. He gestured toward the water. "Now, my dear. Will you jump, or must I resort to this?" An expression of distaste crossed his features. "I pray you choose the former, for I truly have no desire to use this. 'Tis so very messy, you know."

Cassie regarded him in stricken horror. It was just as in her dream, she realized numbly. Behind her was the lake, its waters serene and pristine. But beneath the surface lurked a dark world of gloom and death. Her greatest fear was of drowning, and that was how she would die . . . a slow, choking death.

Slowly she shook her head. "I-I will not jump. You will have to—to shoot me." In truth it was scarcely bravery that prompted her—quite the opposite.

An evil smile crept along Warrenton's lips. Before she knew what he was about, he seized her arm and spun her around. There was a forceful shove between her shoulder blades. A scream welled in her throat as she felt herself flying forward, her feet leaving the safety of the dock.

Frigid water closed over her head. She plummeted deep . . . still deeper through black, murky depths of icy cold. Sheer terror clogged her veins. She managed to surface once, her mouth dragging in one precious gulp of air.

Then she was sinking again. She tried to kick, but her skirts tangled heavily around her legs so that she could not move. She felt herself being dragged down, ever down . . .

Gabriel, her mind screamed. *Oh, Gabriel, help me . . .*

She did not see the two men who raced frantically across the meadow toward the lake. A slight feminine figure trailed distantly behind, her arms clutched around a small, screaming bundle.

Warrenton threw back his head. His sinister laughter turned to a gasp of disbelief as pounding footsteps shook the dock on which he stood.

Christopher reached him first. He lunged for Warrenton and wrapped his arms around the older man. "Hurry!" he shouted to Gabriel. "She just went down again!"

Gabriel tore off his boots and flung them aside, his gaze pinned on the place he'd last seen Cassie. "Jesus," he breathed. "Let it not be too late!" The next instant he knifed cleanly into the water.

Cassie was unaware of the sharp tug at the back of her gown. She panicked, flailing wildly. Searing fire scalded her lungs, so desperate was she for air, but she would not open her mouth to breathe, for she knew what awaited her. Her head swam dizzily. A numbing curtain of unconsciousness began to smother her. She had but one thought. So this is what it was like to die . . .

Somehow Gabriel snared her about the waist. With a mighty kick and an upsurge of power he shot above the surface. His legs churned as he towed his precious burden toward the bank, carefully striving to keep her head above the water. His chest labored with exertion, his muscles straining when at last he succeeded in dragging her ashore.

He scrambled to his knees, cradling her in his arms. His hands were shaking as he pushed aside the streaming hair from her face. Her flesh was milky white and cold. Her eyes were closed, her lashes spiked wetly against her cheeks. His heart leaped in fear.

"Cassie," he cried hoarsely. "Cassie, open your eyes, sweet. Open your eyes!"

Slowly she stirred. Her lungs heaved. She gave a sputtering, choking cough, then a racking, wheezing breath. Her eyes fluttered open.

"Never tell me!" she said with a gasp. "Am I dead then?"

His groan was half-laugh, half-sob. "Why, Yank, do you fancy yourself in heaven once again?" He clasped her tight against his breast.

Awareness returned in full bloom. Though it sapped all her strength, she lifted her arms and tugged his dripping head to hers. "Do you know," she whispered against his lips, "I believe I do."

But it was a moment destined to be altogether short-lived. Nearby there was a resounding blast, and then a high-pitched scream. Gabriel's head jerked up. Cassie strained upward. "No! Don't look, don't look!" He tried to urge her cheek into the hollow of his neck.

She cried out sharply. "Tell me! I must know!"

"It's Warrenton, sweet. He . . . he turned the pistol on himself."

"No! Oh, no! Oh, poor Evelyn . . ." She bowed her head and began to cry. Tenderly, gently, Gabriel gathered her close. The nightmare was over. It was time to go home.

Back in her room at Farleigh, Cassie tightened the sash of her robe. A long hot bath had done much to drive the cold and ache from her muscles, but she was still too restless to sleep.

Her mind strayed to all that had happened tonight. In spite of everything, she could not hate the duke of Warrenton. She felt only sorrow and regret. Her heart went out to Evelyn, for Evelyn had been there to witness her father's choice to end his life. And yet, Cassie sensed that her friend's grief was tempered by Christopher's presence, for it was Christopher who comforted her, in Christopher's arms where she had wept. Christopher loved her, and Cassie did not doubt that Christopher's love would go far in healing Evelyn's wounds.

Edmund had been no less shocked by his friend's deceit and vile intentions. He had listened in stunned silence while Gabriel relayed all that Cassie had told him—all that had happened. Then he retired quietly to his study.

She had nursed Jonathan before her bath, and now, needing the reassurance only the sight of her child could provide, she moved down the hall to check on him.

To her surprise, a candle still burned in Jonathan's room, casting a flickering triangle of light out into the hallway. The murmur of low voices reached her ears. A little uncertain, she hovered near the threshold.

"He resembles you greatly, you know."

Cassie caught her breath. It was Edmund. Turning slightly, she caught a glimpse of the mirror that hung on the opposite wall. Its reflection showed both Gabriel and Edmund bending over Jonathan's cradle.

Gabriel's voice came next. "I pray he does not have my temperament."

"Nor mine, for that matter."

A hint of dry laughter underscored Edmund's tone. Cassie hovered there, close enough to hear, but unseen by the pair inside.

"If he is lucky," Edmund added, "he will grow to be like his mother."

Cassie blinked. When Gabriel said nothing, she had the oddest sensation he was as startled by Edmund's observation as she.

But there was more.

"Do you know," Edmund said softly, "I was determined from the outset that she would be an outsider, so very determined I could never countenance a woman of her station, a Yankee yet! But as the weeks passed, I came to feel something I never thought to feel for her."

There was a small pause. "And what was that?" Gabriel asked slowly.

"Pride," he said quietly. " 'Tis odd, really, for though she was afraid, she did not lack courage. Nor was she afraid to recognize her own mistakes, and she was not afraid to *feel*. And somehow— somehow she made me see myself as I am."

In the hallway, Cassie pressed her back to the wall. She stuffed a fist in her mouth to keep from crying out. Her throat grew achingly tight. A heartrending relief poured through her. To think that she had gained Edmund's acceptance—all that had once seemed so improbable, so impossible!

"Do you remember the night you brought her here? I recalled quite distinctly shouting at you that a change of gown would not make a lady of her." Edmund laughed, the sound dry and rusty, but a laugh nonetheless. "She was a lady already.

And do you know, I do believe she shamed us both."

Edmund seemed to hesitate. His voice came haltingly. "You were right about your mother, Gabriel. I-I did not love her as I should have—as I *could* have, had I only tried. And I truly did not realize her death was no accident—that she took her own life because of me." His tone grew heavy. "I only wish you had told me years ago, though I understand why you did not."

Cassie's heart twisted. So Caroline had chosen to end her life! She had always suspected there was more to her death, and now she knew. But before the thought progressed further, Gabriel was speaking again.

"There is no need to—"

"There is every need, Gabriel. You cannot know the shame I bear when I think of how I treated her and how I treated you, my own son! I felt that your rebellion and defiance were your fault, not mine. But I know now that if you are hard, 'tis because it was I who made you that way. If you are stubborn 'tis because . . . because you are my son. And I know now that . . . you did not turn away. I—I drove you away, Gabriel. With my own arrogance. My own selfishness and ignorance."

He paused. "I would have my son back, if only I could. I have made so many mistakes, mistakes I could never even begin to rectify." To Cassie's shock, there was a telltale unsteadiness in his voice, a catch that rent her heart in two. "I wish for you—and yes, my grandson—the one thing we never really had, Gabriel. A family—and happiness. A bond of trust and love and commitment.

I believe that with Cassie, you and Jonathan have that chance."

Cassie. It seemed such a small thing, but to Cassie it was everything. She swallowed a half-sob and shook her head, still disbelieving. Then she caught sight of Gabriel in the mirror. He held Jonathan against his shoulder, one big hand rubbing tiny circles over his back.

He was staring at his father, his expression solemnly intent. "You are not the man I once knew," he said quietly.

Edmund smiled slightly. "Nor are you."

For a moment, silence drifted. Cassie squeezed her eyes shut, and when she looked again, she beheld a most unexpected sight.

Gabriel placed his son gently in his father's arms.

"I think," he said softly, "it's time you got to know your grandson far better."

For Cassie, the simple, heartfelt scene was too much. Her eyes were streaming so that she could scarcely see. She walked quickly away before she was discovered.

In her room, she wiped away her tears with the back of her hand. She had thought no good would come of this day.

She was wrong, thank God. For the breach between Gabriel and his father had finally ended . . .

Perhaps it was time she healed the rift with her husband.

There had been no chance to speak with Gabriel alone tonight. But there was still so much left unsaid . . .

A rustle nearby snared her attention. She raised

her head to find that Gabriel had just come through the connecting door between their rooms. Her heart caught painfully. Never had he been so handsome, with the candlelight flickering over the striking beauty of stark, masculine features.

Never had she loved him more.

"Gabriel, I—I have something I must say to you. I should never have doubted you. I-I don't know how I could have thought it possible that you would harm me. For what it's worth, I shall regret it forever . . . and, oh, I know I do not deserve another chance, but I must know . . . Do you truly want me to leave?" Unbidden, the question tumbled forth.

The tension spun out endlessly. Everything inside her was wound into a knot. It took an eternity before he answered.

His reply was so low she had to strain to hear. "If you are wise, you will, Cassie." He paused, then said gently, "You need not worry. I will not take Jonathan from you, though it's my hope I can still see him. And I have told you—I will provide for you—always. You will never want for a thing."

Nothing, except you. He might well have struck a killing blow to the heart. There was an aching lump in her throat. How she found the courage to stand her ground, she did not know.

"That's not what I asked you." She hated the way her voice wobbled. "Do you want me to leave, Gabriel? Do you?"

She was just standing there, her slender shoulders shaking, silent tears sliding down her cheeks. Gabriel gazed across at her pale, beautiful face, knowing full well he deserved nothing from her. He had hurt her again, he realized . . . he was always hurting her . . .

He closed his eyes to shut out the sight of her tears. "No," he whispered. "Though God help me, I should. It's what's best for you."

"If it's not what you want, then why must I go? Oh, please, Gabriel, just tell me what you feel. Do not tell me what you think I want to hear. Do not withhold what you think I do *not* want to hear. Just—tell me what's in your heart." Three tentative steps placed him within reach.

He opened his eyes then. A surge of emotion rose inside him, too powerful to contain, too powerful to deny.

"*You* are in my heart, Cassie . . . You as no other . . . only you . . ."

For all the softness of his tone, he was fiercely intent . . . Joy surged in her breast. Her eyes were suddenly shining. She placed her fingertips on his chest and gave a choked little cry.

"Gabriel—"

He threaded his fingers in her hair and tipped her head back. His gaze was exquisitely tender as it roved her features.

"I love you," he said quietly. "You are my lady, my bride . . . my life."

It was all there in his eyes, in his voice, in the touch of his hands as they drew her close. A half-sob of sheer bliss escaped. "Oh, Gabriel, I love you, too . . . I have for so long now! Oh, please, tell me again!" She was laughing, she was crying, and nothing had ever been so right.

"I love you," he said against her lips.

"Again." She begged shamelessly.

His arms tightened. "I love you . . . God, how I love you!" he whispered, and then it was a very long time before either of them was able to speak again.

It was much later, as the moon brightened the night sky, that Cassie recalled what Gabriel had said only a few short days ago.

"*Sometimes,*" he had whispered, "*there comes a time to forget—a time to start anew.*"

Cassie smiled.

That time was already here.

Avon Romances—
the best in exceptional authors and unforgettable novels!

FOREVER HIS   Shelly Thacker

77035-0/$4.50 US/$5.50 Can

TOUCH ME WITH FIRE   Nicole Jordan

77279-5/$4.50 US/$5.50 Can

OUTLAW HEART   Samantha James

76936-0/$4.50 US/$5.50 Can

FLAME OF FURY   Sharon Green

76827-5/$4.50 US/$5.50 Can

DARK CHAMPION   Jo Beverley

76786-4/$4.50 US/$5.50 Can

BELOVED PRETENDER   Joan Van Nuys

77207-8/$4.50 US/$5.50 Can

PASSIONATE SURRENDER   Sheryl Sage

76684-1/$4.50 US/$5.50 Can

MASTER OF MY DREAMS   Danelle Harmon

77227-2/$4.50 US/$5.50 Can

LORD OF THE NIGHT   Cara Miles

76453-9/$4.50 US/$5.50 Can

WIND ACROSS TEXAS   Donna Stephens

77273-6/$4.50 US/$5.50 Can